Don't Try This at Home

Katie Pearson worked in television as a producer and director of documentaries. She lives in London with her husband and two young daughters. This is her first novel.

D0560713

KATIE PEARSON

Don't Try This at Home

Best wishes

Katie Pearson

FLAME
Hodder & Stoughton

Copyright © 2003 by Katie Pearson

First published in Great Britain in 2003 by Hodder and Stoughton
A division of Hodder Headline

The right of Katie Pearson to be identified as the Author of the Work
has been asserted by her in accordance with the Copyright, Designs
and Patents Act 1988.

A Flame paperback

10 9 8 7 6 5 4 3 2 1

All rights reserved. No part of this publication may be
reproduced, stored in a retrieval system, or transmitted, in any form
or by any means without the prior written permission of the publisher,
nor be otherwise circulated in any form of binding or cover other
than that in which it is published and without a similar condition
being imposed on the subsequent purchaser.

All characters in this publication are fictitious and any resemblance
to real persons, living or dead, is purely coincidental.

A CIP catalogue record for this title is
available from the British Library

ISBN 0 340 82703 3

Typeset in Formata Light
by Palimpsest Book Production Limited,
Polmont, Stirlingshire
Printed and bound in Great Britian by Clays Ltd, St Ives plc

Hodder and Stoughton
A division of Hodder Headline
338 Euston Road
London NW1 3BH

For my Father, who showed me the way.

Acknowledgements

With thanks to Polly Samson for getting me started and reminding me about apostrophes, my agent Clare Conville for her exceptional hard work and inspired guidance, Mari Evans and the team at Hodder & Stoughton for their patience with a first-timer, Professor Smith and the oncology team at the Marsden, Gosia and Doroteja for being there when I wasn't, Britt Harrison for giving me the idea to write in the first place, Maddie and Isabella for being a constant reminder of the important things in life and especially Marcus for his tremendous support and encouragement.

Chapter One

'You know more than you think you do.'
Dr Benjamin Spock

To: **Jay@mybestfriendisgay.com**
From: **Dot.com**
Subject: **Do I need to change my life?**

The plan was to be home by 6.00 to bath the girls and read the next nail-biting chapter of *How to Be a Perfect Princess*. Instead I'm stuck here writing a memo to Nikki Soda, the Cruella De Vil of documentary television, updating her on my meeting with the firm of eminent divorce lawyers, Split Savage & Ruck. Nothing to worry about, my marriage is fine. I'm just negotiating access to film a documentary series which will follow a year in the lives of a firm of divorce lawyers and their clients. Obviously there are a lot of sensitive issues involved and most people going through a divorce don't want the sordid details of their lives exposed in front of millions. I simply can't imagine why.

Perhaps we could follow it up with a second series called *Second Time Lucky*. If anybody likes the look of the divorcees, or more importantly, the size of their settlements they could write in and we'd film them on their first date. The meeting was tough. I was dealing with two of the firm's partners who looked like Rose Red and Rose White of the legal profession, in suits so sharp you could file your fingernails on them and personalities to match. There was a lot of straight talking, cross examination and quite a few personal insults, as they branded me a cynical, sensationalist media person with no interest in the pursuit of truth. It was hard not to agree with them, but I defended myself admirably and even managed to convince myself of my own integrity. The problem, which I omitted to mention, is the ruthless Nikki who will stop at nothing to manipulate every situation, however small, to satisfy the preconceptions of the largest audience possible. She would happily sacrifice her own child to the God of Ratings. So Nikki will fit their stereotype as snugly as her delicate hands fit her Anya Hindmarch gloves.

At the end of the meeting both sides agreed to think about the proposals and discuss them with the relevant parties (I'm even beginning to sound like a divorce lawyer). Just as I was leaving, the tougher of the two – Rose White, a platinum blonde called Sophia – put her hand on my shoulder and said, 'Dorothy, can I just say . . .' I braced myself for a final crippling comment '. . . I love your shoes. Are they Prada?' That's what I love about working with women. I can't imagine George Bush saying to Ariel Sharon after a fifteen-hour summit meeting, 'Do you think the cutaway collar works on a man with a fuller figure?'

I've lost it Jay. I found it hard to concentrate today. I found it hard to care. I just wanted to say to the lawyers, 'Yes, you're right, what is the point? I've got two lovely girls at home, and a talented supportive husband. I want to be with them, not sitting round this table pretending to be someone I used to be.' Easter was a disaster as I was so busy at work I didn't get time to work out the egg hunt properly. The children found all of the eggs in about two minutes and then looked at me as if to say, 'Now what?' Luckily Alex saved the day by organising a hunt for the Easter bunny, but I was surprised how useless I was with the girls. I'm out of touch. It's not just that. After everything that happened last year surely I should be having a radical rethink? I read interviews with celebrities: 'How I changed my life' 'It was a wake-up call'. For me it's more like a bloody car alarm going off in the middle of the night that I can't switch off and the message keeps coming through loud and clear.

It was when I should have been making notes in the meeting that I found myself jotting down a few thoughts on how to improve my life.

1. Spend more time with the children.
2. Make sure that Alex and I go out at least once a week on our own.
3. Eat five portions of fruit and vegetables a day (excluding cabbage – not even the fear of getting cancer again will make me eat cabbage).
4. Take up yoga to find balance in my life.
5. Drink two litres of water a day while working simultaneously on pelvic floor exercises.
6. Get veins done on legs.
7. Give up work.

To: **Jay@mybestfriendisgay.com**
From: **Dot.com**
Subject: **Massive cock-up (don't get excited)**

Oh shit, shit, shit, shit. By mistake I've just sent the earlier e-mail to now soon-to-be-ex-boss Cruella instead of the memo about the meeting. What shall I do? Apart from the less than flattering remarks about her, it's obvious I'm not exactly dedicated to the job at the moment. Now I think I'll have to resign, but maybe that's not such a bad idea. I can't imagine what Alex will make of it. I'll keep you posted.

To: **Alex@himindoors.com**
From: **Dot.com**
Subject: **What shall I do?**

Alex, Sorry to interrupt your creative juices and I hope the storyboard is going well. I just tried to reach you on the mobile but it's not connecting. I've done something so stupid I could slap myself.

While joking with Jay I sent an e-mail, meant for his eyes only, to Nikki. Apart from a few ungenerous remarks about her, I sort of indicated, by mistake, that I would quite like to give up work and, clichéd as it might sound, spend more time with you and the children. The funny thing is, now that it's happened that is what I want to do. I want to resign. What do you think?

To: **Alex@himindoors.com**
From: **Dot.com**
Subject: **Giving up work**

No I'm not resigned *to* anything. I want to resign my job. I can't quite believe this is happening quite so quickly, but if I think about it rationally you and I have been talking about this for a while. Matilda is going to be five and it seems more like five months not five years ago, you were yelling at me to keep breathing when it felt like the equivalent of someone grabbing my top lip and stretching it right back over the top of my head. Having survived that, twice, I feel like I'm missing out on all the other important stages, especially the day-to-day routine of them growing up. I want to be the one they tell their stories to. I want to know what happened when Michael pulled down Phoebe's knickers in the school canteen. I want to know why Matilda got a star for finding Emily's blood-soaked tooth in the playground, even though she was the one responsible for pulling it out. I want to know that the reason they have a stomachache might have something to do with the four chocolate Easter eggs, three packets of Skips, followed by two out-of-date fruits of the forest Frubes they ate before tea. I'm missing out on the details. All I get when I come home from work and rush upstairs to kiss them goodnight and ask, 'How was your day?' is a paltry, 'Fine'.

On top of everything I'm fed up with being an emotional Houdini, rearranging filming schedules just so that I can see Matilda play her recorder, out of tune, at the school concert and then realising that all she cares about is whether you and Nanny Sarah saw it. I'm worried about the relationship I have with my children. It all comes so naturally to you – Easter was a perfect example – and because you are so good with them I've used work and being ill as an excuse. You can clock in and clock off without any emotional fall out but I find it impossible. I no longer have the passion and commitment that I used to have for work. I want to save that for you and the children.

To: <u>**Alex@himindoors.com**</u>
From: **Dot.com**
Subject: **Big life changes**

I suppose I must have really meant it when we had those conversations. I'm sorry you thought it was all idle chat. It's the sort of thing we all talk about but never really do, like giving it all up and going to live in a commune in a remote corner of the Scottish Hebrides, or running a hotel in Antigua, or converting to Islam. I think you've got off pretty lightly. I do know last year was tough on you. It's not much fun being married to a woman 'who doesn't suffer the best of health' as your mother so elegantly put it and I know you put your career on hold to be with me and the girls, and you were spectacular.

I completely understand that now you've got to move on with your career. This is partly why I think I should give up work. I want to be able to concentrate on you and give you my full support. Think of me as an emotional Wonderbra – great support and lift. (OK, maybe in my current condition a slightly wonky one.)

To: **Alex@himindoors.com**
From: **Dot.com**
Subject: **Ripple effect**

Alex, I am sorry. I do put you through it but at least you can't say life is boring with us. Maybe you're right and ultimately I'm not cut out for domesticity but please let me give it a try. I'm sorry I didn't prepare you for this but I hadn't even prepared myself. It was a genuine mistake, which now seems to make complete sense. Financially it will be a pressure but I'm sure we can cope. You are great at what you do, you'll have no trouble getting the right jobs. If I give up work I can make sure that you can put all your energies into directing that big drama (when you get it, which you inevitably will) with no domestic distractions.

To: **Jay@mybestfriendisgay.com**
From: **Dot.com**
Subject: **Reluctant partners**

Stop press. I don't think I can go through with it. Alex is less than happy and is certainly not reconciled to the idea. It wasn't part of the deal. He married a successful career woman who would faint at the thought of a soiled nappy and doesn't know the difference between braised and chargrilled, but Jay I really can't go on going through the motions. I know Alex's life is going to change radically but maybe I can persuade him it will be for the better. I need a clincher to really persuade him. Any thoughts?

To: **Jay@mybestfriendisgay.com**
From: **Dot.com**
Subject: **You bastard**

You're right. I suppose it is time to bring out the emotional big guns. Here goes . . . ready, aim . . .

To: **Alex@himindoors.com**
From: **Dot.com**
Subject: **The bottom line**

Being ill took such a lot out of me. Chemotherapy in particular was devastating. Did I ever tell you that essentially it's mustard gas converted into chemicals? Honestly, it really is. So think of me as a survivor of the First World War, and Ambitious Productions as my trenches. I can't do it any more. I can't stumble through the no-man's-land of programme commissions, sidestepping the flak from savage reviews. Always lurking in the back of my mind is, what if the cancer comes back? I don't want to have any regrets about the way I spent the last few years of my life.

To: **Alex@himindoors.com**
From: **Dot.com**
Subject: **Not the end of the world**

Agreed. Let's view this as a trial period. If I prove to be a useless wife and mother, the children sue for a divorce from us and we have to remortgage the house, then I'll just go back to work. I'm certain that Nikki would have me back. Let's face it, how many people would put up with her?

To: **NikkiSoda@ambitiousproductions.com**
From: **Dot.com**
Subject: **Resignation**

Nikki, keep calm. I'm sure you don't mean it when you say, 'If you go that's it'. I'm very sorry that you received my e-mail. Of course you're not the Cruella De Vil of television. It was just one of those really stupid things I say to make Jay laugh. He didn't think it was at all funny. In fact he thought it really rather childish and stupid. As for your integrity, I've always admired the way you chase a story and make the facts fit. It's what makes you such a great documentary producer and it's why you have a shelf full of awards at the office, whereas I have one for services to the Canadian Tourist Industry. As for the rest of the e-mail, it wasn't my intention to give up work immediately but with deep regret I must formally hand in my resignation. I'll never forget how supportive you were last year. Working for Ambitious Productions has been exciting and challenging but being ill has forced me to change my priorities. I want to spend more time with Alex and the children. This could be the biggest challenge of all. I hope this isn't letting you down. There are a lot of young producer/directors who have the right killer instinct to take over the divorce lawyer project. I'm sure you understand that for me, at this stage in my life, this is the right thing to do.

To: **NikkiSoda@ambitiousproductions.com**
From: **Dot.com**
Subject: **My mental health**

No, as far as I know the chemotherapy hasn't affected my brain cells. This has been one of the hardest decisions of my life. I know you managed to juggle work and motherhood but at the moment I'm not being very good at either. We go back a long way, Nikki. We've been stranded in Bosnia, manhandled by orang-utans in Borneo, and survived *Children In Need*. I've watched you juggle the demands of work and the children, but you have always loved the job with a passion. I'm not saying that you don't love your children but you are linked to work by an invisible umbilical cord that seems to be as strong as your biological one. I used to be like that but something seems to have cut the work cord and maybe that 'something' was cancer. I need your support and it goes without saying that just because we're not going to work together it doesn't mean that I resign our friendship as well. We'll always have e-mail, and yes, of course Alex is worried about the situation but even though the financial implications are huge, the emotional ones are even greater. It might not be a permanent decision. If I changed my mind you would have me back, wouldn't you? For the time being I'm convinced this is the right thing to do. Isn't it?

To: NikkiSoda@ambitiousproductions.com
From: **Dot.com**
Subject: **Small sacrifices**

We can e-mail every day if you like and thank you for the open-door policy. I'll probably be knocking on it within a month. Of course I'll drop the company car back today, although God knows what I'm going to do without it. I'm very touched by your suggestion of a leaving lunch – our version of 'The Last Supper'. I'm going to miss you all but I'm not wavering, just drowning.

To: Delissa@splendidmums.com
From: **Dot.com**
Subject: **A major life change**

I'm not sure where you are at the moment. When we last spoke you were off on your abseiling course in the Welsh mountains, so I hope you receive this as I've got some interesting news for you. It's easier to do this by e-mail because you'll have time to consider your response. All I can say is that I need a lot of support at the moment so please don't be too damning. You'll be imagining the worse by now. No, I haven't left Alex, I'm not having a torrid affair and I haven't had a nervous breakdown. Well at least, I don't think I have. I have given up work and have made the big decision to become a full-time mother. I know what you'll be thinking. You've always stressed the importance of having a career and of being financially independent. It all happened by mistake but, without sounding a bit off the wall, I feel it was meant to be. I think I've got my priorities right, well at least for the moment. When the children are older I'll definitely go back to work, even if it's doing something different. It is time to move on.

I think I feel happy with my decision but I'd be lying if I said we weren't experiencing a few teething problems. We'd all love to see you.

To: **ProfwarmhandsHarrison@marsden.com**
From: **Dot.com**
Subject: **All clear?**

Thank you for your expertise last year. I wanted the best breast cancer specialist and I certainly got it. Your tone was, well, unique and I must admit I didn't expect the football analogies. When I asked you whether the cancer would come back and you replied that you weren't sure, but if you were to put me in any club I'd be more Manchester United than Manchester City, I suppose I did find that vaguely reassuring. I'm imagining my friends and family practising their Mexican waves. For your records, if you need to contact me use my home address and phone number as my work numbers are now redundant. See you for my next check-up and here's hoping I don't score any own goals in the meantime.

To: **Bethearthmother@rooted.com**
From: **Dot@noplacelikehome.com**
Subject: **I'VE DONE IT**

I'm feeling a bit tipsy after a splendid send-off courtesy of Nikki Soda and Ambitious Productions. I feel elated at the prospect of the future but I suppose three bottles of Rioja might have something to do with it. I wanted to let you know that at last I have joined your club and I've even changed my e-mail address to prove it. I am now an official but unpaid member of your group of social rejects, otherwise known as full-time mothers. Painting, baking cakes, and feeding ducks with children seem infinitely preferable to travelling to obscure countries, dealing with difficult people having tantrums, who don't want to be involved in making documentaries – and that's just the crew.

It's all because of you. The turning point was spending the evening with you a couple of weeks ago. Coming to your house is like coming to the sort of home I always dreamt I'd have, but it was only the other day that it really hit me how much I crave the atmosphere you've created. It wouldn't matter where you lived, it would still feel like home. I watched you cook tea, listen to Ella's music practice, help Josh with his homework, run through Will's big speech for the debating society, and then cajole the kids to bed, without losing your temper once or making me feel neglected. To top it off you cooked a delicious golden root vegetable casserole, with strands of saffron hand-picked from the souks in Marrakech, nestling on a bed of couscous, followed by an orange and almond cake and *home-made* banana ice cream. I didn't even know it was possible to make your own banana ice cream. It was a revelation. It was impressive. It was inspiring. I envy your relationship with Ella. I know she's older than Matilda but apart from the love, which is a given, you have a mutual respect. At the moment that's not a word that exists in our family's vocabulary. I hope it's not too late to change.

As a result of our evening together I have worked out a new five-year plan. I have set targets for the children and myself, and in my spare time I can write my novel. On my last day of work I smuggled out sackloads of office stationery so the kitchen is awash with wall charts and post-it notes reminding me of routines and personal goals. I've set up a sophisticated star chart system for all of us, and following the rules of good office practice I consulted the girls on how we should work the charts. After a healthy debate we've decided on silver stars for good effort, gold stars for exceptional behaviour/work, and black circles for bad behaviour. Alex is gritting his teeth. (I'm debating whether to give him a black circle for his negative attitude.) I must confess to feeling excited about my new career.

To: **Bethearthmother@rooted.com**
From: **Dot@noplacelikehome.com**
Subject: **Great expectations**

What do you mean, naïve? I thought you of all people would thoroughly approve of my decision. As you say, you've known me since we were four, but I can't understand why nothing has prepared you for this change of heart. Don't you remember the way I felt about the baby rabbits in our Year 3 science project? There is a sensitive soul lurking in me somewhere. It's just never had a chance.

To: **Jay@mybestfriendisgay.com**
From: **Dot@noplacelikehome.com**
Subject: **A big mistake?**

Does anyone think this is a good idea? I knew Nikki would think it strange and Alex would take some persuading but of all people I thought Beth would approve of me giving up work. I haven't heard back from my mother yet, but I think I know what her response will be. Am I mad?

To: Jay@mybestfriendisgay.com
From: **Dot@noplacelikehome.com**
Subject: **Howling at the moon**

I'm not 'barking' but I might concede on 'slightly unstable'. I know you're just jealous. You used to go on about giving up your shallow existence and doing a teacher training course. I'm now going to live your dream. I've got an idea – why don't we do it together? The Style column in the Sunday papers could survive without you, whereas I'm not sure I can. You could do your work experience with Matilda and Daisy, for a minimal fee to be negotiated. It would be such a pity to waste those fabulous child-friendly skills. While Matilda and Daisy have their very own fairy godfather, you can have unlimited access to their Ken and Barbie collection and full use of accompanying wardrobes. Is it a deal? Matilda's birthday party is coming up and it's my first chance to show off my creative skills in a domestic environment. Any tips gratefully received to make it the best party ever. I'm thinking along the lines of fairies or princesses.

To: Jay@mybestfriendisgay.com
From: **Dot@noplacelikehome.com**
Subject: **Right sort of fairy**

Thanks for the offer of friends to provide fairy entertainment. I think I would have remembered if you'd introduced me to a transvestite who wears carnival costumes, Union Jack hot pants, silver platform boots and goes by the name of Tallulah. Matilda would love her, but I think I want to preserve her innocence for a few more years. Having said that, she's so direct it's frightening. Yesterday as we were walking to school we caught up with her friend Molly and mother Kate. Matilda was shouting at me for stepping on the lines on the pavement. Kate said kindly, 'Matilda, be gentle with your mother. She's been a bit poorly.' To which Matilda replied, 'No she hasn't. She's had breast cancer.'

Chapter Two

Forward planning and organisation is the secret to success and party preparation is all part of the fun.'
Annabel Karmel's *Complete Party Planner*

To: **Bethearthmother@rooted.com**
From: **Dot@noplacelikehome.com**
Subject: **The change**

I hoped you'd come round to thinking it was a good decision. I know you've always perceived me as a career girl but motherhood is going to be my new career. As you've always pointed out, it's a question of priorities. If I can do as good a job as you in bringing up my children, I'll die happy – not that I'm intending to do that for a good few years. Funny how the most innocent remark takes on new meaning after the sort of scare I've had. When people ask me, 'How are you?' I have to stop and think. Do they know I've been ill? Should I mention the cancer and thoroughly embarrass everybody if they didn't know? Or shall we all just be polite and respond with the usual 'I'm fine'? But they might genuinely want to know if I'm better. The simplest things are exhausting. On the subject of exhausting, any tips on how to deal with children generally would be helpful. I'm re-organising my life on the assumption 'a busy child is a happy child'.

To: **Grouchomediatrendy.com**
From: **Dot@noplacelikehome.com**
Subject: **Fond farewells**

Sadly I will not be renewing my annual subscription. I've enjoyed rubbing shoulders with the great and the B list. I've achieved many a successful deal over a few bottles of champagne at the Groucho. Still, who knows? I may be back . . .

To: **Tumbletots.com**
From: **Dot@noplacelikehome.com**
Subject: **New recruits**

I'm interested in registering my daughter, Daisy, for Tumbletots. Please send application form and list of clothing requirements. She is of athletic build and judging by the displays off the back of the sofa I think that she is a natural gymnast. She certainly knows how to fall well.

To: **Nobudeliciousgrub.com**
From: **Dot@noplacelikehome.com**
Subject: **No more lunches**

Please cancel my regular Friday reservation for the foreseeable future.

To: **Father.nigel@stpeters.com**
From: **Dot@noplacelikehome.com**
Subject: **Playing with Jesus**

I'd like my daughter, Daisy, to attend your Friday lunchtime church playgroup. Is belief in God a criteria for joining the playground and are we talking about the parents and/or the child? If so, it's early days for us to tell with Daisy but she does seem to be something of a zealot.

To: **Monkeymusic.co.uk**
From: **Dot@noplacelikehome.com**
Subject: **Sound of music**

Have you got a space for a two-and-a-half-year-old in Monkey Music? She has an excellent repertoire ranging from 'Twinkle Twinkle Little Star' to The Smashing Pumpkins. We feel she would now benefit from a more classical training.

To: **Manolo.blahnik@sexyshoes.com**
From: **Dot@noplacelikehome.com**
Subject: **No credit**

It is with deep regret that I write to inform you that I must close my account. Can I pay off my £1,337 debt in monthly instalments at £5 a month? Please notify me if you consider designing a range of sensible shoes for the practical woman.

To: **Ubiquitousboden.co.uk**
From: **Dot@noplacelikehome.com**
Subject: **Change of image**

Having just given up work I need to address image accordingly. Please send latest catalogue asap.

To: **Bethearthmother@rooted.com**
From: **Dot@noplacelikehome.com**
Subject: **Mrs Efficient**

Feeling pleased with myself as have enrolled Daisy in thousands of local activities in attempt to keep her occupied. It will give me a chance to meet a few like-minded mums. Have even ordered a pair of sensible Timberlands from Boden, but draw the line at those unattractive pull-ons which may be practical for the school run but are a stylistic disaster. (Do you wear them?) Have also ordered trunkloads of books from a variety of catalogues including: *The Secret of Happy Children*; *More Secrets of Happy Children*; *How to Talk So Kids Will Listen & Listen So Kids Will Talk* and *How to Behave So Your Children Will, Too!* I still haven't had a response from my mother, she's either not read the e-mail yet or she's so disgusted that she's decided to break off all communication with her impossible daughter. The good news is that Nanny Sarah has agreed to stay on for a month to help me acclimatise and give me a chance to swot up.

To: **Nanny.sarah@indispensable.com**
From: **Dot@noplacelikehome.com**
Subject: **Minor bombshell**

Leaving next week? Of course I'm absolutely delighted you've managed to find such a great job, I just hadn't planned on you going so soon. I'm only a third of the way through *The Secret of Happy Children*, but the flat in Kensington will make a refreshing change from the boxroom in the attic, and of course the trips to the Bahamas in the winter months will be wonderful. Oh and don't let the disappearance of that young English girl in Nassau worry you. She was eventually found, though admittedly in four different parts of the island. I don't know how we'll cope without you. Matilda and Daisy will miss you, as will we all. It's such a shame you'll be leaving before Matilda's party. You mustn't worry. We'll send you all the pictures.

To: **Bethearthmother@rooted.com**
From: **Dot@noplacelikehome.com**
Subject: **Hurdles**

Disaster. Disaster. Disaster. I've been in floods of tears all day and have to keep rushing upstairs and mop my eyes with cold water and pretend that I'm OK. The old 'something in my eye' excuse is wearing a bit thin. Sarah is leaving. Maybe it's best to make a quick clean break, but Daisy in particular will be devastated. I hope I can compensate. I'm interested that you think the pull-ons are a good idea. As you say, I'm not supposed to be making a style statement every time I walk out of the front door. Practicality is what's important for my new life. Smartie Artie clown for Matilda's party sounds like a great idea.

To: **Smartie.artie@wowwhataparty.com**
From: **Dot@noplacelikehome.com**
Subject: **Best party in the world**

Are you available to entertain twenty-five demanding five-year-olds (mainly girls) on February 28? I gather there are nine of you, and have been reliably informed that number nine is the best.

To: **Smartie.artie@wownotaparty.com**
From: **Dot@noplacelikehome.com**
Subject: **A rethink?**

We are very disappointed you have no one available for our party. My husband and I have useful connections in show business that could further the careers of all your Smartie Arties from one to nine, if you reconsider. Otherwise I shall be forced to try Mr Lolly.

To: **Dickdaringdesigns.com**
From: **Dot@noplacelikehome.com**
Subject: **Exciting new commission**

Dick darling. Thought I'd call in a little favour after those exciting designs you did for the opening title sequence of *If You Didn't Laugh You'd Have to Cry/Hitler – The Sensitive Years*. It's my little girl's fifth birthday and I want her to have a cake she'll always remember. Her name Matilda means 'brave little maid', maybe that will give you some inspiration. Send through designs asap.

To: **Dickdodgydesigns.com**
From: **Dot@noplacelikehome.com**
Subject: **Disappointment**

Dick – just because I don't work at Ambitious Productions any more I would have thought our history together counted for something. Making one child happy is just as important as providing entertainment for millions on a Saturday night. If not more so. Furthermore I don't take kindly to your comment that she has an appropriate name for dealing with a mother like me.

To: **Nanny.sarah@indispensable.com**
From: **Dot@noplacelikehome.com**
Subject: **Domestic crisis**

Sarah, I can't find Daisy's baby Betty anywhere. I've searched the house from top to bottom and Daisy is distraught. I have managed to locate Amelia, Whoopi and Megan but no Betty. Any suggestions? Matilda is convinced you gave her a 'fruit winder', chocolate biscuits and a packet of crisps every day in her lunch box. Is this true? Have you got the contact numbers for Sam her swimming teacher, the Will to Win tennis club and Mrs Noyse the piano teacher? I remember you talking about a 'Siblings and How to Survive Them' seminar for children, have you still got the details? Also, any idea where the Calpol is?

To: **Alex@himindoors.com**
From: **Dot@noplacelikehome.com**
Subject: **Wasted talent**

On no account must you accept another contract with that dreadful soap opera *T-Junction*. You only directed some episodes before because of the horrible uncertainty of last year. I would hate to think that my decision to give up work has compromised your career. Please wait a few weeks and see if anything comes up. Apart from a few essentials I have to sort out, I promise I'll start economising immediately.

To: **Ubiquitousboden.co.uk**
From: **Dot@noplacelikehome.com**
Subject: **Spendings and savings**

I would like to order the following:

Suede pumps (lavender) £69 size 5
All-weather hardy rucksack (taupe) £45
Women's original mac (stone) £99 size 10
Sensible plain sweatshirt (navy) £39
Two pairs of women's pull-ons (pink spots/lavender checks) £29 each

Is postage and packaging free if I spend over £300?

To: **Partybags.com**
From: **Dot@noplacelikehome.com**
Subject: **Original ideas**

Please can I put in an order for your most original party bag collections. Although cost is an obvious consideration I want party bags with a decent present that is educational as well as entertaining, along the lines of those mini book classics or glittery pens, stickers, or fairy wands. I don't want to waste my money on tasteless tattoo transfers, useless trinkets that end up in the bin on immediate arrival home, or too many sweets or chocolate, which is hardly inventive and produces an unfortunate sugar rush. Many thanks for your assistance.

To: **Balloonswithoutpuff.com**
From: **Dot@noplacelikehome.com**
Subject: **Helium balloons**

Having scrutinised your catalogue I would like to order twenty-five pink and five blue helium balloons to make the party go with a bang. How much more would it cost to order a personalised Happy Birthday message on the balloons? Please advise.

To: **Fancyfrocks.co.uk**
From: **Dot@noplacelikehome.com**
Subject: **Dresses for princesses**

Please could I place an order for two pink Sleeping Beauty dresses to fit ages two to three and five to six. In addition, to save on future postage, could I order two of the silver fairy dresses in the same sizes with beaded slippers to match? Are tiaras and wings included?

To: **Girlieparties.com**
From: **Dot@noplacelikehome.com**
Subject: **Entertainers**

Smartie Artie and Mr Lolly have prior engagements. Do you have any girls free on February 28 to come and entertain?

To: **Girlieparties.com**
From: **Dot@noplacelikehome.com**
Subject: **Misunderstanding**

I need entertainment for a five-year-old, not adult erotica. Advise you rethink e-mail address.

To: **FairiesRus.com**
From: **Dot@noplacelikehome.com**
Subject: **Respectable entertainer**

Good news that your fairy is free on February 28. It is essential she is blonde, thin and under twenty-five. I presume songs, bells and glitter inclusive. We can provide fairy lights and atmospheric candles. Please send production schedule including the running order of events, timings, words to songs, lighting and music cues and a list of props and costume changes. A picture and any accompanying publicity material would be appreciated.

To: **Bethearthmother@rooted.com**
From: **Dot@noplacelikehome.com**
Subject: **Missing links**

Urgent. Sorry to interrupt dinner but please fax p.125 of the bible according to St Nigella immediately as mine is stuck together with cake mix. Why didn't I just buy everything from Marks and Spencer like everyone else? Somehow now that I'm at home full time that seemed to be cheating and of course I've got to economise. Alex is infuriating. He promised he'd help me get everything ready for tomorrow. Instead he's been facepainting the girls. Matilda is now transformed into a purple witch complete with all the stars in the galaxy and a crescent moon, while Daisy is her cat with luminous whiskers. They've taken every pillow off every chair and sofa in the house and all the sheets and duvets off the beds to make witches' caverns. The biggest saucepans are being used as cauldrons to make exciting potions and I'm left playing my new role of nasty policeman, trying to get the girls into bed while stuffing twenty-five inventive party bags, melting chocolate to make rice crispie cakes and blowing up balloons. I've still got to make the cheese stars, fairy cakes and the pièce de résistance, jelly boats (orange peel for hulls, cocktail sticks with painted paper flags for sails), as well as the house to clean up. Alex has now come in to tell me he's got a temperature and has disappeared upstairs to bed. Can't he at least take the children with him?

To: **Jay@mybestfriendisgay.com**
From: **Dot@noplacelikehome.com**
Subject: **Hyperventilation**

Darling Jay. Your phone is permanently engaged. I need you NOW.

To: **Welshwidows.com**
From: **Dot@noplacelikehome.com**
Subject: **Accidental coverage – acts of fairy**

Due to unfortunate incident at the weekend need to check out our policy as regards fire and domestic furnishings. Please could you send relevant forms immediately?

To: **Bethearthmother@rooted.com**
From: **Dot@noplacelikehome.com**
Subject: **Survival**

I'm exhausted. I don't have time to write shopping lists let alone the novel. How did J.K. Rowling manage it? My hands are raw from washing up and the house is a permanent tip. Just getting the children out of the front door takes hours and all my powers of diplomacy. My daily schedule is ruined before it's begun and my fantasy of inviting seven like-minded mums and their delightful children over for tea is shattered. I cleared my diary this week to leave enough time to make Matilda's birthday cake. After three attempts I had to abandon the fairy castle idea. The pink fairy was over-ambitious, so I eventually commissioned the local bakers to make a fairy wand cake. Sod the expense. The other mothers were very impressed and following in the tradition of the old Birds Eye advert I didn't let on that I hadn't made it myself. The party was what you might call 'interesting'. The entertainer turns up at the front door, disappears upstairs and comes down transformed into Susie Starlight.

'You look exactly the same as the girl who just knocked on our door. Same. Same,' chanted Daisy.

Susie Starlight looked a bit taken aback but took a deep breath and explained inventively, 'I'm her fairy twin sister. She misbehaved and has to stay in the human world. She might come back again later.'

Matilda adopted the expression Jeremy Paxman assumes when tackling Michael Portillo with only a few seconds to go at the end of *Newsnight* – unconvinced but prepared to let it go.

I was still in the kitchen unwrapping cocktail sausages, mixing marmite and butter for the sandwiches, putting the finishing touches on the personalised home-made biscuits and trying to remember exactly who was coming to the party. Matilda ran through the guest list several times and each time the names changed.

'You haven't got an Esmerelda in your class.'

'No, but there is an Emily so it won't be wasted.'

'I've already done an E.'

'No, that's for 'Enry.'

Alex staggered downstairs, looking as though he had polished off a bottle of vodka, to help open the door and be in charge of the video. I managed to manoeuvre as many of the mums and dads as I could into the kitchen to show off the sumptuous feast I'd laid out so beautifully, but they were keen to get away and make the most of the two hours of freedom that lay before them. Jay arrived just in time to relieve Alex of the camcorder, which he was swaying in the direction of the children while at the same time trying to blow his nose.

'I feel awful,' he whimpered, sweating all over the fairy cakes.

'Not as bad as you look,' I said unsympathetically, 'oh go back to bed.'

I despatched him upstairs armed with a box of tissues, numerous packets of Lemsip and a bottle of whisky. He retired moaning, but not before sneezing life-threatening germs into the fairy cocktail.

Jay's first job was to light the candles, which I'd strategically placed in the bookcases, on the mantelpiece and on top of the curtains. I'd already draped the living room and kitchen with five sets of fairy lights (lucky we went for the eleven-foot tree last year). The fairy lights made it look like the Father Christmas grotto in the Arndale centre, but the candles had the right magical atmosphere.

'Do a shot from outside the house through the window,' I hissed at Jay, handing him back the camcorder. Susie Starlight started her party piece by singing a magic song and introducing an invisible fairy called Trixie, who was so shy she didn't want to be seen.

'Are you sure you're a real fairy?' demanded Matilda as she prodded Susie's leg with her own customised fairy wand (fairywand.com from the *May All Your Dreams Come True* catalogue, a snip at £18.99).

The jangling bells and the fairy dance proved no better and the children were beginning to get restless. It was a little worrying. If they were bored now, what hope was there for the rest of the party? What I failed to notice was that 'Enry, a hobgoblin, had gone roaming and on his travels had discovered a bowl of mini gem biscuits. The first purple gem narrowly missed Susie Starlight as she twirled, shaking the bells above her head and pointing her toes. Then another ricocheted off her arm as she waved her magic wand, sprinkling gold glitter everywhere, and as so often happens in an urban riot it took only a few seconds for one small spark to ignite the violence. In the time it takes to say, 'Abracadabra,' all the children started hurling their mini gems at Susie Starlight who was forced to retreat behind the sofa. The air was full of tracer fire of purple, green, pink and orange, flying fast and furiously towards their target. I stormed into the middle of the room and just managed to resist the temptation to pick the hobgoblin up by his red-and-white spotty neckerchief and hurl him by the scruff of his neck out of the French windows. The lesson I'd learnt in the Borneo jungle when dealing with baby orang-utans came flooding back. I'd been taught to use the male authoritative NO. Firm and strong and using as deep a voice as possible to command respect, I screamed SILENCE. It worked. The children were stunned into a few fragile seconds of silence, which gave Jay and me enough time to restore some semblance of order and to coax Susie Starlight out from her hiding place.

There was worse to come. As Susie Starlight continued her act, Daisy, who was sitting behind her, very carefully began to pick out the feathers one by one from her splendid fairy wings. It didn't take long before one side began to resemble Benjie the bald budgerigar I had when I was a child (remember?). I was still in the midst of making sandwiches, popping out at every possible moment to check that things were relatively OK. I mean, what is the point of spending a fortune on an entertainer, a specialist one at that, if they can't keep the children under control? By the way, please, please don't mention to Alex that she cost a fortune. I pretended that as an actor she was hoping to make an impression on him which might lead to future employment and had accordingly reduced her prices. All nonsense of course. I kept trying to attract Jay's attention to get Daisy to stop but he was laughing too much to notice me. What I noticed was the smell of burning and the thin veil of smoke wafting through the room.

'Oh my God, the sausages.' I rushed into the kitchen, threw open the oven expecting to see rows of black lumps, only to discover them sizzling happily and barely bronzed. A shriek pulled me back into the fairy grotto.

'Behind you,' the children were shouting.

'Please children,' pleaded a rather tearful Susie Starlight, 'this isn't panto, you know.'

'Look at the curtains.'

'FIRE. FIRE. FIRE.'

'Enry ran round the room stirring the children into a frenzy while I stood paralysed amidst the screams, watching £600 of Designer's Guild curtains going up in smoke.

'Quick, use this,' said Jay, passing a jug to me which I threw at the curtains. We swiftly established a human chain and after the third jug the fire was out.

The children had decamped to the kitchen where they were cramming fairy cakes into their mouths. BANG went the front door and I caught a glimpse of Susie Starlight hotfooting it in the direction of the tube still dressed as a fairy, leaving a trail of feathers behind her.

'What shall we do?' I wailed at Jay. 'We've still got an hour and thirty-seven minutes to go. They can have tea now but that won't take long – just look at them.'

'Leave it to me,' says Jay, and I do because it's now that the demands really start.

'Can I have a drink?' they all chorus.

Rallying, I say, 'Who would like some fairy cocktail?'

'Nah, I want Ribena,' says 'Enry.

I go in search of my fairy cocktails to realise that the empty jugs by the bedraggled curtains are all that remain of my ingenious drink. With a fantastic display of self-control (Target No. 3 – Attainment Level 1.5 – I have to stop swearing in front of the children) I go back into the kitchen and get out the Ribena.

'Ribena everyone?'

'Nah,' says 'Enry, 'I want fairy cocktails.'

I offer everybody sandwiches, which are mainly rejected. We get into a bit of a muddle with the personalised biscuits, especially when Molly eats Matilda's one that she specially designed for herself as Birthday Girl. I offer a P to Phoebe.

'Have you got any teddy bear crisps?' she asks innocently and I admit defeat.

Jay is desperately trying to keep up morale by inhaling the helium from the balloons and speaking in a Mickey Mouse voice, which amuses the children for at least two seconds.

The doorbell rings and Jay tells me to go and answer it as he's too busy picking the chocolate icing out of Chloe's hair. Standing before me, resplendent in a purple-and-gold butterfly carnival costume, is an exotic creature the likes of which the suburbs have never seen.

'Dorothy,' purrs a deep voice, 'Tallulah's here to party. Lead on.'

Too shocked to argue, I take Tallulah into the kitchen where he/she is received with a stunned silence.

'Follow me you darlin' little pixies. I've got a wonderful secret to show you.'

I feel myself twitch involuntarily and glance anxiously at Jay who throws back a reassuring smile. Tallulah produces not one, not two, but three glittering balls out of her sequinned bag which she juggles effortlessly as she walks, ducking under the partition that divides the kitchen from the living room so that her glorious head-dress remains intact. Mesmerised, the children follow. For the rest of the afternoon she holds them spellbound. Now that's what I call a real children's entertainer. Apart from some magic tricks she lets the children take turns trying on her platform shoes, she paints toes and fingernails with butterflies and flowers, smothers them in glitter, braids their hair and paints their faces in all the glorious colours of the Caribbean. Even 'Enry was happy having play fights, imagining Tallulah's feather boa as a real boa constrictor. No one wanted to leave so the parents (confused by the change in personnel) had to drag their reluctant, overexcited and exhausted children home. I heard Molly say to her mum, 'It was brilliant. Can we have a real fire at my party?'

The house looks like it's survived a tornado, but only just. I opened the fridge to get a well-deserved beer for Tallullah to see twenty-five uneaten jelly boats like landing crafts waiting for disembarkation on D. Day.

So the party was not entirely orthodox but an original success . . . Must go as I can hear Daisy crying for Calpol. Is it normal that the girls still call for Sarah at night? Giving up work was definitely the right thing to do . . .

Chapter Three

'There are times when parenthood seems nothing but feeding the mouth that bites you.'
Peter de Vries

To: **Jay@mybestfriendisgay.com**
From: **Dot@noplacelikehome.com**
Subject: **Indispensable friends**

I owe you one. Do you think Tallulah would consider part-time child care? All the mothers have asked for her/his phone number. I've got a check-up with Professor Harrison tomorrow. Have noticed that Manchester United are not doing as well as they used to in the Premier League, which is a bit worrying. The reserves, in the form of Alex's parents Jack and the scary Sylvia, are coming to play at home. Jack is taking me out for a celebratory lunch to remind me how normal people live and Sylvia has offered to look after Daisy. I'm not sure why I find her so intimidating. She always looks stylish. Even when Daisy was a baby she wouldn't have dreamt of being sick on Sylvia's immaculate shoulders. I can't help feeling I'm being judged, especially when the children behave badly. Before, she could blame it on the fact I was an absentee mother – 'So unsettling for the poor loves' – and then because I was ill. Now there's no excuse. I'm just a bad mother. I know, I know, I shouldn't complain as the children adore her and she was a fantastic help last year but I do have to brace myself. Please be truthful, am I a terrible mother? Also I've been meaning to ask, have you noticed the veins on my legs? Is this age or the effects of cancer?

To: **Jay@mybestfriendisgay.com**
From: **Dot@noplacelikehome.com**
Subject: **'Veinity'**

I didn't want you to be *that* honest but thanks anyway for the list of local family therapists and reputable laser surgeons. I think I've had enough of surgery for a while. I can't afford it and I don't want to ask Alex for any financial help unless it's for essentials. I'm hoping he hasn't noticed the lines on my thighs, which are beginning to resemble rivers on an ordnance survey map. Rest assured our bedroom lights are quickly dimmed when we go to bed. At last I've had a response from Delissa to the e-mail I sent weeks ago. She's only just got it and to be honest I think she's in shock.

To: **Delissa@splendidmums.com**
From: **Dot@noplacelikehome.com**
Subject: **Being there**

Thanks for the offer of coming with me to the hospital for my check-up but I think I'm going to go alone. I've got to get used to it at some point and I can't rely on you every time. It's not fair and you've got your own life to lead. It was fantastically supportive having you there through chemotherapy and you made a great impact with all the nurses. The fact that you baked them a regular assortment of scones, biscuits and fruit fancies every time we went, ensured that I was the most popular cancer patient in the history of the hospital. But we're now at a different stage. I'm getting on with the rest of my life. The idea of e-mailing you my news rather than telling you on the phone was so that you would have time to think about it. Now that was not what I'd call a considered response. I'm afraid I can't change anything at the moment. It's such early days. I only gave up work a few weeks ago and my boss, Nikki, is keeping an open-door policy. Besides, I want to give this a go. No, Alex isn't desperately happy but he respects my choice. This might not be what you would wish for me or for yourself, and I know how important you think it is to be independent. You've always warned me not to put all my eggs in one bastard but you must remember that Alex is not Dad. It's not like I'm putting myself at the mercy of an unreliable Lothario. You must realise I'm a grown woman and I should be able to make my own decisions in life without always having to consult you first. I'll call you later and let you know how the check-up went.

To: **Jack@finefigureofafatherinlaw.com**
From: **Dot@noplacelikehome.com**
Subject: **Out to lunch**

I just wanted to confirm our lunch. My check-up is at 11.30 so the timing is perfect. My friend, Jay (the children's fairy godfather as you so aptly called him), has offered to come over and help Sylvia out if she needs it. He's interviewing a leg waxer extraordinaire on Richmond Green for his regular Sunday column and would welcome any excuse not to have to go back to the office. My mother has finally got the news that I've given up work and she's a bit upset. Judging by the number of messages she's left on my mobile I think by lunchtime I'll need a drink.

To: **Bethearthmother@rooted.com**
From: **Dot@noplacelikehome.com**
Subject: **Offloading anxieties**

Thanks for your thoughtful note. Yes, it's check-up time today and I always feel a little anxious. Most of the time I try not to think about being ill but my overwhelming fear is that the cancer will come back. Alex has managed to move on. I sometimes think he's blocked it out of his mind. 'Dot had cancer. We all coped with it, but she's better now and we can all get on with life.' I had to remind him this morning about the hospital appointment. Of course he's very concerned once he's reminded and even offered to come with me, but it's probably his way of dealing with it. It must be so boring for him.

As the months go by it is getting easier for me, but there are still issues that worry me. For example I'm sure there is a connection between mind and body and there have been moments I've wondered whether I caused the cancer, and if so, worrying about it coming back could actually make it come back. That thought is then processed and pushed to the back of my mind where it festers. Then of course I'm repressing my feelings, which we all know gives you cancer too – so it's a bloody vicious circle. I know I've got to confront it and work it through. That terrifying phrase 'positive thinking' is such a pressure. If only I knew what caused the cancer. Is it late pregnancy, underwired bras, underarm deodorant, chemicals in the water, soft plastics, pesticides, too much dairy food, stress or forgetting to cross yourself and whistle when you walk out the front door of a morning? The list is endless and it can drive you insane. There are no definite answers and it could be a combination of all these factors or just bloody bad luck. Some you can fight and some you can't, but unless you know what's caused it how can you stop it coming back again? All I know is that I never want to go through chemotherapy again.

Anyway, enough said. On to more important issues, how did Will's speech go? Did he win the debate? When can we co-ordinate our busy conflicting school schedules and come and see you? Lots of love.

To: **Jay@mybestfriendisgay.com**
From: **Dot@noplacelikehome.com**
Subject: **Life, death and George Clooney**

Sorry to miss you this afternoon but thanks for looking in on Sylvia. She thinks you're wonderful. I obviously haven't told her any of the more sordid details about your life, but if she starts waxing too lyrical I'll have to break my silence. The check-up went well except I had to wait for an hour which was nerve-racking. I have to steel myself to walk into the hospital because a Pavlovian wave of nausea wells up from the pit of my stomach. It's something to do with the smell of the place. There's an air of gentility in the waiting room with people reading glossy magazines and sipping cups of tea. Everybody is very polite and quietly spoken, smiling at each other as if to say, 'I'm fine. I'm going to be fine.'

There was a handsome middle-aged woman with a young girl of around sixteen years old, whom Matilda would have thought was a perfect live Barbie. The mother looked pale and was anxiously picking at a thread beginning to unravel on the sleeve of her jacket. They sat in silence, occasionally catching each other's eye and giving a reassuring smile. A rather cheery nurse with an ample bosom called out a name and I expected the mother to answer but it was the young girl who got up first. She was the one with cancer. I felt my stomach lurch in sympathy, hating myself for observing their tragedy. They were obviously first timers as the nurse was showing them the way and explaining procedures to them both. The two women smiled eagerly, desperate to 'do the right thing' when all they probably wanted to do was break down and cry.

As I watched them I knew what lay before them in the next few horrifying months of treatment and gradual disclosure. I felt the tears well up. I had to bite my bottom lip to stop myself from crying. Whatever happened I mustn't break the waiting-room etiquette as that would never do. You mustn't cry, you mustn't embarrass anyone, most of all yourself. But she was so young. Maybe manners are a means of survival. In the face of catastrophe people cling to etiquette. Stiff upper lip and all that, which is so British. In fact I've never seen anyone sobbing or shouting in the waiting room and yet I've watched people walk out of the consulting room having been told they have only a few months to live. I wonder if it is the same all over the world? I can't imagine the Italians or the Americans being so composed. Maybe when death is close there is a calm acceptance or maybe you just don't believe it's going to happen to you. It's like the descriptions of the millions of Jews meekly accepting their fate and going to their deaths in the gas chambers. I don't often have these profound thoughts. Most of the time I sit there playing 'Spot the Wig' and wondering whether George Clooney is more attractive than Brad Pitt.

To: **Jay@mybestfriendisgay.com**
From: **Dot@noplacelikehome.com**
Subject: **Eye of the beholder**

No, you're wrong. It's definitely George Clooney.

To: **Bethearthmother@rooted.com**
From: **Dot@noplacelikehome.com**
Subject: **Fly the flags**

Thought you'd like to know that the check-up was good and nothing untoward seems to be happening in my body, as far as they can see. Highlight of the day was lunch with Jack, and who should we see but Alex being wooed by Jessica Bedmeigh, one of the rising star producers at the BBC. She was interviewing him as a possible candidate to direct an exciting new project, which obviously I can't tell you about, except to say it's a modern version of *Tess of the D'Urbervilles* for BBC2, with an all-star cast and masses of money being thrown at it. We didn't interrupt Alex and Jessica as they were deep in conversation.

I had an extraordinary lunch with Jack. He talked about the Second World War and how fear and death became familiar. These days we're protected from it. When I was first told I had cancer it felt like a death sentence, but what was worse was that that was what everyone else thought including Alex, Mum, my friends and, yes, perhaps even you, dear Beth, although you were nice enough not to say it. There were a few who were in denial, who refused to accept that it was anything except a temporary blip, and in some ways that was reassuring and in other ways irritating. It was as if they couldn't or wouldn't understand the implications of having cancer.

Maybe it isn't such a big deal. There are thousands of people living their lives who've had it, dealt with it and moved on. It's the people who die who become high profile. Why can't I reconcile myself to it? The obvious answer is the children. I can't bear the thought of not seeing them through those crucial stages in life: going to big school; meeting their friends; celebrating birthdays; dealing with first boyfriends, exams, careers, marriage, grandchildren; the whole damn business of life in all its ordinariness and its most spectacular. But there's something else much more basic and more fundamental. I simply can't comprehend that I'm going to cease to exist. I remember talking to Emma, the breast cancer nurse, just before my operation.

'I'm here to answer any questions. Is there anything that's worrying you?'

'Yes' I replied, 'Linda McCartney.'

Emma looked a little rattled. 'What do you mean?'

'One minute she's in remission, riding her horse, and then two days later – she's dead? I don't understand the speed of it.'

Emma patiently explained that Linda's cancer was much more advanced than mine, her prognosis was never very positive, but she still didn't tell me how it happens so quickly. One minute you're laughing, breathing, riding and the next you're dead. I could understand if it was an accident or a heart attack but how does the cancer suddenly accelerate to such a degree as to kill you? What happens? I'm not sure it bears thinking about and frankly, I've never had the courage to ask.

I've never seen death. The closest I've come to it was visiting Lenin in his mausoleum in Moscow. He was so small and wizened, his skin a strange salmon-pink. He looked like he'd been stolen from Madame Tussaud's. He didn't seem real, but I know you've seen death close up. You had to deal with it all with your mother. Maybe it's all to do with growing up, or rather not being able to grow up. I realise now that when your mum died, somehow you managed successfully to negotiate that crucial developmental stage and emerge a fully-fledged adult. I'm still in my adolescence, thinking the world revolves around me, being spectacularly moody and slamming doors (and not just metaphorically).

Maybe it's only when your parents die you can accept you're

mortal and you move into the front line. Mum hasn't had a day's illness in her life and Dad's not dead, he's just missing in action. I got a postcard from him last week. It's been years now since we've seen each other. He seems happy enough in America, and of course we spoke on the phone when I was ill, but he was one of the ones who refused to believe how serious it really was. In many ways I feel closer to Jack than to Dad, who's never been there for me. From a very early age I learnt not to expect anything different.

Jack asked me what I'd learnt from being ill. I was so intent on proving to everyone that I was the best cancer patient in the world, I haven't had time to stop and really assess what has happened to me. I was determined to minimalise the effects of being ill on Alex and the children. I didn't want to be too demanding. Business as usual, both at work and at home, and apart from the afternoon sleeps I think I succeeded. I never complained at the hospital. I bought out Kew Gardens for all the staff on the last day of chemotherapy. I was always cheerful and positive.

Every morning for five weeks the radiographer would say, 'Good morning, and how are we today?'

Resisting the urge to say, 'Well actually, we've got cancer . . .' I'd always say '. . . Fine, and how are you?'

But the trouble is that now everyone has moved on. I didn't make the most of the sympathy when it was offered and now it's too late. Professor Harrison suggested cancer counselling and gave me a contact. What do you think?

To: **Bethearthmother@rooted.com**
From: **Dot@noplacelikehome.com**
Subject: **Next stop The Priory**

I get the feeling you think it's long overdue. I'll have a think about it but I'm not going to rush into anything just yet. There's enough happening in my life at the moment without opening Pandora's Box, but I take your point that it might be an important move in my rehabilitation, post-cancer. Mum has finally caught up with my big life decision and she's horrified, as you can imagine. We've been such a close unit all my life and I've always done everything I could to make her proud of me. She approved of my career and now she thinks I've thrown it all away. I fear her disapproval more than anyone else's.

To: **Alex@himindoors.com**
From: **Dot@noplacelikehome.com**
Subject: **Successful schmoozing**

Thanks for the concerned message. I had a good check-up. Everything was absolutely fine, so we can now relax for a couple of months. That's fantastic news about the job. Lunch looked like it was going well. Given her incredible reputation I was amazed by how young Jessica is, and she looked fantastic. I know you hate the networking side of the job, that was always my speciality. As much as I hate to say it, and Cruella would have to put me on the rack before I admit it, I miss the social side of working. Although I'm delighted with our family, I miss having a work family. I miss the gossip. There's a limit to how much teething, pooing problems and how to get into the local school can stimulate the old brain cells. I even find myself analysing the way

Teletubbies is shot just to keep my eye in. Sorry I didn't warn you about Mum. I should have thought that she would call you once she'd finally come to terms with the earth-shattering news in my e-mail. But it obviously didn't affect your meeting. I thought she'd be on the warpath but I trust you were suitably supportive of me. I'm just about to e-mail her again. I'm avoiding the phone as I know how persuasive she can be. Until tonight then, and I can't wait to read the script.

To: **Delissa@splendidmums.com**
From: **Dot@noplacelikehome.com**
Subject: **Double whammy**

Two causes for celebration. I've been given a clean bill of health and Alex has been offered a big new job, which we're all very excited about. Come to supper tomorrow to help us celebrate. We can talk about everything then.

To: **Bethearthmother@rooted.com**
From: **Dot@noplacelikehome.com**
Subject: **Alex's new job**

Big excitement. Alex has been offered a wonderful job directing a top-notch modern adaptation of *Tess of the D'Urbervilles*. Come to a celebratory supper tomorrow night. See you at 8.30.

To: NikkiSoda@ambitiousproductions.com
From: **Dot@noplacelikehome.com**
Subject: **Baftas in the making**

Thought you'd like to be the first to know that Alex is going to be directing the prestigious new drama for BBC2. Come and have supper tomorrow. The champagne's on us.

To: Jay@mybestfriendisgay.com
From: **Dot@noplacelikehome.com**
Subject: **Celebration**

Hurrah! Alex got the job. Dinner's on us.

To: Alex@himindoors.com
From: **Dot@noplacelikehome.com**
Subject: **Sealed lips**

Of course, darling, I haven't mentioned it to a soul. Discreet is my middle name.

To: Bethearthmother@rooted.com
From: **Dot@noplacelikehome.com**
Subject: **Jumping the gun**

Cancel earlier e-mail and erase all information from memory. It was classified information. Will notify you when files are opened for public consumption in year 2057. Apologies about dinner.

To: **NikkiSoda@ambitiousproductions.com**
From: **Dot@noplacelikehome.com**
Subject: **Dinner**

Sorry, dinner's off, and do you mind not mentioning Alex's job to anyone under any circumstances? Apparently there's another director who's going to be very disappointed, and Alex's appointment still hasn't been approved by the writers, commissioning editors, drama executives, Greg Dyke, President Bush and God. You know what it's like. Let's get together soon.

To: **Jay@mybestfriendisgay.com**
From: **Dot@noplacelikehome.com**
Subject: **Careless talk costs jobs**

Tonight's off and please don't mention to Alex that I told you anything about his new project. Apparently it's all supposed to be hush-hush at the moment. I'm off to buy a modest celebratory dinner for two and to stock up. I can feel some home-made apple and oatmeal muffins coming on. (I think I *am* turning into Alex's mother, but unfortunately without the elegance.) Come to tea Saturday?

To: **Delissa@splendidmums.com**
From: **Dot@noplacelikehome.com**
Subject: **Mum's the word**

Ignore earlier information about Alex's job. We'll tell you officially soon. You were a fantastic role model for me and I must confess I'm finding being a full-time mother quite a challenge but you've always encouraged me to respond well to challenges. I don't know how you did it alone. I know you only had one child and Granny Lloyd helped out a lot, especially when Dad left and you set up the business, but I depend heavily on Alex and you didn't have Dad from when I was eight. I can't imagine he was much help before then. Babies weren't his thing. What was his thing, exactly? Can you remember? I don't think I want to know. Did he ever take a real interest in me or in your life at home? It seems like ages since we've seen you so I'm glad you can make it over for tea on Saturday after your Spanish lesson and before the theatre. What a life you lead!

To: **Bethearthmother@rooted.com**
From: **Dot@noplacelikehome.com**
Subject: **Tantrums in Tesco's**

This full-time mothering business is not easy. I'm still recovering from a trauma at Tesco's. Daisy screamed for no reason I could discover from the fruit and vegetable section right through to freezer foods. Bribes of Baby Bel cheeses and copious mini boxes of raisins had no effect whatsoever. Old women tut-tutted at me, mothers with angelic children in trolleys glided past throwing, at best, sympathetic smiles in my direction, at worst reproving frowns. Everyone convinced child abuse taking place, which it nearly did.

My embarrassment reached a crescendo when a voice behind me said, 'Having fun, Dorothy?' I turned to face Nikki Soda, now ex-boss.

'I can see how those early days working as a researcher on Michael Barrymore must have come in very handy.' Her expression could only be described as a smirk. 'Exciting news about Alex. I just happened to be having lunch with Sophie, the Controller of BBC2, and mentioned the good news to her. She didn't seem to know anything about it.'

'Oh God,' I shrieked, trying to make myself heard over Daisy's screaming. 'Didn't you get my second e-mail?'

Nikki looked at me blankly. I could see she was resisting the urge to put her hand across Daisy's mouth to muffle the sound.

'The job's not confirmed. I should never have told you. It's going to happen but it has to be cleared through all the important channels. Alex is going to kill me.'

'Oh, I shouldn't worry. By the time he's sharpened the knife or bought the poison the job will probably be his.' She laughed at her little joke.

I picked up Daisy in a desperate attempt to calm her down and to show that actually I am a very good mother and giving up work was the best thing to do after all. She went rigid in my arms and purple in the face. Nikki watched, without offering to help, as Daisy continued to scream and I rather brutally crammed her legs through the holes in the front of the shopping trolley before it slid off towards pastries and savouries.

'So, no regrets about giving up work?'

'None whatsoever,' I snapped back.

'Well, if you change your mind I might have something that would interest you. It's an executive producing role which you could do part time, so you could still be with the lovely Daisy.'

We both stared at this child, now squirming in the front of the trolley with brown rivulets of tears running down her cheeks and snot pouring out of her nose.

'Let's e-mail.' She turned on her brown suede boot heels and left in a cloud of Calvin Klein's Obsession, her fashionable floor-length brown, soft sheepskin coat sweeping behind her. Have you got a spare copy of *Toddler Taming*?

To: **NikkiSoda@ambitiousproductions.com**
From: **Dot@noplacelikehome.com**
Subject: **Brief encounters in Tesco's**

Yes, wasn't it funny meeting like that and I thought it was very kind of the store manager to speed us through the checkout – it must have been Daisy's big blue eyes that charmed him. I don't know why they call it 'giving up work', as being at home is much harder work than anything I've done before. Of course I love every single minute and wouldn't swap it for anything in the world but the job you mentioned sounds intriguing. Sorry about dinner tonight but why don't you come to tea on Saturday? We can discuss it then. It will also give you a chance to see Daisy and her sister in their natural habitat and check me out in my new role as domestic goddess.

To: **Jack@finefigureofafatherinlaw.com**
From: **Dot@noplacelikehome.com**
Subject: **Giving up already**

Thanks for lunch yesterday. I appreciate having the chance to have a grown-up conversation with no interruptions. It's amazing how much you become tunnel visioned by being at home. I felt like a prisoner blinking in the sunlight having just been let out of solitary confinement for a few hours. Alex has some good news, but I'll let him tell you about it himself.

Now, in your capacity as a headhunter I need some professional advice. My ex-boss, Nikki, is tempting me with talk of a part-time job. As yet I don't know what it is but she wouldn't offer me anything silly. My mother would be delighted as she's very worried at the thought that I'm throwing away a career I worked so hard to establish. Can I give up so easily? It's not giving up exactly, it's just finding the right balance, and I know Alex secretly would be relieved if I do go back to work. I'm sure he's feeling the strain. He has no interest in the minutiae of my life. Yesterday he wandered off when I was mid-story. (OK, it was a slow starter but the punch line was very funny – and it was about his children for God's sake.) Jack, promise to tell me if I become boring?

To: **Jack@finefigureofafatherinlaw.com**
From: **Dot@noplacelikehome.com**
Subject: **Silver tongue**

You smooth-talking father-in-law. But thanks for making me feel better. You're right, I shouldn't make any hasty decisions until I know what Nikki has to offer. If I do go back to work part time, I'll need some help with the children. Child care – the eternal problem. I don't think I appreciated how lucky we were to have Sarah.

To: **Alex@himindoors.com**
From: **Dot@noplacelikehome.com**
Subject: **Away with the fairies**

God, how weird that the Contoller of BBC2 knew about your appointment. Perhaps she's close to Jessica? I'm sure it's going to be OK. By the way, bumped into Nikki Soda in Tesco's, of course I didn't tell her anything about your new job, but she might have a part-time job for me. I don't think I want to do it but I might just follow through and see what she's got to offer. Could you do a supermarket run for me on your way home? I forgot most of the essentials and I can't face the thought of going back there.

I also need some help on an urgent parenting problem. Susie Starlight and the party experience hasn't dampened Matilda's enthusiasm for fairies. I knew we should have been prepared for this and clarified our position. At this very moment she is down in the kitchen composing a letter to Floss, the tooth fairy. What should I do? Should I write back? This inevitably will lead to lengthy correspondence, requiring a great deal of creative effort, but I suppose it might be an interesting project for me. I am worried that, what with Father Christmas, the Easter Bunny and now the fairies, we're putting more spin on childhood than Alastair Campbell does on New Labour. On the other hand, I do think it's important to create some magic. Just because we have had to face some realities I don't see why they should. It's a difficult time with Nanny Sarah having left. What do you think?

To: **Alex@himindoors.com**
From: **Dot@noplacelikehome.com**
Subject: **Fairies and the spycatcher**

No, I don't think I should take up Nikki's job offer immediately. You may think the fairy issue is trivial, but I think it's important. We need to present a united front. Today it's fairies, tomorrow it'll be sex education. And no, sorry to disappoint you, I won't be wearing my fairy outfit when you come home from work as I'm trying to make chicken stock. I'm sorry Jessica's fuming about the leak. Perhaps the phones are tapped at Television Centre. Have you discovered who is the Controller's source?

To: **Alex@himindoors.com**
From: **Dot@noplacelikehome.com**
Subject: **Clean slate**

Ah, sorry. OK, I'll come clean. I was excited for you and wanted to tell the world, which in my inimitable fashion I did. Of course if I'd stopped to think, Nikki was the last person I should tell, but strategic thinking isn't part of my daily routine at the moment. I'm working on a basic instinct level with disastrous results. Have you told Jessica that I'm the link to Nikki? Will it jeopardise your chances?

To: **Alex@himindoors.com**
From: **Dot@noplacelikehome.com**
Subject: **All clear**

Hurrah! What a relief it's now official. Thanks to me. If I hadn't mentioned it to Nikki and she hadn't passed it on they probably would have prevaricated for weeks. Beth's away so I thought I'd check out the fairy issue with Nanny Sarah. There probably is an official Penelope Leach line to take on this one.

To: **Nanny.sarah@indispensable.com**
From: **Dot@noplacelikehome.com**
Subject: **Urgent**

Any ideas on how to deal with fairies? What did they teach you in your training? Is it OK if I pretend to be a fairy and write back to Matilda? Also, do you have the contact numbers for your nanny network. Despite Tumbletots, Monkey Music and playgroup I think

Daisy might be missing her friends. I feel her social life is suffering.

To: **Bethearthmother@rooted.com**
From: **Dot@noplacelikehome.com**
Subject: **At home with the fairies**

Thank God you're back from your long weekend in Ireland. Cruella is waving an offer of a part-time job in front of my nose, and although she may be deliberately taunting me it's unsettled me all week, especially as I don't know what the job is. All was supposed to be revealed when she came to tea on Saturday. It was the first chance I had to talk to Mum face to face since I told her the news. I think her reaction to this has been worse than when I told her I had cancer. Thank God Jay came. He and Mum get on brilliantly, and I needed an ally as I'm not sure Alex is entirely reliable at the moment.

I had planned to write Matilda's first fairy letter on a leaf with silver pen. Of course I'd researched this in some detail looking at my early copies of J.M. Barrie and the famous anthology of case histories of fairy sightings in the Victorian era. Mum was always so imaginative and inventive when I was growing up. I hazily remember something about magic circles made out of foxgloves and beautiful daisy bracelets with jewels embedded in the stems, which she claimed were left for me by the fairies. I couldn't go quite that far on my first attempt at creating some magic but I thought the leaf idea was simple but effective. I wanted the others to be there when Matilda discovered it. I hid it in the garden, which meant I had to keep her inside until teatime. She was immediately suspicious but dogged in her determination to discover the truth about fairies.

'Do you believe in fairies?' demands Matilda when Jay arrives.

'Of course I do, darling.'

Mum arrived laden with cakes, home-baked bread, pasta sauces, treats for the children and enough food to last us for weeks. Alex and the children fell upon them with desperation, as if they were prisoners in a concentration camp receiving their first Red Cross parcels in months. I suppose being a good cook is an integral part of being a good mother. It's somehow part of the job description. It's something I'm going to have to work on.

'How are you, my darling?' Mum looked at me with genuine concern, searching my face for those tell-tale signs of exhaustion that only a mother can see. 'You look a bit peaky.'

I'd never introduced Delissa to Nikki before. It was a deliberate decision, as I suppose it was the one area of my life I didn't want her to influence. Of course I'm very proud of her, but you know what she's like. She's such a formidable force, it's hard to match up to her and perhaps secretly I knew that it was inevitable that she and Nikki would get on famously. Nikki spent part of her childhood in Spain and can speak Spanish fluently. She was delighted to discover that Delissa was studying for a Spanish degree.

I didn't get a chance to talk to either of them as they were both so engrossed. Matilda kept interrupting their conversation in a desperate attempt to make them watch her and Daisy do a show. Daisy was dressed in a nurse's outfit, with a tiara on her head and a bandage round her knee. Matilda wore her Sleeping Beauty costume and a Captain Hook plastic attachment on her left hand. There was no logic to the story and as usual there was no beginning, middle or end (these shows infuriate Alex – I think they offend his professional instincts) but a lot of strange songs and dancing. Alex coped for about three minutes before he retired upstairs to read scripts. I know he's still cross with me for telling Nikki about his job. Personally I think he's being over-sensitive about the whole thing. I do miss his involvement. I never thought Alex would become one of those absentee fathers, there physically but not emotionally. Since I've given up work it's somehow become all my responsibility and when Jay's around he tends to pass the parental baton on to him.

The children kept calling to their inattentive audience, 'Granny Delicious, look. Look at me.' Nikki and Delissa continued to talk at each other without pausing for breath, much to Matilda's fury. Her singing became louder and more insistent. Then in an inspired attempt to liven up the performance she went to get the hamster from her room, telling Daisy to keep singing in her absence. Once the hamster had made an appearance and been admired by the audience, Daisy, keeping in character, attempted to bandage the poor rodent who clearly was not happy with being cast as patient to a method-acting nurse. Matilda kept grabbing her pet and Daisy kept trying to pull her back. Jay had taken over teamaking duties, while I was trying to keep up with Delissa's and Nikki's conversation at the same time as rescuing the hamster. Daisy was desperate to hold her.

'I love her.'

'OK, you can hold her gently while I go and help Jay bring the tea in.'

After a few seconds Daisy followed me into the kitchen. 'Fluffy's sleeping now,' she said.

'That's good, darling,' I said as I took some shop-bought muffins out of their cases and put them in ones that looked like they could have been home-made. I glanced at Fluffy lying in the palm of Daisy's tiny hand and realised with horror that Fluffy wasn't going to wake up ever again. Daisy must have squeezed a little too tight.

'Oh my God. Give her to me, darling, I'll look after her now,' I said as calmly as I could to Daisy, trying not to show how horrified I was. Daisy skipped back happily to the sitting room oblivious to her crime. 'Christ Jay. Look.'

Jay put the lid on the teapot and turned to look at the dead hamster I was carrying. He screamed.

'Everything all right in there?' called Delissa.

'Yes, everything is fine. I just burnt my hand on the teapot,' replied Jay.

'What are we going to do? Matilda will be distraught,' I said tearfully. This was yet another thing I could do without.

'Leave it to me,' he hissed and I did, as I always do. What would I do without Jay?

Jay went upstairs and put the dead hamster back in its cage. 'I think it's the best thing. When Matilda discovers her, you can tell her that she died in her sleep during the night. I thought about burying her in the garden and saying she'd run away but you know what Matilda's like, she'd organise search parties and have the entire neighbourhood out looking for Fluffy for days.'

It made sense. After all that's half the point of having pets, so that the children can learn about life and death.

After a somewhat impressive tea (mainly thanks to Granny Delicious's contributions) I had a communication breakdown with Daisy. She kept tugging at my leg and saying repeatedly, and each time more emphatically, 'Alloll.'

'Ah, apple,' I said, passing her one.

She looked at it in disgust, shook her head and screamed, 'Alloll.'

'Your doll?' I said, rushing to get Betty. Daisy was practically apoplectic by this point.

'No, it's Calpol she wants,' said Matilda, with the sort of tone usually reserved for dismissing the village idiot. 'Mama, can I go into the garden now?' and she headed off, pulling Daisy behind her. It was only a few seconds before she was back waving the fairy leaf letter. 'Look what Mama's done for me.'

We all tried to laugh it off, but what with Fluffy's death and the disappointing reaction to my carefully crafted fairy letter I felt an acute sense of failure somehow, and it was all so public. I never got the chance to talk to Nikki about the job. She left arm-in-arm with Mum, vaguely saying she'd call sometime next week. Everything I do seems to go wrong. At least when I was working I was competent and sometimes even inspired, but these days I can't even manage the simplest tasks. I'm worried about Daisy. Do you think she's addicted to Calpol? As I put Matilda to bed that night she said, 'Are you happy, Mama?'

I don't know. Am I?

To: **Jay@mybestfriendisgay.com**
From: **Dot@noplacelikehome.com**
Subject: **Fluffy memorial service**

Your presence is requested, not to mourn, but to celebrate the life of Fluffy the hamster on Friday, April 10. No flowers necessary but financial contributions can be made to the Knight family charity fund.

Thought you'd like to know how your goddaughter coped with the news of Fluffy's death. She discovered the lifeless Fluffy and brought her to our bedroom first thing in the morning. She was sobbing her heart out but quietened down as we both explained that hamsters often die like this, that Fluffy'd had a good life and that Matilda had made her very happy. I suggested we buried her in the garden and she could visit her whenever she felt like it. There was a pause while she thought about what we had said.

'If you like you can have another hamster,' suggested Alex

thoughtfully. 'You might want to wait a bit, though.'

'Oh no,' said Matilda, brightening immediately, 'I'd love another hamster right now. Can we get one today, and this time can I have a white one? I always thought Fluffy was a bit too brown.' And without an appropriate moment of mourning she rushed off to wake Daisy up and break the good news. I wonder if she'd react the same way if it was me. 'I always thought Mummy's hair was a bit too brown. Next time, can we have a blonde one?'

To: **NikkiSoda@ambitiousproductions.com**
From: **Dot@noplacelikehome.com**
Subject: **Job offer**

Lovely to see you on Saturday and sorry we didn't really get a chance to chat. I'm glad my mother impressed you. Yes, it is strange you haven't met before but you've obviously heard me talk about her. She was abroad a lot when we first started working together, setting up her business in Paris and Rome. Anyway I'm glad that you found Saturday to be a grand meeting of minds. As far as the job offer goes, thanks for thinking of me for the series of six thirty-minute documentaries. Let's face it, you know as well as I do that it couldn't possibly be part time. I'd just be trying to squeeze five days' work into three. I've decided that I want to be at home for this interesting period in the girls' development but please keep those sexist joke e-mails coming. They make an interesting diversion from domesticity.

To: **Alex@himindoors.com**
From: **Dot@noplacelikehome.com**
Subject: **Career flushed down the pan**

I can't bear these sexist joke e-mails that Nikki keeps sending me but I thought I'd pass on the latest offering to make you feel good about being a man:

'What's the difference between a golf ball and a clitoris?'
'Men will spend hours looking for a golf ball.'

At last I've found out what Nikki's job offer is. She wants me to be an executive producer (yes, thank you) working three days a week (it sounds better and better but hardly realistic) on a series of documentaries (home territory) and the subject matter is (cue roll of drums) *'Are You Sitting Comfortably – a History of Great Toilets of the World*. The treatment was surprisingly detailed, covering a variety of fascinating facts about toilets all over the world, ranging from the loo at Chartwell where Winston Churchill was rumoured to have made his decision to bomb Dresden, to the public convenience where George Michael was arrested. I didn't have to think about it for long. What was it that made her make the immediate connection. 'Toilets . . . ah . . . Dorothy Davies'? Anyway, I think I'm doing the most important job by being with the children.

To: **Delissa@splendidmums.com**
From: **Dot@noplacelikehome.com**
Subject: **Glad to be grey**

Thank you for your more considered e-mail. Of course I know you only want the best for me, and as you said, you can only imagine how much being ill has affected me. It goes without saying I'd love any help from you if you can fit us in. It's always wonderful to see you, and the children adore you. I'm so pleased you enjoyed meeting Nikki last week. What a great opportunity being Programme Consultant on her strand of programming for the over sixties. Clever old you. *Glad to be Grey* is a good title. Not that it applies to you. You may be over sixty but there isn't a grey strand of hair that I can see, and as for wrinkles, I think I've got more than you. So this could be the beginning of a new career for you. Nikki is always quick to recognise potential. This year Spanish degrees, next year the Baftas. I'm really happy for you. Enjoy.

To: **Bethearthmother@rooted.com**
From: **Dot@noplacelikehome.com**
Subject: **Sad to be green**

Why my mother? There must be thousands of dynamic mature women out there who would have fantastic ideas about the sort of programmes they want to watch. I hate myself, and why should I begrudge her this opportunity? I should be thrilled for her. She's amazing, she can always turn everything to her own advantage, it's quite admirable. Remember that time she was spotted in the shop by the scout from the advertising agency, and next thing we know she's plastered all over the sides of buses as the new mature face of Gap? That's just typical of her. Also, the time when she went to photograph the Masai in Kenya. She lived with them for six months and when she came back the photographs were snapped up by *The Observer Magazine*, and it was the first time she'd pointed a camera at anything other than my naked five-year-old bottom. I can go on for ever about the marvellous exploits of my mother. She lives life with such gusto. She was fantastic when I was growing up – exciting and loving – and whenever we did spend time together she always had an exotic story to tell or an adventure planned for me, but I could never be like her.

Funnily enough, the one thing she never did was stay at home with me. This is my chance to do something she's never done and won't be able to do at this stage in her life. I need to embrace being a mother and not hanker for my old lifestyle. If I'm going to do it, then I'm going to do it well. Nikki always said there were two types of women in the world – those who do, and those who don't – and it was nothing to do with sex. It was about women who have children and carry on working, and those who give up and become full-time mothers. She always put me in the first camp, and to be honest I put myself there. Maybe she was right, I do belong there, but now I've made the decision I've got to keep to it. I'm determined to prove her and my mother wrong, but please help!

Chapter Four

'Life is an Incurable Disease.'

Abraham Cowley (1656)

To: **Bethearthmother@rooted.com**
From: **Dot@noplacelikehome.com**
Subject: **Churlish whispers**

What's got into me? As far as I know I haven't got cancer for God's sake, unless there's some determined stray cell that somehow managed to escape the surgeon's knife, chemotherapy, radiotherapy and a ruinous phalanx of antioxidants. I should be skipping down the road singing, 'Hello birds, hello trees, hello sky,' but all I feel like saying is, 'fuck off everyone.' How ungrateful can you get? What's happened to Dennis Potter's blossomiest blossom? What's happened to my wake-up call? Don't get me wrong, I *do* want to be with the children but I'm weighed down by domesticity. Alex rang me this morning at 10.00 a.m.

'Sorry, did I wake you?'

What does he think I do all day? Retire to my bed to take naps, abandoning Daisy in front of *Teletubbies*, or lie on the sofa, gossiping on the phone with friends, buffing my nails? This is my normal day starting at 7.00 a.m. Get all three of us dressed.

'It's my turn to wear the sparkly hairband.'

'I hate that skirt, I want to look cool.'

Make breakfast, one Ready Brek with raspberries and one with banana.

'Can I have the Barbie spoon?'

'I want Postman Pat.' Unpack dishwasher, pack Matilda's lunch box.

'Molly has crisps every day and 'Enry has a big chocolate muffin and chocolate biscuits with big chips in them. They've got nice mummies.'

Brush hair and teeth (make note not to confuse brushes). Try to stop Matilda taunting Daisy by swinging favourite doll Betty round and round her head like a shotputter before she decides where to 'putt'.

'Matilda, I don't want to have to ask you again.'

'Well then, don't.'

Then it's out of the door into the pouring rain to walk to school, back again because we've forgotten her reading folder.

'Shit, Matilda, we forgot to do your reading last night.' Oh shit, swearing policy back to Attainment Level 2.

The journey is punctuated by cries from Daisy in the buggy, 'No buggy. Get out NOW,' as she struggles to unclip the harness and jettison herself into the path of oncoming cars.

Discourage Matilda from taking detours to look for fairies. Apologise to Mrs Steel for being late, again. Overhear two mothers, without toddlers, making arrangements to have a cappuccino in the café after drop-off (oh, the luxury of it) and three other mothers, with toddlers, arranging to meet but not asking me. Rush back to put on washing, clean up kitchen, ready for next onslaught. Check list Nanny Sarah left stapled to fridge, and pack bag with juice, raisins, tissues, spare set of clothes, nappies and wipes (potty training not entirely reliable) ready for exhausting Tumbletots session. Just as I am negotiating with Daisy to leave behind Betty, Teddy and an entire china teaset with accompanying wicker basket, the phone rings. I answer it and take deep breath to shout at insensitive husband. Sleep, if only.

I'm sorry to go on but there's never any time off. Seven days a week you're on duty, and it's hard to be a confident, inventive and understanding mother on those terms. At the moment the children still regard me as an interloper, a replacement for their beloved Sarah.

'When's Sarah coming back?'

Resisting the urge to say, 'Never, because she doesn't love you. She never has, and I'm your mother,' I try to patiently explain the situation. She's never stepping foot in this house again.

To: **Nanny.sarah@indispensable.com**
From: **Dot@noplacelikehome.com**
Subject: **Babysitting**

Could you babysit Thursday next week? We've got a babysitter crisis. You needn't come until 8.00 as it's a late launch party for Alex's drama. Trust all is going well with you.

To: **Alex@himindoors.com**
From: **Dot@noplacelikehome.com**
Subject: **A few ideas?**

Just to let you know, despite a busy schedule of naps, manicures and champagne cocktails with friends, I've arranged (as a last resort) for Sarah to babysit the night of your launch party. I've sneakily asked her to come later on so that the children will be in bed. I'm worried that seeing her may upset the status quo.

I read the *Tess* script last night while you were out. I was rather impressed. I had a few ideas about casting and a couple of plot changes. I think Angel should come to terms with his homosexuality at the end while Tess embraces and accepts this part of his nature and understands his attraction for Alec. Have you thought about shooting the flashbacks on Super 8? It gives it that nice grainy nostalgic feel. Julian would be the best designer for the project. His Trollopes are always good, but maybe you want a more contemporary feel. Will you be using Stan as Director of Photography? Think about Jake, my documentary cameraman. I've heard from Nikki that he's keen to get into drama and he would bring a fresh look to a period piece, although I suppose he would be a risk. See you tonight. Dinner on the table as usual (hah!).

To: **Alex@himindoors.com**
From: **Dot@noplacelikehome.com**
Subject: **Great minds . . .**

Glad to hear that Jessica has already suggested so many changes that are the same as mine. Shows I haven't completely lost it. Maybe my casting ideas were a bit extreme but I think Brad Pitt needs a change in direction and Angel Clare would be a challenge. Alec needs to be sexy and cruel. What about George Clooney? I'll come back to you on other attractive leads. It will keep me mentally exercised during Monkey Music while singing our regular medley of 'Do you know the Muffin Man', 'Three Blind Mice' and 'Humpty Dumpty' (crippling for the knees at my age).

To: **Jay@mybestfriendisgay.com**
From: **Dot@noplacelikehome.com**
Subject: **You know how to whistle . . .**

Thinking about casting ideas for Alex's drama, and trying to work out who's sexy and why, has stirred things up. I think there must be something wrong with me. This morning I started ogling the men in the Boden catalogue and Christopher Plummer suddenly seems irresistible in The Sound of Music. I thought his bosun's whistle was a good idea and have found my old stopwatch, which I'm using to time the children in the morning. The first day it worked fantastically well. They thought it was a great game. Matilda ate her Ready Brek in ten seconds (probably terrible for the digestion). A week on, the novelty has worn off but it's been nice to see the look of surprise on Mrs Steel's face when we actually turn up on time for school.

If I'm lusting after the men in Boden it's not going to be long before I catch Alex fondling the girls' Barbie collection. Our sex life is non existent. There's never a good time. In the evening we're exhausted. In the morning I usually wake, with a start, to see an eye close up, staring at me intensely, and hear a little voice whispering, 'Can I wear my pink spotty dress again today with my purple tights and pink sparkly hairband?' Then the girls come in. Sorry, my little joke, but you can see what a passion killer it is.

It's been strange since my operation. Everything is in the right place but I've got some spectacular scars along the top of my breast and across into my armpit (did you want to know details?). Things sag where they never used to. Pert is no longer a word to be used in connection with my body unless you're describing my eyelashes. Alex made such an effort to begin with to make sure I didn't feel like Mrs Frankenstein, but to be honest I felt too sick to respond during chemotherapy and was convinced I smelt bad. It was as though the poison was seeping out through my pores. I overheard Matilda tell Alex that, 'Mama smells different.' I could never bring myself to ask him about it. The sad thing about sex is that once you get out of the habit it's really hard to get back into it.

To: **Jay@mybestfriendisgay.com**
From: **Dot@noplacelikehome.com**
Subject: **Lonely hearts**

I know you're absolutely right. I'm incredibly lucky. Alex is a lovely man, blah, blah, blah . . . He's not lovely all the time but I suppose no one ever is. So you want to fall in love. I never thought of you wanting to settle down, you seem to relish the excitement of the new. Of course everyone wants a Mr or Mrs Special. Although there's never a problem finding someone to have fun with, it is much harder finding someone to do nothing with. When I was single I used to long for those cosy Saturday nights curled up with a significant other on the sofa, sharing a takeaway and watching TV. But there's nothing I like better than a challenge. Can I help you in your search for love? Let me play Cilla and see what I can come up with. Won't be hard as you know I think you're eminently lovable.

In fact, there is someone who you might be interested in. He's very good-looking, which could be a problem, and although I haven't actually spoken to him I see him most days as he lives round the corner from us. He works as a nanny to two boisterous boys and he's quite magnificent with them. All us exhausted mothers watch him in admiration as he's so physical. So that's one thing you would have in common. I don't mean the physical bit, as your idea of exercise is to walk to the car, but at least you share an amazing ability to get on with children.

Enough of your emotional problems, what about my more practical ones? I've made contact with the inner circle (Sarah's nanny circuit) and Daisy and I are meeting them tomorrow morning for coffee. You don't think there'll be any strange initiation ceremonies do you?

To: **Bethearthmother@rooted.com**
From: **Dot@noplacelikehome.com**
Subject: **Sartorial savvy**

Have just returned from disastrous shopping expedition with both girls. A big mistake. I thought they might enjoy it as I remember being mesmerised by my mother trying on beautiful dresses in elegant shops. We went to a local shop where you can buy all the big designers. We were greeted by an assistant.

'How are you today? Can I be of assistance?'

Matilda was awestruck at the lovely dresses hanging around the shop walls. Daisy began to grab at anything pink, 'Lovely 'ink.' The shop assistant flinched as Daisy touched everything. She fondled a pink silk ballgown, rubbing the fabric against her cheek which still had the remains of her boiled egg and marmite soldiers stuck to it. The dresses worked as efficiently as a dry flannel.

I quickly tried to distract the assistant by saying, 'I need something for a party. Nothing too elegant, just something to look good.'

Matilda had taken off her trainers and was tottering around the shop in a pair of horribly high-heeled satin, strappy black evening shoes, accosting customers as they came into the shop and mimicking the shop assistant, 'Can I be of assistance?'

We'd already overstayed our welcome. I don't know what I was thinking of. Special party, buy new clothes – it's a reflex reaction, but these days of course I can't afford to buy anything new. My Manola Blahnik overdraft is eating into my savings and I spent far too much on my Boden pull-ons. Since the day I started working I have never had to ask anyone for money. The idea of going, Prada beret in hand, to Alex appals me. How humiliating.

Can you lend me anything for Alex's party? All I've got are my tired timeless classics from Nicole Farhi circa 1997. They're hardly exciting and I want to look good on what will be my first foray into the land of social intercourse for months. An honest look in the mirror doesn't reveal 'the fairest of them all' but a rather dilapidated version of a once-quite-attractive woman. My hair has recovered from the chemotherapy but it's grown back wavy and lacklustre. My eyes are shot through with little red veins (well at least it's a variation on the thighs). Lines have appeared either side of my mouth and on my forehead. I'm sure it's nothing to do with having cancer, they seem to have appeared since I gave up work. It's all that frowning at the children. (Make mental note to be more jolly.) I need some cosmetic assistance.

To: **Hari@hairsculpture.com**
From: **Dot@noplacelikehome.com**
Subject: **Some colour in my life?**

Hari – I haven't seen you for ages. Domestic goddesses don't usually require much attention, everything just falls into place naturally. Yet again I'm feeling follicly challenged. Can you squeeze me in?

To: **Jay@mybestfriendisgay.com**
From: **Dot@noplacelikehome.com**
Subject: **When shall we three meet again . . . ?**

I was looking forward to the coffee morning, minus the coffee now that I've given up caffeine post-cancer. That was my first mistake. By refusing the coffee, and they having no alternative (herbal tea was dismissed snootily as lesbian tea), I immediately alienated myself. What I've come to recognise is that there's a clear social divide between nannies and mothers, and it's very hard to cross the boundary. It's as if we, the mothers, are encroaching on the nannies' territory. They are the professionals, after all, whereas we are mere untrained amateurs who just happen to have biology and natural instinct on our side which, as we all know, can be very unreliable.

We sat around watching our charges developing their social skills, which consisted of, 'I want that. You've got it. So I'm going to hit you or push you until you give it to me and once you've given it to me and gone on to play with something else, I'll change my mind and want the next thing that you're playing with.' Daisy shone at social skills. I kept trying to intervene but ended up feeling as redundant as Nato forces in Kosovo. After a few preliminary questions about teething and potty training the first of the witches, Angela ('Ange to me friends.' Angela to me), said, 'Have you seen that Philippe? The French bloke that looks after Henry and Charles. I think he looks just like Robbie Williams.'

'I don't think it's right. I don't think boys should be nannies. It's just not in their nature. I know I wouldn't trust him, Robbie Williams or not,' said Louise.

'Give over. He's brilliant with those boys. He takes them swimming, skate boarding, bowling and plays footie for hours on the common. You wouldn't do that. There's only so much of painting and making shell pictures that boys can take.'

I realised that they were talking about my perfect match for Jay. Now was a perfect opportunity to discover his sexual preferences.

'Does he have a girlfriend,' I asked, then realising immediately that they thought I fancied him, 'because I have a friend who might be interested,' I quickly added.

They looked at me unconvinced. What could Sarah have possibly told them? Maybe she has a vivid imagination and didn't believe me when I said I had to work late at the office.

'I think he's gay,' said Louise.

I resisted shouting, 'Yes. Result.'

She continued, 'That's another reason I wouldn't have him near those boys.'

'Oh, come on,' I said, and then stopped myself because I could see it could easily blow up into a terrible argument. Louise glared at me.

So, I was right and all I've got to do now is arrange for you to meet him. You, on the other hand, must invest in a French dictionary for research purposes. *Ça c'est le frisson*.

In the meantime Daisy had seized the opportunity afforded by my having distracted the nannies and was aggressively prising off little Lucy's fingers from a doll she particularly admired. Angela commented on her behaviour.

'Funny, I've never seen her do that.'

'Me neither,' I laughed quickly. The conversation came round to Sarah, as I knew it inevitably would.

'Have you spoken to Sarah?' asked Louise.

'Oh yes, we're always in touch.'

The three witches looked at me knowingly. They think (actually they know) I can't cope without her.

'Has she told you about her book?' asked Michelle, the final and possibly most lethal of the three.

I tried not to choke on my glass of water, and to say nonchalantly, 'Oh yes, she might have mentioned it – what is it again? A guide to good nannying?'

Michelle sharpened her talons and tossed back her dark hair, 'She's writing a novel.'

My stomach literally lurched. Then they started to shriek and cackle and dance around me, laughing and pointing while the children joined in. (OK, not really, but it felt like that.) I have a bad feeling about this book.

To: **Alex@himindoors.com**
From: **Dot@noplacelikehome.com**
Subject: **Poor communication**

I've been trying to get you on your mobile all day. Every time I ring up, the phone goes dead as though you've switched it off, leaving me feeling foolish and personally affronted on the end of the line. I know you're busy but it wouldn't take a minute to give me a quick call back. I don't have time to chat because the phone acts as a cue for the girls to start fighting to get my attention, so I wouldn't keep you long.

Anyway, that's fine about you going with Jessica to the launch. It makes absolute sense to go straight from the office, especially if you've got things to talk about. I'll get a cab and maybe we can go out to dinner afterwards? Thought you ought to know that I've had my hair cut for tonight. I was quite pleased with it, until I picked up Matilda from school and she said, 'You look just like Maria in *The Sound of Music*.' In my opinion that's a disaster, and she's being fairly inscrutable about whether it's an insult or a compliment.

The important news of the day is that Sarah is writing a book. Did she ever mention anything about this to you or ever hint that she had any literary aspirations? I have a horrible feeling that we're going to be involved in this somehow, and to make it worse she's got an agent.

To: **Trustytaxis.com**
From: **Dot@noplacelikehome.com**
Subject: **Call me a cab**

Can I book a cab for 8.00 p.m. tonight. It is imperative that you are punctual. If possible I'd like a BMW or a stretch Mercedes and not a battered old Skoda.

To: **Bethearthmother@rooted.com**
From: **Dot@noplacelikehome.com**
Subject: **Times they are a changin'**

What happened to those days when you just got up in the morning, put on something that you knew would look fine during the day, then with a few choice accessories and change of shoes, could transform you into a sex kitten for the evening? Why am I spending so much time thinking about trivia? Why should it matter what I look like tonight? Hari, my highlighting hero, has managed to put some life back into my locks. Trussed up in tin foil like a turkey ready for the oven, I read an article in *Marie Claire* about hair colouring being carcinogenic. It was too late to do anything about it. Honestly, it is a minefield out there. Soon they'll say breathing causes cancer. What happens when I go grey (if I'm lucky to get that old)? I suppose I'll just have to accept it gracefully. Maybe there are natural alternatives. I should get Mum to look into it for her programme. Must go as I can hear the cab knocking on the door – it's turned up early. What a relief. I'll give you a full debriefing tomorrow.

To: **Bethearthmother@rooted.com**
From: **Dot@noplacelikehome.com**
Subject: **Best laid plans**

When does a cab ever turn up early? I'm living in la la land. It was Sarah who wanted to come early to see the children. This wasn't the plan. Of course they were beside themselves with joy and excitement. They flung their arms around her and shouted, 'Sarah, Sarah,' and I felt like I'd been stabbed through the heart. I know it's silly. Nothing ever phases Sarah. She arrived looking gorgeous in jeans, armed with two horrible cute teddy bears holding appropriate initials for the girls. They were something I would never dream of buying them but the girls were delighted. They climbed up her knees and did tumble turns. She took them off to the kitchen to whisk up some 'Sarah Specials,' otherwise known as pancakes.

'But they've just brushed their teeth,' I said lamely.

'Don't worry, Mummy, we'll brush them again,' pleaded Matilda. 'Please can we have pancakes, we haven't had them for ages.'

Another blow to my mother-shaped ego. Must remember to look up pancake recipe tomorrow. Defeated, I retired upstairs. On the plus side it's given me some extra time to have a bath, slap on some make-up and talk to you. What was good was the children's reaction to me in a dress for the first time in months.

Matilda gave me a big hug, 'You look so pretty. I think Daddy will marry you all over again.'

The effect was slightly ruined by the splodgy purple handprint she left on the back of the dress but you never know it might start a new fashion. Just looked at my watch, it's five past eight. I must go. By the way, don't worry about your dress, I'm sure the paint will come off when it's dry-cleaned.

To: **Trustytaxis.com**
From: **Dot@noplacelikehome.com**
Subject: **Where are you?**

Your phone is permanently engaged. Where is my taxi? It is now ten minutes late. Send someone immediately.

To: **Trustytaxis.com**
From: **Dot@noplacelikehome.com**
Subject: **!!!!!!!!!**

Where the f**k are you? I'm now twenty minutes late.

To: **Untrustytaxis.com**
From: **Dot@noplacelikehome.com**
Subject: **Hell hath no fury . . .**

I was supposed to be having dinner with the Prime Minister but I'm too late to go now. Rest assured, questions will be asked in the House of Commons and Cherie has offered to act as my solicitor. My husband and I are extremely influential members of the community and will never use your company again. You will be blacklisted. I must warn you, I have extensive contacts at the BBC and I shall make sure you feature in a *Watchdog* special, exposing rip-off car companies.

Chapter Five

'Cancer is the new black.'

To: **Bethearthmother@rooted.com**
From: **Dot@noplacelikehome.com**
Subject: **Midnight vigil**

I haven't been up this late for years unless it was to tend to the girls. The evening started disastrously with the cab failing to turn up. I took a deep breath and went by tube (don't laugh), but it meant I was late and stressed, and I was nervous too. I was determined I wasn't going to talk about being ill as it's so boring. But what should I talk about? When you're working you don't have time to stop and think about socialising, it's just part of the lifestyle, but tonight it felt like two alien worlds colliding and it takes a massive mindshift. I wasn't prepared for feeling rusty, but I have a little tactic that I've adopted over the years. If I'm worried about a social situation I just pretend to be someone I particularly admire, but tonight Lindsay Duncan let me down. I probably should have used Kate Winslet.

There were lots of familiar faces there. 'Darling Dot,' two air kisses, and a hug that was meant to be bolstering but was just a clash of bones, and Nikki enveloped me. 'What's it like to be back in civilisation?' she asked, looking suspiciously at my dress (sorry, your dress). 'Ghost, circa 1983?' she quipped.

'God knows,' I replied, 'It's Borrowed, 2002.'

Alex waved at me from the bar, but I needed to build up my strength before fighting my way across to him through the seething crowd of producers, actors and hacks.

Nikki continued, 'I was disappointed you didn't want to do *Toilets.* It's going to be very exciting. We've just heard we've got George Michael as an interviewee.'

'That's wonderful,' I enthused. 'It was probably too soon for me, but don't count me out of the equation for ever,' I replied as breezily as I could. I saw Tom Hooper, Head of Comedy, making his way over.

'Hello Dot, looking lovely as ever. Haven't seen your credit for a while. Working on anything interesting at the moment?'

'My children,' I replied.

'Ah yes, we all think of our programmes as our babies,' he said earnestly.

'No, I mean I've given up work to be at home with my two girls.'

He looked baffled, as though the concept of me not working did not compute, 'So you've gone independent then, but you're not getting the commissions? Come and see me. You always have interesting ideas, if not exactly mainstream. Let's do lunch, or better still an evening drink at the club.' With that he strode off purposefully to continue to work the room.

'Lecherous toad,' snorted Nikki.

'How's Richard?' I asked.

She laughed, 'Good connection. I haven't seen him for months. I expect we'll get divorced one of these days but you know how it is, we don't seem to have the time.'

'How are things working out with my mother?' I asked as casually as I could.

'God, darling, she's an absolute gem. I can't thank you enough for introducing us. I'm thinking of sending her off with her own film crew. She's up for anything and totally dedicated to the work. She's even put the Spanish degree on hold until things calm down a bit. Oh, look, there's Mark Thompson. I must go and schmooze. See you later darling.'

A concerned voice behind me called my name. I turned to face affable, well-meaning Janet Clark, Head of Publicity.

'Dorothy,' she murmured intensely, while clutching my hand, 'how *are* you?'

I always know I'm in trouble when the head moves to one side in sympathy.

'You look amazing. It must have been a nightmare for you. You've been so brave.'

'Oh, not so brave,' I mumbled, 'you just deal with it. You have to. How are things with you?' I said, trying to change the subject.

'Well, nothing as bad as you obviously, but my mother hasn't been well. They think it's early stages of dementia and it's just not as fashionable as Alzheimer's these days, so there's very little information or support. I mean, at least the good thing about breast cancer is there's so much money being piled into research. It's so high profile, even Prince Charles is involved.' She paused, realising she was on dangerous territory. She looked at me anxiously, 'I'm sorry, I didn't mean . . .'

'Oh, don't worry,' I replied breezily, trying to edge my way towards the bar.

I tried to see if there was someone I could bring into the conversation so that we could change the subject. I really didn't want to talk about illness tonight or ever again. But Janet seemed intent on holding my attention. It's as if she thought that because of what I'd been through I'd be more sympathetic. Maybe I'm just a horrible person but I didn't want to hear all the depressing details about dementia.

'I am sorry about your mother but I think I should go and find Alex now. Lovely to see you,' I started to walk away, but she came with me continuing the conversation.

'Oh well, you've been through much worse. It's not as though she's young. She's had her life. She doesn't have to contemplate the idea of leaving behind two small children.'

I find it intriguing that there is a scale of human misery. Breast cancer rates higher than Alzheimer's, but I suppose death in the Twin Towers would be right up at the top of the scale. How do you assess whether your misery is worse or better than another person's tragedy? Determined to move on, I turned to Janet and said, 'Have you spoken to Alex yet, he's very keen to discuss the publicity campaign for *Tess*. Oh, look, he's over there.'

As she headed off in Alex's direction I grabbed onto Sally, a producer whom I'd worked with at the BBC Features department at least five years ago.

'So what's it like being at home all day? Don't you get bored?' she asked.

'Well, it's much harder work than I thought it would be. I do think it's making a difference for the kids, especially Daisy, my youngest. I mean the other day we were in the playground and she actually stopped kicking all the stones off the gravel path when I asked her, whereas a few months ago she wouldn't have listened to me at all. I do find it a problem keeping their diet healthy. Do you buy organic?'

I'd lost her. She was doing exactly what I'd been doing a few minutes earlier with Janet, desperately searching for an excuse to walk away. Not only had I lost her, I'd lost myself. What was I doing talking about playgrounds and organic vegetables?

'Ah, there's Mark Thompson. I've been trying to talk to him for weeks. Bye Dot.' She left so quickly I didn't even have time to say, 'See you later, Sally.'

'For God's sake, Dot, you can do better than this,' I said, mentally reprimanding myself.

The next person I engaged in conversation was Mike, a lovely graphics designer who I should have asked to do Matilda's cake designs rather than dastardly Dick. We talked about the project he was working on and I managed to steer clear of the subject of domesticity. I was doing pretty well until it was obvious our conversation was coming to its natural conclusion.

'Give me your address,' Mike said, 'I can send you my programme cards so you know when the programme will be transmitted.'

'I'd love that,' I replied, 'It's 24 Acorn Avenue. That's A for Annie apple, C that's a curly C not a kicking K, O for Ollie . . .'

I suddenly realised what I was doing. Mike couldn't stop laughing and I flushed what I hope was a delicate shade of pink. I'm not sure I should be allowed out in grown-up company.

'Ah, found you.' It was Alex come to rescue me. 'How are you doing? Good haircut.' Under his breath he started to sing 'How, do you solve a problem like Maria?'. I glowered at him.

'Alex,' a resonant voice called across the sea of faces, 'I need you,' and there she was – the immensely impressive Jessica Bedmeigh making her way towards us, looking stunning in a dark Armani suit with clearly very little underneath. It was sexy in the way that it revealed little and intimated much. Just undo one button and it would show everything, and we're talking Agent Provocateur rather than Marks and Spencer.

People moved out of Jessica's way as they would have done if it had been a royal procession. That was the kind of awe she inspired. She walked in slow motion with her glossy blonde hair rippling over her shoulders, looking like a perfect advertisement for L'Oréal hair shampoo. Alex and I stared at her as she made her way towards us, both caught up in our own personal thoughts. I didn't want to know what he was thinking, but judging by the look on his face he didn't need to spell it out. I, on the other hand, now realise that Jessica Bedmeigh is trouble with a capital T for Tantalising Totty.

Once she reached us she turned to Alex, completely ignoring me, 'I've got to do my bit in a minute and I need you with me. Talked to anyone interesting?' she asked him, still with her back to me.

'Oh . . . um . . . Jessica, meet . . . um, um . . . Dorothy, my wife.' For a minute I thought he'd forgotten my name. She turned and looked me up and down and then switched on a smile.

'Oh God. How lovely to meet you,' but as I put my hand out she wrapped her arm around Alex. 'We'd better go as they're just about to start.'

Alex gave me a sheepish grin as he was led off. I didn't have a chance to say anything, but I noticed as they walked towards the screen, looking every bit the handsome couple, Jessica put her hand proprietorially on his shoulder.

Managing to control the overwhelming urge to shout after her, 'Oy, you. Hands off my husband,' I made my way to the bar. By this time I needed a drink to clear the bad taste in my mouth. As I was standing by the bar Jessica stood up to speak. There were a lot of programmes being launched but *Tess* is obviously going to be the proverbial jewel in the crown. Clips were shown of series that had already been made or were in post-production, and Jessica was going to announce the cast and filming dates for *Tess*. She was very impressive. Informal, funny and very complimentary about Alex, saying how talented he was and how long she had wanted to work with him. He looked suitably embarrassed and pleased.

It was interesting looking at Alex across a sea of people. OK, he's not the tallest man in the world, his battered leather jacket has seen better days and his dark hair never gets touched, but he has an energy, which is exciting. He also looks younger than his years (a great source of irritation to me, people often think he's my toy boy). I was proud of him. We've been so cemented together for the past few years, dealing with the shock of having two small children and my cancer, that I haven't stood back and looked at him properly for a very long time. I felt an overwhelming desire to kiss him but I couldn't get anywhere near him. I'd have to save it for later.

Then I saw Jake. You remember the cameraman with whom I got stuck in Bosnia. We'd had a brief affair before I met Alex and there's always been some electricity between us. Now you know me, I'm never going to pass up the opportunity for a good safe flirt, and after my introduction to Jessica Bedmeigh I was in need of a boost. I went over and touched his arm. He leapt as if the electricity was tangible and then just about managed to say, 'Hello.' Looking uncomfortable, he stuttered some inane remarks about hoping to work with Alex as he was keen to get into drama.

'So have you completely given up on documentaries? You're such a natural in compromising situations. Remember that bar in Bosnia? You just have the right instincts.'

I expected a reaction but it was like talking to a stranger. I was finding it hard to make eye contact with him because he kept staring uncomfortably at the ground. I gamely struggled on, 'So what are you working on at the moment?' I got nothing back, I couldn't understand what was going on. Did I smell funny or was my haircut so terrible that he couldn't bring himself to look at it? He didn't ask me a single question and just as I thought he was going to say something, he made a feeble excuse and left me standing alone. I was shocked and then it dawned on me that he obviously knew about the cancer but he didn't know how to deal with it or what to say, particularly because it was breast cancer. I suppose I can't blame him but it made me feel like a leper.

Nikki loomed into view. 'Want to meet the Controller of BBC2, darling? She's awfully nice. Sophie, this is Dorothy. She's Alex Knight's wife.'

I flashed a look of fury at Nikki but she missed it as she was already half-way across the room in hot pursuit of Ruby Wax, no doubt hoping to get her involved in *Are You Sitting Comfortably?* I heard her saying, 'George Michael has agreed . . .'

I felt as if my whole career had been wiped out in the space of a few months. 'Nikki and I used to work together,' I muttered unconvincingly, 'but I've just given up.'

'Why is that?'

Her eyes were straying over my shoulder. I knew she was asking out of politeness rather than genuine interest. What was it about tonight? Nobody wanted to talk to me. For a few seconds I wavered. Did I really want to go there, but as I saw her eyes scanning the room over my left shoulder I knew I had to do something drastic.

'I've just had breast cancer.'

I'd done it. I'd resorted to playing the cancer card, something I'd never done before. I felt a twinge of guilt but it was almost worthwhile as the effect was instantaneous. It was as if I had magically metamorphosed from boring housewife into interesting woman. I now had her complete attention. Her whole manner softened. She looked shocked but curious. I knew I had to be careful how I continued but I was enjoying her sympathy. She didn't get to be Controller of BBC2 without having an inquisitive mind and being prepared to ask the difficult questions.

'God, how awful. You poor thing. Are you all right now? You look absolutely wonderful of course,' and within seconds I felt a firm gentle hand on my back as she guided me to some chairs around the side of the room as if I was a fragile person who needed special treatment. 'When did you have it?'

'Well, I've been clear for a while now,' I said cheerily, 'and of course I have the regular check-ups.'

'How did you discover it?' She wanted to know every little detail, concern evident in her eyes. 'What was the lump like. Did it hurt? How long before you were treated? What was chemotherapy like? How did you tell your children?'

I fielded the barrage of questions as well as could be expected, 'Well, if you're going to have cancer it's the one to have. So fashionable these days.'

'Has it changed you?' she wanted to know.

I began to feel pressurised and a bit of a fraud. It was as though I held the secret of life and death in my hands, but all I could mumble was, 'Well, I suppose it made me give up work. So something is changing. I don't know yet. I think it's too soon to tell.' I hoped this wasn't going to disappoint her.

A couple of independent producers had been standing near us, keen to get their five minutes with the Controller. Sophie, her eyes slightly wide and shiny, called them over.

'Have you met Dorothy Davies? She's quite extraordinary. You don't mind me saying, do you?' she said, without waiting for me to answer, 'but she had breast cancer last year and she's just dealing with it so well. I'm just filled with admiration.'

The first producer was quick to join in the conversation, 'Oh, I've been there. I know exactly how you feel. I found a lump last month. I couldn't get to see a specialist for a week. I was absolutely terrified. It was undoubtedly the worst week of my life. God you must be brave.'

'Are you OK?' I asked.

'Oh, yes. Turned out it was just a cyst, but it was terrifying.'

'My mother died of cancer a few years ago,' said the other producer, her eyes beginning to water.

'Was it breast cancer?' I asked uneasily.

'No, lung cancer, but it was awful. She decided to go the alternative route. I expect you've heard about the Max Gerson diet – vegetarian, lots of juices and grapes?'

I assured her that I had, and that I'd done a lot of research and was on my own diet of sorts. I said knowledgeably, 'I read a book by a woman called Jane Plant, called *Your Life in Your Hands*. She was given two months to live after constant recurrences. Infuriated by the medical profession, she set about trying to understand why she had the disease. To cut a long story short she advocates giving up all dairy and beef as well as a variety of other things I won't go into here. I think it's made a big difference. She's been clear of any cancer for the past eight years.'

'Has anyone bought the rights to this book? Her story sounds fascinating,' said John Hopkins, another producer who had just joined us. 'God, it would make a feature film. Who do you want to play you, Dot?'

My favourite game. I thought for a moment, 'Michelle Pfeiffer ten years ago would be my first choice, but Jennifer Connelly would be good. Or perhaps Gwyneth Paltrow would be better, her English accent is very convincing.'

They all nodded furiously. I couldn't believe they were taking me so seriously. If I'd said Robbie Williams, Tom Cruise or Eddie Izzard in drag they still would have agreed.

'The interesting thing is whether there is such a thing as a cancer personality?' said the first producer.

'Oh-oh' I thought, 'this could be the beginning of a backlash.' Here was someone about to blow the gaff and say it was all my fault anyway that I got cancer, so why give the girl any attention? I was beginning to feel we'd done enough cancer talk for one evening but everyone else was riveted. Over by the screen I could see Jessica laughing excessively at something Alex had said. She kept touching her neck and putting her fingertips to her lips as if to say, 'Look at these. Would you like to try them?' I tried to catch his attention but he was too far away, although I think the only way I could have distracted him would have been to strip off, and even then I don't think it would have been a guaranteed success.

'Susan Sontag's *Illness as Metaphor* is a very interesting essay on cancer. She had it years ago and refutes there is such a thing as a cancer personality.' Sophie was defending my corner far more intelligently than I could have done. 'Dot, have you read the Louise Hay books *You Can Heal Your Life* and the follow-ups?'

I nodded. By now we'd gathered quite a crowd and they were all hanging on my every word. 'This could go to a girl's head,' I thought to myself. I wasn't used to so much attention.

'Did you lose your hair?' asked a young researcher

'Well, I suppose I was lucky in that I didn't lose it all but I became like one of those sad balding men who pull a few straggling strands of hair across their foreheads, in a pitiful attempt to hide their predicament. I had a wig in case of emergencies, but whenever I tried the wig on in the privacy of my own home I looked like I was wearing a badger on my head. It's now been let loose in the children's dressing-up box. I was never quite brave enough to do a Sinead O'Connor. It was lucky for me that headscarves suddenly became fashionable. The gods were really on my side.'

Everybody laughed encouragingly and it felt like it wasn't just the gods but the whole room urging me on and encouraging me to talk about the one thing I'd been determined not to talk about.

A rather large woman who I recognised as a former children's TV presenter said, 'You look so well now it's hard to believe it was only last year, and you're so gloriously thin. It's almost worth getting cancer to have a figure like that.'

Sophie shot her a look that signified the final nail in her career as a presenter on the BBC2 daytime cookery show. Noticing the gathering crowd it didn't take long for Nikki to join us. She basked in the reflected glory of playing the role of good friend to the brave cancer patient.

'Yes, I went to as many of her chemotherapy sessions as I could.' I heard her say to John Hopkins. The fact that she had offered to come once, and spent most of the time in the loo on her mobile because she hated the sight of the needle, was not mentioned. 'This is fantastic,' she whispered to me, 'it could be very useful. They all think you're amazing.'

By now I wanted to leave. I felt as if things had spiralled out of control. Alex was nowhere to be seen and I was feeling a bit shamefaced. Nobody had thought I was wonderful until I played the cancer card. Surely it is undignified to have to resort to such methods. Can't I be interesting for who I am, rather than for what programme I work on, who I've married or how ill I've been? Exhausted, I felt it was time to leave. I made my excuses and managed to extricate myself from the crowd. For one brief second I got the distinct feeling that people were going to start applauding me as I left.

'Let's hear it for Dot the Brave who stared cancer in the face and survived.'

I eventually found Alex, Jessica still by his side as if stuck with superglue.

'I'm off,' I said.

He looked worried, 'I can't go yet.' I was almost past caring.

'Don't worry, I'll see you at home.' One of the producers who'd been part of my audience was talking to Jessica and nodded in my direction. I saw the look of surprise on her face as she stared at me, and I felt an overwhelming sense of triumph.

'I bet you haven't stared death in the face,' I thought to myself. And I pulled myself up to my full height, stuck my slightly lopsided chest out and walked proudly out of the door.

Alex came back late, but I waited up for him. He gave me a big hug.

'Well, you were a bit of a star then?' he said. 'I got the sympathy vote from every woman at the party. No one was interested in *Tess* after you'd gone, all they wanted to talk about was you and how brave you are.'

'Sorry,' I apologised, 'I didn't mean to steal your moment of glory.'

'Don't be silly,' he said, kissing my forehead, 'I'm very proud of you.'

This wasn't the time to remind him that he'd almost forgotten my name earlier in the evening. But exhausted as I was, I also felt in need of a hug from Alex. In the taxi back from the party my euphoria had worn off, leaving me with an uncomfortable realisation that this wasn't a film. It was real and I wished to God it wasn't, but Alex gave me the briefest kiss and then disappeared into the bathroom saying, 'Sorry, I'm desperate.'

When he got into bed I snuggled up to him, enjoying the feel of his body against mine, but he switched off the light and within seconds he was snoring. The thought of watching his back as he drifted off to sleep excited by his new job and the gorgeous Jessica Bedmeigh was too depressing. Do you think he's interested in her? She was all over him tonight. What man could resist those 'Come to Bedmeigh' eyes? She's younger, more successful, and better-looking than me. I bet all her body parts are pert. I can't bear it.

Chapter Six

'For what do we live but to make sport for our neighbours and laugh at them in our turn!'
Jane Austen, *Pride and Prejudice*

To: **Bethearthmother@rooted.com**
From: **Dot@noplacelikehome.com**
Subject: **Cold light of day**

Apologies for hysterical e-mail of last night. A lethal cocktail of wine and rejection made me overreact. I haven't said anything to Alex but I'm going to have to be vigilant as regards Miss Bedmeigh. Since giving up work my confidence has been battered. I feel like my life has very gently slipped out of gear. I'm floundering and last night didn't help.

Out of interest, when people ask you what you do, do you say, 'I'm a housewife,' or, 'I'm a full-time mother?' Are you content to say that, not feeling any need to justify your existence any further? I found last night that it stuck in my throat. I had to keep referring back to my former glorious career to feel of value. It's ridiculous that motherhood is seen as an indulgence of the middle classes. Society doesn't value any of the caring professions any more. Nurses and teachers aren't paid properly and mothers aren't appreciated because they're not economically viable. It all comes down to economics. Here ends a party political broadcast on behalf of the Disenchanted Party. Your dress is at the dry-cleaner's and if you look on your doorstep there is a big bunch of purple tulips to say thank you for everything.

To: **Bethearthmother@rooted.com**
From: **Dot@noplacelikehome.com**
Subject: **Proud to be Mum**

I can see that you love being a mother but I'm interested that there's no dilemma and that you feel absolutely confident that when the time comes to work you'll have no trouble finding something that's interesting. Granted it won't be a glittering career, but so what? We all know how frustrating glittering careers can be. As you say, look at Mum. She's had an amazing mix of careers but the point is, she never took her eye off the ball. She never did stay at home as she knew it would drive her mad. She also had to work to keep us financially, as Dad's meagre offerings weren't enough to keep us in the style we hadn't become accustomed to.

Your confidence is encouraging. It's interesting what you say about the mothers at school and how the ones who didn't stay at home now feel that they've missed out on something that can never be recaptured. I suppose the intriguing thing would be to look ahead ten years and see how they feel then.

To: **Jay@mybestfriendisgay.com**
From: **Dot@noplacelikehome.com**
Subject: **Strange Meeting**

I've just come back from the school run, wearing my Boden pull-ons. (Yes, I've succumbed – it just saves so much time not having to work out what to wear. Maybe I should lay out my clothes the night before as you suggested I do with the girls.) I was pushing the buggy, walking a few strides ahead in an attempt to disown Matilda, who was singing loudly 'He's got the whole world in his hands'. (It's the price you pay for a free education at a church school.) I was spotted by the overbearing Arabella, who is determined to recruit me onto the PTA. I dodged round some parked cars but like a determined pit bull terrier she quickened her step to catch up with me. I quickly crossed the road without stopping to look.

A blast of a horn stopped me short and a man started yelling, 'You stupid cow. Look where you're going. You shouldn't be allowed out with children.'

'In case it has escaped your notice, these are school gates,' I said in my most controlled talking-to-an-irrational-member-of-the-public BBC voice.

'Bloody hell,' said the voice, 'Dorothy? Dorothy Davies driving a buggy? Holy shit.'

The angry man disintegrated, just like the Wicked Witch of the West after Dorothy throws a bucket of water over her. In his place stood a tall Scottish comedian with the face of a fallen angel. Mothers walking by with their children looked shocked. 'Holy shit' isn't the usual sort of language you expect to hear outside a church school.

'Luke Lloyd. How extraordinary. What are you doing here?' I exclaimed disingenuously. I'd forgotten quite how attractive he was.

'Haven't you heard, I've given up showbusiness to become a teacher?'

'Really?' I said in amazement.

'No, you daft thing, my kids go to the school.'

I laughed politely while kicking myself for being so gullible. He was always very good at winding me up. We worked together years ago when I was a researcher and he was an aspiring comic, fresh down from Dundee. I knew he'd do well because he had a presentable edge. He wasn't so political that he alienated his audience and he was always very sexy, which helps. Nowadays he presents a cult game show but it doesn't really suit him. It was a shock to see him out of context and you could feel the other mothers were only too aware of this celebrity in their midst.

He was staring at me and Matilda was beginning to get restless.

'Can we go now, Mama?'

As I turned to follow her, he said, 'It's great to see you. Look, what are you doing after drop-off? Let's go for a coffee?'

I glanced down at my pull-ons and thought how awful I must look. 'Yeah, OK. That would be nice. I'll see you at the café in the village.'

There followed an agonising moment of indecision. Should I go home and change out of my Boden pull-ons and put on make-up? But then he's bound to notice I've made an effort, and why would I be bothering? If memory serves me well he's a cocky bastard. Probably worse now that he's a fully-fledged TV celebrity. The alternative was to turn up wearing the aforementioned pull-ons with no mascara and pallid complexion. Vanity, vanity. What would you have done? Yup, you're right, I'm back here making myself presentable, changing into jeans, putting on make-up and then wiping a lot of it off to achieve that natural look. Daisy, on the other hand, has no qualms about looking like Joan Collins on a particularly scary day, resplendent in pink lipstick, not just confined to her lips. I'll report back later.

To: **LukeLloyd@talent.co.uk**
From: **Dot@noplacelikehome.com**
Subject: **Proposals**

Receiving you loud and clear. Yes, it was great to see you this morning. It sounds as though your production company is developing some interesting projects and of course I'd be happy to help with proposals if you can make it worth my while. I hope you'll be able to afford my consultancy fees and of course I've got so much free time. I'll get my people to call your people! You made a great hit with Daisy. The teaspoon trick worked a treat. She has been happily blowing on spoons and sticking them to her cheeks and nose for the past half-hour, which didn't make her the most popular member of Monkey Music but she doesn't seem to mind. OK, let's make it a regular date – Wednesdays are usually good for me. See you next week, if you don't run into me before. (Hah!)

To: **Jay@mybestfriendisgay.com**
From: **Dot@noplacelikehome.com**
Subject: **My little filip/Philippe**

Coffee with Luke Lloyd surprisingly good. He still is sexy and he's a terrible flirt.

'Dotty,' he said, calling me by the affectionate name he used to have for me, 'it's all because of you. If you hadn't spotted me that sweaty night at the Comedy Store, I would have been on the first train back to Dundee.'

'That's rubbish, Luke Lloyd, and you know it. The club was crawling with scouts that night, I just happened to be pushier than the others.'

'And prettier,' he added quickly.

This was more like it. I hadn't had a good flirt for years and I was still feeling bruised by my failed attempts with Jake at the party. It's obviously in the genes as Daisy was unbelievably flirtatious, putting on a cute face and playing peek-a-boo with Luke. He was wonderful with her. I think comedians probably have a direct link to children. It might have something to do with sharing the same mentality.

'She's a gorgeous thing and utterly captivating. You've done a great job with her.'

At first I was taken aback and then I felt pathetically grateful. Not only was someone attractive and semi-famous flirting with me, he was also complimenting me on my skills as a mother. No one ever tells you you're a good mother, least of all your husband, your children or your parents. It's not like other jobs where you have an assessment. Every day is judgement day. At this stage the only way you can measure your success is by how your children behave and by the quality of the relationship you have with them. We're all so paranoid about whether we are good parents, we're disinclined to be generous and supportive to each other. When was the last time I told a friend she was being a good mother?

To: **Bethearthmother@rooted.com**
From: **Dot@noplacelikehome.com**
Subject: **Praise where praise is due**

Beth, just wanted to let you know what a great mother you are.
Love
Dot
XXX

To: **Delissa@splendidmums.com**
From: **Dot@noplacelikehome.com**
Subject: **It's good to write**

Have been thinking about you a lot lately and just wondering, how's the job going? Keep me posted.

To: **Delissa@splendidmums.com**
From: **Dot@noplacelikehome.com**
Subject: **Is there still a spring in the step of Saga holidays?**

Well, I'm dying to know, is there? Let's hope the clients aren't 'dying' to find out. Apologies for the particularly poor joke. How lovely to be in sunny Florida when all it does is pour down here. Are you surrounded by geriatrics, purple rinses and zimmer frames or has that all changed? I must say, Saga holidays are hardly your style. Are you actually involved in the filming, or are you there as a consultant? Can I help? Do you need any tips? Could I just come and lie by the pool for a few days?

To: **Alex@himindoors.com**
From: **Dot@noplacelikehome.com**
Subject: **Summer holidays and fancy a date?**

Don't you think we need a family holiday? We're all exhausted. But we need to book it now otherwise everywhere will be taken. I know it's going to be difficult with finance and filming dates etc., but is there any chance you can take a week? Two would be better but I imagine that will be impossible. Also, the idea of my leaving work was to spend more time with you, not just the girls.

I seem to be seeing even less of you. I need some quality time with my husband. Fancy a night out? Have you remembered that we've got a teacher's talk about Matilda's progress with Mrs Steel tomorrow evening at 6.30. How about going to see a film afterwards?

To: **Moneytoburn.holidays.co.uk**
From: **Dot@noplacelikehome.com**
Subject: **Summer holidays**

Please send brochure of holidays in the sun including hotels with kids' clubs and English-speaking assistants.

To: **Moneytoburn.holidays.co.uk**
From: **Dot@noplacelikehome.com**
Subject: **Extortion**

Am sending back brochure as you have no holidays for less than £7,000, which is clearly ridiculous, even if you do provide luxury resorts with exclusive care for exclusive children. It's more like expensive care for expensive children.

To: **LukeLloyd@talent.co.uk**
From: **Dot@noplacelikehome.com**
Subject: **Indecent number of proposals**

Just to let you know that I received your e-mail with six programme proposals (are you sure you can afford my expertise?). I will look at them asap. When we talked about summer holidays you mentioned a fantastic campsite in Cornwall that you'd been to. As you said, the girls would love it. It's not exactly my style but I thought I could book it as a fall-back. That is, if I'm not too late already. See you Wednesday.

To: **Jay@mybestfriendisgay.com**
From: **Dot@noplacelikehome.com**
Subject: **Making contact**

I'm so excited I've had to dump Daisy in front of a *Tweenies* video to e-mail you immediately. We just came back from what I thought was going to be a normal trip to the playground. As to be expected, it started to rain just as Daisy and I got to the swings. She was keen to splash in puddles and I couldn't see a good enough reason why not. I forgot about getting home in time to put baked potatoes in the oven, or worrying about her feet getting cold. I just went for the moment and you know, it was fun. Why do I try to force the children to do what I think they ought to do? When do we just hang out? Have I ever asked them what *they* want to do? I was beginning to demonstrate to Daisy the climax of the Gene Kelly dance routine in *Singing in the Rain*, when two boys shot past on bikes covering us both from head to toe in cold muddy water.

'My apologees, Madame.' I looked up to see an Adonis in what looked like a shell suit but was probably a very expensive range of French sports clothing. As he got off his bike he shouted, 'Boyz, come 'ere and say sorry to the lovely Madame and her petite.'

To my amazement he produced a towel. He tried to dry Daisy off but she squealed with indignation.

'What is your name, leetle one?' Daisy wasn't having any of it.

'And you, Madame?' He fixed me with his brown eyes, stopping himself as he was just about to start drying me off as well. He laughed and passed me the towel.

'My name is Dorothy,' I said.

'And Dadda's name is Alex,' said Daisy emphatically.

'Well, I am Philippe. Sorry to ruin your fun. See you around, Madame Dorothee.'

He's gorgeous, Jay. You would love him and I'm sure he's gay. I have an instinct for determining sexual preferences even if Daisy hasn't. Now all I've got to come up with is a cunning plan for a rendezvous.

To: **Jay@mybestfriendisgay.com**
From: **Dot@noplacelikehome.com**
Subject: **A big Philippe**

I shouldn't worry about him being too energetic. I expect by the end of the day he's exhausted and desperate for some entertaining, sympathetic and intelligent company. But until he finds it, you'll have to do. (Joke!) As I said, I think you're perfect for each other and I have an instinct for these things. So Philippe is your 'fillip'. You *shall* go to the ball.

To: **Bethearthmother@rooted.com**
From: **Dot@noplacelikehome.com**
Subject: **Burst bubble**

And I thought things were getting better. I've found myself slotting into a domestic routine. Daisy and I have defined our boundaries. At her age they're all a bit like Jekyll and Hyde (fact verified by

Christopher Green in *Toddler Taming*). One minute they're angelic and the next a monster. I'm learning to deflect the moods and to be one step ahead. She is still a timebomb waiting to explode, but the impact of the shock is less now that I'm more prepared. The problem is Matilda. Last night we had a parents' interview with Mrs Steel, Matilda's teacher. I was confident as she has always done really well at school. She's the original teacher's pet. Alex managed to make it to the school by 6.15, which these days is something of a miracle.

We had to wait outside the door to the classroom, which immediately made us feel five years old again. This effect was enhanced by having to squeeze our adult bottoms into two small chairs. We got a bit giggly as we waited. Alex started flicking elastic bands at me, and I put my hand up and said in a silly voice, 'Miss. Miss. Alex is flicking elastic bands at me.' The classroom door opened, I quickly put my hand down and we immediately sat up straight, or as straight as you can when your bottom is being held in a pincer-like grip by plastic. Mrs Steel was saying a curt goodbye as she released the previous prisoners. I recognised Helen, 'Enry Carter's mother, but only just. She looked like a deflated balloon, as if all the hopes and aspirations for her child had been sucked out of her. 'Enry's father, on the other hand, was pale and tight-lipped with fury. Whether this was directed at Mrs Steel or 'Enry, I wasn't sure.

'Ah, Mr and Mrs Knight.' I looked round to see if Alex's parents had walked in and then realised with a jolt she was talking to us. I'm still not used to hearing my married name. I'm used to being Dot Davies. Alex started to giggle again.

'On time for a change,' Mrs Steel said with a cold laugh as she indicated where we should sit down around a miniature desk. Resisting the urge to slap her, and without pausing for breath, I decided attack was the best method of defence.

'We're very pleased with Matilda's progress. Her reading is very good and her numeracy skills have definitely improved.'

Mrs Steel stared at me. Alex was trying to stop giggling. 'Well, I'm glad *you* think she's doing so well.' She glared at Alex, which had an instant effect. You can see why she has such a reputation. The control she must exercise over those children is formidable. I must watch and learn.

'To be honest with you,' she continued, 'I have been worried about Matilda. I know it's early days but rot can set in at the beginning and, before you know it, bad habits have formed and . . .' she trailed off, leaving images of drug-dependent drop-out children hanging in the classroom air.

'Are you saying there is a problem with Matilda?' I asked.

A deep sigh, 'She's a changed child, Mrs Knight. I mean, her work is of a very high standard but not as high as I know it could be. She used to be the one child I could always count on to help me with the others, to do exactly what I asked, when I asked. Now I notice a rebellious streak and a lack of enthusiasm. It may be a playground problem, but I suspect not. She has many friends and is something of a group leader. I know she could do better. Do you mind me asking if anything has changed at home?' I could feel Alex's eyes burning into the side of my neck as I flushed red. 'Is there anything that could be bothering her?' An uneasy silence was broken too quickly by Alex.

'Well . . . my wife has given up work to be with the children and our old nanny, whom we've had since Matilda was three months, has moved out. Could it be something to do with that?' said Alex.

'Traitor,' I wanted to hiss at him.

'Oh, very interesting. Behavioural problems are often the result of a lack of confidence, which in turn is often because a child is feeling insecure.' Mrs Steel smiled at him in what I thought was a sympathetic manner. They were ganging up on me. I wouldn't have been surprised if she'd asked him, 'And how are you coping with your wife being at home? It must be very difficult for you.'

I interrupted their supportive moment. 'Without wishing to be impertinent, perhaps it's something to do with your teaching methods. We all recognise that she's a bright child. She's in her third term and maybe now she's bored and needs more stimulation.'

Mrs Steel's features hardened into a withering glare, honed and perfected through years of dealing with parents like us and their troublesome offspring. 'I don't think so, Mrs Knight. I've been doing this job for many years and I know in Matilda's case, as I said before, she could do better, Mrs Knight.'

I hated the way she kept repeating my married name. She's the sort of woman who finds your weak spot and then works on it until you crumble. Alex intervened.

'The important thing is to find out if anything is worrying Matilda. Let's not personalise this.'

'You started it,' I wanted to say to him, but I resisted.

The rest of the ten minutes allocated to us was spent with Mrs Steel showing us Matilda's books and my desperate attempts to prove that in fact she was doing excellent work, while Mrs Steel kept referring to earlier examples to prove her point.

'Let's all try to encourage her. Boost her confidence. Maybe you should have a talk with her *Mr* Knight,' said Mrs Steel pointedly, as she herded us out of the classroom. After ten minutes precisely our meeting was over. I knew that this was one job interview I wasn't going to get. I had failed to be a good mother. We walked out of the school in silence.

'Dot . . .' Alex said.

'Don't say anything,' I replied grimly.

'But we've got to talk about this. It's important.' Alex tried to keep up with me, 'Dot, wait.'

Out in the street there was an explosion. Or at least that was how it felt. The tears I had been fighting back sprang into my eyes. Beth, I didn't just cry for a few minutes, I cried for two hours. (You know I never cry except at the bit when Maria comes back in *The Sound of Music*.) I cried for Matilda and her misery. I cried for the damage I would inflict on Daisy. I cried for Alex and the future of my marriage. I cried for my lost career. I cried for being a bad friend. I cried for being a disappointing daughter. But most of all I cried for being ill, for being weak and sickly, for having had cancer. All the tears that had been dammed up over the years poured out of me and ran down my cheeks, splashing away into the gutters of suburbia. Alex held me and stroked my head and mopped up what he could. He gently guided me along the dark streets, holding me as I sobbed. We passed one or two people but I couldn't focus on anything or anybody through the waterfall of tears.

Once home he poured me a glass of wine and ran me a bath while I continued to cry. I stopped crying to get undressed but once in the bath, like the walrus in *Alice in Wonderland*, I felt as though I was sitting in a bath of my own tears. Self-pity overwhelmed me and I started sobbing again.

'What about our film?' I said in between sobs.

Alex perched on the side of the bath. 'I'm not in the mood. Anyway, I don't think we've got enough tissues to get us through the first half-hour if you keep this up. Dot, don't let her get to you. She's a frustrated cow,' he said.

'It's not just her, it's everything, and you . . . (sob) . . . didn't . . . (sob) . . . help.'

'Let's not talk about this now, you're exhausted. I'll make us some supper and it's early bed. We'll talk tomorrow.'

But of course it's now tomorrow, and we haven't talked as he had a meeting first thing with Jessica.

To: **Jay@mybestfriendisgay.com**
From: **Dot@noplacelikehome.com**
Subject: **What have I done?**

I've made a terrible mistake. I've made everyone miserable by changing everything. Is anyone benefitting from my decision? I don't think so. Matilda is losing her confidence, Mrs Steel's words, 'She could do better,' ring in my ears, and Daisy is obviously addicted to Calpol. Alex comes home to a house in chaos and an exhausted wife. We have no money. And me? I'm ragged with it all. Why did I do this to us? The awful thing is that it's too late. I could never get Sarah back. We can't offer her a holiday home in Barbados and an extortionate salary. If I go back to work I'll have to find another nanny – a thought which fills me with horror. I don't even know if Nikki would have me back. I can earn a bit on Luke's proposals but it's not a full-time job, unless any of the ideas get commissioned and that can take ages. I'll have to get my CV together and start sending it out, touting for work. I feel sick to my stomach.

To: **Jay@mybestfriendisgay.com**
Bethearthmother@rooted.com
From: **Dot@noplacelikehome.com**
Subject: **Solidarity**

Thank you for coming round today. I've thought a lot about what you both said. My gut response to going back to work is not good. I don't think it's what I want to do, but is that just because I've lost confidence and energy? I've only been at home for a couple of months. It's bound to take a while for us all to get used to it. I made the decision to give up work because I knew instinctively that my life had to change. It was a question of survival. You both made the point that change is always unsettling and not necessarily a bad thing. But I hate to think I'm jeopardising the happiness of my children and my marriage.

To: **Alex@himindoors.com**
From: **Dot@noplacelikehome.com**
Subject: **About last night**

Thank you for taking Matilda to school this morning. I don't think I could have faced Mrs Steel again so soon. I know our life has changed dramatically these past few months since I gave up work. I admit it has been a shock for us all and I know you're worried about Matilda. So am I, but I don't think we should be reserving our place at The Priory quite yet. Let's keep this in perspective. I'm going to make a big effort to support and encourage her. The past couple of weeks I have begun to feel like I'm getting into my stride. Having said that, I'm also tempted to throw in the towel and go back to work if Nikki will have me, but I know in my heart I don't want to waste this opportunity that you've given me.

I think what I'm asking for is an extension on that trial period we talked about when I first mooted the idea of giving up work. Jay's offered to have the girls tonight for their first sleepover. Matilda is so excited by the idea that she has already packed the entire contents of the toy cupboard and her wardrobe. It's the weekend tomorrow, so I think it'll be fine. He can have some quality time with Matilda, which would be good for her at the moment, and we can have some quality time for ourselves. Let's go to that film we were supposed to see last night. We can talk afterwards.

Chapter Seven

'If you want knowledge, you must take part in the practice of changing reality. If you want to know the taste of a pear, you must change the pear by eating it yourself.'

Mao Tse-tung

To: **NikkiSoda@ambitiousproductions.com**
From: **Dot@noplacelikehome.com**
Subject: **Grapevine gossip**

'How many men does it take to tile a bathroom?'
'Two. If you slice them very thinly.'

Thanks for your latest offering. Feel I haven't been very proactive in the sexist joke department, so accept the above as a peace offering. Your instinct that I'm about to make a return to the workplace is, I'm afraid, wrong. So what was the name of this instinct? Who told you? Still, it's a relief to know that you're still interested in me professionally. I am going to do a little bit of work, at home, on some proposals that Luke Lloyd has put my way. Have you ever worked with Luke? He's certainly made the school run a little more exciting. Mind you, that's not hard.

Glad to hear that Mum is still in America. I haven't heard from her for a while and was wondering where she was. Interviewing Native Americans in New Mexico sounds fascinating. I'm used to her disappearing for months at a time but it would be good to talk to her. If you manage to make contact, could you ask her to phone or e-mail?

To: **Delissa@splendidmums.com**
From: **Dot@noplacelikehome.com**
Subject: **Your brilliant career**

Just heard from Nikki that you're in Taos discovering the secret of long life amongst the Native Americans. If you discover the elixir of youth or something similar please let me be the first to know. I could do with a little boost. When are you coming home?

To: **Bethearthmother@rooted.com**
From: **Dot@noplacelikehome.com**
Subject: **Marital friction**

Darling Jay had the children for a sleepover last night. It was the first time Alex and I had been alone for months. I made an effort and tried to look sexy, even though we were only going to a film (French, charming and feel-good) and out for a modest supper afterwards as we can't afford anything else. I still felt cross with him for being unsupportive at the interview with Matilda's teacher so the evening was a bit scratchy. He thinks he knows me better than I know myself. I'm not sure he's right. Nothing stays the same, but can you change your character? Can something like illness affect your personality? Surely you have to change to deal with everything that happens in life. You learn. You adapt. You move on. It's the secret of survival. Maybe it's not your character but your attitudes that change.

Alex is under a lot of pressure. They've started casting *Tess*. I enjoyed playing the name game and making suggestions. I pride myself on being good on ideas and casting but most of the names I came up with Alex would say, 'Yeah, Jessica was keen on him/her.' Jessica Bedmeigh is driving me mad. Alex of course finds her very impressive. Apparently she is very astute, good with the script, and supportive of his ideas. She never says, 'That's going to be too expensive.' She's brilliant at manipulating a budget to make it work for the creatives. I hate her. Work was neutral territory. Neither of us was keen to start talking about our current situation. As we drove home he mentioned that he's invited his parents over for Sunday lunch.

'Oh, bloody hell, Alex. You might have asked me first,' I snapped at him.

He replied calmly, 'Don't worry, I'll help you cook.' It's not what I need at the moment.

Once home Alex started his offensive. I know him too well. 'Your casting ideas are great. It's so good to be able to talk to you about all this. (Pause) Don't you miss work at all Dot?'

I knew I'd be lying if I said I didn't, but I don't miss the stress of it all so I said, 'Not really. If I went back I'd have to do something radically different. I feel too old.'

'It just seems to me it's such a waste of your talents.'

'Surely being a creative mother is a way of exercising my so-called talents.'

'Yes, but that's the point. You're not being a creative mother. It's not working. Why are you doing this, Dot? Is it really for us, or is it just a selfish experiment?'

It was out there. He'd said it. I felt stung.

I could see by his expression that he immediately regretted what he had said. He looked at me anxiously, no doubt worried that I'd start to cry again. But I didn't. Instead I felt the anger surge up inside.

'Give me a chance, you bastard. It's been two months. Two months of upheaval. Two months of you being completely unsupportive. It would help if you were around a bit more. I know you're busy but you could at least read to the children one night a week. You could help tidy up occasionally or offer to take the children to the playground. You've abnegated all responsibility. Why does it have to be all *my* fault? It hasn't even occurred to you that Matilda's unhappiness could be because you're no longer here for her like you used to be. Think about that before you start accusing me of ruining our lives.

'You think that dealing with the children is my job now that you're the sole breadwinner. You may be the one bringing in the money but you're still their father, for Christ's sake. Do you know what I think? I think you want me to fail so that your life can return to the way it was before. Well, I'm sorry, it's not going to happen. No, you're right. I'm not doing it very well but I can't do it all on my own and I shouldn't have to. Even bloody Miss Perfect, Sarah, didn't have to do it all. She had us at the weekends and in the evenings, but I have no one.'

I stormed off to bed, leaving Alex to reflect on the way his life is changing. I got undressed and into bed as quickly as possible and turned the light out, fuming in the darkness. When Alex finally came to bed I was still awake. He got in quietly and then very gently snuggled up and put his arm around me. I deliberately started breathing heavily as though I was in a deep sleep. I was tempted to start muttering words as if sleeptalking like, 'Bastard . . . so alone . . .' but I resisted, worried that I might not be convincing. He fell into a deep sleep very quickly while I tossed and turned the night away.

Jay brought the girls back Saturday morning, all of them exhausted. I don't think any of them went to sleep before midnight. He organised a sing-along *Sound of Music* and they all dressed up – Matilda as Maria, Daisy as Gretel and Jay alternating as Mother Superior and the Baroness. I think they took it in turns to play the other parts but the highlight was taking Jay's curtains down and cutting them up for playclothes (Matilda's idea). Daisy had her first experience of toffee 'n' pecan popcorn and is now addicted. I suppose it's an improvement on Calpol. I persuaded Jay to stay for the day so I wouldn't have to face Alex alone. Matilda went and snuggled up to her father, who was still in bed.

'Why don't you two spend the morning together?' I suggested. 'Jay and I can take Daisy out for a constitutional.'

Jay groaned, 'Do I have to?'

'Yup. Today's the day you're going to meet the man of your dreams. Let's go find Philippe. We'll use Daisy as bait.'

We walked to the road where Philippe lives. Number forty-eight looked quiet. The curtains were still drawn and there was little evidence of life. We loitered for a while and did a few circuits round the block.

'This is silly,' said Jay eventually, 'it's Saturday, he'll have a day off today. Besides, I feel like a hooker touting for business on street corners. Anyway, I'm not wearing the right jeans. Who would look twice at me in the state I'm in?'

'I don't want to go back yet.' The thought of facing Alex and going through the day not talking was too miserable to contemplate. I said, 'Let's go and walk by the river. Can you take Daisy on your shoulders? You have to be careful as the path is very narrow and it's a steep fall into the river.'

It was a fine morning and the river was full of rowing boats with coxes bullying and bellowing at bedraggled exhausted oarsmen. Bicyclists whizzed past and I checked them all to make sure none of them was the elusive Philippe. As we got to a bend in the river, about fifty yards away we saw a couple kissing passionately beside the river path. Their fingers were entwined and their bodies so close they were welded together. I felt a stab of envy. Jay and I couldn't stop looking at them. Their passion was mesmerising. As we walked closer the man broke off the kiss and tenderly took the woman's face in his hands and stared at her.

Something about the couple seemed familiar. Was it possible that this was Philippe? We were practically level with the couple by now and I tried as surreptitiously as possible to see their faces. They were clearly oblivious to the rest of the world and I couldn't help thinking how lucky they were and how wonderful it would be to be twenty again, experiencing that first 'whoosh' that comes in the early stages of a relationship. As we passed them I looked again, as unobtrusively as possible, and then realised that it *was* Philippe – my lovely gay Philippe, perfect partner to best friend Jay – who was kissing Helen Carter, 'Enry's mother.

'Oh my God,' I gasped.

'What?' said Jay. 'What is it?'

I turned back to Jay just in time to see him walking blindly towards the edge of the embankment, about to fall down the steep slope to the muddy Thames below. Daisy was clutching his head with both her hands covering his eyes the way small children do when they're feeling insecure on your shoulders.

'Jay, STOP!' I screamed, having visions of losing my best friend and youngest child at the same time.

He prised Daisy's hands away from his eyes and lifted her off his shoulders. He looked at me.

'Why are you gawping like a fish? It's not attractive.'

'That was him, Jay. That was Philippe, kissing 'Enry's mother. You remember 'Enry – the one who started the riot at Matilda's party. I'm amazed.'

'So that's another relationship that's not going to work.'

'Well, she *is* married and he must be ten years younger than her.'

'No, I meant him and me.'

'Oh, I'm sorry, Jay. How could I have got it so wrong? I was convinced he was gay. Maybe he goes both ways.'

'I don't think he's my type,' said Jay bravely, 'too pretty. Actually, I've been meaning to tell you something. I think I might have met someone. I didn't tell you before because I didn't want to ruin your scheming as I know it makes you happy.'

'Who is it? I need names, descriptions and full credentials. You do realise there will be a screening process?'

Jay laughed. 'It's early days but I met him through work. I had to interview him about a new club he's opened called 'Stud'. It's like Studio 54 in New York but without the 'io' and the '54'.

I giggled, 'So what's he like?'

'Oh, you know, interesting.'

'Come on, Jay, you've got to give me more than that.'

'It's early days. I only met him last week but it feels good.'

'Can I meet him?'

'Of course you'll meet him, but give me a few more weeks. I don't want to frighten him off. He might be out of my league. He knows everyone and goes everywhere. I'm playing it as cool as I can.'

'You can tell me his name, can't you?'

'It's Kevin,' mumbled Jay.

'Well, it could be worse. Your fillip is now a Kevin.'

For the rest of the weekend Alex and I established an uneasy truce. Sylvia and Jack turned up on Sunday. Jack brought a bottle of champagne.

'What are we celebrating?' Alex asked his father.

'Life,' he replied, 'and your new job or your new wife or whatever you want to celebrate.'

'New wife?' I queried. 'Is there something I don't know about?'

'Well, you've taken on a new role in life. It's like you're a new woman.'

Alex started carving my less than perfect chicken. He was hacking at it, angrily chopping at the legs. Jack, realising he'd touched a nerve, raised his eyebrows at me and I just shrugged my shoulders.

'Well I think it's marvellous,' said Sylvia, taking me by surprise. 'I think Dorothy is doing exactly the right thing by staying at home. You both work too hard. It's not right for a stranger to be bringing up your children. What's the point in having them if you never see them? Honestly, women today think they can have it all.'

Resisting the urge to defend the sisters and cry, 'Well why can't they?' I took a moment to bask in her endorsement. It was the first time I could remember that she had taken my side. Victory was sweet. Alex scowled and continued to hack away at the chicken.

'Can I have the wishbone, Dadda?' asked Matilda.

'Only if I can pull it with you.'

Matilda grinned. I must confess to being worried about Alex. I wonder what he wished for?

Chapter Eight

'Age cannot wither her, nor custom stale Her infinite variety'
William Shakespeare, *Antony and Cleopatra*

To: **LukeLloyd@talent.co.uk**
From: **Dot@noplacelikehome.com**
Subject: **Giving me ideas**

I've been mulling over the programme treatments that you sent last week. Out of the six, I like *First Loves* the best. We all remember our first love. Steven Cox. Just writing his name has brought a silly wistful smile to my face. I had my first proper kiss with Steven Cox. We met through my friend Beth's brother, James, who was always keen to initiate conversations about sex. Only weeks before he introduced me to Steven, James had told us all the intimate details of French kissing. I was quite horrified and disgusted at the thought of it. Imagine putting your tongue in someone else's mouth – how unhygienic. Shocked, I went home and wrote an affidavit stating that, 'I, Dorothy Davies, promise never to put my tongue in anybody else's mouth,' and signed and dated it.

A few weeks later Steven Cox and I found ourselves in a slightly fumbling but passionate embrace. It was such a relief I knew what to do, and if James hadn't warned me I probably would have screamed and bitten it off. Instead, I was a natural. I talked about that kiss for a year afterwards and Beth and I analysed every minute detail on the bus to school: the way we had met; what he had said; how he had held my hand; what he was wearing; what I was wearing. Amazingly there was no real awkwardness, no clashing of teeth or bumping of noses. It was the perfect first kiss and has been a benchmark for every kiss since then. Even now a waft of Brut sends shivers down my spine for all the right reasons, or maybe not. For a whole year the memory of that moment never failed to produce a frisson. In fact I can still feel it now. Our relationship lasted six months, which was an eternity at that stage in our lives and it ended when he did the unforgivable.

Sorry, I digress. You could get a great range of contributors, from the Queen to Kylie Minogue. Perhaps we could reunite people with their first loves. Actually, the idea of meeting Steven Cox again fills me with dread. He's probably a fat, balding computer salesman living in Bracknell and meeting him again would destroy the memory. Still, it might make interesting viewing, seeing how people have changed.

To: **LukeLloyd@talent.co.uk**
From: **Dot@noplacelikehome.com**
Subject: **Personal revelations**

I don't know what came over me, divulging the intimate secrets of my past to a virtual stranger. So, you're intrigued by what was considered unforgivable when I was fourteen. You'll be sorry you asked. I was horse mad as a young girl and spent a lot of time at the local stables looking after a pony called Dusky, whom I loved passionately. I think Steven Cox found this a little threatening and completely incomprehensible. He wrote to me saying, 'It's either me or the horse.' There was no contest, the horse won. What made it particularly painful was that he started going out with my best friend, Beth. I don't know if it determined the pattern of my future relationships but it certainly gave me a taste for kissing. There, you see, I'm off again.

To: LukeLloyd@talent.co.uk
From: **Dot@noplacelikehome.com**
Subject: **First fumbles**

Betty Barnstrop sounds like a bit of a goer. It always makes me laugh when people refer to the older woman when they're only sixteen. When I look at sixteen-year-olds today, they seem so young but I suppose it's all relative. Does the memory of what happened with Betty make you blush with embarrassment or glow with nostalgia? Do you know what's happened to her? Have you kept in touch?

To: LukeLloyd@talent.co.uk
From: **Dot@noplacelikehome.com**
Subject: **Reconnection**

That's obviously one of the disadvantages of celebrity – everyone knows where you live. At least you wrote back, but it all happened a long time ago – the only thing you would have in common is the past. Enough of this reminiscing. After all, we are supposed to be professionals.

As for the other ideas, I wasn't very keen on the animal quiz show but game shows aren't my forte. My expertise is in the quirkier end of the market. I've never been good at mainstream and I thought you wanted to get back to your alternative roots.

We can discuss all this and more when we meet tomorrow at the café. I'll be wearing blue and carrying a screaming child. You can't miss me. If you've got a picture of Betty, why not bring it along? Maybe we could start the series off with you two?

To: **Jay@mybestfriendisgay.com**
From: **Dot@noplacelikehome.com**
Subject: **Young love**

I've been thinking about my first kiss and wondering how you and cool Kevin have been getting on. You've been remarkably cagey about the whole thing. Does he have a significant other somewhere or, even worse, a wife ranting in some loft conversion in Soho? Have you gone off him or is he playing hard to get? Information required on a need-to-know basis.

As you know, it's my birthday next week and instead of everyone getting together and embarrassing me horribly by arranging a surprise party, I thought you and I and the usual suspects could go out locally. I'd offer to pay but you know I'm somewhat financially embarrassed at the moment. Perhaps this would be the perfect opportunity to introduce us to Kevin, or do you think it would be too much for him to meet us all at the same time? I could stagger arrival times to ease him in gently. What do you think?

To: **Bethearthmother@rooted.com**
From: **Dot@noplacelikehome.com**
Subject: **A friendly press gang**

Don't you think it's about time we were introduced to Jay's new love? What if he's made it all up? Do you think Kevin is to Jay what Harvey, the rabbit, was to James Stewart? Perhaps he's spent so much time working on the Style sections that he now believes he's really living the celebrity lifestyle he describes. He's probably never even met Kevin Casey and it's just a big fantasy. I bet he'll find some excuse for us not to meet him.

To: **Jay@mybestfriendisgay.com**
From: **Dot@noplacelikehome.com**
Subject: **In the diary**

Great. I'm thrilled he can come. I promise to be on best behaviour and try not to embarrass you. Don't worry, we'll try to be exciting enough for a man who's used to partying with Kylie. Actually, on second thoughts, maybe you should leave it for a couple of months as I haven't got time to tone my bottom.

To: **Bethearthmother@rooted.com**
From: **Dot@noplacelikehome.com**
Subject: **To tell, or not to tell, that is the question**

Ignore last ungenerous e-mail. Kevin has agreed to come to my birthday celebrations. I can't wait to meet him but I'm not sure why he's such a celebrity. I suppose he's one of those people who's famous for being famous. He's always popping up in *Hello!*. He seems to be a professional partygoer. Will know more when we meet him. I hope you can come as well so we can scrutinise him together.

On the subject of birthdays, I had an embarrassing moment at school this morning. Often we meet up with Kate, Molly's mum (Matilda's best friend), and this morning we started a conversation about birthdays and age.

'Just how old are you, Mama?' asked Matilda, eavesdropping.

I used to hate the way my mother refused to tell me her age. She never even let me see her passport and if pushed she always said she was thirty-two. She was thirty-two for many years, in fact as far as I know she still is thirty-two. I gave up asking.

So, in an effort to be truthful and direct, I replied, 'Now lots of people, especially women, don't like you asking about their age.' Matilda looked at me as if I was exhibiting the first signs of Alzheimer's. I persisted, 'But I'm not one of those women. Getting old doesn't worry me. I'm thirty-seven but I'm going to be thirty-eight next week.'

Matilda said nothing but stared at me thoughtfully. It suddenly seemed as if the playground was packed with young fresh-faced mothers, athletic fathers and teenage nannies fussing, arguing, and kissing their children goodbye. I resisted the urge to put Matilda's reading folder in front of my face, like an actress caught by the paparazzi without her make-up after a long flight. Every wrinkle and telltale grey hair was obvious to the entire school.

As we walked into the classroom Molly shouted out, 'It's Matilda's mummy's birthday next week, and do you know how old she's going to be?'

Moving quickly, Matilda passed me and stood in the centre of the room and said very loudly 'Thirty-two.'

I looked at her in amazement, not sure whether to kiss her for saving my pride or reprimand her for lying, but as she came to the door to kiss me goodbye she whispered, 'Thirty-eight is just too old, Mummy.'

To: LukeLloyd@talent.co.uk
From: Dot@noplacelikehome.com
Subject: **Age cannot wither**

Sorry, but on this occasion blackmail won't work. It wasn't me. I never said I was thirty-two. It was my daughter, Matilda, who was so embarrassed to have such an old mother. You know me, I'm not the sort of person who worries about age. I'm sure thirty-eight is going to be a wonderfully fulfilling year. I'm now mature enough to understand the world, yet young enough to still enjoy it. Anyway, you must be somewhere around that mark, if not a few years older. Besides, what were you doing loitering around other children's classrooms? To be honest, I'm really proud of my age.

To: Bethearthmother@rooted.com
From: Dot@noplacelikehome.com
Subject: **Boundaries and other people's children**

Have you ever contemplated plastic surgery to prevent the signs of ageing? It's tragic. Last year I was worrying whether I'd make it to this year let alone a ripe old age, and already I'm getting defensive about being thirty-eight. It's nothing, for God's sake, and there's still so much to come. I'm determined to embrace each year and treat it as a blessing. If I ever whine about age you have my permission to give me a good slapping – verbally, not physically. Advice time again. Maybe you should start charging me a parenting consultant's fee. I think you could make a fortune (except out of me at the moment). Actually, maybe that's a really good idea. You could start lecturing, write a book (If Nanny Sarah can do it, you certainly can) and go on book tours all over the world. This could be your new career based entirely on your own experience and amazing knowledge and understanding of children. Good, I'm glad we've got that sorted out. What I need to know is how do you deal with other people's children? I'll give you an example.

Matilda's best friend, Molly, came over to play after school yesterday in the one window we have in our week – the rest are chock-a-block with ballet, art, swimming and sibling rivalry seminars. I know it's terrible, but I have to confess I don't really like other people's children. Perhaps it's more that I'm a little nervous of them. It's hard enough to deal with your own children, and at least you have a biological connection and an in-built love for them. Other people's children just upset yours and seem much more exhausting. There are a few exceptions of course, but in my experience they are very few.

Molly brought packets of sweets, obviously worried that the food was going to be inedible. I was making a big effort as I'd love to be a popular mother. So with that thought in mind I said, 'What's your favourite vegetable, Molly?'

'Chocolate ice cream,' she replied, without a hint of irony.

I tried to be more specific, 'Broccoli, carrots, peas or sweetcorn?'

'Yes,' she replied enigmatically.

Oh sod this, I thought, I'll just get on and make whatever, and if they don't like it, tough.

There followed an hour of running up and down stairs (who needs to join a gym) trying to sort out a range of problems and issues that would keep Freud happy for years. In between expeditions I cooked pasta (always a safe bet) and kept some aside, without sauce, as it's inevitable Molly will hate the one I've made.

'Girls, it's teatime,' I called up hopefully.

I discovered Molly already downstairs eating her packet of sweets, sharing the occasional one with Daisy who was sitting panting at her feet like a loyal Labrador puppy.

'Oh, Molly, we're just about to have tea.'

She looked at me defiantly and carried on eating the sweets. Matilda looked at me anxiously, curious to see how I would respond.

'Molly, we don't have sweets before tea in this house,' I said firmly.

'Well, I have sweets whenever I want in my house.'

This was becoming a stand-off that I knew I had to win, especially in front of Matilda. 'Be a good girl and put the sweets down,' I said, resisting the urge to say, 'put your hands on your head and move away slowly.' It's times like these I feel like calling up the childcatcher from *Chitty Chitty Bang Bang* and getting him to take a detour via our house. Molly carried on eating the sweets. I had to act fast and didn't even have time to consult *How to Behave So Your Children Will, Too!*

'OK, no ice cream for pudding then.'

Molly stopped for a few seconds, thought about it, weighed up the choices and then very slowly put the bag of Haribo mixtures down. Success without tears.

While toying with her pasta Molly started talking about school sports day.

'Molly's going to win everything,' said Matilda generously.

'Well, you don't know that, Matilda,' I said, bristling on behalf of my eldest daughter.

'Oh yes I am, because I am the fastest in the class,' said Molly, picking out strands of cheese one by one with her fingers. It wasn't bragging, it was a fact that was obviously accepted by everyone in the class.

'Are you faster than the boys?' I asked, genuinely interested.

'Alexander is good, and 'Enry's quite fast, but I think I can beat them.'

Matilda seemed content not to feature in the sports stakes, so I wasn't going to worry about it, but I hope, just a little bit, that Molly doesn't win every race and learns an early lesson that not everything in life turns out quite as you expect. But seriously, what can you do? It's so hard when it's other people's children. I was so relieved when it was time for Molly's mum, Kate, to come and collect her. I had to stop myself from bundling Molly out of the front door, chucking her jacket and school folder after her.

On a more adult note, I hope you are coming to my birthday. I'm a bit worried I haven't heard back from you yet.

To: **Bethearthmother@rooted.com**
From: **Dot@noplacelikehome.com**
Subject: **A martyr to motherhood?**

What do you mean, you don't feel up to it? I can't imagine celebrating my birthday without you. To tell you the truth, I'm not surprised you're exhausted. You have three children, two rabbits, a puppy, a cat, five goldfish and no help whatsoever. (Those goldfish can be exhausting.) You've probably got one of those savage viruses that have been doing the rounds recently. At least six of Matilda's classmates have been off this week and all the mothers are complaining of exhaustion. Have a think about it. I'm sure by next Thursday you'll be feeling better.

To: NikkiSoda@ambitiousproductions.com
From: **Dot@noplacelikehome.com**
Subject: **Fount of all knowledge**

Why is your phone permanently engaged? Anybody would have thought you had work to do but I know you've probably just been gossiping. I've just turned on Radio 4 for some mental stimulation as I was driving home from Tesco's and heard Jenni Murray finishing an interview, 'Thank you, Sarah Standish.' Now, maybe I misheard but Sarah was our nanny. Does this mean that her book is out already? But to be on *Woman's Hour*, it must be seriously good. As fount of all knowledge, do you know anything about it?

To: Alex@himindoors.com
From: **Dot@noplacelikehome.com**
Subject: **Slander! Libel!**

Sorry to bother you on your recce in Dorset, and I understand you're completely involved in working out how to shoot this drama, but I've got to tell you what I've just heard from Nikki. Sarah's book is being tipped as the biggest book since *Bridget Jones*, and it hasn't even been published yet. Apparently it's about a nanny working for two ambitious professionals who, funnily enough, work in television. Spot the difference? They treat her badly and neglect their children dreadfully. It's basically a romance with the only way out for the nanny being through the love of a good man. (How dated. Oh, no, how cynical of me.)

Nanny abuse is the big topic of the week. Everyone will think it's us. It's ridiculous. We didn't abuse Sarah, we were just busy. I haven't heard from you for days and a phonecall or an e-mail would be appreciated, if not by me by your two daughters who are forever whining, 'I want my dadda.'

'When is Dadda coming home?' is the question most asked, and I realise that you never said when you were coming back. I trust you *are* coming back.

To: **Alex@himindoors.com**
From: **Dot@noplacelikehome.com**
Subject: **Nanny novel**

Lovely to hear from you at last and, no, the book is not non-fiction, it's being sold as a novel, but you know what people are like. They always assume that characters are real, and they don't understand the importance of the imagination. Fact and fiction are always blurred. It's her first novel, for goodness sake. Everyone is going to presume it's autobiographical. What can we do?

To: **Alex@himindoors.com**
From: **Dot@noplacelikehome.com**
Subject: **Don't panic**

I suppose you're right, there is nothing we can do except wait for it to come out and then read the damn thing. I don't think I want to and I'm sure you won't have the time. I'm glad you'll be home for my birthday, but please don't forget Matilda's sports day, which is in a couple of weeks. Apparently her best friend Molly is going to win all the races, but you never know, we might have an outside chance. I'm thinking about putting Matilda into training.

To: **NikkiSoda@ambitiousproductions.com**
From: **Dot@noplacelikehome.com**
Subject: **Competitive instinct**

'Why do boys run faster than girls?'
'They have two ball-bearings and a stick shift.'

As queen of the competitive instinct I thought you might be able to help me with a little domestic problem. Matilda's sports day is coming up and I think she needs encouragement. I seem to remember you telling me you were captain of lacrosse for Middlesex County in your youth. How about coming over and coaching Matilda? I'm sure she'd love it. I'll give you supper as payment, and any advice you might need for your projects. Shall we say Friday at 6.00? Also, I'm glad you can make my birthday meal at Il Traviata. I know it's not the Ivy, but it could be a fun evening.

To: **Delisssa@splendidmums.com**
From: **Dot@noplacelikehome.com**
Subject: **Presents, presents and more presents**

I can't tell you how lovely it is to have you back. America and working for Nikki obviously suit you. It's very kind of you to offer to pay for my birthday dinner and I graciously accept. Of course you mustn't get me anything else, dinner will be quite enough. I hope you don't mind, but it might be quite expensive, as there will be nine of us if Beth and Tom come.

Life hasn't been quite so rosy here, and I think I wouldn't be overstating it to say that Alex and I are going through a bad patch. He's been away in Dorset but he did manage to phone us last night just as the girls were going to bed and as Matilda was quizzing me on the morals in Aesop's fables, so the phone was a welcome relief. He's being very short with me at the moment, and I don't think it's just because he's worried about the filming, although he often gets withdrawn just before a shoot, and this is the biggest challenge of his career to date. I'm cross with him too, and because we don't talk nothing is resolved. Am I wrong to expect him to be more supportive? I don't want much, just the occasional word of encouragement. Is that too needy?

To make matters worse, people are talking already about Nanny Sarah's book, which hasn't even been published yet, but I'm sure everyone is going to think it's about Alex and me and the way we bring up our children. I want to run away and hide.

To: Jay@mybestfriendisgay.com
From: Dot@noplacelikehome.com
Subject: **Good vibrations**

Thank you for my birthday presents. You are terrible. Why do you delight in embarrassing me? You do realise this is war and I'll have to get my own back. I'm glad you gave me the vibrator before my mother and Alex turned up. What am I going to do with it? No, don't answer that. I think I can work that out for myself, but what a bad impression it must have made on Kevin.

'Kevin, meet Dot, my sexually frustrated best friend.'

In fact, my mother gave me a strange look when, later on, I opened the parcel containing the batteries, and even though she hadn't been there for the earlier present opening, I'm sure she guessed what you'd given me. The bracelet, however, is gorgeous and makes up for any previous embarrassment (just).

It was good to meet Kevin, at last. You're right, he is very inscrutable, so inscrutable that I have no idea what he thought of us. The more inscrutable he became the more I rabbited on. I hope he didn't find me boring. Alex thought he was very interesting and they had a long talk about work and second homes in Mauritius (dream on). I thought he was great and you seemed really good together. We can't wait to meet him again. Do send him my love.

To: **Bethearthmother@rooted.com**
From: **Dot@noplacelikehome.com**
Subject: **Kevin**

Cool Kevin was awful. God, I missed you. It wouldn't have been so bad if you'd been there. From the moment he walked through the smoked-glass doors, I knew it was going to be difficult. What was extraordinary was the effect Kevin's arrival had on the atmosphere in the restaurant. He was instantly recognised by the sassy blonde greeter at the door. Jay remained a distinctly defined two steps behind, and for a brief moment I thought Kevin was going to drop his coat in the middle of the restaurant and expect Jay to pick it up. I have no doubt he would have done. The way he was behaving, he would have licked the floor clean with his tongue, if asked. Maybe Jay has a masochistic streak that I've never noticed before.

The other diners tried to continue eating but kept looking shiftily in Kevin's direction, and one couple immediately took out their mobile phones and busily started texting the exciting news that they were having dinner with Kevin Casey. An ageing supermodel who rarely makes the front cover these days made a point of catching his eye and Kevin shrieked his welcome, never for one second thinking of introducing Jay, who waited obediently behind him. The statuesque blonde greeter proudly led them to our table and then, to my irritation, said to Kevin, 'Would you like a better table? We could move you to the corner if you like?'

For a moment Kevin scrutinised the room, and then replied, 'No, this is fine. It's not my party.' Jay nervously introduced us.

'It's lovely to meet you,' I said enthusiastically. Big mistake.

He looked at me as if he was thinking, 'Yes, you're a lucky girl,' but said, 'God, that woman is such a bore, and so yesterday.'

For a moment I thought he was talking about me, but then I saw the supermodel waving at him as she got up to go. He waved back. I can see I'm going to have to watch him. I wonder what the others thought of him?

To: **Delissa@splendidmums.com**
From: **Dot@noplacelikehome.com**
Subject: **Spilling the beans**

Thank you for paying for my big night out. It was much appreciated by us all. I must admit I was so relieved to see you. You looked amazing covered from head to toe in turquoise bracelets, earrings and a neck choker – spoils from filming in New Mexico.

You captivated Kevin, but I don't think he felt quite so enthusiastic about me. I had a rather awkward start with him before everyone else arrived. Initially I was pleased at the thought of having half an hour alone with him and Jay. Oh good, I thought to myself, some time for us to really get to know each other. It was clear he didn't feel the same way as he spent the entire time gossiping on his mobile. So I opened the presents Jay had brought for me and we caught up. I longed for you all to arrive as I was beginning to feel distinctly suburban. As soon as Alex came in, Kevin came off the phone and his opening line was, 'Ah, you're working with Jessica Bedmeigh. Is she as good as they say she is?' I know it wasn't a deliberate jibe at me, but let's just say it didn't help my confidence.

It might just be me, but I thought that not only was he rude but he was also really unattractive. Didn't you think his hair was badly dyed, or is that fashionable now? Under the lights it looked green to me, and did you notice the pockmarks? What do you think – acne or syphilis? I'm sorry, I know I'm being mean, but it was very disappointing. Am I missing something?

To: **Delissa@splendidmums.com**
From: **Dot@noplacelikehome.com**
Subject: **Kevin cont**

OK, I agree, he does have extraordinarily green eyes to match the hair, but didn't you think that it was as if the lights weren't on and he wasn't interested in anyone else except himself? Did you see how he behaved when Nikki arrived late, air kissing all of us? He was so pleased by her reaction when she saw him.

She audibly gasped, collapsed into the seat next to me and said, 'When you said Kevin, I didn't realise you meant Kevin Casey. Do you know who he is? He knows everyone you'd ever want to meet. He's even best friends with Kylie.'

I inwardly groaned, 'So bloody what.'

She continued to gush, 'Hasn't he just opened that new club in Soho?'

I noticed Kevin wasn't so inscrutable as to miss the opportunity of lapping up her every word, while he was pretending to be deep in conversation with Alex. Has she told you what she thought of him? I bet she was impressed, he is a celebrity after all.

Alex says I'm overreacting but I feel it in my gut that Kevin is not a good thing. Of course I want Jay to be happy, but he needs to be with someone who really appreciates him. Jay wasn't himself with Kevin and became rather subservient, as if he didn't think he was worthy of him because he's so fashionable and knows all the right people, blah, blah, blah . . . As if any of that matters. Everyone knows it's all hype.

I really don't understand the celebrity thing. It's fine to be in awe of someone if they have real talent and can sing, write or act fantastically, but just because someone's got big tits or appeared on a TV programme for fifteen seconds doesn't seem enough justification for all the adulation and free tables at Mezzo's. As far as Kevin's concerned, he's just a good businessman who's tapped into the zeitgeist and knows how to schmooze effectively.

To: **NikkiSoda@ambitiousproductions.com**
From: **Dot@noplacelikehome.com**
Subject: **About the other night . . .**

Good to see you last night, and thank you for my present. A voucher for a day of pampering in The Sanctuary sounds blissful, even if there are renovations taking place in all the massage rooms and God knows how I'll be able to organise child care. Did you get a chance to chat to Kevin at all? By the time he deigned to speak to me I was feeling cross and insecure.

'So, Dorothy,' he drawled, 'what do you do?'

The question I most dread these days. Jay obviously hadn't briefed him, or if he had, Kevin hadn't been listening. For a few seconds I contemplated lying, 'Well, I've just completed my first feature film script, and I'm having lunch with Spielberg tomorrow to discuss our deal.' Instead I said, 'I've given up work . . . well, it's not giving up exactly . . . it's just . . . well, a different kind of work. I'm actually at home full time looking after the kids . . . but . . . you know . . .' I'd lost him, he was staring over my shoulder. 'But I used to be in television,' I ended lamely.

'Great,' he said, not listening to a word I said. Am I really that boring?

To: **NikkiSoda@ambitiousproductions.com**
From: **Dot@noplacelikehome.com**
Subject: **Suburban sensibilities**

What do you mean by 'not exactly boring'? I try not to talk too much about the children but they are my life at the moment and I thought having been through it yourself you might be a little more understanding. Anyway this isn't to do with me, I'm just worried about Jay. He delights in calling him inscrutable, which in my language translates into boring. I've never subscribed to the still waters run deep school of philosophy, I suspect it's more a case of still waters run shallow. Anyway I won't go on – I don't want to be any more boring than I am already.

To be honest the whole evening was not as I had imagined it. I don't want to seem ungrateful but I was a little disappointed with Alex's present. I mean to say, anyone can buy an unimaginative bottle of perfume. It was Jo Malone, but still, a bottle of perfume? That says everything about the state of our relationship at the moment. He's usually so imaginative with presents, like the time he found a first edition of *The Wizard of Oz* and gave me some wonderful sparkling red stiletto shoes to match. I don't want him to spend a lot of money, especially at the moment, and I know he's wrapped up with the film, but I did expect something a little more thoughtful. I promise you I'm not being mercenary, I'd be happy with a poem or something personal, but it's just an indication of everything not being right with us. Maybe things are worse than I imagined.

To: **Bethearthmother@rooted.com**
From: **Dot@noplacelikehome.com**
Subject: **Missing in action**

I seem to be in the minority when it comes to crappy Kevin. Everyone else thought he was interesting, funny and astute. I must have missed it, or maybe I've just lost all ability to judge people. Don't tell the others, but I really didn't enjoy the evening at all. At one point I sat back in my chair and looked around the table at everyone laughing and talking animatedly. Delissa was telling another story about the Native American chief who, rather than being reluctant to be interviewed, would never shut up and even rang her in her hotel room after the interview was finished, determined to continue the conversation. Nikki was scanning the room looking for potential films in the making. Alex was relaxed but distracted, his mind elsewhere on his film. Jay was watching cocky Kevin like a commis chef watching a master chef working his magic. They all knew their place and felt comfortable but I felt miserably lost.

By the end of the evening I practically had to bite my lip to stop myself crying from disappointment and worry that my lovely Jay is in a relationship with this cold-hearted, lascivious, mean-spirited, ugly man, but apart from that he was great. I wish you'd been there (are you feeling better?). We all missed you and Mum sends lots of love.

The actual day of my birthday was fine. Thank God for the children. Matilda and Daisy couldn't have been more thoughtful. They woke me up first thing with flowers picked from the neighbour's garden and some lovely home-made cards. Matilda was especially concerned that I wasn't going to have a cake and that I hadn't booked an entertainer for the evening. It's quite hard explaining to someone who thinks birthdays are the most exciting things in the world that once you've had thirty-eight of them the novelty begins to pall. Please can I pop round tomorrow and see how you're feeling? Is there anything I can do to help – perhaps a supermarket shop for you? I'm sure all you need is a couple of good nights' sleep and you'll feel much better. Please, please, please don't tell Jay what I think of cruddy Kevin, as I'm sure it would ruin our beautiful friendship.

Chapter Nine

'From my experience in life I believe my personal motto should be, '"Beware of men bearing flowers."'
Muriel Spark

To: **Jay@mybestfriendisgay.com**
From: **Dot@noplacelikehome.com**
Subject: **All of a fluster**

I'm feeling a bit flushed as I've just had the most wonderful encounter with Luke at the café. As you know, Wednesday morning is our usual rendezvous. I hadn't told him when it was my birthday but he'd done a bit of research. Daisy and I arrived a little later than usual because someone stole our buggy last night and took it for a joy-ride. We found it in the next street with the two front wheels completely buckled. I tell you, life in the suburbs is hard these days. Buggy joy-riding is the next thing Blair is going to have to tackle in his fight against crime. As a result I had to carry Daisy most of the way because she's not the most active of children and she kept moaning, 'My knee, my knee' like a veteran complaining about his old war wound.

Luke was waiting for us in the back section of the café at our usual table. He had already ordered our regulars – a double espresso for himself and a peppermint tea for me, plus a bottle of still water and apple juice for Daisy and a couple of croissants to share. We're already as predictable as an old married couple. I must admit I really look forward to our meetings, as they've become the highlight of the week. We usually just chat and gossip as it's impossible to discuss work with Daisy around. I don't know if you've seen him recently hosting his show, but he's looking good. He's so direct but it always makes me laugh and he has a way of looking at you – well, you know, it's the old cliché but he makes me feel like I'm the funniest, most fascinating woman he's ever met. I'm extremely wary as he must be like this with everybody but I'm such a sucker for a bit of attention. It's all harmless fun, I think.

To: **NikkiSoda@ambitiousproductions.com**
From: **Dot@noplacelikehome.com**
Subject: **Excitement in the suburbs**

Have you ever had any dealings with Luke Lloyd? Is there anything I should know about him? We're spending a lot of time together and it's great but I feel a little worried. What do you think? We meet regularly on Wednesday mornings so I've just come back from seeing him. This morning I was late and as I arrived he got up to greet me. Something was strange but I couldn't work out what it was.

He grinned at me, 'I thought you'd stood me up. Come here.'

He pulled me to him and I felt myself flush crimson and quickly looked round to see if there was anyone I knew in the café. For one spine-chilling moment I thought he was going to kiss me. His face was getting closer and closer to mine so I could feel his breath on my cheek, and just at the point when our lips should have met he turned his head to one side and thrust his neck under my nose. I didn't quite know what I was supposed to do but I didn't think kissing his neck was entirely appropriate.

'Come on, have a whiff,' he commanded, and then it hit me –

the smell of my youth. He was smothered in Brut and was grinning as he watched me go through the various stages of confusion, nostalgia, delight and finally disgust.

'God, it's horrid, isn't it?' I laughed. Daisy couldn't understand why we were laughing.

'Come and smell me, Daisy,' invited Luke, and she climbed up onto his knee and sniffed hard.

'Mm, lovely.'

'She's her mother's daughter,' he said.

'Are you going to wear that all day?' I said.

'If it's going to make you excited, I will. It's my way of saying Happy Birthday. Oh yeah, and there's these as well.'

From under the table he produced a bunch of beautiful, deep red, blowsy peonies and in his other hand he held a package, wrapped up in comic-book paper and tied with plain string. I was quite overcome that he'd made such an effort.

'Open it,' he said, pushing the package in my direction.

Once I'd sawn off the string with a knife the parcel unravelled in front of me and there was a burnished gold photograph frame and in it a photo of a young girl with a clipboard, looking as though she thought she was doing something very important. It took me a while to realise that the fresh-faced earnest girl was me. It was the jumper that gave it away. I thought I recognised it – my favourite comfort jumper – olive-green with black and red Aztek designs. (I know it sounds horrid but it's not. In fact I've still got it.)

'Where did you find this?' I gasped.

'Oh, I rang round some people and pulled a few strings. I'm very well connected you know. I remembered seeing it years ago. It was taken when that magazine came to follow a day in the life of our show. Don't you remember he called the researchers Luke Lloyd's Lovelies? You were furious. I asked the publicity people if I could have a copy at the time, but I can't remember what happened to it.'

I looked at the young woman in the picture. Are we the same person? I hope so because I quite liked the look of her, but I'm not sure I feel the same way about myself at the moment. Is that too weird?

'You've weathered quite well for an old woman,' he teased and then, as if to make up for interrupting my thoughts, he put his hand over mine. It seemed such an intimate gesture but I didn't take my hand away and for a moment I forgot where we were. Daisy broke the spell by putting her hand on top of Luke's, eager to join in the hand-holding game. I pulled mine out and put it on top of hers and Luke followed suit. Daisy quickly got the hang of this game but then ruined it all by slapping any hand she could get hold of. I'm amazed he went to so much trouble, but I can't imagine what his wife must have thought about the Brut. We never talk about our spouses, it's not in the rules, but I wish I knew what sort of game we're playing

To: **NikkiSoda@ambitiousproductions.com**
From: **Dot@noplacelikehome.com**
Subject: **Not so boring after all**

I knew you'd be interested. He is very attractive and charming but I must keep him at arm's length, which is quite hard when he's working hard to disarm me. What am I thinking of? We all know the price of dallying with celebrities. It's not worth it, but he does seem to be different from the others I've worked with – more genuine somehow.

To: **Jay@mybestfriendisgay.com**
From: **Dot@noplacelikehome.com**
Subject: **Guilt – the price you pay for having fun**

I'm feeling guilty about encouraging Luke. It's not that I'm encouraging him but I'm not exactly saying NO. If I think about it I haven't been very supportive of Alex over the past few weeks and that was part of the deal when I gave up work. I think I need to make more of an effort with Alex. Maybe it's my fault we're not getting on. He starts filming today and I didn't see him last night as he spent the whole evening pinched and pale, huddled over his storyboards. There must be something that I can do to help.

To: **Alex@himindoors.**
From: **Dot@noplacelikehome.com**
Subject: **Break a leg**

I missed you this morning and I just wanted to wish you all the best for today. I know you'll do a fantastic job, and remember, only forty-one days to go until it'll be a wrap and then you've just got the edit, the viewings, the dub and the reshoots to worry about. No, seriously, I know it's going to be wonderful and I'll wait up for you tonight to see how it went. The girls send good-luck kisses, albeit wet ones.

To: **NikkiSoda@ambitiousproductions.com**
From: **Dot@noplacelikehome.com**
Subject: **Go girl go!**

Thanks for the coaching effort yesterday. What do you think Matilda's chances are, and do you think I'm wrong to be pushing her like this? I just think a little encouragement goes a long way. If she can learn to start quickly and focus on the end she might find it easier. Her problem is she is a bit of a daydreamer. As you said, it's all about concentration and determination but unfortunately Matilda is more interested in whether her pink shorts look good and her ponytail swings nicely when she runs. Do you think you're born with a competitive instinct? Can you teach someone to be competitive? More importantly, should it be encouraged? So many questions from a confused mother.

To: **NikkiSoda@ambitiousproductions.com**
From: **Dot@noplacelikehome.com**
Subject: **Again . . . again . . . (too much Teletubbies)**

No! I can't believe it. Can you just run that last sentence past me again?

To: **NikkiSoda@ambitiousproductions.com**
From: **Dot@noplacelikehome.com**
Subject: **Bombshell**

Well, I'm completely amazed. Here I was thinking I knew how things were generally in the world and you've completely wrongfooted me. Are you sure you're right? What I want to know is, did she tell you herself or are you just guessing, and if you *are* right, why on earth hasn't she told me about it? Do you think she's ashamed, or worried I won't approve? Just e-mail me with all the details. I want everything you know, and it'll give me a chance to digest it all.

To: **Delissa@splendidmums.com**
From: **Dot@noplacelikehome.com**
Subject: **How are you?**

I've been thinking about what you said about caustic Kevin and maybe I'm judging him too harshly. Please don't tell Jay what I think, but I know you're discretion itself and I'm glad you got along so well with him. I feel that you and I never get the chance to catch up. I have no idea of what's going on in your life and yet here am I boring you with the intimate details of mine. Please can we try and talk soon?

To: **Delissa@splendidmums.com**
From: **Dot@noplacelikehome.com**
Subject: **Manners maketh (wo)man**

I don't think I was rude to Kevin or in the least bit distant. I was the one initiating all the conversation. He didn't ask me anything about myself. Do you think he hates me then? Has Jay mentioned anything to you about it? Your filming sounds like it was great fun and I'm glad you enjoy going into the office and working alongside Nikki. Another trip to America sounds interesting – is this purely for business?

To: **NikkiSoda@ambitiousproductions.com**
From: **Dot@noplacelikehome.com**
Subject: **She won't talk**

I can't get anything out of her. I think she's been taking inscrutable lessons from conniving Kevin. Do you think she's just teasing me, or perhaps you're wrong and there's nothing to tell? I've got to go. Alex has started his filming, beginning with the later scenes in the script when Tess is a kept woman. They're using a beautiful town house just off the green so I thought I'd take a film survival kit for Alex as a goodwill gesture, and I also thought the girls might find it interesting seeing what Dadda does all day and what Mama used to do. Keep me posted on the Delissa front. I've been meaning to ask you, do you think Kevin just took an instant dislike to me?

To: **Jay@mybestfriendisgay.com**
From: **Dot@noplacelikehome.com**
Subject: **The road to hell . . .**

Determined to be supportive to Alex and still feeling a little guilty about my behaviour with Luke, I took the girls to see Alex on location to give him a little present to wish him luck. It's part of my new initiative to save our marriage. (This is my battle of the S.O.M. – Save Our Marriage.) I came up with the idea of a film survival kit for him and had thought very carefully about what to put in it. I bought a large soft wallet (easy to store) and packed it with the following items:

Five packets of Trebor mints (which he always sucks when he's filming)
PK chewing gum (chewing helps concentration and he doesn't like Wrigleys)
Three sharp pencils to use on the script plus sharpener
One red rubber (his favourite colour)
Three packets of paper tissues with Superman emblazoned on them (he often sneezes when he's nervous, don't ask me why)

One packet of Marlboro Lights (for the really bad days)
One slim lighter
One home-made Good Luck card from the girls, with a passport photo of Matilda, Daisy and me with our thumbs up.

All silly stuff, but at least I'd thought about it. The girls were very excited about seeing Dadda at work, actually they were excited about seeing Dadda, full stop. I managed to park quite close to the location. It was impressive seeing the big trucks, and standing alongside was a group of extras, dressed in nineteenth-century bonnets, crinolines, waistcoats and breeches, sipping coffee out of polystyrene cups and gossiping about *Big Brother*, while checking out the windows in Marks and Spencer. I've never done anything as big as a costume drama but I always love being on location. A complicated crane shot was being set up and the sight of 'my' Jake and a film camera produced a frisson not dissimilar to the one I felt when I smelt the Brut on Luke Lloyd.

I tried to explain what was happening, as simply as possible, to the girls but most of it went way over Daisy's head. For a while we just sat down and watched the action from a distance. It took me a while to see Alex as he had been giving notes to the gorgeous ingénue playing Tess. (First job out of drama school – apparently Jessica spotted her, but I think there's some family connection so it's jobs for the boys. Actually I'm being unfair because Alex thinks she's going to be very good.) Alex was jogging back to the monitor where the tantalising Jessica was waiting for him.

She rubbed his back and I could just make out what she was saying, 'You OK, darling?'

He looked tense, but concentrated as he smiled a positive reply. Jessica was taking off her jacket and Alex went to help her.

'Thank you, kind sir,' she joked.

'God, how nauseating,' I thought. Hasn't he got enough to do without playing lady maid to the producer. Jealous, moi?

The shot they were setting up started with the camera on a tall crane pointing over the rooftops, providing a stark contrast to the Dorset countryside of Tess's innocent youth. (Who says an English degree is a waste of time?) The camera then had to swoop down to discover the villainous Alec D'Urberville leading Tess along the road. The camera tracked with the couple as they walked up to the house. Alec stepped aside to let her in and Tess had to stop and look back, as if searching for someone to come and save her from her destiny, and then stoically follow Alec into the house.

I knew all about this shot as Alex had discussed it with me at great length and had been excited about it. It was a very complicated shot with a long track, which required a great deal of orchestration, as horse-drawn carriages had to be queued and extras walking on the streets had to hit their marks at precise points. As I watched everybody trying to make it work it felt like I was part of the unit, so when a woman passing by stopped and asked me, 'What are you doing?' I knowledgeably replied, 'It's a new costume drama for BBC2.'

She looked impatient. 'No, I mean what are you doing hanging around here? Can you move along, please, we're trying to film.'

Rather shamefaced I had to explain that I was Alex's wife and these were his children and we'd come along to say hello.

She looked suitably unimpressed and then rather brusquely said, 'Ssh, they're just about to go for a take. We've been trying to get it right all day.' She turned away huffily, clapped her hands and shouted loudly, 'Come on everybody, let's get a move on, we're losing the light,' leaving us to watch the action.

Matilda climbed onto my knee, craning to get a better view.

We became completely immersed in the action unfolding before our eyes. The roof shot was good and the camera didn't wobble as it swooped down to find the two protagonists. Carriages passed by and extras looked convincing as the camera tracked alongside Alec and Tess, walking slowly enough for the camera to follow them. Alec stepped aside for Tess to go inside the house. This time he got it right, stepping out of shot to give the camera enough room to move closer to Tess to see her wistful look for help. As she silently sighed her despair a little hand reached into shot and tugged at the beautiful red velvet dress she was wearing and a small but very shrill voice cut through the scene like a knife, 'Scuse me, can I try on your hat?'

To my horror I could see Daisy standing on the highest step beside Tess, still tugging on her dress in her usual insistent manner.

'Cut,' yelled the assistant director.

'For fuck's sake, where did the kid come from?'

There was a beat before a voice I recognised said grimly, 'She's my little girl.'

Alex came out from behind the monitor. I knew that look too well. He was furious. I grabbed Matilda and ran to hide behind the nearest tree.

'Daisy – what are you doing here?' said Alex in anguish. 'Where is your mother?'

Daisy pointed in my direction. 'She's behind that tree.'

Alex picked her up and walked over to the tree where we were hiding.

'Hello Dadda,' said Matilda, 'are you having a nice time?'

If it was possible, he seemed to have gone even paler than he was before. 'What are you doing here?' he hissed.

'I came to give you this present,' I replied. 'I'm so sorry, I was so engrossed in the shot I didn't realise Daisy had slipped away. I'm really, really sorry.'

I gave him the survival kit.

'Thanks,' he said bitterly, and for one second I wondered whether he was going to throw it at me, but with tremendous self-control he deposited Daisy and walked back to the monitor, while we followed behind. He threw the parcel down onto his chair, without giving it a second look, and ran his fingers through his hair. He looked completely shattered.

Jessica turned back to Alex, having been deep in conversation with a man who looked like he might be an exec.

'You remember Dot?' Alex said to Jessica.

'Oh, hi,' she said, obviously not having a clue who I was.

'We'll go now,' I said, trying to pick up Daisy who was just about to do her rigid routine, making it almost impossible to pick her up.

Matilda began to whine. 'But I want to stay and watch this little television,' she said, pointing at the monitor. 'Mama, you said. You promised.'

Alex knelt down and gave her a kiss, 'Dadda's really busy at the moment but I'll see you soon and we'll have a big treat once I've finished all this hard work.'

Matilda wasn't really listening to what he was saying but she was staring hard at Jessica. 'I love your earrings,' she said and Jessica visibly softened.

'Well, that's very kind of you, they're my favourites. I tell you what, do you and your little sister want two of these?' She produced two production baseball caps which she'd obviously had made up for the entire unit. The girls were delighted.

'What do you say? What's the magic word?' I said, prompting them.

'Abracadabra,' said Matilda, too quick for her own good. Jessica laughed while I glowered at Matilda. It was happening already, infiltration from the enemy camp.

'Thank you,' said Matilda and Daisy in one monotonous voice.

'Does that mean we can we stay and watch some more?' asked Matilda hopefully.

'No, my love. It's not the best of times. You'd better go home with your mother and I'll see you later,' said Alex firmly, giving me a look that clearly said, 'Get them out of here now.'

There was a queue of people waiting to speak to Alex and in seconds he was swamped by questions from the production designer, and behind him the assistant director, the make-up lady, the props girl, the sparks, the sound engineer and, last but not least, his cameraman, Jake. He was no longer 'my' cameraman but he waved at me and I could tell he was pissed off because we'd ruined his precious shot. I led the children off before their tears really started to flow, but once we reached the car they were both in full flood crying, 'I want my Dadda.'

I knew exactly how they felt. Luckily, an ice cream soon calmed them down but because of my non-dairy diet I had to make do with a bottle of still water, which somehow doesn't have the same comfort factor. Life can be so unfair sometimes.

To: **Alex@himindoors.com**
From: **Dot@noplacelikehome.com**
Subject: **Sorry, sorry, sorry, sorry . . .**

Big apologies for what happened today. I just wanted to be supportive but it misfired horribly. If it's any consolation there seemed to be a great atmosphere on set and the shot looked like it was going to be great once you got it right. Hope you get this before I see you tonight.

All my love
Dot
X

To: **Jay@mybestfriendisgay.com**
From: **Dot@noplacelikehome.com**
Subject: **Another cock-up**

Can you see a pattern developing in my life? Tell me honestly, has it always been like this or have things changed since I gave up full-time work? It's amazing how quickly I've forgotten what life was like B.C. (before children). If you were planning on running bets on the likelihood of our marriage surviving, I don't think the odds would be in my favour. When Alex came home from filming he was exhausted.

'Thanks for the kit. It was a kind thought, even if your timing was off.'

'Did you manage to get it all done?'

'Nope, we've got to do a reshoot. Your little visit has cost us £35,000. This is only the third day of the shoot and we're already over budget and behind, but Jessica is being very relaxed about it.'

I didn't know what to say. 'Sorry' is hardly adequate but I feel terrible and, needless to say, Alex is under so much pressure that our flailing marriage is the last thing on his mind. Whoever said, 'It's the thought that counts,' was talking bollocks.

Chapter Ten

'Sure, winning isn't everything. It's the only thing.'
Henry 'Red' Sanders (1955)

To: **NikkiSoda@ambitousproductions.com**
From: **Dot@noplacelikehome.com**
Subject: **The will to watch?**

Matilda's sports day is tomorrow. Are you interested in coming along to support your protégée? Obviously Alex can't make it but he's sending Jack, his father, as a substitute and Delissa said she'd try to pop along if you allow her time out of her busy schedule. I just thought the more cheering we could do from the sidelines, the more Matilda would be encouraged. I can't get anything out of Mum, it's so frustrating, but I'll just have to wait until she tells me herself. I think you've probably got the wrong end of the stick. Let's hope Matilda doesn't in the relay race.

To: **Bethearthmother@rooted.com**
From: **Dot@noplacelikehome.com**
Subject: **A sporting chance**

Are you OK? I haven't heard from you in weeks. It's so unlike you not to reply to my e-mails. We haven't had such a long gap in communication since you went to Peru for your year off after exams. I hope I haven't said or done anything to upset you. If so, you must ignore me as I seem to have lost all sense of social skills. I just hope you're feeling better and that you've gone to have a check-up. I'm sure it's nothing serious but it's always worth having an MOT every now and then.

I thought I'd give you an update on the latest sporting news. Matilda's sports day has been worrying me. Silly, I know. I spent an anxious morning checking the weather reports, which were typically obtuse. One minute it was supposed to be sunny, the next raining and for once it was remarkably accurate, so races had to be postponed while we huddled under trees and doorways and enormous picnic umbrellas.

Jack, Daisy and I arrived nice and early to find rows of empty plastic chairs and after a healthy debate about which end would be best, we positioned ourselves by the finishing line, making sure Matilda would be able to see us. As the last of the parents settled into their seats, the children from Reception filed out of their classrooms onto the sports ground. Matilda looked so young and vulnerable as she walked towards us, her long blonde ponytail swinging from side to side. As soon as she caught sight of us she started to wave. Daisy cried out, dramatically, 'Sister, sister,' and waved back with great gusto. Matilda's friend, Molly, was next to her and looked extremely nervous, which I thought strange considering her attitude at tea the other day.

I must confess, I felt rather nervous. My hands were clammy and I had a dreadful sinking feeling in my stomach. This was ridiculous. It was only a primary school sports day. What had got into me? Perhaps my competitive instinct from my working days was resurfacing and because it's had no professional outlet, I've channelled it into Matilda. I thought, 'Oh no, I'm going to be one of those awful pushy mothers. One day sports day, the next

Broadway. Matilda is going to turn into Gypsy Rose Lee or one of the Spice Girls.' Get a grip, Dot.

'You all right?' asked Jack, obviously concerned.

'I'm fine. I'm just being silly, that's all.'

Nikki and Delissa came together, making a dramatic entrance as usual. We'd saved them some seats but Nikki had brought along one of those football rattles and was chanting, 'Matilda Knight is full of grace. She is going to win this race. Rah, rah, Matilda Knight. She is going to win this fight.' She was just about to start, 'Give us an M. Give us an A,' when I leapt up and dragged her to the chair.

'Stop it. It's just too embarrassing. People will think you're drunk.'

She looked hurt, 'I thought you wanted us here for encouragement. You're lucky I left the megaphone in the car.'

'There are more subtle ways of encouraging her,' I whispered as I gave my mother a welcome hug. She did look glowing and I vowed to get to the bottom of Nikki's rumour mongering by the end of the day.

Matilda looked like she was really enjoying herself waiting for the races to begin. I could tell she was excited and that sinking feeling returned in my stomach because I so desperately hoped she wouldn't be disappointed. Molly's mother, Kate, was sitting in the row behind us chewing her nails and looking as anxious as I felt. The first race was a kind of obstacle race. The children started with three beanbags, they had to run to a hoop and drop them in the middle, race back and get the next beanbag until all the bags were in the middle of the hoop and then race to the finishing line. They were divided into groups of five. Molly and Matilda were together and hugged each other, jumping up and down (no mean feat). There were three heats before them and then it was Matilda's turn.

She grinned at us as she found her place at the start and Nikki began coaching her from the sideline.

'Remember what I said, darling, focus, focus, focus.'

Matilda looked confused. Mrs Steel glowered at Nikki and turned her attention to the line of eager competitors.

'Ready, steady . . .' and she blew her whistle, and they were off.

To my delight Matilda was doing well. She picked up her beanbag and was one of the first to put it down in the hoop. She ran back to get the second bag but Molly had caught up with her so they were neck and neck. Molly chucked her second bag down into the hoop and ran back for the third but Matilda carefully placed the second bag down. She stopped for a minute to look at where it had landed and then remembering she was in a race ran back for the final beanbag. Molly by this time had flung the third bag into the hoop and was racing to the finishing line, while Matilda was being overtaken by 'Enry as she started to arrange the beanbags into an interesting pattern in the middle of the hoop.

'Forget the bloody bags, just run,' I screamed, forgetting where I was.

She looked up and saw Molly running over the finishing line and ran as fast as she could. She just managed to beat Chloe, who was trotting along and waving at everyone she recognised in the crowd.

The pattern was set for the day. Matilda is a perfectionist, which is something I don't suffer from myself. She's inherited it from Alex. Nikki leant across Delissa and said to me, 'You should have found out what sort of races they were doing and then I could have been more specific in the training.'

Delissa laughed, 'You two, you're so competitive it's ridiculous.'

Matilda looked like she was about to cry but the school had

cleverly arranged for each participant to have an older child to congratulate them at the end of every race and lead them off for a glass of orange squash or water. Matilda's favourite big girl, Miranda, was there to pat her on the back and offer words of encouragement. Meanwhile I felt horribly embarrassed and guilty about my outburst.

In between breaks for rain 'Enry won the egg and spoon race, but he cheated most of the way by holding firmly onto the egg with his thumb. Matilda came fourth (but not last) because she was determined that her egg was going to be the stillest egg in the race. The children went back to their seats before the final race and Matilda looked utterly miserable. By this stage Molly had three winner's ribbons pinned on her sports shirt and a large grin across her face. Matilda mouthed across to me, 'I haven't won anything,' and all I could do was mouth back at her, 'Don't worry – you've done really well,' and do an emphatic thumbs up.

After the last race Jack, who was holding Daisy, got up to stretch his legs. Nikki said she had to dash as she was having lunch with a new commissioning editor at Channel 4. I turned to kiss her good bye and thank her for coming, and over her shoulder I caught sight of Luke talking to Jack while Daisy wriggled in his arms. Luke took her and put her on his shoulders, where she settled comfortably, and he and Jack strolled towards us. My stomach lurched again, and this time I wasn't thinking about Matilda.

'How'd she do?' asked Luke, nodding towards the track.

'I've only just turned up, my boys are in the next batch.'

'It wasn't a great success,' I replied, 'but she's very good at art.' He laughed. 'Luke, have you met Jack, my father-in-law?'

'Yeah, I introduced myself.' He smiled at Jack, who seemed less than enthusiastic.

Nikki's urgent lunch appointment suddenly didn't seem so urgent. She was hanging back hoping to be introduced to Luke and then, bored of waiting for me to do the honours, just barged in and said, 'Nikki Soda. Dot used to work for me. I am Ambitious.'

'She means her company is Ambitious Productions,' I explained.

Nikki took Luke off to one side, cornering him about possible work. I expect she wants him for the toilet project. Delissa was deep in conversation with Helen, 'Enry's mother, who had been sitting the other side of her, about the difficulties of bringing up boys these days.

Jack was watching me. He indicated towards Luke and leant forward and said in a low voice, 'Be careful, Dot.'

I blushed, 'What are you talking about?' I could feel my neck beginning to flush red. 'I'm just doing a bit of work for him. I knew him years ago.'

Jack gave me one of his knowing looks that Alex has inherited from him, 'I'm just warning you.'

I tried to laugh it off. How can Jack read me so easily? It's funny how men get so territorial. I suppose he's just fighting his son's corner but from that brief talk with Luke how does he know that there's any romantic inclination/intention, which of course there isn't. Well, not on my part anyway.

We were all invited by the headmistress, the glamorous Mrs Goodwill, to give the boys and girls a round of applause and then the children filed back into their classrooms for the rest of the day's lessons. I blew the miserable Matilda a kiss and went to look for Delissa. She had agreed to come to lunch so at last I was to have some time alone with my elusive mother. As we walked home she said, 'I liked Helen, is she a friend of yours?'

'God, no,' I replied, 'she's a boy's mother. We hardly ever talk to them.'

I was tempted to tell her all about Helen and her furtive relationship with Philippe but decided against it. You know me, I'm not one to spread gossip. It was lovely spending some time with her and she told me some amazing news, but I've just looked at the time and I must go collect Matilda from school, so I'll call you later.

To: **Jay@mybestfriendisgay.com**
From: **Dot@noplacelikehome.com**
Subject: **You won't believe this . . .**

Oh my God, my mother has a boyfriend. He's called Carl and she met him when she was filming in New Mexico. She was quite coy about the whole thing, but once I'd prised it out of her she couldn't stop talking about him and became almost girlie. He sounds interesting but I would expect no less of my mother. He has been married and his wife died, but they were together for twenty years so he knows how to successfully sustain a relationship, which is a good sign (I thought that, she didn't say it). He has three daughters, whom she hasn't met yet, but he sounds very keen. Art dealing is a precarious business but I think he's got a few Georgia O'Keefe's so he must be doing quite well. Of course there have been men in her past but she's always kept them separate from me. I think she lost faith in men and was always wary of trusting anyone after Dad left. I suppose so much time has passed now, she feels she has little to lose. It's early days and I think the geographical distance is a bonus at this stage, as it gives them both some breathing space. She said she didn't want to bother me before, as she knew I was preoccupied at the moment. It's a bit of a strange feeling but I think I'm genuinely pleased for her.

To: **NikkiSoda@ambitiousproductions.com**
From: **Dot@noplacelikehome.com**
Subject: **Autumnal love**

You were right. Delissa does have a boyfriend and I think it's a good thing. It feels a bit strange but that's only because I'm not used to the idea. I'm intrigued to meet him.

On the holiday front, please come camping with us. I know it's not exactly your thing but it's not mine either. I think it's good for us to try new things occasionally. Did you see that article in Style about camping in Cornwall being the next big thing in holidays? Forget St Tropez or Ibiza and roll on Rock. Anyway it's an adventure for the children and I'm determined to make it special, but I know I'll need all the support I can get. Imagine sitting out under the stars, white wine chilled in a special cooler, children sleeping exhausted in their sleeping bags after a day on the beach. You and I with splendid all-over tans, all of which costs less than half the price of a plane ticket to Portugal. I think it will be fun.

Thanks for coming today and sorry you didn't get a chance to use your megaphone. Yes, Luke Lloyd is rather lovely but please don't encourage me. I went to pick up Matilda and her friend, Molly, from school dreading the sight that would be sure to greet me of a thoroughly disgruntled girl. I always know exactly what sort of day she's had by the look on her face when the door to the classroom opens to let the little darlings out. I braced myself, but Matilda skipped out of the classroom and greeted me with a big smile. I'm usually not so attuned to other children's moods but I would have been insensitive if I hadn't realised that Molly, champion of the day, was definitely in a grump.

'Look, I got a loser's sticker and Molly wants to swap her ribbons for my sticker but I'm not letting her.'

I silently congratulated the school on making losing seem just as desirable as winning. I felt I ought to congratulate Molly because she had run so well. So I waited for the right moment, just as we were about to drop her at home and said, 'Well done, Molly, you ran brilliantly.' She cheered up and gave Matilda a triumphant smile as she went up the path to her door. Matilda's smile disintegrated and she started to cry.

'Why did you have to say that? You love Molly more than me.'

I quietly tried to explain that they both had done very well and that it wouldn't have been fair not to congratulate Molly, but Matilda remained inconsolable and I was left wondering whether I should have said anything at all. Once home I gave her another sticker. There's nothing like a good sticker to set the world to rights. Maybe that's what I need.

Chapter Eleven

'There is a tide in the affairs of women,
which taken at the flood, leads – God knows where.'
Lord Byron

To: **Jack@finefigureofafatherinlaw**
From: **Dot@noplacelikehome.com**
Subject: **The roller coaster ride aka marriage**

Jack, you are being ridiculous about Luke. There is absolutely nothing going on but I appreciate your concern. I don't know about you but I always look at other couples and assume they have no problems, unless it's glaringly obvious and they're screaming at each other, or the husband is to be found kissing his best friend's wife given any opportunity. I've always thought you and Sylvia were very happy together so I was surprised by what you said. Interesting that your first rough patch was just after the children were born. It's always a difficult time, which undoubtedly puts pressure on any relationship. It *is* about working at it, but somehow it seems strange to talk about working at emotions. Maybe that's something our generation have got wrong. We have the freedom to cut loose but there's a price to pay for that freedom

Don't worry, I knew it wasn't always going to be easy but I'm not planning on giving up on Alex. If anything, I'm worried that he's giving up on me. I know he's fed up and the hardest thing is that we're not spending any time together, so the differences between us grow daily, and any attempt to make things better misfires. You are right, it is all about communication, but it's hard to communicate with a man who is engrossed in his work and will be for at least the next three months. Of course I understand he needs to concentrate – I, of all people, know what it's like. That's the problem. I also understand the temptations when you're working closely with someone on a project you're both passionate about, and that makes me very uneasy.

To be honest, Jack, Alex was so brilliant when I was ill that I really miss him now. I'm trying to be tough and reassure myself he's just cutting a bit of slack, having been incarcerated with the children and me while I was ill and recuperating. At the time I thought it was bringing us closer together, but being married to 'a woman who doesn't suffer the best of health' is not much fun. I hope he loves me for who I am, but I'm worried he loved me for who I was. As far as Luke is concerned, of course I won't let him turn my head. My relationship with him is purely professional and I treat our meetings as a little fillip, or a 'Kevin' (as Jay and I call them), in an otherwise dull and dreary life. OK, not that dull and dreary, but you know what I mean.

To: **LukeLloyd@talent.co.uk**
From: **Dot@noplacelikehome.com**
Subject: **New proposals**

Thanks for your comments on the treatments, which were valid. I'm not sure about developing the *First Loves* idea with *The One That Got Away*, but I'll think about it. There are people I was interested in who didn't feel the same way about me, but there's no one really whom I wish I'd seduced and didn't, and I certainly haven't felt the inclination to marry anyone but Alex. How about you?

To: **LukeLloyd@talent.co.uk**
From: **Dot@noplacelikehome.com**
Subject: **Ridiculous notions**

Now you're just being silly. There was never a moment when you and I could have had a relationship when we worked together. For a start, we were both involved with other people and also you flirted outrageously with all the researchers. Shame on you, Luke Lloyd, you're just a big tease.

On a more practical note, any advice on camping and camping accessories would be much appreciated. I went when I was sixteen with my best friend Beth and some others and I didn't put up tents or do anything useful. We had great fun but I can't remember what we ate or how we cooked, maybe we existed on a liquid diet. All tips greatly appreciated.

To: **Jay@mybestfriendisgay.com**
From: **Dot@noplacelikehome.com**
Subject: **Forgetting how to flirt**

Help, help, help! I've just had suggestive e-mail from Luke and for a minute got all panicky and practical and ruined the mood but think it was a wise thing to do. Maybe I should be strict with myself from now on and keep all further e-mail correspondence entirely professional. Please advise. I need to throw myself into organising this camping trip for good diversionary tactics.

To: **Hardmancamping.co.uk**
From: **Dot@noplacelikehome.com**
Subject: **Camping essentials**

Have been advised to consult you on essential accessories for camping in the summer. We're planning our trip in the middle of the summer but I've been warned that August in Cornwall can be as cold as Alaska and a lot less welcoming. Could you compile a list of products asap?

To: **Wildwolf@surviveordie.com**
From: **Dot@noplacelikehome.com**
Subject: **Catalogue queries**

Have been very impressed by your web site and am planning expedition of my own. Are you interested in assisting?

To: **Wildwolf@surviveordie.com**
From: **Dot@noplacelikehome.com**
Subject: **Small scale enterprises**

Dear Mr Wildwolf

I'm sorry, I didn't mean to mislead you. No, we're not attempting the north face of Everest and we don't need any sponsorship, especially not from Annie Oakley female-friendly sleeping bags. Although, I'm intrigued by the phrase 'female friendly'? Ours is a modest expedition to a domestic campsite in Cornwall but I have no equipment except for an old lilo my mother has agreed to lend as a sleeping mat. Please advise.

To: Bethearthmother@rooted.com
From: Dot@noplacelikehome.com
Subject: **Survival skills**

Have been completely immersed surfing the net for companies to help set me up for this camping holiday. I've always fancied myself as a survival expert facing nights in the jungle with only a handy pocket mirror and a box of matches. Actually, cancel the matches, I'd make my own fire with twigs and old bits of material. It is amazing the amount of equipment you need, I never realised camping was so technical. Are you planning to come down for a few days with the kids? We could have a chance to catch up, and the children will be blissfully happy playing on the beach so we could talk. If you are thinking of coming do you have any tents, sleeping bags, stoves, Teasmades or cuddly toys? (Cue Bruce Forsyth, 'Didn't she do well?' God, Matilda's right, I am old.) We don't need too much stuff as I'm determined to keep it simple.

To: Wolfman@surviveordie.com
From: Dot@noplacelikehome.com
Subject: **The final list of basic camping essentials**

Dear Wolfie. Have taken on board your invaluable advice and require the following:

1. Rapid-fire stove – for quick turnaround on dinner for kids £25.99
2. Three gas cylinders for above £12.99
3. Aluminium fold-up table £33.99
4. Four longback chairs £39.99
5. One roll-a-stool £9.99

6. One Annie Oakley female-friendly sleeping bag £39.99
7. Two child-friendly sleeping bags £35.99
8. Three sleeping mats (spend more for good insulation) £59.99
9. Three camp towels £29.99
10. Nexus safety whistle (you can never be too careful) £6.99
11. Butane lighter that can even take a swim £19.99
12. Six-man (or, in our case, woman) tent from Medieval Pavilion Resources (interesting design but easy to assemble according to catalogue) £500
13. 'Light up your life' lantern for evenings outside the tent £24.99
14. Washing line £5.99
15. Campagas electric coolbox (plug into cigarette lighter) £43.99
16. Three packets of emergency rations (chicken casserole) £9.99
17. First-aid kit £11.99
18. Car roof-rack to accommodate all the above. £149.99

TOTAL: £1062.83

I can take my own saucepans, cutlery and disposable barbecue. I'm undecided about the rope and the binoculars but I think that might be a bit excessive, and I've definitely decided against the blue-check plaid shirt. This holiday is supposed to be about cutting costs. Actually, I am interested in your book on emergency medical procedures which might be more useful than *Basic*

Essentials of Survival, which I hope won't be appropriate for Cornwall.

To: **Bethearthmother@rooted.com**
From: **Dot@noplacelikehome.com**
Subject: **Second mortgage**

I've just spent a fortune on camping equipment and consequently I feel a bit sick. This camping holiday was supposed to be my way of economising but I think I'll have to sell the house and live in the tent at this rate. I went for the medieval pavilion style because I was fed up with everything being priced at –99p. At least it was an honest £500. I also thought it might be useful for parties in the garden when it's raining. I could even rent it out and start my own marquee business. Still, we could have had two weeks in sunny Mallorca for the cost of all this equipment but I've been persuaded that it will last for life. So when I'm sixty-four I'll still be able to use it – whether I'll want to is another matter. I just hope the children appreciate this holiday as I'm only doing it for them.

What's more worrying is all this nonsense your doctor has been telling you. I'm glad you went to see him as you've been feeling bad for weeks now, but I really think you should get a second opinion. I'm your best friend and I think I'd know if you were depressed. Just look at your life. You have one of the best marriages in London, your children are clever, charming, talented and beautifully behaved, you love being a mother, you live in a splendid house and Tom's work is going very well, so you are financially secure. What is there to be depressed about? I'm sure it's a virus. Maybe what you need is some regular exercise, or take up yoga, but I expect a week with us camping in Cornwall will soon sort you out. I haven't seen you for ages – I'll try and pop in tomorrow.

To: <u>**Jay@mybestfriendisgay.com**</u>
From: **Dot@noplacelikehome.com**
Subject: **Baking or barking?**

As Miss Clavel says in *Madeline*, 'Something is not right.' I went round uninvited to see Beth yesterday because she's been a bit strange and her doctor thinks she's depressed. I found her making cakes – nothing strange in that as she loves baking – but she had bought boxes of cake mixes, which is so unlike her as everything is usually home-made. It wasn't just one box of cake mix but nineteen. I thought she must be having a party, or making them for a school cake stall, but she looked at me as if I was the one who was mad and it was the most normal thing in the world. Apart from that, she seemed her usual self. Do you think I'm being oversensitive? Maybe she's just fed up with doing it all herself, and that I can relate to.

To: <u>**Alex@himindoors.com**</u>
From: **Dot@noplacelikehome.com**
Subject: **Teacher from hell**

I've just come back from Matilda's Open Day and I have to admit, I was impressed. I wish you could have been with me to see it. Two girls from Year 6 greeted me at the gates and gave me a guided tour around the school – I went to places I never even knew existed. The girls were unbelievably confident, witty and intelligent without being cocky. I wasn't like that at eleven – I'm not like that at thirty-eight. They asked me who my daughter was, and I said Matilda Knight. Both their faces lit up and they said, 'Oh, we love Matilda – she's such a character.'

I enjoyed their company so much that I was a bit late for Matilda. She was standing by the entrance staring mournfully through the large window. If she'd been old enough to wear a watch she would have been constantly checking it and tapping it to make sure it was working. When I arrived she looked at me as if to say, 'This really isn't good enough.' It took two seconds for her to rally and she delighted in showing me all her work, which seemed, in my opinion, to be excellent. I kept trying to sneak a look at the other children's workbooks to put it into context. Around the classroom she had lots of pictures on the wall. The best was her self-portrait which was worthy of Matisse (me, biased?).

What was so encouraging was the reaction of all the other children as we walked around the school. Everywhere we went people would say, 'Hiya, Matilda,' and she'd give a little wave or stop for a chat. I was impressed, and I thought back to that conversation with Mrs Steel. There's nothing wrong with Matilda. I don't think I've ever seen such a well-balanced, confident and content child. Maybe I wasn't the problem after all. Silently fuming for all those sleepless nights I've had, worrying about our damaged child because of Mrs Steel, I made my way back to the classroom. There was a visitors' book open on Mrs Steel's desk for the parents to make comments. I read some of the entries.

'Couldn't have done it without you, Mrs Steel. Thank you for making our child's first experience of school such a happy one.'

'The work is of a fantastically high standard, but it is Mrs Steel who couldn't be more patient and observant. She should be congratulated for all her hard work.'

I looked up and saw Mrs Steel herself, with an unbearably

smug expression on her face. This was her day not the children's day. I picked up the pen and wrote as clearly as I could, 'Could do better.' I didn't sign my name, which is a bit cowardly, but she'll know I wrote it and you know, I really don't care. Revenge is sweet. I can't wait for next term when Matilda will have a new teacher and things can only get better.

To: **Delissa@splendidmums.com**
From: **Dot@noplacelikehome.com**
Subject: **Where the buffaloes roam**

Off to the land of the free again. How I envy your lifestyle – please pack me in your suitcase as Cornwall doesn't sound nearly as appealing as New Mexico. So you're going to be allowed to meet the girls this time. It must be getting serious. You don't have to worry, they'll love you. Is there any chance Carl will be coming over? I can't wait to vet, I mean meet, him. Just suppose you two decide to get married, I'll have three sisters, which is something I've always craved. Funny to think I might acquire a new family at the age of thirty-eight without having to go through teenage quarrels and jealous tantrums. I hope they're lovely women, not just for your sake but for mine as well.

To: **Delissa@splendidmums.com**
From: **Dot@noplacelikehome.com**
Subject: **Jumping-the-gun weddings**

Sorry. It was only a thought. No, of course it's early days and I completely understand that you're nowhere near even contemplating the thought of marrying Carl. In future I'll keep my thoughts to myself. Have a good time and see you in September.

To: Jay@mybestfriendisgay.com
From: **Dot@noplacelikehome.com**
Subject: **Time of the month**

It was check-up time today. I think it does get a little bit easier each time I go. I suppose it has become routine, like going for a check-up with the dentist. What is annoying is that for a couple of months I can almost forget what has happened. I can block it out and get on with life. I've stopped checking myself daily, because that way madness lies, and now I only examine myself the night before so that if anything is worrying me I can show Professor Harrison. I feel less anxious that way. What I hate is the thought that a twinge in your back is bone cancer, a cough means it's spread to your lungs and every headache is a definite brain tumour. I'm playing a waiting game.

I decided to take Daisy with me to the hospital today. I know the routine so well that if there is anything sinister they'll do a needle test and we'll have to wait a couple of days at least for the results. With the sort of cancer I've got it's hardly going to be immediate emergency surgery with Daisy having to scrub up and assist the anaesthetist.

Afterwards I was taking her to her first party and she was dressed in a beautiful party frock that Matilda used to wear. It is dark midnight-blue velvet, lace trimming at the collar and cuffs, with a big silk bow which ties at the back. It's a hand-me-down from Alex's mother, and his older sister, Rebecca, wore it when she was a little girl. Daisy looked gorgeous with her hair tied back in a

French ponytail and was the centre of attention at the hospital with all the nurses stopping to talk to her and admire her outfit. She must have been a welcome relief from the grey tense faces they usually have to deal with. Daisy, on the other hand, was confused and every time a nurse greeted her she launched into 'Happy Birthday to You' thinking that this was the party. Of course she has no concept of what a party is. All she's been told by Matilda is that at a party you give presents, play games, sing Happy Birthday and eat cake.

'Can I have cake now?' she kept asking, and I tried to explain that this was not the party, it was a hospital, and that we were going to the party very soon.

While she was serenading one of the nurses (I had the best child care possible during the hour I was there courtesy of the NHS) I started chatting to a middle-aged woman sitting opposite. I've never talked to anyone in the waiting room other than the nurses because you don't know what emotional minefields you could detonate, but she initiated the conversation and seemed fairly relaxed and sane.

'You here just for a check-up?' she asked.

'Mm,' I replied warily, 'how about you?'

'I've been clear for six years,' she replied, holding up her crossed fingers.

'That's fantastic.' Now this was what I wanted to hear.

'I always get a little anxious before check-ups,' I confided to her.

'It gets easier as the years pass,' she reassured me.

'I've sort of lost faith in the future,' I confessed, surprising myself by vocalising the thought. I hadn't realised what I felt until the words came out of my mouth.

'Oh, you mustn't think like that. I know exactly how you feel, but there is another way of looking at it. Now whenever I get worried about doing anything, I say to myself, "Well what have you got to lose? You might be dead in a couple of years so just give it a go," and though it might sound strange, I find that thought liberating, it gives me confidence.'

It certainly was a different way of looking at the whole experience. She leant forward and patted me on the knee, 'You've got to make the most of the moment.' She indicated towards Daisy, who by this stage was sitting on the receptionist's knee. 'She's lovely, is she your only one?'

'No, I've got two girls. How about you?'

'I've got two boys but they're in their twenties now,' she replied with a smile.

'It's what's important, isn't it?' I said. 'When I was diagnosed it was fantastic having the children there. They grounded me and so did my husband. Throughout the whole business it was always wonderful to come back and have a hug from the girls.'

'Oh no, when I was told about the cancer I did the exact opposite. I left my husband, decided to go travelling, had lots of affairs and had a marvellous time. I even sailed across the Atlantic, didn't quite make it across, but at least I tried.'

I was speechless. I looked at this plump, tawny-haired, jovial woman who looked like a typical housewife (oh, that's me now) and could visibly feel that my jaw was hanging open.

'What about your husband? How did he cope?'

'Well, there wasn't a lot he could do about it, poor thing. I suppose he understood really. He was very patient and just waited for me to get it all out of my system, which I did eventually. I came back to him but I didn't want to have any regrets, and now I haven't and I've never felt better. For once in my life I acted completely selfishly and the world didn't collapse, it understood. I don't think I'll do it again though.'

A nurse called my name and for the first time I was irritated that they were seeing me so promptly as there were so many questions I wanted to ask this extraordinary woman. I scooped up Daisy and said good bye and the woman smiled at me. I felt that something important had passed between us. Everything was fine with Professor Harrison. We had a nice chat about Ireland where he'd just come back from holiday. I quizzed him about camping (I'm asking everyone about it at the moment, I am in danger of turning into a camping bore) but he had no valuable insights. He checked me all over but if there was anything amiss I'm not confident he would find it. He does have fantastically warm hands so, except for the worry of what he could find, it's actually quite a pleasant experience. Oh, I am a sad woman.

How are you and the inscrutable love of your life? I haven't heard from you for weeks. Is everything OK? Do you fancy a week's camping in Cornwall? (Ignore, obvious joke.)

To: **Jay@mybestfriendisgay.com**
From: **Dot@noplacelikehome.com**
Subject: **Camping in Cornwall**

It's fantastic news that you can come to Cornwall for a few days even though you will be parted from your loved one. Will you cope? I so need your help, especially with packing all the equipment into the car, the drive down and putting up tents, and with general morale. At best we will have the chance to spend some quality time together. I can't wait. Why don't you e-mail me a list of things you want to bring? The children are very excited you're coming, and so am I.

Have you spoken to Beth recently? I don't quite know what's going on. She called me three times on one day and left messages on the answer phone. When I rang back she denied she'd ever called. Will you try talking to her? Alex has gone to Dorset for three weeks and is already behind because of the rain. They worked the whole schedule around the long summer evenings and now it's a washout. I bet Jessica Bedmeigh isn't smiling at the moment and I only hope she's not seeking consolation in my husband's arms. Enough of this self torture. Alex hasn't mentioned her for weeks but I'm not sure whether that's a good thing or not.

Luke Lloyd is flirting outrageously with me and I have to admit I find it disconcerting. I'm treating it like it's a game but it feels like my stomach is trying to perform a series of impressive backward somersaults whenever I see him. I'm wondering whether these feelings are dangerous, especially considering the state of my relationship with Alex at the moment. The words play and fire, come to mind. I need to develop an effective, well-tuned internal sprinkler system and fire alarm. What I want to know is, what does Luke really feel? Do you think he's in love with me? Maybe he's suffering sleepless nights tossing and turning, unable to get me out of his mind, waking up exhausted in the morning and feeling in complete turmoil. Oh God, do you think he's wondering whether he should leave his wife? I can't imagine our children getting on. He has got older boys, after all, and how would they cope in our world of pink and purple?

To: **Jay@mybestfriendisgay.com**
From: **Dot@noplacelikehome.com**
Subject: **Swollen head**

Point taken. Of course you're right, Luke is just having a good old-fashioned flirt. He can't help himself, he's always been like this, trying it on with everyone, and I'm reading far too much into the whole thing. But he did go to a lot of trouble with my birthday presents and he always makes a point of seeking me out in any social situation. You mustn't tell anyone, but sometimes I imagine what it would be like to have an affair. Maybe I should try it, just for the experience. Oh my God, what am I saying? Just writing that last sentence makes me feel so scared. Why jeopardise my marriage and my children's happiness? Yes, you're right, I'm taking this far too seriously. I need to get away. Actually, looking at your list of essentials for our holiday I have to say, Jay darling, I don't think we'll be needing champagne stoppers, trifle bowls, your poster of Kylie, even if it has been personally signed, or your weights. Just lifting the children up fifty times a day will keep your muscles toned. I am looking forward to this holiday so three cheers for the simple life in Cornwall, some wholesome adventures and lashings of ginger pop!

Chapter Twelve

'Summer afternoon – summer afternoon . . . the two most beautiful words in the English language.'
Henry James

To: **Delissa@splendidmums.com**
From: **Dot@noplacelikehome.com**
Subject: **Wish you were here**

This is an exciting first for me. I've never done this sort of thing before but, tuning into the twenty-first century zeitgeist, I'm sending this to you via an Internet café. I feel like I'm part of a vast communication network connecting the whole world. I think Cornwall to America is pretty cosmopolitan. Consider this more of an e-mail postcard without scenic photo (it's hard to focus through a sheet of rain).

We were splashing along the picturesque streets of Penzance in search of a bucket shaped as a castle (not hard to find) and one in the shape of a puppy (so far, impossible) when I saw this old tea shop advertising Internet facilities. What a great combination – Cornish pasties and international communication with your loved ones. The children are happily slurping hot chocolate with Megan, Gary, Ocean and Sky (all will be revealed later) while I take time out to get my e-mail fix. Do you think I might be addicted to e-mail? I feel so much better after I've sent one and I get all confused and frustrated if I can't express myself. A day without my laptop is like going cold turkey.

Thank God Jay came for the first four days, as I couldn't have coped without him. Going camping is worse than organising a film shoot and far more complicated. We woke up to a beautiful summer's morning, everyone excited about the adventure ahead. In the spirit of our old holidays, when we'd have to get up at 4.00 in the morning to drive to catch the ferry over to France, I had planned an early start. I wanted to get there by lunchtime. Jay was to be with us by 7.30 to help pack the car. The night before, I'd written an inventory of everything we were taking and drawn a map showing where it would fit in the back of the car.

By quarter to nine I was still arranging bags. The girls started arguing because they were bored and I could tell Jay was getting a little irritated with me when I snapped, 'No, look at the map, the balls go in the right-hand corner not on top of the games box.' By 10.00 I'd thrown away my map in a temper. As you know, geography was always my worst subject and maps have never been my strong point – I've never been very good on scale and I think that's where I went wrong. By 10.30 we still hadn't fixed the bikes on the back. When I walked back into the house there was a pile of essential toys in the hall that still hadn't found their way to the allotted space.

'This is ridiculous,' snapped Jay as he started wedging saucepans, pillows, macs, babies, Betty and essential fluffy toy kittens into any available space. Just as we had got everything into the car Jay remembered his emperor-sized double duvet, complete with lifesize print of Michaelangelo's David, which I thought highly impractical but eventually the kids used it as a blanket and spread it over their knees in the back of the car. Obviously there was no room for my laptop, but this is supposed to be a complete holiday where I concentrate on providing fun and games for the children.

Did I say holiday? At 11.05 precisely we drove away from the house and by 11.10 we were back again because the girls had forgotten to have a wee. In an effort to calm our jangled nerves Jay waved a couple of CDs and said enigmatically, 'I think they're ready for the next stage. This will get us in the mood.' Mood was the right word for the way I felt as the lyrics of *My Fair Lady* filled the car.

The first stage of the journey was surprisingly quick, the roads were clear and our spirits began to rise. What was worrying were the clouds that were beginning to gather, and the closer we got to Cornwall the darker they became. I started driving faster, determined to get there before the rain, until we hit the point where the A30 narrows. We were stuck in a queue that stretched down to Cornwall for all we knew, and the girls had eaten all their picnic provisions in the first ten minutes of the journey. All I had left were a couple of bruised apples and some soggy digestive biscuits, which had been packed too close to the leaky water bottle. Stupidly, I'd packed some travel games in the games box, which was underneath the mountain of luggage in the boot. The traffic was crawling so slowly that I sent Jay out on a seek and rescue mission. It was a diverting ten minutes, Jay running behind the car with the boot open, desperately trying to get to the box of games while picking up all the odds and sods that kept falling out into the middle of the road.

'I'm dicing with death out here and you're not being very sympathetic,' he shouted when he heard us all giggling.
The cars behind hooted every time a fluffy kitten or a saucepan tumbled into the road and Jay shouted obscenities back at them. In true Starsky and Hutch style he ran alongside the car and leapt back in.

'You're . . . not . . . going . . . as . . . slowly . . . as you think,' he panted accusingly, as though it was my fault he had failed in his mission.

After that we tried everything to keep our spirits up but there aren't a lot of games you can play with very small children once we'd exhausted I Spy, with colours not letters, and Guess the Tune. How I long for the days of civilised car journeys when we can play Botticelli. After an hour we discovered the only reason for the delay was people slowing down to look mawkishly at a stationary Volvo on the hard shoulder, hoping to spot some dramatic crash complete with battered and twisted metal and spots of blood on the road. To their disappointment it had simply broken down and the only evidence of violence was a blown gasket.

Once in Cornwall the inevitable slow tractor practically brought us to a standstill. I think they hang around the fields in groups, skulking behind hedges waiting for the busy tourist times.

'Your turn, Giles, the road's been a bit too clear for my liking, time to slow it up.'

You'd think they'd be more considerate. By the end of the journey the girls knew all the words to *My Fair Lady* better than Jay. They wound down the windows and sang gustily, 'All I want is a room somewhere . . .' not realising quite how prophetic that would prove to be. We eventually made it by teatime. I think I understand now why you never took us camping – we could have flown to America in the time it's taken us to get down here. Trust you are well and that your journey was relaxed and luxurious. One day, no doubt, I'll look back fondly on this time. Have a good summer. We all send our love.

Dot

To: **Bethearthmother@rooted.com**
From: **Dot@noplacelikehome.com**
Subject: **Mud, glorious mud**

Well, we're here and it's not quite what I expected. Luke had recommended the campsite and I thought it would be something unusual not just . . . well, a campsite. Surely celebrities don't go to the same sort of campsites as everyone else? At first I put it down to the weather as it had been raining continuously for two weeks. We were faced with a muddy field and not the horn of plenty which the name Rustic Camping – A Cornish Cornucopia optimistically suggested. Actually, it is a horn of plenty of mud. I began to wonder whether Luke had been joking when he recommended it.

Inevitably, our spot seemed to be the worst, situated in a dip in the field where all the rain had collected. It was like camping in the waterhole rather than beside it. Any minute you expected rhino and antelope to come and drink. Our neighbours (dreadlocks and sandals) viewed us suspiciously when we arrived, annoyed that someone was going to be pitching quite so close to their tepee (or maybe they just didn't like our taste in music). They were veteran campers and through years of experience had obviously mastered the organisational skills necessary for a successful camping trip, which so far seemed to elude me.

It took Jay and me two fraught hours to put up the easy-to-assemble tent but once up it looked pretty splendid in a medieval pavilion sort of way. There was only one problem, there didn't seem to be a groundsheet which, considering the state of the site, was going to make the difference between a tolerable couple of weeks and pure hell. Putting it down as a design fault (or maybe I should have read the small print) I admitted to Jay I hadn't a clue what to do. The girls were whining so I told them to put on their wellington boots and go and explore.

'I can't find my boots,' moaned Matilda.

'Do I have to do everything?' I snapped, but an hour later with the entire contents of the car strewn across the campsite, I had to acknowledge that I had forgotten to pack the boots. Meanwhile, Jay had come up with a brainwave.

'Necessity is the mother of invention,' he muttered as he started to cut up the bin bags I had remembered to pack, sticking them together with Barbie plasters from our first-aid kit. Just as I was worrying whether there were going to be enough bin bags and plasters for our rather large tent, Mr Dreadlocks splashed his way over to us.

'If he's coming to gloat, I'm going to pull his hair,' said Jay maturely, but he didn't gloat, he just held out a plastic sheet which meant that we had enough groundcover until we could fix up something more professional.

'Cool tent,' he said, and then waded back to the tepee.

'Thanks very much,' we shouted gratefully at his retreating back. Mrs Kaftan waved a response. Looking at the rest of the campsite with the array of neatly presented tents and caravans our section could definitely be described as alternative, which at least meant we were interesting.

By now the children, dressed in trainers, were exploring the facilities, the most obvious being an enormous sandpit in the centre of the field. I borrowed Jay's mobile to ring Federal Express to see how much it would cost for the boots to be sent by courier to us. £83.00 plus VAT was obviously far too much, especially considering our current financial situation. We'd just have to go and buy some more boots in Penzance.

We set up the stove and the table and chairs, and just as we were frying some sausages for tea to check that the stove was actually working, the most terrible blood-curdling scream echoed across the field. I knew instinctively that something or someone was attacking my child. Jay and I ran as fast as we could towards the sandpit. By now a group had gathered around them and we managed to fight our way into the middle to see Daisy bawling her eyes out with Matilda cradling her in her arms, rocking backwards and forwards.

'What is it, what happened?' I shrieked at Matilda.

'It was awful, Mama.'

'What, what was it?'

'It was a big fly and it flew so close to Daisy it almost ate her up. Look, like that one.'

A normal-sized housefly did a victory loop-the-loop before it headed off towards the open fields. I stopped checking Daisy for bites, stings or burns. The large crowd of anoraks and woolly hats began to disperse and I realised that my children weren't what you'd call natural country girls. The tiniest midge produced shrieks from both children and plodding back to our tent, Matilda burst into tears when she fell over and got mud on her favourite purple jeans.

By this point Jay had retreated to the car and was doing the alternate nostril breathing he'd just learnt in yoga. Interrupting his karma and irritated by my children's faint-hearted attitude, I pretended to start packing up the car saying, 'Right. No more adventures. We're going home if you're going to carry on with this ridiculous behaviour. They're tiny flies, they are not going to hurt you, and a little bit of mud is hardly the end of the world, for goodness sake.' Jay, sensing my frustration, took the girls to check out the other amenities while I salvaged the sausages that had been sizzling furiously while we were rescuing the girls from their terrible ordeal.

After half an hour, and just as I was beginning to wonder what had happened to them, they returned with big smiles brandishing their newly acquired cuddly pig (!), a handy penguin keyring and a tin of baked beans. Jay looked sheepish.

'Sorry, I couldn't resist. I just love spoiling them.' My heart sank. At this rate my holiday budget would be blown in a few days. 'Come here and look what I've got,' Jay carried on enthusiastically. 'You know when you go on holiday and stay in a hotel, one of the first things you do is look at the freebies in the bathroom?' he said as I was rummaging around for the tomato ketchup.

'What are you talking about?'

With a flourish, he opened a plastic bag he was carrying. It was full of soap, hair bands, hair ties, shampoo and novelty flannels.

'Here are our freebies. We found them in the shower block.'

'You can't do that. People will recognise things if you wear them and I, for one, don't want to use someone else's flannel. Put them back,' I said indignantly. 'What was the shower block like anyway?'

'Oh, you know, smelly. Wet but functional. Have you ever watched *Bad Girls*? They must have modelled the prison showers on them. I think I would have chosen more interesting tiles, brown is so suggestive.'

'Mama, I'm hungry,' said Daisy, doing her impersonation of Roly, the podgy puppy in *101 Dalmations*. Everyone managed to perch on a chair or sit on a mat and at last, as I got ready to serve the sausages, I realised that I had also forgotten the plates and cutlery. We improvised using saucepans, fingers and my handy penknife. By now Federal Express was beginning to look like an absolute bargain. Just as well I'd left our key with a neighbour.

With only a few minutes left of the day I was determined to see the sea. We all squelched and Daisy skidded down a small path, which looked like a promising route to the coast. It took a while to untangle ourselves from the final bramble bush, but once clear, the path opened out to a beautiful cove with a sandy beach, surrounded by gentle hills with farmhouses dotting the fields into the distance. The clouds were moving quickly across a mackerel sky, and for a while it looked as if the rain would hold off. As soon as they hit the open space the children ran, arms open wide, the wind blowing their hair off their faces, and started to collect stones and shells. As I watched the sea crashing onto the beach I took a deep breath and felt all the worries of the past few months pour out of me, and my shoulders dropped at least five inches.

'That's better,' I said, almost to myself. Jay smiled and put his arm round me.

We joined the girls in their hunt for novelty shells and I started explaining to Matilda how, if you held a big shell to your ear, you could hear the sea. She looked at me a little non-plussed.

'But the sea's right here and I can hear it now without listening to a shell.'

Jay joined us, 'Here, for you, Dot,' and he handed me a pale yellow stone with mottled edges, worn soft by the sea, but what made it unusual was the small hole through the middle.

'It's supposed to be lucky,' he added. I kissed him a thank you and made sure the stone was safe in my pocket.

I wish you were with us, Beth. I'm not sure I can remember the last time we went for a walk together. Children, husbands, work, illness – it all gets in the way, and we don't have the same kind of intimacy we used to have. When we were younger there wasn't a day that passed when we didn't talk on the phone, often more than once. I remember Delissa, worrying about the size of our phone bill, saying, 'You two girls have been together all day at school. What more can you possibly have to say to each other?'

I suppose once you know someone really well, you develop a

shorthand – there's no need for explanations, you have complete understanding. There would have been no point in ringing another friend because you'd have to explain the background to whatever was the issue of the day. What is your issue today? You see, I have no idea what's worrying you or making you happy. I can guess, but that's not good enough. Spending a few days with you would have given us a chance to recharge the friendship. We must try and organise something soon. Having said that, it's hardly going to be the relaxing holiday I predicted, but we do miss you.

All the fresh air and the stress of avoiding low flying insects exhausted the children so they were ready for an early bed, and they were so excited about spending their first night in a tent. We decided to set up a dormitory in the back section of the tent and all sleep together, at least for the first few nights. Jay read them a story each, doing a very lively rendition of *Peepo* for Daisy and a frighteningly good *Eloise* for Matilda, and they snuggled down into their sleeping bags. I went in to kiss them goodnight. We've developed a night-time ritual of kisses, which to the casual observer must appear absolutely nauseating but I find endearing. We start with a butterfly kiss (fluttering of eyelashes on cheek), next an Eskimo kiss (rubbing of noses, to be avoided during colds), finishing with a grand finale of the fairy kiss (lips fluttering). I was just moving onto the finale when Daisy asked,

'Where's my blanky?'

There was no point in looking for it. I knew exactly where it was, as I could see it in my mind's eye on the bottom of the stairs where I had put it to make sure we wouldn't leave it behind. This was definitely one of those 'bad mother' days.

I felt terrible, if there was one thing I should never have forgotten it was Daisy's blanket. It was irreplaceable. Daisy had never spent a night apart from her special blanket. They were inseparable, like Paul and Linda McCartney (except for those few days he spent in a Japanese prison on drug charges). Daisy started to sob and it was obvious that Cornwall was to be for Daisy what a Japanese cell had been to Paul. We'd have to open an account with Federal Express in the morning. I'd have to call our neighour with a list of all the things we'd forgotten so she could get them ready to be sent down to us. How stupid of me, and I thought I'd been so organised. It took Daisy hours to get to sleep. Eventually she snuggled into my sleeping bag and we had an uncomfortable night together, compounded by the fact I woke up in the middle of the night realising that I'd forgotten to take off my bra and knickers.

The next morning Jay and the girls went to get the ice and some milk for breakfast while I tried to get the tent organised. I'd just managed to work out a laundry section where we could keep the dirty clothes separate from clean clothes, when they returned with two I Heart Cornwall T-shirts, *Girl Talk* magazine, ice but no milk.

'Jay,' I said, exasperated.

'Sorry, it's just they wouldn't stop pestering me and I didn't want a scene. You know how loud and persistent they can be. You go with them next time and see how you like it.'

On the second morning Daisy discovered the Nexus safety whistle and woke up the whole campsite with her own version of the dawn chorus, which didn't help our position in the popularity stakes. The sight of sleepy faces peering over their windbreaks in our direction at 5.30 in the morning will stay with me for a long time. This morning it was my turn to go to the shop. I waited until the girls were distracted by a search for early blackberries on the bushes behind our marquee, and tried to sneak off, but Matilda, forever alert, said,

'Mama, where are you going?'

It was hopeless to pretend, so they came with me and after a matter of minutes, even I had to admit defeat. We came back with packets of Refreshers, two pairs of bright pink waterproof shoes for the rocks and some felt tip pens, all of which I tried to hide from Jay. I despair, but at least Alex isn't here to see how cavalier we're being with his money. Trust the children are well. I'll try and e-mail again before you go on holiday. Thinking of you, as always.

To: **Alex@himindoors.com**
From: **Dot@noplacelikehome.com**
Subject: **You don't know what you're missing . . .**

OK, so this is not the holiday of my dreams. Thought you'd like to know how we're getting on and what you're missing. Every day is spent planning what to eat, shopping, cooking, eating, washing up and then planning the whole thing again. Thank God, Jay is quite domesticated – you'd hate all of this. We take it in turns to wash up. My highlight of the holiday is being the one who has a day off and sometimes I get half an hour to read a paper, but only very occasionally. Usually I have to try to stop your youngest child eating poisonous berries or flinging herself off the nearest cliff, lemming style.

Yesterday I was standing in the washing-up block waiting for our neighbour who's camping in a tepee (say no more) to finish. Jay and I have called him Mr Dreadlocks for obvious reasons.

'Look at this,' he said proudly, and I peered into the sink to see what he was talking about.

'That's my skillet. I've had it twenty years, since I was a boy. It's great, you can put bacon on top and lamb chops underneath at the same time. It's also got a detachable handle so it folds away. I wouldn't go anywhere without it.'

I made suitably impressive noises but I couldn't help wondering, why would you want to cook bacon and lamb chops at the same time? It also changed my attitude to Gary as he later introduced himself. I had them down for vegetarians. Just goes to show, you can't judge by appearances. Megan, aka Mrs Kaftan, was very friendly and they soon got used to our continual questions and requests while we waited for our Federal Express deliveries. (I'll explain about that when I see you – but it was an emergency.) They lent us crockery, cutlery, lighters (Jay lost the waterproof lighter when testing its efficiency in the sea) and they seemed to have two sets of anything essential (including toothbrushes). I don't know where they stored it all but it was impressive. Whatever the weather Gary always wears open-toed sandals and shorts, and despite a great deal of effort on our part, we have never once spotted a goosebump. Their skins must be made of leather. Sartorially I must confess that every morning I say a silent prayer of thanks to Johnny Boden for inventing the pull-ons.

To be honest, the children are getting restless and Jay and I have found it very hard work. You know what it's like, at the best of times holidays with small children aren't as holidays used to be, they're more a change of scenery without the back-up of the usual toys and the distractions of home. I'd promised them adventures but it's hard to get enthusiastic about fairy trails and the like when it does nothing but rain. I find it so dispiriting, apart from one brief moment on the beach on the evening we arrived, it hasn't stopped raining since we got here three days ago. So what with dew, rain and condensation inside the tent, nothing ever gets completely dry. The first night I left my shoes outside the tent so that the next morning they were sodden and they've never had the chance to dry out. I dream of central heating, radiators and drying machines.

Yesterday we were woken by Megan who had come to tell us that our Federal Express deliveries had been sent to the Outer Hebrides due to some clerical error, but would we like to go over for an early-evening drink that evening? It appeared that the campsite manager had delivered the message to the wrong tent, but how you can mistake a medieval pavilion for a tepee beats me. Inviting us for a drink sounded deeply suburban but we accepted their offer, as it was becoming obvious that they were integral to our survival. With the thought of waiting another day, or maybe two, for Daisy's blanky we definitely needed a drink.

After much consideration I took some elderflower cordial and they offered us organic beer. I think I've lost my ability to read people. Their children, Ocean and Sky, are a bit older than our girls and of indeterminate gender. I think Ocean is a boy, but his hair is as long as Matilda's and a great deal curlier. Gary took Jay off to compare stoves and Megan and I were left to chat. Alex, this will amuse you.

'Matilda looks very like Jay,' said Megan, 'she's got his aura.'

I realised that she thought Jay and I were a couple. 'Oh no, you've got it wrong. Jay is gay.' This didn't phase her.

'You know, I thought Gary was gay for a while. Like you, it wouldn't have worried me. You suit each other.'

I couldn't be bothered to explain that I wasn't living in a lavender marriage. Can you imagine what that would be like? The children seemed to be getting on well singing songs together, until I heard Matilda shout, 'Move your bloomin' arse,' and realised that perhaps they are a bit too young for Jay's CD of *My Fair Lady*. Jay and I giggled about their misconceptions as we walked the five hundred yards home. That night we had a long talk about relationships, but you would have been proud of my self-control as I resisted saying anything about cringe-making Kevin.

The next morning Jay was up earlier than the rest of us. As I walked out of the tent he called, 'Morning, darling,' and I laughed and said, 'Morning darling,' and gave him a kiss. You and I are never that affectionate first thing in the morning. I was quite enjoying this. At first I didn't see Megan cooking porridge for breakfast, but she poked her head round the tepee and smiled at me, obviously thinking what a great couple we were. For the next few days Jay relished his new role and whenever Gary or Megan came within earshot he would start discussing our plans for the children's education and whether it was the right time for Matilda to begin piano lessons.

On Jay's last evening with us he played his part with gusto. He told Megan that we had met through the lonely-hearts page in the *Independent* and that he knew as soon as he saw me that I was the one for him. I found it hard to keep up with his charade but even harder not to giggle. He claimed it was something to do with the shape of my ears. It was like those early days when Beth and I had just left school and used to pretend to be airhostesses for a laugh. Apart from Jay becoming a little overenthusiastic, I suppose he *is* a surrogate father and husband. Having said that, I do miss the real thing.

As the children lay sleeping Jay and I sat in the front section of the tent while the wind howled and the rain battered against the tarpaulin. Not once have we been able to sit outside watching the stars and feeling relaxed. We talked about you and wondered how you're getting on, about my giving up work and how life was going to change for me when Daisy eventually started going to nursery school. Inevitably we got round to talking about Kevin. This time you wouldn't have been so proud of me, but he did ask.

'What do you really think of him?' asked Jay.

'Mm,' I mumbled, while taking a sip of hot chocolate made

with my soya milk and using it as an excuse for not replying immediately.

'Does it really matter what I think? What's more important is what you think of him. How's it going?'

'It's amazing. I've never met anyone like him and I feel like I'm learning so much from him. I miss him when we're apart.'

'Does he feel the same way about you?'

'Well, he says he does. I mean, he's always very busy but, yeah, I think he likes me being there when he comes home.'

'You're not living together?' I said, trying to keep the note of alarm out of my voice.

'As good as. Why, do you think we should?'

'No,' I said, too quickly.

'You don't like him, do you? Go on, be honest. As my friend you should be honest with me,' he said, sounding about ten years old.

'All right, if you really must know, I don't like him and I know he feels the same about me. You mustn't read anything into it. We can't all get on . . .'

Jay interrupted, 'You're impossible. Just as soon as I feel happy with someone you have to ruin it all,' and with that, he got up and got straight onto his lilo and pulled his duvet over his head.

'Jay,' I called, trying not to wake the girls, 'I'm sorry. Will you forgive me? It doesn't matter what I think, if you're happy – I'm not the one going out with him, thank God,' I muttered under my breath.

'I heard that,' said a muffled voice. 'Leave me alone, I'm going to sleep.'

I was left with my hot chocolate, fingering the stone in my pocket that Jay had given to me on the beach, and wondering when the good luck was going to start. Hope you're having a better time than us, and don't worry, I don't expect a reply. Call me if you have time.

To: **Bethearthmother@rooted.com**
From: **Dot@noplacelikehome.com**
Subject: **Côte de Cornwall**

I think I've really offended Jay by being too honest about Kevin, but the silly boy did ask me. I could kick myself. He left us saying that he had forgiven me, but I knew it wasn't from the heart. I felt miserable as we waited for Nikki to arrive on the fast train from London (first class). Typically, she came with an enormous Louis Vuitton suitcase on wheels which didn't stand a chance in our muddy campsite. After two minutes it looked more like a missing part of the local farmer's plough than a stylish piece of luggage. Nikki was trying her best to be positive but looked up at the sky and said, 'Has it been like this all week?' We all nodded. 'Forecast any good?' We all nodded again, but not the way she wanted.

In spite of the rain, our pavilion-style tent looked stylish, even if it did shriek Townies' Tent, and I think Nikki was impressed. Once inside she decided to change while I played a game of giant Snakes and Ladders with the girls. She reappeared wearing pink Versace jeans and a psychedelic, tight-fitting shirt and sat down beside me for two seconds before she said, 'No, I don't feel right. I'll be back in a minute.' Thirty minutes later she was back in a striped cream-and-blue Joseph boating jumper with a crew neck and blue flared lycra trousers.

'I think this is a bit more Cornwall – don't you?'

Matilda was refusing to go down the longest snake on the board, trying to find ingenious ways to avoid it such as cheating the dice and changing the level where her marker was placed.

Nikki disappeared again for another thirty minutes. By now the children were suffering from cabin fever, or rather tent fever. I had to get them outside, despite the rain. Nikki had changed again and was complaining that we didn't have a mirror.

'I have got a mirror,' I said indignantly, producing Matilda's purple daisy pocket mirror that came as a freebie with her *Girl Talk* magazine. By now Nikki was wearing a pair of beautifully pressed Gucci jeans with a gold belt bedecked with roman coins and the breast cancer awareness T-shirt. When she saw me look at it she said, 'I bought it with you in mind, darling.' It was as she struggled to put on her Prada wellingtons saying, 'I really don't think they go with these jeans,' that I lost my temper.

'Nikki, for Christ's sake, we're going for a walk on the beach in Cornwall, we're not promenading down the Champs Élysées. Now, are you coming or not?'

It was bad enough having one fashion diva (Matilda), now I had two. We passed Gary and Megan on the way to the beach and I felt annoyed that Nikki rolled her eyes and nodded her head towards Megan as if to say, 'What *is* she wearing?' Nikki and Matilda grumpily walked along the path to the beach, complaining that their jeans weren't comfy in their boots, and I began to regret ever having invited Nikki.

By nightfall there was no doubt in my mind that it had been a bad idea. Needless to say, she lasted one night in the tent, which she spent reminiscing about her last camping expedition on an upmarket safari in Kenya where it never rained and she had servants to satisfy her every desire. First thing the following morning she was on her mobile getting Julia, her poor assistant, to look into local accommodation. An hour later she was in a taxi.

'I've booked into a little local B&B. Here's the address and number,' she said, thrusting a piece of paper into my hands, 'Call me.'

Before the children got a chance to say goodbye, the taxi had screeched out of the campsite, wheels revving in the mud.

The next day Daisy's blanky finally arrived, and we celebrated by checking out Nikki's new accommodation. From the outside it didn't look like a B&B to me. It wasn't just one cottage but a group of white-washed stone cottages, which had been converted into one of the most stylish and comfortable hotels you can imagine. Nikki's face fell when she saw us, but I was determined to make the most of our (or should I say Nikki's?) new facilities. The hotel was simply a haven. Every room was unique and luxurious although, to be honest, after a week at our rustic campsite Crossroads Motel would have seemed like luxury. As soon as we got into her room Matilda said, 'Thank goodness, a television,' and both girls sat mesmerised by Teletext for half an hour. I lay down on the enormous king-size bed and savoured the comfort of a mattress and the smell of crisp clean linen. Nikki was looking at her reflection in the long mirror, relieved to be able to see herself again in all her designer glory. I think she finds it reassuring. If she can't see herself she's not sure she exists.

'Oh, I feel old, old, old,' she said self-pityingly.

'Nonsense,' I replied, turning on the gleaming taps to run a bath for myself, 'You're not old, old, old. Just tired, tired, tired.' (I think it's time to move on from *Eloise*.)

I ran my hands along the clean white, soft warm towels, all with individual motifs of lighthouses and anchors. Never has a warm towel rail seemed so wonderful. I undid the stoppers on all the bottles of bath oil and moisturisers, relishing the smell of almond, lavender and rosemary. I finally decided on natural sea salts and poured huge amounts into the bath. I placed my damp shoes under the towel rail to dry out while I soaked in the best bath I've ever had. The one advantage of camping is that it makes you appreciate the simple things in life.

After twenty minutes of paradise I wrapped myself in Nikki's enormously comfortable white towelling bathrobe and scrutinised the room service menu. Heaven on a plate. While we were waiting for our fresh crab and king prawn sandwiches to arrive, I read the hotel brochure offering á la carte picnic hampers, cooking classes and a private cinema. I spent the next ten minutes wondering, if I was staying here, whether I would plump for a day on the eight-seater speedboat or the magnificent forty-eight-foot classic yacht with skipper and mate. Am I mad? If I went back to work all this could be mine, if only for a day. If only I'd known what sacrifices I'd have to make when I resigned, would I have followed through with it? Nikki was watching me carefully and when I looked up she had a triumphant gleam in her eye, as if she was saying, 'Told you so.'

It was time to say good bye to luxury. The children made a dreadful fuss when we left but I didn't want them to get used to the comfort. I'm sure it can't be good for the soul.

'Oh, please, can we stay? It's *Scooby Doo* on next.'

As we walked down the stairs, past the terrace made of decking with its huge terracotta pots bursting with white geraniums, men in blazers and women in elegant chinos and white shirts quietly sipped their gin and tonics. I said to the girls, 'You'd have to be very quiet if we stayed here. That wouldn't be much fun, would it?' They said absolutely nothing, as if to prove a point, and we drove back to the campsite in silence.

I must sign off as I've run out of time but we may be coming home earlier than expected. Hope you've had a second opinion and that all is well with you. Lots of love from us.

To: **Bethearthmother@rooted.com**
From: **Dot@noplacelikehome.com**
Subject: **Gobsmacked**

Have just received your e-mail. I had to keep re-reading it because I thought I might have misunderstood. I would never have thought Will would be the sort of boy to steal anything. Someone must have put him up to it. What are his friends like? Of course I can understand why you find it so upsetting. It's not every day you get a phonecall from your local police station telling you that your son has been caught shop-lifting. Thank God they've let him off with just a caution. I'm sure there is a simple explanation, and I know you'll be able to sort this out. Maybe it would help if Tom spoke to him alone to discover what's going on? Or sometimes it helps if it's someone outside the family that he really admires. I'd offer to talk to him but I'm not great with boys – I don't really know how their minds work, and although I've always liked him I don't think we've got a particularly close relationship. I'm thinking of you and send lots of love and positive thoughts. Have a good holiday in Greece and remember to try and relax.

Chapter Thirteen

'I wasn't kissing her, I was just whispering into her mouth.'
Chico Marx

To: **Jay@mybestfriendisgay**
From: **Dot@noplacelikehome.com**
Subject: **How much time have you got?**

Are you still talking to me? I hope you're not too upset about what I said about Kevin. I'm a terrible judge of character and I'm probably completely wrong about him, but you did ask me to be honest. Everyone else thinks he's great. I think I just need to spend some more time with him, getting to know him better. I expect he was delighted to see you. It's been a tempestuous time here, and I'm not just talking about the weather.

Things were even more miserable after you left. The rain began to get on my nerves and the sight of holidaymakers in T-shirts and swimming costumes with large expanses of flesh turning blue, determined to expose themselves because it was summer after all, began to pall. The sandpit got soggier and soggier along with our clothes. Nikki lasted three days in Cornwall, despite the fact she abandoned us and stayed in one of the most exclusive hotels in the South of England, and then booked herself on the first available flight to the South of France. She's depressed because her divorce has come through and her teenage children, through force of habit, have organised the summer holidays without her presence being required. I realised why Nikki wanted to come with us, because wretched Richard and his new girlfriend were taking the children clubbing to Ibiza for three weeks. Nikki could hardly contain her venom.

'She had a terrible fake tan – St Tropez gone mad – but do you know what was the worst thing about her?' Nikki could never bring herself to mention her name . . . 'She had a diamond in her belly button. That about says it all. I bet he bought it for her. My belly button doesn't need jewellery. It's perfect as it is. He looks ridiculous with her. It's obscene. He really should grow up.'

This carried on for the whole time Nikki was with us right up to yesterday, which was her last day, and we decided to attempt a coastal walk. Because of Daisy's stamina, or lack of, it only lasted half an hour and most of that was spent sitting at a scenic spot looking out to sea, or to a sea mist to be more accurate, talking about Richard and 'her'. To my initial relief she changed the subject.

'Have you heard from Alex?' she asked with a tone of voice that made me think she knew something I didn't.

'No, but I didn't expect to. He rang our first night here on the mobile to check we got down safely,' I replied confidently, wishing that she hadn't stopped talking about her ex-husband and his new squeeze. What is it about certain people that when their personal life is in tatters they can't help hoping yours might be too?

She continued to stare out to sea while I kept a cautious eye on Daisy to make sure she didn't wander too close to the edge. Matilda was collecting daisies to make a chain.

'Darling, I think you should know I've been hearing things about Alex and . . .' her voice tailed off. She didn't have to say anything more. I would have preferred a punch in the stomach than what I was about to hear. I was torn between wanting to know all the sordid details and refusing to listen to what she had just said, blocking it out of my mind.

'You know my friend, Amber, is the make-up supervisor on Alex's drama,' she continued, determined to tell me everything she knew. I was tempted to put my hands over my ears while shouting, 'Woooooo,' so I wouldn't hear any more of her gossiping.

Nikki continued, 'Well, she had to come back from Dorset because her best friend is having a baby. Amber promised to be there at the birth. The father's not around, I think he's even denying that he is the father – the bastard. Why are men such bastards? Anyway, she knows that we're friends and she just thought she should mention it. There's probably nothing in it. You know how people gossip.'

I resisted the urge to strangle her with Matilda's daisy chain but I could feel the panic rising in me. All she had done was to confirm my suspicions. She had no details, just a general rumour, and I feel I can't ring him up and confront him. I've already put him in an impossible situation by making him go over budget, and what if she's completely wrong? I'd feel so stupid and neurotic. It started to pour down again and I herded the children down the path back to the campsite.

Nikki left yesterday afternoon and I can't say I was sad to see her go. I spent the rest of the evening debating tactics. The children fell asleep remarkably quickly and I had to resist the temptation to wake them up to have some company other than my bleak thoughts. As the rain beat down on our medieval pavilion I decided that the next morning we'd definitely go home. I contemplated stopping off in Dorset to see Alex but remembering the last disastrous visit to the film set, thought that would be inadvisable. I need to come home, regroup and see if Delissa is back from America. Perhaps she could come and look after the girls for a weekend so I could spend a few nights alone with Alex. What do you think I should do?

To: **Jay@mybestfriendisgay.com**
From: **Dot@noplacelikehome.com**
Subject: **Change of heart**

Thank you for your concerned e-mail and I'm sorry I didn't get back to you immediately but as you probably gathered by the fact I didn't come banging on your front door, circumstances have changed. I was all set to come home immediately and that night after my chat with Nikki I had terrible, troubled dreams. I could see Alex walking through a long corridor of doors and when I tried to follow him the doors would close and the handles disappear. Don't need Freud for that one.

The smell of eggs and bacon woke me up the next morning. Apart from the sound of sizzling bacon and birds singing it was remarkably quiet and peaceful. At first I couldn't work out what was wrong and then I gradually realised it was the first morning we hadn't heard the rain pounding incessantly on the roof of our tent. The delicious smells seemed to be coming from directly outside the tent but that couldn't be possible. The children were still asleep as I made my way through the main section of the tent. As I opened the door flap I had to narrow my eyes against the light for the first time in a week. Sun. Oh, the relief of it. Once my eyes had got accustomed to the light I realised that there was a familiar form, crouched in front of the stove. For a second in my sleepy state I thought it was Alex, but the rational, barely functioning part of my brain realised it couldn't be because he didn't even know where the campsite was.

'Well, good morning. It certainly is a lovely one,' he said, looking at me. 'You look like you've been shagged by a rhino.' The Scottish consonants and direct approach gave him away. It was Luke.

I can't begin to tell you how pleased I was to see him, it was all I could do to stop myself from flinging my arms around his neck. His two boys, Hamish and Dougal, were at the far end of the campsite throwing sticks for their dog, Gameboy, a friendly, shaggy mongrel.

'It's a lovely, day,' I said sleepily.

'Thank you,' he replied, 'breakfast is served.'

'God, that smells good. That's better than anything I've made all week.'

I woke up the girls and Matilda was delighted to see Dougal. (Year 2 at her school, 'He's OK, he's cool.') Daisy was just delighted to see the food, and so was Gameboy who sat by her feet, pretending she was his best friend while he surreptitiously tried to take bits of eggy bread and bacon off her plate. She was an easy target until she howled at him in fury and he scurried back to Hamish's side.

I could see Gary and Megan with their children, watching us enjoying our breakfast, and invited them over. We shared out some more eggs and bacon, Luke tossing the rashers of bacon as if they were pancakes, while simultaneously doing impressions of Jamie Oliver, Delia Smith and Nigella Lawson all rolled into one. They were obviously a bit overwhelmed by Luke, although I don't think they had a clue who he was. They were just intrigued by our relationship. They probably thought I was being unfaithful to my gay husband. Still, I was sure Megan would understand. She looked sympathetic enough and gave me an understanding hug before returning to her tepee.

The boys, who knew the campsite well from previous visits, took the girls off to show them a secret path to the beach while Luke and I washed up. Hamish had obviously inherited his father's natural ability with children and was being fantastic with Daisy. She was looking up at him wide-eyed, impressed by the attention she was getting and obviously developing a big crush. He gave her a piggyback and ran to catch up the others. Maybe it was going to turn into a Famous Five holiday for them after all.

'I didn't know you were coming down here. You never said?' I quizzed him.

'My plans changed,' he said enigmatically.

'Staying long?' I asked, as casually as I could.

'Until the wind changes,' he replied.

'I was thinking of going back to London today,' I said.

'Now that's a great idea, considering the sun's out and we've just arrived. Do you want a hand packing up?' he said dryly.

'Well, perhaps we'll see how it goes with the weather,' I suggested. 'We'll give it a few hours.'

We've had four wonderful days. We built the biggest sand canoes and mermaids Cornwall has ever seen (apparently, according to Hamish, castles are 'so twentieth century'), had picnics on the beach, wandered round coastal villages window shopping and getting the girls' hair braided. The children have eaten tub-loads of Cornish ice cream and mountains of pizza while watching the fishing boats come home after a long night's trawl.

'I could do that,' said Luke as we watched the fishermen sort through their catch.

'All right then, catch us supper tomorrow night,' I challenged him. Luke took the boys fishing in the estuary and they came back three hours later with smug expressions and a pair of sizeable salmon trout.

That evening we decided to have a barbecue on the beach. Luke scoffed at my pathetic disposable effort and sent the boys off to find some large stones, which he placed in a circle on the beach making sure the edge of the cliff provided a natural windbreak. They dug a hole in the middle, which they began to fill with driftwood.

'You've done this before,' I said, impressed. We all had a happy afternoon collecting driftwood for the fire and feeling at one with the elements. The children paddled and built dams and I dozed in the sun, utterly content, my problems with Alex feeling like something I'd read in a bad novel.

At teatime Luke lit the fire. 'It will take a good hour to get going.'

Hamish agreed to tend to the fire while we all went swimming. The water was freezing but bracing and we had races with Luke carrying Daisy on his back while I pulled Matilda along with one arm. To our amazement, and with the help of a freak wave swamping the others, we shot over our imaginary winning line first. Matilda was delighted as it's the only time she's won anything remotely sporty. Afterwards, in an attempt to get some feeling back in our arms and legs, we played Stuck in the Mud and British Bulldog, or British Bollocks as Luke wanted to call it. He was determined to get his own back after losing the swimming race and tackled me at every opportunity. I felt like a teenager again.

Once the fire was good and hot, we boiled new potatoes in salty sea water, made vegetable kebabs, which we barbecued alongside corn on the cob and the splendid fish. I don't think I've ever tasted such fresh fish, even the girls liked it, although Daisy couldn't resist asking for ketchup. Pudding was a huge watermelon, nectarines, cherries and chocolate and as the night began to close in we toasted marshmallows on long sticks. Luke showed the girls how to make a marshmallow sandwich using crackers and squares of chocolate, melted by the heat of the roasted marshmallows. It was the height of indulgence but we felt we all deserved it. Hamish, Dougal and Matilda went off to play Hide and Seek, and Daisy lay down exhausted, days of not having a buggy finally catching up with her. Within seconds she was asleep with her head on my lap.

It was the magic hour when day slips into night and there we were, Luke and I, sipping beer, our stomachs full, skins tingling after a day of sea and sun. He got up and walked away from the fire towards the sea. I could just make out his silhouette as he stood at the water's edge. He turned round, his back to the sea, and was watching me by the fire. I began to feel self-conscious under his gaze and tried to create the impression that I was staring dreamily into the fire, while silently praying that firelight was flattering to a woman sliding towards forty. After what seemed to be ages, he walked back dragging a large piece of driftwood and flung it on to the fire so that sparks shot up into the sky like baby fireworks. He sat down and I drew back to avoid getting burnt and turned to look at him. He smiled and then, looking a little more serious, he leant forward and kissed me. His lips tasted of salt and beer and he smelt of summer and smoke.

'Mmmm . . .' he murmured.

I broke away, saying, 'I'm not su–'

He kissed me again, this time less tentatively, and I found myself putting my hands over Daisy's eyes just in case she woke up. It was the sound of the children shouting that brought me back to my senses and I knew I had to stop now before it was too late. I pulled away from him and called to all the children. It was beginning to get quite dark and it wasn't safe for Matilda to be out playing Hide and Seek. They came running and laughing, and collapsed by the fire, oblivious to what it had just witnessed.

'I must get them to bed,' I said, as practically as I could. Somewhere an alarm was ringing and I realised it was in my head, not a wake-up call this time but a siren shrieking, 'Warning! Warning! Luke Lloyd alert.'

'Oh, Mama, please can we stay up longer?' pleaded Matilda. The boys joined in, trying to persuade me while Daisy, who had woken up, tried to eat a marshmallow covered in sand. I could see Luke wanted me to stay, and of course I really wanted to. Why ruin the perfect end to the best day of summer, in fact the best day I'd had in years? Was this so bad? I thought of the woman I'd met in the hospital waiting room. Would she be encouraging me to stay? It was only a kiss, and surely kissing doesn't count. I unconsciously put my hand to my lips at the memory. Luke said persuasively, 'We're on holiday, let them have fun.'

I was wavering when a mobile phone began to ring. Matilda, who was sitting by my basket, saw the phone and answered it.

'It's Dadda,' she shouted.

Chapter Fourteen

'There cannot be a crisis next week. My schedule is already full.'

Henry Kissinger

To: **NikkiSoda@ambitiousproductions.com**
From: **Dot@noplacelikehome.com**
Subject: **Timing**

> 'Why do female black widow spiders kill the males after mating?'
> 'To stop the snoring before it starts.'

No, I haven't had a talk with Alex yet. He only got home last night and I have to pick my time carefully. Besides, I'm not sure what I'm going to say. He came home exhausted, hung over, and he seems like a stranger. It's worrying how easily we have got used to functioning as a family without him, and it takes a while to make the adjustment. Not that he's been around much. He spent most of the weekend sleeping off the hangover, for which he got little sympathy from me. The end of shoot party was obviously a success, but I haven't asked for details as I don't want to imagine how he and Jessica must have celebrated. The girls found it inexplicable that he didn't want to spend every minute of the day with them watching their shows and listening to their stories. Matilda was desperate to tell him all about Mr Poppy, her new teacher, who despite initial reservations ('He's a boy') has now turned out to be the best teacher in the land.

'I love Mr Poppy. I'm going to marry him.'

Alex went through the motions of listening but you could tell it was washing over him. It's strange having him in bed with me as I'd got used to spreading over both sides, but it is reassuring to feel his arm around me when I sleep, in spite of the snoring. Please will you stop worrying about my domestic problems when I'm sure you've got enough of your own to sort out.

To: **Jay@mybestfriendisgay.com**
From: **Dot@noplacelikehome.com**
Subject: **The worst friend in the world**

I've done a terrible thing. As soon as we came back from Cornwall we were sucked into school runs and the usual routine. Today was my first official meeting with Luke since Cornwall and I was a little nervous. Cornwall was special and unresolved. I keep telling myself that it was a bit of midsummer madness, but just the thought of him produces a whoosh. I deliberately make myself channel hop as soon as one of his shows come on television, but the other day the children's video stopped when one of his repeats was transmitting, so for a few guilty seconds I indulged myself. I try not to read all the magazines at the supermarket checkout, packed with articles about the wonderful, funny but sexy, Luke Lloyd. Inexplicably I find myself queuing behind the woman with the biggest overflowing trolley with the young toddler who insists on helping her unpack the trolley at his own steady pace and has a screaming fit if she tries to speed him up. With all that time on my hands waiting in the queue I have to do something, so I might as well read the magazines and gaze at his picture, while pretending not to be the slightest bit interested.

I changed five times this morning and ended up putting on the Gap cropped trousers I was wearing when he kissed me. As I was walking out the front door, at least fifteen minutes behind schedule, the phone rang. I let it go onto answer machine but as I shut the front door I could hear it was Beth, sounding upset.

'Dot? Are you there? Pick up, please, I need to see you now. I've got to talk to someone . . . if you get this message come over right away . . .' There followed a long pause, and then she said more briskly, 'Oh, forget it. It doesn't matter.'

I hesitated. She did sound strange, but I was going to be late for Luke. We had spoken on the phone a few days previously, just after I had got back from Cornwall, and I thought she was sounding a little better since her holiday in Greece. She said she'd had a lovely time. I put the key back in the door to go and pick up the phone but then I stopped because I knew if I rang her we'd be incapable of having a quick conversation and then I'd be really late. What could be so urgent that it couldn't wait an hour? I wasn't planning on spending all morning with Luke, so if I cut short my time with him I could ring her after our meeting and pretend I'd just picked up her message and I'd be with her by lunchtime. It would only be an hour or so later than if I went straightaway. I convinced myself that it would be fine. By now Daisy was halfway down the street, determinedly pushing the buggy as if she'd made my mind up for me. I followed her, with a nagging feeling that I was doing the wrong thing, but I put that down to the fact I was excited at the prospect of seeing Luke.

At the café Daisy gave Luke a big kiss and I felt jealous that she could fling her arms around him and touch him unselfconsciously. He kissed me on the cheek and lingered for a moment. I wanted to follow Daisy's example, but with great restraint I made myself let him go and sit down. We sat there grinning at each other.

'Good to see you,' I ventured.

'You too. Your holiday has done you a lot of good,' he replied, still grinning.

'Must have been the company.'

His little finger was resting on mine. I could see he wasn't going to make this easy for me.

'Good news. Our *First Loves* proposal has got through the first round of offers. Fingers crossed we could get a series. We'll know in a few weeks' time. If it happens, you will do it with me, won't you?'

Why had I never noticed his beautiful mouth before? I was so busy concentrating on his lips as he talked that I hadn't listened properly to what he was saying. The lips had stopped moving and I realised that it was my turn to say something, but all I had heard was, '. . . do it with me?' Oh God, what should I say? I fumbled around for the right words. He was being so direct. He looked at me and repeated the question, 'Dottie, if we get the programme, you will do it with me, won't you?'

I felt stupid. 'Oh, the programme,' I said, trying to hide the disappointment in my voice, 'let's see what happens. Who knows if it will get commissioned, and I'd have to get child care.'

I could see his eyes glaze over. He didn't want to be bothered with the details, and who could blame him? Neither of us talked about Cornwall, or what had or hadn't happened. I suppose there was nothing to say, but when I looked at my watch I saw that I'd been with him for an hour and a half and then I remembered Beth's call.

'I've got to go. Same time next week.'

'Don't go, Dot, I want to talk to you,' he pleaded.

'We've been talking for an hour and a half. What more could you possibly have to say to me?'

'Oh, you know, stuff.'

'I'm sorry, I've got to go. Call me.'

'Yeah, right.' He looked downhearted, but I knew I had to go.

Out in the street I rang Beth on my mobile and Tom answered, 'Oh, Dot, it's you. I thought you were the Doctor.'

'What's happened, Tom?' I asked, my heart sinking at the tone of his voice. 'Where's Beth, is she all right?'

Tom's voice started to crack and I could hear he was trying to fight back the tears, 'No,' he said flatly. 'I don't know what's happening, Dot. I've never seen her like this. I called the doctor and he told me to call an ambulance. She won't talk to me or to anyone. I came back from work when the neighbours called me. She's smashed every plate and cup in the house.'

It just didn't sound like the Beth I knew. If only I'd gone round straightaway when she called me, maybe I could have helped her. Instead I was indulging a stupid flirtation and I let down my oldest, dearest friend. How could I be so selfish? I put my hand under my armpit. I often do it when I'm upset, it's unconsciously reassuring like I'm giving myself a hug. It was then that I felt it. I tried to focus on the conversation with Tom and told myself to stop being silly.

'Look, Dot, I'd better get off the phone. I'm waiting to hear from the doctor.'

'Please send her my love, and anything I can do – if you need help with the children, with anything at all, just call.'

I put the phone down, took a deep breath and checked again. It was still there, hard like a large frozen pea. Horribly familiar, but bigger than before. For a moment I thought I was going to be sick. Jay, I think it's back.

Chapter Fifteen

'It is only with the heart that one can see rightly;
what is essential is invisible to the eye.'
Antoine de Saint-Exupéry, *Le Petit Prince*

To: **ProfwarmhandsHarrison@marsden.com**
From: **Dot@noplacelikehome.com**
Subject: **Wednesday appointment**

Thank you for fitting me into your Wednesday clinic. Maybe I'm overreacting, but there's definitely something there and as you say, best to get it checked out as soon as possible. Fingers crossed this isn't God's way of showing me the yellow card.

To: **LukeLloyd@talent.co.uk**
From: **Dot@noplacelikehome.com**
Subject: **Wednesday rendezvous**

I won't be able to make our next Wednesday meeting but see you the week after, if not before, at school.

To: **LukeLloyd@talent.co.uk**
From: **Dot@noplacelikehome.com**
Subject: **Wednesday rendezvous**

Of course it's nothing personal, I just have another urgent appointment that I can't miss. You haven't said or done anything wrong. I'll see you the week after – usual time, usual place.

To: **Jay@mybestfriendisgay.com**
From: **Dot@noplacelikehome.com**
Subject: **The waiting game**

So now the waiting game begins. I've got four days until I know about my future prospects. Actually, that's not strictly true because I'll have to wait a couple of days, at least, for the results of all the tests. I hope I don't have to have a bone scan again. It was one of the worst I had first time round. I don't know if I told you about it? Not that it was painful, it was just I had no idea what to expect so I wasn't prepared. I lay down on a bench, having been injected with a special dye, and read in small print on the information leaflet, 'Do not have contact with small children for at least twenty-four hours.' They were pumping me full of radioactive material, and I couldn't even hug my children for fear of contamination.

I had to be completely still. On the screen in front of me my skeleton materialised. At first I felt the urge to laugh and was tempted to wave my little finger at myself but the nurse was very serious and I didn't want to ruin their tests. The minutes passed and the more I stared at the essential me, the more miserable I became looking at my skeleton. Was this it then? What about all the thoughts, feelings and experiences I'd had throughout my life that had felt so important? Where did they feature on the picture in front of me? No contaminating chemical could possibly reveal them because they weren't tangible. They only exist in my memory, and in the memories of the people who shared those moments, and even then their memories are from a different perspective. Lying there immobile with my brain whirring, staring at my skeleton, for forty-five minutes made me feel insignificant and ridiculous. Stripped to the bone I am like everyone else, an ordinary skeleton with no distinguishing features – nothing special. It was the most sobering forty-five minutes of my life.

I must stop thinking about the last time I was ill. I'm going to try and deal with this myself and not tell everyone until I know what I'm dealing with. That includes Alex, because he's got too much to worry about at the moment. It just seems so unfair to burden everyone else with my fears, especially if it turns out to be nothing. I'm sorry, but you're going to have to bear the brunt of my emotional outpouring. I'll try not to do it to you again. Alex doesn't seem to have a clue that there's anything wrong. I think he puts any sign of tension down to my being worried about Beth. I thought about telling him last night when he came back from his first day in the edit, but he's so exhausted and distracted that I couldn't find the right moment. It didn't seem appropriate while serving up the remains of the fish pie, which the children had refused to eat at teatime.

'Oh, by the way, darling, I think my cancer is back. Yes, I know it's annoying, but enough of me. Tell me, what was your day like?'

I find it easier to write it, but I can't say it. Saying it makes it a reality. I'm certainly not going to tell Luke. I don't think he even knows I've had cancer, as I haven't told him and we have never talked about it. I didn't want it to sully the innocent flirtation. With Luke I feel like my old self, untainted by surgery and self-doubt.

Now it seems so frivolous. Perhaps this is God's way of bringing me back down to earth. Maybe flirting gives you cancer. Anyway, I haven't got the heart for it at the moment.

The most reassuring thing for me is my routine. I'm glad Matilda is back at school and I'm filling up Daisy's diary for the next few days so that I don't have time to think about anything. I haven't been able to talk to Beth yet, and I don't want to bother Tom, but I keep wondering whether I could have done anything to stop this happening. If only I'd read the warning signs earlier. I think I've let Beth down, and in my bleaker moments I feel I deserve everything I get. On a more practical level, how do you show concern without being obtrusive? I've dropped round some food for them all, as that seemed the most positive thing I could do. It certainly helped me when I was ill.

Delissa is back, which is a great relief, and we've left messages for each other. She wants to come over but I know if I see her I'll just cry and tell all, and why worry her, perhaps unnecessarily? She's a bit of a paradox. In some ways she's very open. When I was growing up I could talk to her about boyfriends, contraception, sexual attitudes or politics, but on personal, emotional matters she was like many other people of that generation. It's almost as if she doesn't have the vocabulary. She would be embarrassed if I told her how much I loved her, and she doesn't often say it to me. Having said that, she doesn't need to, as I know how much she loves me. I wonder if it's a post-war attitude. There just weren't the words to describe what happened during the war, and no one was spared the tragedy, but you just had to get on with life and not make a fuss.

When I was diagnosed we never talked about how she felt, but I'll never forget how difficult it was to ring her and tell her I had cancer. Trying desperately not to cry, I remember saying,

'Well, it could be worse, at least it's not one of the children. That would be really hard.'

And only then did I hear the sadness in her voice as she quietly said, 'Yes.'

It was so insensitive of me. Oh, Jay, I don't think I can go through it all again, especially chemotherapy. If it *has* come back then it shows it didn't work, it just bought me a few extra years, most of which I felt terrible. I'd think very carefully before doing that again. Oh God, I must stop this and work on living one day at a time. Maybe I should adopt a post-war attitude.

To: **Delissa@splendidmums.com**
From: **Dot@noplacelikehome.com**
Subject: **Breakdowns**

I'm so pleased you're back. So you saw Nanny Sarah's book at the airport. I was wondering when it was going to be published. Now there's something else for me to worry about. You read it and tell me all about it as I haven't the heart for it at the moment. On a more positive note, it was interesting receiving the joint e-mail from you and Carl. He sounds nice, if not a little Californian, but he seems to be genuinely fond of you. I particularly enjoyed his comment that it was, 'So lovely to meet a wonderful woman who wakes up every morning and says yes to life.' I didn't want to destroy the illusion by telling him that's not exactly my memory of you at 7.30 on those damp, dark and dismal January mornings before school when I was growing up. But I know what he means, you do have a fantastic energy, and I'm just pleased he appreciates it.

You sounded a bit hesitant on the phone. I'd love to catch up with you and hear all about your time there. What were his daughters like, and how did they take to you? Life continues at a traumatic pace over here. Alex is back from filming but he may as well be away. He is still immersed in his work but it's only four weeks to go until he finishes the edit. Although he then has the dub, life will start to become more normal (she says hopefully). It's like someone's pressed the pause button in our relationship and I'm not sure how the rest of the video will turn out. I've got to wait until someone comes and presses the start button. Of course, I could do it myself but I'm not sure that would be a good idea.

The most distressing news is that Beth has had a breakdown and has been booked into a clinic to recuperate. Tom says that it's all happened gradually but what triggered her complete breakdown was the discovery that Will, their lovely, charming middle child, has been skiving off school for months. He's lied to everyone and forged letters from Beth to the school claiming fake doctor's and dentist's appointments. I find it hard to believe. Beth has taken it deeply personally as she's devoted her life to being a good mother, whatever that means, and now she thinks she's failed.

Why is everything in life such a pressure? I really thought when I gave up work that my life would become less stressful, but it hasn't happened. It's a more subtle kind of stress with this constant worry in the back of your mind that you could be doing irreparable damage to your children, which will take years of therapy to sort out. We know too much and too little nowadays just to be able to relax and enjoy the everyday business of mothering. Good mum, bad mum – why can't it just be mum who has good days and bad days? I can't imagine you worried about all this when I was growing up.

Tom thinks there must be a chemical problem as well. Did you realise that her mother suffered from clinical depression at one stage in her life? You were never great friends but I suppose you could see what was going on. You never said anything to me about it but Tom thinks it may be something Beth has inherited. I always thought her mother was a bit strange. I remember one tea in particular when I told my favourite joke at the time, 'How do you know when an elephant is in bed with you? By the embroidered E on his pyjama pocket.'

Beth's mother started to laugh hysterically and then the laughter turned to sobbing and Beth looked embarrassed and we both concentrated really hard on the shepherd's pie we were eating. We didn't talk about it, but maybe we were too wrapped up in our own problems. Emotionally disturbed mothers weren't uncommon in nineteen-seventies' suburbia, and we were all fairly accepting and disinterested. Beth's relationship with her mother was strained, which is why she always loved coming round to us. She adored you. But Beth in a clinic – can you believe it?

To: **Delissa@splendidmums.com**
From: **Dot@noplacelikehome.com**
Subject: **Visiting Hours**

I'm not sure about you visiting Beth. According to Tom, she's not talking to anyone yet. Why don't you leave it a few days and then give him a ring? A dose of Delissa might be just what she needs. It was lovely to hear from you and you mustn't worry, I'm absolutely fine, just a little tired. I'm a bit busy this week but I'd love to see you next weekend?

To: **Jay@mybestfriendisgay.com**
From: **Dot@noplacelikehome.com**
Subject: **Once upon a time . . .**

What did the old storytellers have against mothers? Up to now, neither of the girls has been interested in having the old fairy tales read to them. They're convinced that they're all written by Walt Disney, and as they've watched practically every Disney film available on the market they've been there, done that. However, last night Daisy wanted me to read *Cinderella*. Inevitably, Matilda wanted *Snow White* so I read both of them, wondering why the mothers have to die so young, and trying to stop myself casting Jessica as the wicked stepmother. What would be worse is if they love Jessica more than me.

I could hear Blondie's wheel squeaking as she did her evening work-out, and I thought about poor old Fluffy, her untimely death and Matilda's delighted reaction when she realised she might get a new and even prettier hamster. Would she feel the same about me? I picked up Daisy and swung her over my shoulder like a sack and she squealed in delight.

'Come on, girls, it's past your bedtime.'

Once tucked up in bed she put her arms around me and we did our evening kissing routine. As I turned out the light she said, 'Mama. Will you stay with me forever and ever?'

I thought I was going to break into a cold sweat. I can't believe this is happening to me again, and the worse thing is that the children are older now and able to comprehend the implications of serious illness.

'Of course I will,' I said, crossing my fingers behind my back.

I went back into Matilda's room and she pleaded with me to have what she calls a 'hugsy hug', which means I have to lie down with her and we talk about the day's events. We lay there, face to face, while she chatted away and I watched her expressions change with each new tale she had to tell. Being with the children full time is so tactile and sensual. I've never had so much constant physical contact – holding hands, hugging or kissing. Sometimes it can be cloying but mostly it's uplifting. Tonight Daisy gently stroked my hand absentmindedly, while I read the story to her. This physical closeness is what I missed when I was working, and despite the frustrations of dealing with small children there's no denying my relationship with the girls has really improved. Nowadays I feel physically and emotionally comfortable with them. It would be terrible if, just as I'm getting to grips with motherhood, I got ill again.

What I found so hard the first time round was not so much the sickness after chemotherapy, which wasn't pleasant, but the lack of energy and the feeling of a permanent hangover. I mean, a really serious hangover, the sort you get after drinking at least three bottles of tequila, followed by a bottle of champagne and topped off with a cheap brandy. (Not that I've ever drunk that much, but now I know how awful it would make you feel.) The one thing you need with children is energy.

I had a bad night fretting about whether I've brought this on myself. I keep thinking about Alex's launch party and the way I talked about being ill, playing the cancer card as I joked at the time. Part of me feels I've been cavalier and not paid due respect to 'it'. If by 'it' I mean the cancer then I'm treating it as though it's a living thing, but it's not – it's a disease. I feel like I've tempted the gods, the fates or whatever. Rationally I know this is ridiculous, but that doesn't matter at four o'clock in the morning.

Unable to sleep, I climbed out of bed as quietly as I could so as not to wake the exhausted Alex and went into Matilda's room to watch her as she slept. I stupidly started to play the What If? game. What if it is bad news, I might not be here for her next birthday or to buy her next pair of shoes? Who would really understand the intricate workings of her mind as I feel I do? Who would cope with her strength of character without crushing her spirit? I went into Daisy's room. She was lying on her back, her arms stretched like a starfish above her head and the bedclothes falling onto the floor, breathing heavily in a deep innocent sleep. I stroked her cheek and thought that despite my world collapsing around me, I was so lucky to have two extraordinary girls. I know I'm being self-indulgent, and if I want to live a normal life for the next couple of days these thoughts have to stop until I know what I'm dealing with.

The next day, ironically, Matilda was doing living things and non-living things in class. They all had to draw examples of both categories. On the way home from school Matilda told me what her friends had drawn.

'Molly did a cat for the living thing and a castle for non-living, and Chloe did a baby and a bottle.'

'What did you do?' I asked, feeling every moment with her to be precious, and that every thought and word should be burnt into my memory forever.

'Oh, for the living thing I did the Queen and for non-living the Queen Mother.'

I laughed for the first time in days.

Chapter Sixteen

'It is not to live but to be healthy that makes a life.'
Martial (circa 40 A.D.)

To: **Jay@mybestfriendisgay.com**
From: **Dot@noplacelikehome.com**
Subject: **A sense of tumour**

I didn't want to wake up this morning, but at least by lunchtime I was going to be put out of my agony and I would know either way. Rather amazingly Alex offered to take Daisy into the edit this morning as the receptionist had said she wanted to meet her, and apparently there is a fantastic playground just round the corner. He never asked where I was going. I think he just presumes it's all to do with Beth. It's a little annoying that here I am exercising fantastic self-control, being strong and coping on my own (with your help as well), and he doesn't even appreciate it. It's totally against my nature, I usually have to tell everyone everything, and the irony is that no one can give you credit for it because they don't know you're being brave.

To make matters worse, as I was reading the paper this morning I saw a fantastic review of Sarah's book. 'Hysterically funny, poignant, wonderfully satirical and shocking . . . raising serious issues about the way we raise our children . . . a refreshing first novel.' I don't know why I don't just end it all now.

My mind was racing as I was driving to the hospital. I heard a police siren behind me and I slowed down and pulled in to the kerb to let them overtake, but to my amazement they swerved in front of me and stopped. A woman police officer came over and tapped on the window and I immediately felt guilty, but I didn't know what I'd done wrong.

'Do you realise, Madam, that you've just driven through a red light?'

'No,' I gasped, 'I'm sure I haven't.'

'Are you calling me a liar, Madam? We were right behind you and couldn't believe our eyes. This is a serious offence.'

'I'm terribly sorry. I can't believe that I would do such a thing.' And then I went for it, as it was an emergency, 'I'm going to be late for my appointment at the Marsden hospital.' I let the name register. 'It's very important.'

'I see.'

'Breast cancer,' I said, and apart from looking a bit shocked by my forthright attitude she visibly softened.

'Let me talk with my colleague.'

I sat in the car, feeling guilty for going through the light but also for playing the cancer card again. Hadn't I learnt anything? She came back a few minutes later.

'OK, you were obviously distracted, but maybe next time you should let someone else drive you. We'll let you go on this occasion but, please, in future drive with due care and attention.'

'Thank you. I promise I'll really concentrate. It's just around the corner.'

It was a good sign. I might have cancer but at least I still had a clean driving licence. I found a parking meter straight away. Things were looking good but I felt anxious as I crossed the road and made my way towards the steps that led up to the hospital. A builder leaning on the scaffolding which masked a smart new housing development across the road shouted at me as I passed, 'Cheer up, love, it's not the end of the world.' I stared at him. Do you think he knows he's working opposite a cancer hospital?

I didn't have to wait long to see Professor Harrison. If not for the circumstances I'd quite enjoy our meetings. He always has a reassuring smile, and as I walked in I realised that he's probably only a few years older than me. Because he's always been a figure of authority I've assumed him to be much older.

'Let's have a look at you?' he said, indicating the couch.

I took my shirt off and felt exposed as I lay down with the nurse smiling benignly at me. I never know whether to cross my arms to modestly hide my breasts, which seems silly considering he's going to get a full view in a few minutes, or to lie there brazenly flashing everything I've got. I try and do a mixture of both. He lifted up my left arm and felt all around the breast and deep into the armpit.

'You show me where you think it is.'

I prodded my armpit worried, perversely, that it might have disappeared and I'd be wasting his time, but it didn't take me long to find it as I had felt it hourly since I first discovered it. That seems like months ago, each day stretching into eternity. Professor Harrison followed my finger to find the lump within the armpit already sunken from surgery.

'Hmm . . .' he said non-committaly.

He checked the other breast and the armpit. I sat up while he felt my neck and tapped my back to see if the lungs were clear. I lay down again, heart pounding against my ribcage as he went back to check the armpit. I watched his expression.

'There it is. That's your problem.' So I was right, there was something wrong.

'Is it bad?' I asked, as calmly as I could.

'It's not bad. It's the bony bit at the top of your ribcage that you're feeling. The surgery has made it more prominent, which is why you never felt it before.'

Relief surged through me as I started to laugh. Days of emotional and mental torture inflicted on myself, all for the sake of my ribcage.

'It's understandable,' said Professor Harrison kindly, 'you're bound to have scares like this, and you did absolutely the right thing by coming to see me. It's always worthwhile getting these things checked out.'

'You're absolutely sure that's all it is?' I checked.

He nodded, 'You look in good shape.'

I had trouble walking down the corridors to the exit because I wanted to skip and dance and tell everyone I met, 'I'm OK. I'm OK.' Once out in the street I wanted to shout, sing or scream my joy. It was as if for the last few days I'd dived into a dark pool but now I'd burst up to the surface and could breathe again. Everything was sparkling in the September sunlight. A girl walking past smiled at me, her hair sleek and shiny, the black railings glistened, even the bus stop seemed dazzling as the sun's rays were reflected in the plastic of the shelter. The world was truly beautiful. I saw the builder who had shouted to me from the scaffolding, and to his surprise I waved at him. He was right, it wasn't the end of the world. Not yet. Nothing else matters. Now that I know I'm healthy, I'm never going to worry about trivial things again.

To: **Jay@mybestfriendisgay.com**
From: **Dot@noplacelikehome.com**
Subject: **Not another crisis**

Thanks for your e-mail. We can both heave a huge sigh of relief. This recent scare has taught me a lesson that I must never panic again until I know what I'm dealing with. It's unfair on both of us and so exhausting. I feel like I'm being stalked by cancer. For a while you can forget it ever happened and live life normally, but one day you feel a lump or a bump and it's like opening the front door or glancing out of a window and seeing your stalker is back, watching and waiting. It will always be there. I have got to learn to live with it.

After this morning I thought I'd never worry about anything ever again, and now three hours later I'm feeling anxious. I nipped out to collect my order from the health food shop. I decided to stock up on basic essentials as I don't think I'm looking after myself nutritionally – I must be getting thin if I can feel my ribcage. I needed to be back in time for Alex, who was bringing Daisy home. As I parked the car I saw Jessica through the window in my house, picking up my Daisy and tickling her. She was giggling and wriggling while Alex looked on smiling. They looked the perfect family unit. I felt sick for the second time today and thought about getting back in the car and just driving off. Learning to face my fears was the lesson for the day, so I walked into the house. I felt like I was weighed down, with 'Sad, desperate woman trying to get healthy and stay young' emblazoned on my bags from the health food shop. I dumped them in the kitchen as quickly as possible while fixing my smile.

'We needed a break from the edit,' said Alex.

'Hi, Dorothy,' said Jessica. It was the first time she had recognised me, but I suppose it wasn't hard seeing she was in my house and the odds were that I wasn't young enough to be Matilda, nor exotic enough to be an au-pair.

'What a lovely house,' she said, trying to ingratiate herself. Daisy started to climb up her long legs.

'Let's do the upside down game again,' she pleaded. Jessica, laughing, took her hands and let her walk up her legs and flip over in a somersault without worrying once about the tassles on her leather jacket. She smelt of success and confidence.

'Daisy, it's time for your sleep,' I snapped.

Alex said, 'We must get back – see you later, Dot. Oh, and don't worry about Sarah's book. Jessica thinks it's a flash in the pan. By tomorrow people will have forgotten about it.'

Oh no, he'd discussed it with her. I wonder how many more intimate details she knows about our private lives? She probably even knows about the unsightly thread veins on my thighs. I managed to maintain the smile as they walked out the door. Daisy was trying to run after them.

'Kiss, kiss,' she was shouting after Jessica, and she ran to her and gave her two kisses. She turned round and ran back into the house. How could she do it to me? I had to remind myself she's two-and-a-half years old and just a generous, happy soul. What do you think?

To: **Jay@mybestfriendisgay.com**
From: **Dot@noplacelikehome.com**
Subject: **Space**

Yes, of course I understand that you need time to get on with your own life. You've been very supportive, and if Kevin is feeling neglected then of course you must devote more time to him. I know I've put you through it, and you're right, I have become too dependent on both you and Beth. I must stop running to you every time I have a problem. It is time to take responsibility for myself.

Chapter Seventeen

'Jealousy is all the fun you think they had.'
Erica Jong

To: **NikkiSoda@ambitiousproductions.com**
From: **Dot@noplacelikehome.com**
Subject: **Nanny Sarah's reincarnation as brilliant novelist**

Oh my God, she's everywhere. This morning, driving Matilda to the dentist, there she was in technicolour – an enormous poster of Sarah advertising her book, looking attractive in her usual, understated way. After dropping Matilda off at Molly's house, I rushed into the local bookshop and scoured the shelves for a copy of *Don't Do That* by Sarah sodding Standish. My plan was to go round all the local bookshops buying out all copies so that no one round here who knows us would be able to read it. To my delight there was nothing on the shelves between Zadie Smith and Steinbeck. Relieved, I walked out of the shop thinking to myself, 'It's probably not that good.'

Call it instinct, but something made me glance back at the shop window and I saw to my horror not just one but hundreds of copies of the dreaded book, prominently displayed. There were too many to buy and too many to miss. For a brief moment I was tempted to firebomb the shop, but I knew it was pointless. I felt like I was standing in front of a giant tidal wave about to engulf me, and I realised the inevitability of what was going to happen.

There was to be no escaping the shame of it. As I was standing there transfixed, overbearing Arabella from the PTA joined me.

'Looks good, that book. I was reading about it in the *Sunday Telegraph*.' Pause . . . 'Didn't she used to be your nanny?'

'Yes,' I said, unable to think of a suitable retort.

'Should I read it?' she demanded.

'Suit yourself,' I replied sulkily, and left her stunned by my rudeness.

To: **Delissa@splendidmums.com**
From: **Dot@noplacelikehome.com**
Subject: **Honourable intentions**

Thanks for the update about Sarah's book. From what you say I think she's got nappy brain, reading *Cinderella* one time too many. We never treated her like that. What is very worrying is that when I went to collect Matilda from school, I'm convinced people seemed to be avoiding me. No one smiled, let alone talked to me. Then a terrible thought occurred – do you think they've read Sarah's book? I just hope I'm being paranoid.

To: **NikkiSoda@ambitiousproductions.com**
From: **Dot@noplacelikehome.com**
Subject: **Putting the question**

I saw her again this afternoon – there's no getting away from Sarah and her bloody book. Matilda came home from school feeling sick, but she didn't want to go to bed so I set her up on the sofa in front of a video with a hot Ribena (sugar free) and spoonfuls of Calpol. I turned on the television, and there was

Nanny Sarah confidently talking to Richard and Judy about her blasted book and reaching the punch line to a hilarious story.

'. . . I can wipe my own, thank you.' Richard and Judy and all the technicians fell about laughing and Richard was even wiping the tears from his eyes.

'Now, I have to ask you,' Judy said, crossing her legs while trying to move the interview onto a more serious level, 'was the book based on your personal experiences when you were working as a nanny?'

Sarah looked coy, 'Well, obviously a lot of the book is based in reality but I used my experience as a springboard.'

The girls dropped the box of tissues which they had been fighting over and cried out, 'Look, it's Sarah,' and Daisy rushed over and tried to kiss the television screen.

I switched on the video as quickly as I could. It was *Matilda*, a present from Delissa, and I hoped Miss Trunchball and Miss Honey would prove a big enough distraction from the girls' beloved Sarah. You would have thought that after all this time they would have forgotten about her. I thought children were supposed to have short memories. Alex brought her book home last night and has left it lying on the kitchen table. Maybe you should read it for me and then tell me whether I should be really worried. I have no intention of wasting my time reading it.

To: **Delissa@splendidmums.com**
From: **Dot@noplacelikehome.com**
Subject: **'Don't do that' to ex-employers**

I'm on page twenty-two and the heroine has already been locked in her bedroom twice by the wicked parents, and the husband is wandering around semi-naked making suggestive remarks. In her dreams. It's ridiculous – why would we have wanted to lock her in her bedroom? I was delighted when she went out in the evenings, as it meant that Alex and I had the house to ourselves. There were times I felt like Princess Diana, 'With three of us in this marriage . . . it was a bit crowded.' (Not that she and Alex were having an affair, as far as I know, but we never felt entirely alone.) I'm not going to read any more.

To: **Jack@finefigureofafatherinlaw.com**
From: **Dot@noplacelikehome.com**
Subject: **Nanny Sarah's book**

Lovely to hear from you and thank you for the review you scanned from *The Times Literary Supplement* of our ex-nanny's book. I've heard mixed reports, but I suppose it will appeal to a certain kind of market. I only wish I had time to read it.

To: **Delissa@splendidmums.com**
From: **Dot@noplacelikehome.com**
Subject: **More tales of the unexpected**

I'm on to chapter seven: 'I watched her face twist into a cruel smile as she dangled little Gemma upside down. The poor child's desperate screams reverberated around the house while her sister cowered in her hiding place under the bunk beds in her bedroom, too frightened to move. I knew I had to keep calm or else she might pull the knife on me again.' I wish I had pulled a knife on her, if I'd known she was going to write such rubbish while she was living with us.

To: **Jay@mybestfriendisgay.com**
From: **Dot@noplacelikehome.com**
Subject: **Slimy Sarah's slander**

Yes, thank you, I did know that Sarah's book has been published. You'd have to be blind, deaf or cast adrift on a desert island not to know about her book. Of course I haven't read it, I've got better things to do with my time and so, I expect, have you.

To: **Delissa@splendidmums.com**
From: **Dot@noplacelikehome.com**
Subject: **Betrayal**

I've finished it and I can't get rid of the horrid taste in my mouth. I feel tainted. How could she do it to us? We paid her regularly by direct debit and even gave her a couple of pay rises during her time with us. She even came on holiday when we went to Portugal. Admittedly, we weren't being completely altruistic, but still, she had a couple of days off. We were nothing but kind and considerate, and our only crime is that we were working too hard. What can I do? I could write an article, but people won't believe it and I don't want to get into a public slanging match. This book is pure fantasy and it's making me very cross. I'm going to rise above it and impress everyone with my dignified behaviour, content in the knowledge that my friends and family know the truth.

To: **Delissa@splendidmums.com**
From: **Dot@noplacelikehome.com**
Subject: **The shame of it**

Have just been caught trying to steal Sarah's book out of Kate's handbag. She'd left it by the door of the classroom at pick-up, and seeing Sarah's 'I'm so clever I've written a book' expression, taunting me from the back cover, was too much. I didn't really stop to think but I hoped if I picked it up quickly enough I could throw it in the bins on our way out with no one seeing. OK, it wasn't the most perfectly planned crime of the century, more of a spur of the moment kind of thing, but why should she be allowed to carry on humiliating me like this? I thought Kate might think she'd dropped it. Just as I managed to pick the book up, Matilda's voice said, 'What are you doing with Molly's mum's handbag?'

'Shh,' I hissed at her, 'I'm looking after it for her.'

'Isn't that Sarah on the back of that book?' she continued loudly, and grabbed it from me before I could chuck it into the nearest bin.

Kate turned round and, thinking on my feet, I said, 'Someone knocked your bag over, I was just picking everything up for you.'

Kate, looking at the book in my hands, said a little guiltily, 'I've just bought it. I couldn't resist it, but I haven't had time to read it yet. Sarah was such a nice girl. I'm glad she's doing well.'

'Yes, so am I,' I replied with great self-control, and before I could stop myself I said, 'It *is* a novel you know. Nothing to do with us.'

'Oh, Dot, of course not,' she said, laughing at me as I flushed a deep magenta.

To: **NikkiSoda@ambitiousproductions.com**
From: **Dot@noplacelikehome.com**
Subject: **Putting the question**

I'm glad you're enjoying Sarah's book as I have heard that it's not very well written. Still, that's the least of my problems at the moment. I hate to admit it, but you were right, I should have talked to Alex about the whole Jessica issue. By not talking about it and bottling it up my imagination has run riot. Last night when Alex came home he was in quite a good mood and totally unaffected by the fall-out from Sarah's book. The film is looking good, he's caught up on his sleep and he was being affectionate. He had thoughtfully brought home a Thai takeaway so that I wouldn't have to worry about cooking.

We were all set for a relaxed evening watching television. I was exhausted after the trauma of dealing with Sarah's book, and over the past few days the encounter with Jessica had kept nagging away at me. We ate our takeaway while watching *Help, I'm a Celebrity, Get me Out of Here*. Alex ate hungrily, finishing his first plate in only a few minutes. He leant back on the sofa and pronounced, 'Jessica says that these sorts of programmes will be the death of drama. The suits think, "Why bother to spend all that money on period dramas when you can get it all with real people, or celebrities desperate for publicity, for half the price."'

Now this was my territory, and the combination of Jessica being scathing about the sort of programmes I used to make while trying to steal my husband from under my nose was all the encouragement I needed.

'For Christ's sake, does she have any idea how hard these programmes are to produce? You don't just point a camera and follow things as they unfold. It takes months of research and preparation and a certain amount of manipulation once you're shooting. In many ways, it's much easier if you have a script to follow. You drama people have had it so easy up to now with your obscene budgets and lorry-loads of labour to help you. It's so profligate. We have to do everything ourselves. For years there's been no money for us, it's all been sucked up by the big drama productions. It's always drama that gets all the awards. I think it's about time factual entertainment and documentaries got a look in. Bloody Jessica.' I viciously stabbed a prawn with my fork.

Alex looked at me, surprised, but he laughed when he said, 'Mrs Chippy. You can't blame Jessica for the way finances are allocated in the wonderful world of television.'

'Why not?' I muttered, trying to catch a stray noodle which hadn't quite made it to my mouth and was floating towards my chin.

'Well, it's not her fault. She's just a good drama producer trying to get as much money for the projects she feels passionate about.' Alex was nonplussed by my vitriol.

'I think this,' I said, pointing at Tony Blackburn stacking up his log pile in the middle of the jungle, 'is just as important as drama, if not more so. All those people poncing around in crinolines and bonnets. If you ask me, it's a waste of money. These programmes are . . .' I paused as Tara Palmer-Tomkinson told Darren Day how unattractive he was because he couldn't control his farts '. . . important social documents.' I knew I was on thin ground but I was determined to hold my position.

Alex sat stunned, and then he began to laugh, 'You don't mean it. Dot, you are funny.'

'I do.' My voiced raised because of his patronising tone. 'I think period drama is a load of crap and a waste of money.' I'd never attacked his work in this way before.

'I didn't realise you thought I was just wasting my time and other people's money.' I'd ruffled his feathers.

'I hate drama. I've never liked it and I don't trust the sort of people who make it,' I muttered.

'You're being ridiculous. You loved *Wives and Daughters* and all those Jane Austen and Trollope adaptations. How many evenings have I had to sacrifice watching the football for your obsession with costume drama?' He paused and then, thinking about what I'd said, followed it with, 'So am I one of those people you don't trust?'

'Is there any reason why I shouldn't trust you?' I said pointedly.

'What are you saying, Dot?'

'Nothing.'

'Oh, not nothing. I hate bloody nothing. Nothing always means something. Go on, what's bothering you?'

On the screen love rat Darren was complaining to the pugilistic Nigel about the obscene notes It Girl Tara had written to him.

'I've got a girlfriend who I am very happy with. She knows that. I wish she'd stop bothering me.'

I was tempted to shout at the screen. Bloody typical – he'd been flirting outrageously with the poor girl and as soon as she started criticising his behaviour he was being spiteful, putting in the knife. I wished I hadn't started the conversation with Alex but now that I had, there was no turning back. I had to know if my husband was also a love rat.

'Is there something going on between you and Jessica?'

'Yes,' he said, looking me straight in the eye. My stomach churned and it was nothing to do with the Pad Thai I was eating.

'We're working together and making a very difficult drama, for God's sake.'

'That's not what I've heard.'

'What? So I haven't been working with Jessica?' he said, taking me literally. 'This whole drama is an elaborate alibi so that we could embark on a tempestuous affair without you ever finding out? What are you talking about?' He was getting frustrated with me.

'It was Nikki. She knows Amber, one of your many make-up supervisors.' He groaned.

'I might have known Nikki would have had something to do with it. Look, I don't know what people have been saying, but they always talk – you know what it's like. If I believed all those sorts of rumours, I'd think you'd had an affair with every cameraman you've ever worked with.'

For a moment I flushed red. It wasn't every cameraman, and anyway I wasn't married then. It's different. But I didn't want to start talking about that. We were moving off the subject.

'You just don't get it, do you? You don't know what I've been going through the last few months. I've just had the worst scare of my life. I thought the cancer was back but I didn't want to bother you with it because you were busy with Jessica.' I snarled her name.

'I wasn't "busy with Jessica" as you put it. I was busy shooting and editing *Tess*, the most important project of my life. But I'm sorry I didn't know you'd just had a scare. It's OK, though?' he asked suddenly, looking anxious.

I nodded, 'No thanks to you.'

'Dot, you can't blame me for not being sympathetic about something I didn't even know about.' He was becoming exasperated.

'Well, you should have known about it. You don't seem to care about anything other than your precious career.'

'What's happening, Dot? Come on. I don't recognise you like this.'

'You mean, you don't recognise our bank balance. I haven't

changed, it's you that's changed,' I muttered.

'But all this stuff about me and Jessica, this wouldn't have bothered you before. Since you gave up work you get obsessed with . . . nothing, things that aren't important.' I had wondered how long it would be before he brought up my giving up work.

'I don't think my husband having an affair is unimportant.'

'I don't mean that – I mean you're totally wrapped up in yourself. You're in your own little world. Look at Beth. You didn't even notice what was happening there. Oh no, nothing could be wrong with your perfect friend, Beth, because that doesn't fit the picture – your picture. You've become self-obsessed. It's sort of understandable, but you've got to realise other people have lives. We've all got to move on. Life can't just stop because you've been ill.'

For a minute I was speechless. I'd heard what he said but I didn't want to believe him. Besides, love rats always go for the throat when cornered, but I wasn't going to let him put me off the scent. I was determined to discover the truth about him and Jessica.

'Well, are you? You haven't answered my question.'

'Am I what?' he snapped at me.

'Having an affair with Jessica?'

Barely concealing his irritation he said in a sarcastic voice, 'Oh, for God's sake. Now let me see, why would I want to have an affair with Jessica?' He paused, 'Well, she's bright, funny, good-looking and most of all she's independent,' he taunted. 'She doesn't need anyone because she can look after herself, but you know what? What I really find attractive about her is that she reminds me of you – the way you used to be.' He stood up as though he couldn't bear to be in the same room a minute longer, and without even looking at me he went upstairs to bed. In the background Rhona, the gay Scottish comedienne, was being buried alive in the jungle. She started to scream, 'Get me out. Get me out.' Maybe Alex had a point. I remembered Jay's last e-mail and I thought about dear Beth, my closest friend for over twenty years, sitting alone in her room in the clinic.

Chapter Eighteen

'Under all speech that is good for anything there lies a silence that is better. Silence is deep as Eternity; speech is shallow as Time.'

Thomas Carlyle

To: **Bethearthmother@rooted.com**
From: **Dot@noplacelikehome.com**
Subject: **You**

My Dear Beth

I'm listening now.

Dot

Chapter Nineteen

'Marriage is a wonderful invention; but, then again,
so is a bicycle repair kit.'
Billy Connolly

To: LukeLloyd@talent.co.uk
From: **Dot@noplacelikehome.com**
Subject: **Greta-Dot-Garbo**

No, I haven't been deliberately avoiding you and, yes, tomorrow is still on. Good news that *First Loves* has got through the first round. When will we know if it will be commissioned as a series? Tell me all tomorrow.

To: Jack@finefigureofafatherinlaw.com
From: **Dot@noplacelikehome.com**
Subject: **Wedding anniversary**

Thank you and Sylvia for the Frank Sinatra e-mail celebratory message. It's not exactly a romantic image but a very practical one. 'Love and marriage, goes together like a horse and carriage.' Which one of us is which, do you think? I feel like a reluctant horse is dragging me along and that there's definitely something stuck in the spokes of my carriage wheels. Ol' blue-eyes certainly knew something about marriage as he had enough practice at it. I wonder if he ever got his wedding anniversaries mixed up? 'Oops, sorry, darling – that was number one not number three.' Both Alex and I forgot it was our anniversary and we've got no excuse.

It sounds as though your trip to Egypt was fascinating, but you mustn't overdo things. I know you resist any concessions to age but the occasional afternoon nap does not mean you're due to be packed off to the old people's home at the top of the hill. Sylvia is right to nag you.

Your suggestion that Alex and I go out tonight is a good one. Can you put in a good word with your son, as I don't think he's talking to me at the moment?

To: **Delissa@splendidmums.com**
From: **Dot@noplacelikehome.com**
Subject: **Babysitting**

This is making me feel terrible. If everyone else can remember our anniversary, why can't we? Thanks for your offer to babysit tonight. I haven't managed to get hold of Alex yet to see if he's interested in spending an evening with me. We had a horrible conversation last night and I don't think he'll be rushing to make a reservation for this evening. Do you think being ill has changed me? Alex thinks I've become self-obsessed and that I worry about nothing. It's supposed to be the other way round. You have a serious illness and get a perspective on life so that you don't waste time worrying about the little things that shouldn't matter. I don't know if he's right or feeling guilty about something.

I know that I've been relying too heavily on my friends. Jay has borne the brunt of my fears over these past few years and has had enough, and I certainly haven't been much help to Beth. I tried to write to her last night but after writing nine inarticulate, sentimental pages I realised there are no words to tell her how I feel, so I kept it brief. Watching Matilda and Molly together makes me think about her every day, and wonder how she's feeling and why this has happened? When I was ill I never thought, 'Why me?' Terrible things happen to people all over the world, things far worse than coming down with a dose of cancer, but I did wonder, why did I get it? I feel that if I can understand why I got it, then perhaps I can prevent it coming back.

Alex thinks I've changed but I don't feel any different. I still feel like the old Dot. I've changed the superficial things in my life as a direct result of being ill. I look after myself, and maybe I've learnt to read my body better. I used to enjoy pushing myself to my limits but nowadays after two nights out in the same week I feel like I've been running in a marathon. The more interesting question, I suppose, is should you change? The only reason to change is if you were doing something wrong that brought on the cancer, and then we're back where we started, with the, 'Why?' question. I wonder if it is a chemical thing with Beth?

As far as Alex is concerned, we need to go away together on our own but that doesn't look likely for a while, and we can't afford it anyway. For the short term I'm sure we can work out something for tonight. Come over early so we can talk while the children are having tea (ha, ha).

To: **NikkiSoda@ambitiousproductions.com**
From: **Dot@noplacelikehome.com**
Subject: **Dot abuse**

No, I won't be interviewed for your film on nanny abuse. How could you do this to me? I know I asked you to read Sarah's book but that means reading it, not optioning it and then publicising it so that even more people will read it. I'm sure Sarah must be delighted. You have to remember, I've been on the other side of your negotiating tactics in the past, so that when you say it will give me a chance to put my side of the story, I know how you could stitch me up. I never abused Sarah, whatever that means, and I certainly never behaved like that with my children. It's a piece of fiction, for God's sake. I've got nothing to defend.

To: **Alex@himindoors.com**
From: **Dot@noplacelikehome.com**
Subject: **Hot date**

Happy anniversary to you too. We do need some time together. Can't you postpone the dub? If not, do you really have to be there all the time? Maybe we could eat late? Call me.

To: **LukeLloyd@talent.co.uk**
From: **Dot@noplacelikehome.com**
Subject: **Best news I've had all day**

Fantastic news, and I'm so pleased *First Loves* has been commissioned. Thanks for gallant offer of a celebratory dinner at Oscar's Oyster Bar, but it's my wedding anniversary and there is a thought that I might be having dinner with Alex. Also, Daisy has a bit of a temperature. I think she might have caught the virus Matilda had last week. Have a drink on me and we'll talk in the morning.

To: **Alex@himindoors.com**
From: **Dot@noplacelikehome.com**
Subject: **I give up**

Fine, if you can't make it then you can't. Just to let you know the programme proposal I've been working on with Luke Lloyd has been commissioned, and he's asked me to go and celebrate tonight. Delissa is happy to babysit, and rather than sit around with the memories of how happy my marriage used to be I thought you wouldn't mind if I went. Maybe see you later.

To: **LukeLloyd@talent.co.uk**
From: **Dot@noplacelikehome.com**
Subject: **Dinner invitation**

You're on. I'll see you at 8.30 at Oscar's.

To: **LukeLloyd@talent.co.uk**
From: **Dot@noplacelikehome**
Subject: **Long encounter**

It's only been an hour since we were together but I wanted to say thank you for a wonderful evening. I'm sure I'll regret all of this in the morning, and it's probably the champagne speaking, but I just wanted to keep talking to you and realised that it wouldn't be a great idea to ring you at home.

It was extraordinary spending a whole evening with you without the distraction of Daisy, bonfires and overexcited children. Mind you, there were still countless interruptions from people wanting autographs, waiters who wanted to tell you how funny you were, but not produce any food, producers who wanted you to appear in their programmes, and all those directors and actors you've worked with over the years. Being you is exhausting – you never get any time off. Jude and Sadie look better in the flesh (if that's possible), Madonna seemed nice, but I didn't think Guy was looking very happy. He's probably worrying about his next film.

The big shock for me was seeing my friend Jay's other half, Kevin Casey, out partying alone. He was all over that American fashion designer and looked a little sheepish when he caught sight of us watching him. You're right, he doesn't like me one little bit, but he was torn between ignoring me and wanting to come and meet you. Waving is his idea of a compromise. I wonder if he'll tell Jay what he was up to? I'm certainly not going to get involved, but I do worry about Jay getting hurt.

I wish you hadn't kept filling my glass with champagne – ever since chemotherapy alcohol doesn't really agree with me, but tonight it tasted lovely and the oysters were delicious. I'm sorry I didn't tell you before about having had cancer. There never seemed a right time, and anyway, I didn't want your sympathy. I wanted life to be as normal as possible, and with you I could almost pretend it never happened. Did you mean all those things you said, or was it two bottles of champagne talking? If I was cool I'd just take it all in my stride, but I haven't got a cool bone in my body especially when I'm near you. I think you owe me an apology for kissing me in the street. You don't know who might have seen us. The papers could be full of it tomorrow morning. 'Luke Lloyd snogs mystery housewife.' We must stop our lips meeting like this.

Thank you for putting me in a cab. As I sashayed up the garden path my mother was waiting by the front door looking worried, but as soon as she saw the state I was in her concern quickly turned into anger. Why is it whenever I've been with you

I end up feeling like a teenager again? She hadn't been very happy when she arrived to babysit and realised I was going out with you rather than Alex. Her mood hadn't improved by having to spend the night worrying about Daisy's soaring temperature and pleas for her mother. She'd tried the mobile all night but I never checked to see if it was receiving. I forgot to tell her where we were going, and she couldn't get hold of Alex either.

Feeling guilty, I rushed upstairs to find Daisy high as me, on Calpol not champagne. We cooled her down with a flannel and I stroked her forehead, and she soon fell into a restless sleep. My mother stared at me and hardly controlling her irritation, she said, 'You'd better get to bed and sleep it off.' She paused, and then said enigmatically, 'Dot, don't make the same mistake that I did,' and with a look of disappointment and disapproval she walked out into the dark street.

I couldn't go straight to sleep. I want to make the most of tonight because I know that tomorrow I'll feel hung over and guilty – a lethal combination. What I find so exciting is that I never know when we're going to meet, whether it be in the street, in a village shop or in the school playground. It makes getting up in the morning that little bit more interesting. I can hear Daisy crying again. I must go. Thank you for the second best evening I've had all year. Until whenever . . .

To: **Alex@himindoors.com**
From: **Dot@noplacelikehome.com**
Subject: **Urgent**

Alex, where the hell are you? It's two o'clock in the morning and you're still not back. There's no answer from the dub and your mobile has been switched off. I'm really worried about Daisy, she's got a temperature of 104 and it's not responding to the drugs. She's delirious and keeps talking to lots of puppies that she can see in the bedroom. I'm going to give her a cold bath to try and get her temperature down, but I wish you'd come home.

To: **Alex@himindoors.com**
From: **Dot@noplacelikehome.com**
Subject: **Where are you?**

The cold bath has helped a little bit, although it was agony getting her into it and she yelled when her bottom hit the cold water and pleaded with me to stop. Should I ring the doctor? I've checked her all over for rashes and she's not wincing when you turn on a bright light. Well, no more than you would if someone was shining a torch straight into your eyes. I'm finding it hard to type this . . . m . . . the keys are going all blurry . . . pssk . . . I'm feeling faint and rather strange. Oh no . . . I think I'm going to be . . .

Kboiugdkjha13akjaglkajaitkasgnv,z , kzjzl .(
lzksdgjoi749587q0u0
854js,';Mnkasjdfhaiu9875ns,67tghvyrgj6eoscnwpscmvkhksgaq
w2SGM
gjghaitoanvnri75409qjaslnvnai0092jflkskdfhfghjtuirkhgkdnvnr
eio458549565uu5yujhjkgbknbnbnb,ngkjgfl..................................

To: **Jay@mybestfriendisgay.com**
From: **Dot@noplacelikehome.com**
Subject: **Too sick to talk**

HELP.

To: **Alex@himindoors.com**
From: **Dot@noplacelikehome.com**
Subject: **We need you**

Where are you? I feel terrible. I've been up all night being sick and trying to get Daisy's temperature down. At the height of the sickness I tried to leave the bathroom to look after Daisy, but I couldn't even make it to the door before I was sick again. As I was clinging to the side of the loo on my knees, dreading the next wave, my stomach rumbling ominously, a little voice said, 'Are you alright, Mama?' and I turned to see Matilda looking anxious in her Angelina Ballerina pyjamas. I was sick again and the next thing I knew she had a flannel and was holding it on my forehead.

'This is what Granny Delicious did to Daisy,' and for the next couple of hours she ran between Daisy and me trying to make us both feel better.

After being sick more times than I care to remember I managed to crawl into our bed and the girls came too, and by 6.00 a.m. we all managed to sleep. I am never ever going to eat oysters again.

Where are you? Oh God, I hope you haven't had an accident. You're probably lying in hospital with concussion, with your wallet stolen so no one can identify you. If I had more energy I'd ring round all the hospitals, or maybe you're with Jessica. Of course why, didn't I think if it before? You bastard, I never thought you of all people would be so cruel or such a coward. You didn't even have the guts to tell me to my face. If that's the way you want it, we don't need you. We've managed perfectly well without you all summer. Don't bother coming home.

Chapter Twenty

'Well now there's a remedy for everything except death.'
Cervantes

To: **Delissa@splendidmums.com**
From: **Dot@noplacelikehome.com**
Subject: **In shock**

I can't quite believe it but Jack died last night. Alex has just called me from the hospital where Jack was taken by ambulance, complaining of pains in his chest. For a while he seemed comfortable, but in the early hours of the morning he had a massive heart attack and died. It was all over very quickly, and luckily Sylvia and Alex were with him. We're numb with shock. Jack dead – it's just plain ridiculous. Alex is going to stay with Sylvia so I've packed some clothes for him and he's dropping by to pick them up. I'm so sorry about last night. It's the first time I've drunk champagne for years and it went straight to my head. I've never had oysters before but I don't think I'll be in a hurry to try them again after being violently sick all night. Is there any chance you can come over today? I feel terrible.

To: **Alex@himindoors.com**
From: **Dot@noplacelikehome.com**
Subject: **Constancy**

I hated seeing you so briefly this morning when you came to pick up your bag, and I'm sorry I didn't say much. Holding you seemed more important. You know how much I loved Jack, and like you I can't believe he's dead. I'm worried about you as you looked exhausted. Please try to get some sleep at home. Alex, I'm so desperately sorry about the e-mail I sent the night he died but I didn't know what to think. Please delete it immediately and ring me when you can. If you're fielding all the phonecalls for Sylvia you may want to e-mail. Just keep in touch. Send all my love to Sylvia and if I can do anything to help, I will. I do love you, I've just forgotten how to say it.

To: **Jay@mybestfriendisgay.com**
From: **Dot@noplacelikehome.com**
Subject: **Jack**

Thanks for your phonecall, it was so good to hear from you. I suppose we're all in shock and disbelief. Jack was my champion and he adored all his children, especially Alex, who's finding it hard to come to terms with his death. I can only begin to imagine what he must be feeling. I decided to tell the children today because I was worried Matilda would hear me on the phone, or listen to conversations between Alex and me, and know something was going on. I remember that feeling of exclusion as a child when grown-ups never told you what was really happening. People speaking in hushed voices and going quiet when you walked into a room was upsetting and disconcerting because you ended up thinking it was your fault.

It's the unknown that is frightening. When I was ill I thought it was very important that Matilda knew what was happening to me without any unnecessary or gruesome detail. I was going into hospital to have medicine that would eventually make me better, but it had to make me ill first. She wasn't the only one who was confused, but it meant that when my hair began to fall out it wasn't a shock to her, and we could go and buy scarves together.

I waited until Matilda came home from school and just before tea I sat them both down and tried to tell them as gently as possible. I wasn't sure how they would react, as Daisy is too young to understand and Matilda has a rational streak, which would override her emotions in the short term. After Fluffy she's mentally prepared for death, but I was worried that I might cry and that would in turn upset them.

'Girls, I've got some sad news.' Daisy was scribbling on the tablecloth and Matilda was trying to fold a piece of paper to make a fortune-teller. 'Papa was taken to hospital last night and he died.' The girls looked at me and I looked down at my hands in my lap to stop my eyes from filling with tears. There was a pause as they tried to digest the information.

'Will he still bring me a present at Christmas?' asked Daisy.

'Oh, Daisy,' I said, 'I don't think so,' and with that she burst into tears.

'Grandma will still bring you a present,' I said quickly, and with that news bulletin she brightened.

Matilda had gone quiet, and I could almost hear the cogs in her brain working hard. 'Will he be in heaven?' she asked.

'I'm sure he will. He and Fluffy will be having a nice chat.' Certainty is what children need in these situations.

'I don't think so,' said Matilda, looking at me as if I'd gone mad.

'Oh, why not?' I said, wondering whether she was already cynical about the idea of heaven.

'Fluffy can't talk.' She carried on colouring in her fortune-teller and then paused, 'If God loves us, why does he let us die?' This was a real challenge. I felt it was time to be straightforward.

'We've all got to die at some time. It's nothing to be frightened of.'

Daisy clutched me dramatically, 'I don't want you to die, Mama.'

'I have no intention of dying for a long time, not until I'm very old, and by then you'll be glad to get rid of me,' I said as lightly as I could.

That afternoon I took Matilda to her ballet lesson. Mrs Johnson who plays the piano is straight out of central casting. She was having a chat with Matilda and I heard her say, 'How old are you, darling?'

Matilda said confidently, 'Five.'

'How old do you think I am?' asked Mrs Johnson sweetly.

'A hundred,' replied Matilda emphatically.

When I went to pick her up she said very loudly, 'Is Mrs Johnson going to die soon?'

I quickly changed her shoes and bustled her out to the car. I have to keep reminding myself that Jack is dead. You expect the world to stop and acknowledge what has happened, but it doesn't. Business as usual – except for us.

At bedtime, after the girls had brushed their teeth following a protracted argument about who had spat the toothpaste out first on each other's hands, Matilda snuggled under the covers and asked 'Will I ever see Grandpa again?'

'No, darling. But you can always remember him. He can live on in your memory, and that's important.'

'It's the circle of life,' she said in a matter-of-fact voice, and seeing my look of surprise she said, '*The Lion King*.' Then, making the connection, she asked wide-eyed, 'Was Papa killed by stampeding Wildebeest?'

'No, nothing like that.'

'Do you think he can see us now?'

'Maybe. You never know.'

Later, as I was tidying up the bathroom, I heard sounds coming from Matilda's bedroom. I listened at the door and realised she was talking to Jack on her pretend mobile phone.

'Papa, I'm sorry you've died. Are you having a nice time?' There was a pause while she pretended to listen to his answer. 'A hole in one, really, that's wonderful. Listen, I'll call you tomorrow just in case you feel a bit lonely – all right?' she said in a tone of voice I recognised as my own. Heaven is obviously a place where you can score a hole in one every day. As I took the washing downstairs, considering whether I had the energy to roast some vegetables for my supper, I thought about *The Lion King* – I wonder if having a heart attack does feel like being trampled by a herd of stampeding Wildebeest.

I will send your love to Alex, and thank you for the lovely letter you wrote to him. He was very touched by it and read it to me over the phone. I think he's quite amazed by the reaction he's had to Jack's death. Sack-loads of letters have been arriving daily. If only Jack was there to read them, he would have appreciated all the things people have written. It was the way to go – he enjoyed his life and had just had a great holiday. It was over pretty quickly with no fear and, as far as we know, little pain. It's just hard on Sylvia and the children, who had no time to prepare and make that mental adjustment. Part of me envies him his quick death. I long for a death like Jack's or, even better, to pass away peacefully in my sleep. Is that a thing of the past? Do people still die in their sleep?

Have a lovely holiday with Kevin. I'm not surprised he's exhausted, as he must lead such a hectic life. Think of us as you're drinking cocktails in front of a Californian sunset. You do realise you're going to a place where the people applaud the sunset? Have a nice day.

To: Delissa@splendidmums.com
From: **Dot@noplacelikehome.com**
Subject: **I've been wondering . . .**

These past few days have been emotionally exhausting but strangely cathartic. It's been important to me to spend so much time with you, and the children adore Granny Delicious. Last night after you left, I was thinking about the night Jack died. What did you mean when you said, 'Don't make the same mistake I did'?

To: Delissa@splendidmums.com
From: **Dot@noplacelikehome.com**
Subject: **Is there a cure for genetic infidelity?**

Why didn't you tell me this before? I had always thought Dad just walked out on us, it never occurred to me that he left because you had an affair. Do I know the friend? How and why did it happen and more crucially, if it hadn't happened would you still be married to Dad? I feel like I'm watching a play I've seen a thousand times. The characters are the same but I'm no longer sure whether I understand the play, it seems like a very different story. And now you're worried that history is going to repeat itself.

Oh, Mum, I'm so confused about everything. Nothing is as it should be.

To: **Delissa@splendidmums.com**
From: **Dot@noplacelikehome.com**
Subject: **Pulling up the drawbridge**

I suppose you're right, these things are complex. I don't really remember Peter but I've seen photos of him with you and Dad. So he was the friend who died in the helicopter crash when he was working for BBC news. That must have been hard for you, or was the affair over by then? I can see how Dad's work wasn't conducive to a happy marriage. Being a foreign correspondent meant he was always travelling, and when he was at home he was either sleeping or working on his books and articles. It was always, 'Shh, you'll wake your father,' or, 'Don't make a noise, your father is working.'

What I remember is, sensing that you weren't happy with him but not understanding why. It wasn't just the work. He was completely obsessed with his career and he was always very remote with me so that I felt like I was a nuisance, which I probably was. I don't remember ever climbing on his knee or going on special outings. You were both much younger than Alex and I when you married, and we managed to get a lot out of our systems before we settled down. It must have been hard in the late sixties and early seventies – I wonder if many 'open' marriages survived? From what you say, Dad was the one who considered it an open marriage, but you fell in love.

Despite everything, I know you found it difficult when Dad left – we both did. Single parents were something of a phenomenon in those days and I felt isolated at school, but at least I always had Beth. In some ways it helped that Dad went to live abroad. It made it easier to cut him out of our lives. Thinking about it now from a purely personal perspective, I haven't had an example of a happy and loving marriage to emulate. I'm not sure how to go about repairing my own marriage. It's possibly the only thing you haven't taught me – not that I'm blaming you, as there are some things in life I have to sort out for myself. From the moment you realised Dad wasn't coming back your philosophy was self-sufficiency at all costs. You and I became a strong unit, and no one was allowed to penetrate our protective walls. We did OK, though. It's just hard to let anyone else get close. Do you think I've become totally self-obsessed?

To: **Delissa@splendidmums.com**
From: **Dot@noplacelikehome.com**
Subject: **Aftermath**

Thank you for being so supportive – I suppose you're right, I shouldn't be so hard on myself. I'm just exhausted. It's been over a year since I finished my treatment and I thought that would be enough time to completely recover, but chemotherapy quite simply sucked the lifeblood out of me. The simplest task, such as making tea or taking the children to the playground, consumed all my energy. Maybe Alex is right, I have become selfish, but without being dramatic it was necessary in order to survive. I had to conserve all my energy to get better and anything that was left over went to the children and to Alex. Friends and family suffered as a consequence, but I hope they understood. Most of them seemed to at the time. But that was then, and maybe I need to have a little rethink.

I remember the breast cancer nurse saying that it can take up to two years to feel back to normal, but still, I'm not ill now. I'm well, and the sooner I forget about what happened and how I felt, the better. I think I will take you up on your offer of seeing your acupuncturist, Dr Arr. I'll try anything to make me feel stronger. At least Alex and I are communicating again. He e-mails me every night from Jack's desk and for the first time in years he's confiding in me.

Last night he described sitting in Jack's chair, reading through letters and documents. He finds it strange using his father's favourite pen, speaking into the phone knowing that Jack was the last person to talk into it, looking at the photos that smiled at Jack every day from the desktop. Alex found a scribbled note for me, probably the last thing he ever wrote, not realising that in twenty-four hours he would be dead. It was stapled to an article on 'Women Who Want it All'. I think it was a shock seeing his handwriting and realising that he would never have a welcoming hug or hear his voice again. How can you ever prepare for the death of a parent? I can't begin to think about losing you. Even though I know it's inevitable it will be unbearable, so you'd better stick around for a bit longer.

Sylvia is being very British and concentrating all her efforts on organising the funeral with Alex's sister Rebecca, who has just flown over from Australia. At least they don't have to worry about jelly boats, helium balloons, partybags or booking a good entertainer – that's the vicar's responsibility. Sylvia has always thrived in a crisis and I think the funeral is a good diversion with no time to think. God, it is so important to make the most of the time we have.

To: **Alex@himindoors.com**
From: **Dot@noplacelikehome.com**
Subject: **Jack**

My dearest Alex, don't worry about us, we're all fine and the girls both send you all their love. Daisy is recovering but is now obsessed with those syringes that look like needles and help to squeeze Calpol down children's throats. We've never needed one before, but Delissa used it when Daisy was ill and she now thinks it's great and won't leave the house without it. It's like walking around with a heroin addict. It sounds as if you're being a great comfort to your mother, helping organise the funeral and just being there, it would be very lonely for her without you all. I'm very touched to be asked to read. What do you think of Joyce Grenfell's poem, 'If I Should Go'? It's short and to the point, but most of all I think Jack would appreciate the sentiment. If you or Sylvia have a better idea then I'll do whatever you want.

How is your speech coming on? It's a hard thing for you to have to do. I have lots of memories of Jack but nothing that would be interesting enough for a speech. When I was first diagnosed I remember he was the one who brought it up at Sunday lunch. He didn't make a fuss, he just asked how I was feeling, listened to me and then told me a positive story about a friend of a friend who'd been clear for years. He then steered the conversation onto a happier topic. He understood completely that it was a relief for me to talk about it, but I didn't want to dwell on it. He was very *simpatico*. It's no accident that there isn't really a word in English that means the same, but Jack was quintessentially English in every other way. What I'll miss about him is his humour. He always knew how to lighten a difficult situation. He was amused by the world and never took it too seriously.

Why don't you do word association and see what you come up with? Here's a few thoughts: the smell of Imperial Leather soap, hot curries, his deep chuckle, silver hair, tailored suits, terrible ties, filming at awkward moments with his old Super 8 camera, Frank Sinatra's 'You Make me Feel so Young', interesting articles that he kept to show people, driving too slowly, always welcoming, and those big comforting bear hugs. If Jack had any fault it was that he was too soft, but in a critical world that was a comfort to all of us.

I know he died suddenly, but what did you need to tell him that he didn't know already? He was exceptionally proud of you. You had your arguments but he took that in his stride, they always upset you more than they did him. I think he quite enjoyed the challenge. I remember him telling me that because of the war he felt like he was living on borrowed time. In a strange way, because of his experiences, he prepared for death by making the most of his life. I'll e-mail you later.

All love
Dot
X

To: **Alex@himindoors.com**
From: **Dot@noplacelikehome.com**
Subject: **I remember Siena**

How could I forget Siena? It was the best holiday I've ever had. How lovely to find the postcard that we sent to your parents. I'd love to see it. Can you still smell the sun and Chianti? I think I was six months pregnant with Matilda and we very wisely decided to have our last holiday together before our lives changed dramatically. Everything in my life was perfect. I was having a Martine McCutcheon 'Perfect Moment'. It was still relatively early days for us. In less than a year we'd met, decided to have a baby and get married. I know most people do it in a different order but it seemed the right thing at the time and there wasn't any point in waiting. We'd both been around long enough to recognise when something was special.

I felt so lucky to be having a baby, let alone a healthy one and I was loving being pregnant – at last I had an excuse to have a big stomach. We'd just heard that our offer on the house had been accepted and I'd finished making the best film of my career. I couldn't believe my luck. We had no idea what was about to hit us. I think we were totally unprepared, but it had all happened so quickly. I wonder if you ever have any regrets? I know I don't. But we've hardly had time to catch our breath, what with two children, work, cancer and now this.

Do you remember those long lazy lunches in the Tuscan sun, eating freshly cooked pasta, and those delicious tomatoes – I still dream about them. I had a craving for those tomatoes all through my pregnancy with Daisy – I almost sent you out to Tuscany to bring back a crate for me. When I was having chemotherapy I would sometimes imagine that I was sitting on the terrace under the vine, watching the peacocks strutting through the olive groves, the gentle June sun on my face, the baby warm in my belly and you immersed in a book beside me.

When was the last time we were alone together, apart from the odd jaunt to the cinema or a few brief seconds in a car going out to supper? I miss you and I miss our lazy days. Will we ever have them again?

To: **Alex@himindoors.com**
From: **Dot@noplacelikehome.com**
Subject: **Spending your inheritance**

Yes, we deserve it. It's a fantastic idea. In the spring we'll go back to Siena together, but without the children. I'm sure either Delissa or Sylvia would help out with the girls. That's wonderful news about the money Jack left you, at least it takes some of the pressure off and makes me feel less guilty about not earning. I'm sure he would definitely approve of us spending some of it on a holiday for just the two of us. Now you must get some sleep, or you'll be exhausted after all that sorting and clearing. I love you so much and long to see you.

To: **LukeLloyd@talent.co.uk**
From: **Dot@noplacelikehome**
Subject: **Wednesday meetings**

Sorry I haven't replied earlier to your e-mails but Alex's father, Jack, died the night we went out to celebrate, and since then I've been helping organise the funeral and giving all the support I can to Alex. Apologies for the drunken e-mail I sent the other night, and on reflection I think it would be better if we stopped our Wednesday meetings. Pre-production on *First Loves* won't start until next year, which will give me a bit of time to work out whether I want to go back to work full time or help you as an executive producer or consultant on a part-time basis. I hope you understand and feel, like me, that this is for the best.

Chapter Twenty One

'"What is the answer?" No answer came. She laughed and said, "In that case what is the question?"'
Gertrude Stein's last words

To: **Bethearthmother@rooted.com**
From: **Dot@noplacelikehome.com**
Subject: **We have contact**

I can't tell you how wonderful it was to get your e-mail after all these weeks, and of course I understand that you've got to take it gently and recover in your own time. Tom sounds as if he's coping well and the children are responding to the nanny. It's the first time you've had someone else looking after your children. Don't worry, and make the most of it – be selfish. I know what you mean, it's like telling children when they make horrid faces that the wind might change and they'll be stuck like that for life. You're worried that if you start being selfish it might never stop and you'll become an unlovable self-centred woman. Take it from someone who knows, it could happen – but if it does, someone inevitably will tell you.

Tom never mentioned the letters that you wrote to the children when you were very low. Strangely enough, one of my worries when I was ill was about writing good-quality farewell letters to the girls. In all the best books and films the dying mother always writes these incredibly poignant letters with invaluable insight and good advice. Whenever I tried it was a gibbering, embarrassing, sentimental mess of, 'I love you so much.' As far as good advice to guide them through the 'slings and arrows', the best I could come up with was, 'Sodium bicarbonate is great for sticky eyes if you want to avoid antibiotics.' Now that's something really special to carry with you throughout life. I'm so pleased we've established contact. Take it easy and e-mail me when you feel up to it.

To: **Delissa@splendidmums.com**
From: **Dot@noplacelikehome.com**
Subject: **Beth and the funeral**

Don't be alarmed by the above subject – there's no connection. I've just had my first e-mail from her. It's made me so happy, it's like being reunited with a long-lost sister after being separated at birth. I've missed her so much. Are you coming to Jack's funeral? We'd love to see you there, but I'm just wondering what to do with the children? I think they're too young for it all, especially Daisy. Sylvia's cleaning lady has offered to look after them during the service, but if you're not coming I could leave them with you for the day.

In answer to your question, no, I haven't spoken to Nikki as I'm still angry with her for even contemplating making that film. Am I being unreasonable? If I think of the number of nannies she's got through in her time, and the stories they must have to tell of life in the Soda household, I'm amazed she can look me in the eye. I don't know why I'm surprised as I've worked with her for so many years and know how unscrupulous she can be when it comes to work. I suppose I just thought it would be different with me. In retrospect it's surprising that she didn't try to film me dealing with chemotherapy and all the cancer treatment, but I suppose these days cancer confessions are rather passé. We've all seen it, heard it and bought the T-shirt.

To: **Bethearthmother@rooted.com**
From: **Dot@noplacelikehome.com**
Subject: **The last party**

Well, I suppose that's it. A funeral lends an air of finality to everything. It's official – we won't be seeing Jack again. Each morning I've woken up and half-expected his death to have been a dream, but this week has given us all a chance to come to terms with it. I won't bore you with too many details, but as funerals go it was pretty splendid. Sylvia made sure of that. I drove down on my own having dropped off the girls at Delissa's first thing. It was a beautiful October morning with a clear blue sky, the roads littered with conkers ('honkers' as Daisy calls them), and the smell of bonfire smoke wafting into the car as I drove through patches of mist, signalling the burning of the first leaves of Autumn.

We had agreed that I would go to the house before the funeral and I was a bit nervous about seeing Alex again. It felt like months since we had been together. He opened the door as soon as he heard the car on the gravel drive. Dressed in his one and only suit he looked unfamiliar, but he wrapped me in his arms and I wanted to laugh with relief. Every touch or gesture felt reassuring. We're still here, even if Jack isn't.

It was a strange atmosphere in the funeral car as we travelled slowly behind the coffin the few miles up the road to the local church. I've never really been involved in a funeral before. Obviously I've been to funerals but always as a guest, never as part of the family. What do you say when you're sitting in a car with a family in shock, just about to make a very public appearance?

Alex broke the tension, 'Do you think they could go any faster? Dad would hate to be late for his own funeral.'

We all giggled. I had the rescue remedy that you gave to help calm me during chemotherapy, so I passed round the bottle and we all took deep breaths as the drops settled on our tongues. I suppose it's the twenty-first century's answer to smelling salts.

I noticed that Sylvia had a small ladder in the back of her tights. It fascinated and worried me at the same time. It's the first time I've ever seen anything out of place on Sylvia. I wondered if it was the beginning of her life literally unravelling. I was torn between mentioning it and ignoring it. After all, a tiny ladder wasn't important on a day like today, except I knew it would have mattered desperately to Sylvia when Jack was still alive. I decided to keep quiet, as there was nothing we could do about it now, but I watched the ladder develop as we walked behind the coffin. It was like walking down the aisle at a wedding but with more personnel, and black being the order of the day.

Luckily my reading was one of the first, and it was with relief that I heard the vicar introduce me. I wasn't sure how long I would be able to control my emotions but the thought of making a fool of myself in front of the congregation stopped me from bursting into tears. Thank God the reading was almost over before it began. I speak quickly at the best of times and although I tried hard to slow it down the words came tumbling out. Sylvia looked puzzled but Alex was smiling encouragingly, and I felt for the first time in months that we were a team. I didn't care about the others. He was all that mattered. I made my way back to the family pew, and as I sat down beside him Alex reached for my hand. Rebecca's reading was a poem she had written herself. Listening to her read you could hear the slight lift at the end of her sentences that ten years in Australia had induced, but she never once stumbled or hesitated over a word and I marvelled at her self-control.

The vicar knew Jack, as he was what you might call a closet worshipper. We never talked about it as I expect he thought it was nobody else's business. The vicar spoke well and made it heartfelt and personal. I could see Alex's feet tapping nervously beside me. He was shaking with the effort to control his emotions, but when it was his turn his speech was incredible.

He started by talking about his father's war record and how that had shaped the rest of Jack's life, but he was also marvellously honest about his more irritating, or shall we say quirky, characteristics. Jack drove very slowly as if he had all the time in the world. If he saw people queuing at bus stops he would pull in and offer them a lift into town. He hated the idea of waste. If he was driving into town with an empty car and people were going in the same direction, it seemed perfectly natural to him to stop and offer them a lift. The rather bemused individuals would either decline, thinking he was a lunatic, or the more adventurous would accept the lift. Hours later, and overtaken by at least three buses, they would regret their decision and beg Jack to let them out at the first opportunity.

Everyone laughed remembering Jack's idiosyncrasies, but the mood changed as Alex came to the end of the speech and his voice began to break. The whole congregation seemed to lean forward collectively in a supportive gesture, willing him to continue. He stopped to try and take hold of his emotions, and then finished very simply, 'A day won't go by when I won't think of him and feel how proud I am to be his son.' I wanted to run up to the pulpit and take him in my arms, but for once I resisted making a spectacle of myself and as soon as he came back to the pew he took my hand again. It nestled into mine and I felt safe and home again.

I thought about Jack and his life. He achieved many things. Would people say that about me when I die? What have I achieved? I've made some interesting and entertaining television programmes, but nothing groundbreaking. I've tried to be a good friend, and despite our recent problems I love my husband very much. I'm extremely proud of the children, although I'm not sure how much credit I can take for them, but I suppose at this point in my life my biggest achievement is survival. The combination of that thought and the final hymn, 'Dear Lord and Father of mankind forgive our foolish ways . . .' was all the encouragement I needed to start crying. It felt like a personal message from Jack. Sylvia passed an immaculately pressed linen handkerchief down the pew to help me mop up while I downed the whole bottle of rescue remedy.

After the last prayer Alex and I walked out behind Sylvia and Rebecca, and as we came to the final pews I saw her. Jessica Bedmeigh was looking her splendid beautiful self in an understated black suit which had Joseph written all over it. She smiled sympathetically at Alex and I tightened my grip, clutching his hand firmly.

'I'm not letting you go,' I thought to myself.

Outside the church we were separated and I was cornered by Jack's elderly sister, who was telling me how much she had enjoyed my reading but wished I'd slowed down a bit. Over her shoulder I could see Jessica talking to, or rather draping herself over, Alex. Aunt Jane continued to chatter on: 'Wasn't it a lovely funeral'; 'We're so lucky the weather held off'; 'Jack would have loved it' while I tried to manoeuvre her closer to Alex and Jessica so that I could be in a better position to lip read. Jessica didn't stay long, but with a lingering parting kiss for Alex she walked to her soft-top black Mercedes coupé and drove off down the road to London. When will it stop? I thought about the hymn we had just finished singing and about the service. I was being stupid. Alex and I fit together, I must stop torturing myself. Just think of Siena.

Only family went to the burial and there's nothing to say except it was miserable. I defy anyone to remain teetotal, after that experience we all needed a drink. There were a lot of people at the house, most of whom I didn't know, but having to socialise dulled the misery and was a useful distraction for all of us. Jack's presence was still palpable, possibly because we all talked about him so much. The last of the guests left around six o'clock and Alex and I helped clear up. We left an exhausted Sylvia in Rebecca's capable hands.

Driving home together we didn't talk much. The children were staying overnight at Delissa's, so when we opened the front door the house was eerily quiet. Alex walked through the rooms, reminding himself of the smells and sounds of the old house.

'It's strange here without the children,' he said, looking a little lost.

'Have a bath while I cook supper,' I suggested.

'That would be nice,' he replied.

We were being careful with each other, polite almost like strangers, as it seemed so long since we were last alone together. We ate in companionable silence and went straight to bed. Lying side by side we stared at each other and then very gently he put his arm around me. He pulled me close to him and started kissing my forehead, then each eyelid, followed by the tip of my nose and every part of my face, and when we eventually made love, although everything was familiar, it felt different, more tender and profound.

When it was over, Alex started to sob. They were big, racking, heart-breaking sobs that rippled through his entire body. I hadn't seen him cry since Matilda was born. We used to lie side by side on the sofa, the baby straddled across my chest, close to my heart, and cry at the adverts, every emotion new and raw. I'd never heard a cry like this but I did what I could to comfort him, stroking his head and smoothing back his hair as you would a child's.

Eventually the sobs subsided and after a while, thinking he was asleep, I carefully tried to move my arm, which had gone dead. He held onto me and whispered like a boy, 'I was so frightened when you were ill.' He said it so quietly that I wasn't sure I'd heard correctly what he had said. 'I don't ever want to lose you, Dot.'

Relief washed over me. He still loves me.

'I know,' I whispered back, 'I know.'

When we finally slept I didn't even mind the snoring. I could put up with anything just to be close to him again.

Chapter Twenty Two

'The happiest women, like the happiest nations, have no history.'

George Eliot

To: **Jessica.bedmeigh@sultrysirens.co.uk**
From: **Dot@noplacelikehome.com**
Subject: **Hands off my husband**

Dear Jessica
Without wishing to be rude I would really appreciate it if you would stop flirting with my husband. His interest in you is entirely professional and despite appearances to the contrary he is basically a one-woman man – and that woman is me. Also, you have to consider that Alex comes as a package. Love him, love his children. Could you really consider taking on someone else's children while trying to maintain your busy career? So please stop all of this nonsense and find someone of your own to play with.
Best wishes (not)
Dorothy

To: Jay@mybestfriendisgay.com
From: **Dot@noplacelikehome.com**
Subject: **Jessica Bedmeigh (see attachment)**

Glad to have you back. At last I feel like everything is beginning to return to normal. Have just written e-mail to Jessica Bedmeigh which I will never send, but I enjoyed writing it anyway. Have enclosed it for your perusal and wondered if you'd like to add anything. Speak soon.

To: ProfwarmhandsHarrison@marsden.com
From: **Dot@noplacelikehome.com**
Subject: **Facts of life**

Thank you for calling me back – I just wanted to clarify what you said on the phone. I know it sounds ridiculous at our age, forgetting to use contraception, but from what you say it's really nothing to worry about because of the probable effects of chemotherapy and my age (menopause, here I come). By the way, how is Manchester United doing at the moment?

To: Bethearthmother@rooted.com
From: **Dot@noplacelikehome.com**
Subject: **Does Miss Turner ring any bells?**

I'm so pleased you're beginning to feel better. If the pills are working, don't stop popping them.

I thought of you today, you're often in my thoughts at the moment. You know how you remember the strangest things? Often, it's inconsequential days when nothing remarkable happens that stick in your mind. Well today, looking at Matilda's RE classwork book I was suddenly reminded of Miss Turner, our old RE teacher, who had black-rimmed glasses that made her look like Nana Mouskouri. It was one particular lesson I remember. Walking into the classroom, I think I was discussing Steven Cox's kissing technique or whether an Eggbutt snaffle or a Pelham bit was a more effective way of controlling a frisky pony. On the blackboard, written in large letters, was a selection of words and our task was to put them in order of priority. I can't remember all of them but they definitely included: Love, Friendship, Wealth, Health, Happiness and Faith.

After a good twenty minutes, to allow us time to really think about our answer, Miss Turner got up from her desk, and as she walked to the front of the classroom she caught my eye.

'Dorothy, come and share your thoughts with us.' She handed me the marker pen and said, 'Write the order you have chosen on the board.'

I think I put Love first, followed by Friendship, Happiness, Wealth, Health and ending on Faith. Miss Turner smiled as she read out the list in the order I had chosen.

'Who else put Love first?' she asked the class. I think every girl put up a hand. 'Do you all agree with Dorothy's order of words?'

Generally there was a consensus, but some had put Wealth higher than Friendship (it was that sort of school) and Wendy Parker, our resident communist, asked why Politics wasn't one of the words listed. Miss Turner then swung round on the class with real passion in her voice.

'What you have all forgotten is Health. It's way down on all your lists, but just think about it. How easy is it to love someone if you feel ill all the time? How can you enjoy your wealth if you feel sick? How can you be happy if you have no energy? You're all lucky you have never been seriously ill. But please don't take your health for granted.'

It certainly got us all thinking and we all agreed that Love deserved its place at the top of the list but, as if to prove a point, six months later I got glandular fever. Years later when I was diagnosed with cancer I remembered the lesson. Her words rang in my head and haunted my dreams, and I thought about it again when I heard you were ill. Talk about learning a lesson, it's more like having our noses well and truly rubbed in it.

Please don't be hard on yourself about Will. I don't think this has anything to do with your mothering skills. I hate this concept of the perfect mother. The more I think about it the more nebulous it is – blaming us for everything that goes wrong and giving credit where it's not necessarily due. What is a good mother? Ultimately so much comes down to character and personality.

If I'm honest and look carefully at Matilda and Daisy, they haven't changed in character from the day they were born. Matilda came out wide-eyed, looking around eagerly as if to say, 'Where's the party?' She gave me a terrible night after the birth, nothing would satisfy her, she wouldn't latch on, she didn't want to be cuddled, her nappy was pristine but still she bawled her eyes out. In desperation I started to sing to her, and for some inexplicable reason the only song that I could remember was 'Downtown', but it seemed to do the trick and by the morning she began to settle. We got through it together, and as we stared at each other I had a vivid sense that this was how our life would be – extraordinary, but it wasn't going to be easy. Daisy, on the other hand, was a content and happy baby from day one (if you ignore her addiction to Calpol). She was happy to feed, happy to sleep, happy to be cuddled. I suspect that will be the pattern of her life.

Would anyone watching that class over twenty-three years ago, seeing us sitting together in our short grey-flannel skirts and white shirts, cuffs flapping, top buttons undone, ties loose around our necks, earlobes still pink from just having had them pierced, and grey socks falling around our ankles, have predicted what would happen in our lives? Or that all these years later we'd still be good friends? I don't think I could have coped without you. We've survived Steven Cox, exams, work, marriage, children, and cancer. I know we can survive this too.

To: **Delissa@splendidmums.com**
From: **Dot@noplacelikehome.com**
Subject: **'There's a bright golden haze on the meadow . . .'**

Wasn't it a beautiful morning? Blue, blue skies with the odd cloud looking like it's been painted onto the perfect picture, and a chill in the air which means it's time to pull out your favourite jumper. I love the autumn. There's something about this time of the year which ironically feels full of promise. It reminds me of new beginnings, maybe it's to do with starting a new class at school or going to university. I always seem to start new projects at this time of year. I'm feeling rather content. The children are being delightful and you'll be pleased to hear that Alex and I feel back on track. It's made me realise quite how miserable I was when we weren't talking.

I went to see your Chinese acupuncturist, Dr Arr. I now know how he got his name. It's the noise you make when he puts in the needles, 'Ahh!' I thought you said it doesn't hurt. I did get used to it and found him very interesting. He asked about my illness and how I had coped and why I wanted to see him now.

'I want to stop a recurrence and get my energy back,' I told him.

After he'd felt my pulse and looked at my tongue he started placing the needles. At one point I looked at what he was doing but I could feel myself beginning to faint so I looked away quickly.

'Very good for immune system,' he said, his accent still quite thick.

'Sounds good.'

I couldn't stop myself talking about how I'd discovered my lump and how I still found it hard to stop worrying about it coming back. He put in the last needle and then said casually, 'Do you want to live with cancer or die with cancer?' I was shocked but it certainly shut me up. Are you sure he's any good?

Last weekend we went back to Sylvia's to help sort through Jack's clothes. She kept trying to persuade Alex to take some of his more recent jackets or shirts, but apart from the fact they're not really his style the thought of wearing his dead father's clothes did not appeal. The only thing he kept was a battered old Panama hat. Passing on the crown.

As Sylvia was serving up lunch she said, 'Alex, you sit here,' indicating the chair where Jack usually sat. I saw a look of horror cross Alex's face as if his mother had suggested something indecent. He deliberately walked round the table and sat next to me, and I realised that being back home so soon after Jack's death was difficult for him. In fact there's a lot I'm beginning to realise about Alex. He coped so well when I was ill, I didn't appreciate how frightening it was for him. I think it's much easier having to deal with trauma yourself – you cope because you have to – but I never realised how difficult it was for all of you until now.

Great news that Carl is coming over for Christmas, as I can't wait to meet him. Everyone must come to us for Christmas lunch at Acorn Avenue, which will be a first for me but I'm looking forward to it. I've got a day off today. I've just waved goodbye to Alex and the children, who are going to see a film and indulge in a McDonald's (but I'm not supposed to know that). They are going to have a day of unhealthy eating without me fussing over them, and I'm going to have a day to myself for the first time since I gave up work. I've already had breakfast in bed, which feels like luxury, and I'm seeing Beth this afternoon. It feels strange knowing I can walk out of the house on my own and do whatever I like. Ah, freedom. This sort of thing could go to a mother's head.

To: **Bethearthmother@rooted.com**
From: **Dot@noplacelikehome.com**
Subject: **The maternal link**

I really enjoyed our walk this afternoon and I've been thinking about what we were talking about. Yes, you're right, having children has made me understand my mother better. I can see why everyone thinks she's a splendid woman. She's a very strong character who has had to learn to fend for herself. But you know, although I feel terribly disloyal saying it, I'm not sure that splendid women make the best mothers because they're too busy being splendid. There's too much ego involved.

You talked about feeling you'd lost sight of who you are. It was your choice to be at home with the children and I know, up to now, you haven't regretted it for a minute. I think the difficulty we all face, if we're lucky enough not to have to work in order to feed and clothe our children, is how much our desires and needs have to be sublimated for the sake of the children. We decided to bring them into the world and we have to accept the responsibility that goes with having children. But they have to see us as individuals too, with our own needs. If we do our job properly the children will leave home and lead their own lives, and then where will that leave us? I think that's what really worried Mum and Alex when I gave up work. What happens later on? We want to be ourselves but we want to be there for the children as well. Tricky, isn't it?

To: **NikkiSoda@ambitiousproductions.com**
From: **Dot@noplacelikehome.com**
Subject: **Rapprochement**

I can't say I'm sorry to hear that you've abandoned the idea of making a documentary based on Sarah's book. I know you have a good nose for popular documentaries, but surely you could see this one was too close to home and also basically untrue. I'm sure there are lots of stories about families behaving despicably to their nannies but we weren't one of them, and I had always thought our friendship was worth more than fifty-five minutes of sensationalist television. I'm glad you've come to your senses at last. Of course I'm still talking to you, and as an olive branch do you fancy coming to us for Christmas lunch? I know it's a few months away but you'd be very welcome. It's all going to be different this year as Sylvia will be on her own, Mum is bringing Carl and it will be the first time I've cooked a turkey. All in all, it could be anthropologically interesting. Obviously I'll see you before then, and we'll speak soon.

To: **Nanny.sarah@indispensable.com**
From: **Dot@noplacelikehome.com**
Subject: **Request granted**

I received your e-mail and was a little surprised at your suggestion after everything that's been happening, but I expect the girls would like to see you as it has been quite a few months since your last visit. So you may as well come for tea – on Friday?

To: **Delissa@splendidmums.com**
From: **Dot@noplacelikehome.com**
Subject: **Strange meeting**

Have just had e-mail from Sarah wanting to come and see us. I'm amazed she has the nerve to step into the lioness's den but I'm intrigued to see how she will handle it. Do you think I've been wise?

To: **Jay@mybestfriendisgay.com**
From: **Dot@noplacelikehome.com**
Subject: **Catching up**

Have you seen Beth yet? She seems to be making good progress but is still coming to terms with what has happened. She's speaking in psychobabble but at least she's communicating, so I'm not complaining. Alex and I feel back on course, the Munchkins seem happy and all is well in the land of Dot, so I do believe Mum's acupuncturist is beginning to have an effect.

The girls have a new obsession, which is gathering as many leaflets as possible. Shopping with them is never easy at the best of times but now we're weighed down with leaflets from the bank, the chemist's and Claire's Accessories. I have to frogmarch them past travel agents as quickly as possible as I glance nervously at all those catalogues and special-offer leaflets/tantalisingly close to the shop window. At least they're free, but I don't understand why they find them so fascinating. It just means Acorn Avenue is very popular with Jehovah's Witnesses.

'Have you heard the word?'

'No but, boy, have we got the leaflets.'

The recycling lorries have to do a couple of trips a week past our house. I'm sure there'll be complaints from the council soon, and our already hefty council tax bill will treble.

Surprise, surprise, we had a visit from Nanny Sarah yesterday and I wish you could have been there to see it. She arrived looking nervous and for the first time ever she brought me a present. I looked at the book-shaped parcel, not wanting to open it, dreading the thought that it was going to be a leather-bound copy of her book, which would have added insult to injury. I reluctantly tore the tissue paper to reveal a beautiful hand-crafted notebook with blank pages made out of parchment paper. She looked embarrassed.

'For you to write your book. If I can do it, anyone can, and I know you've always wanted to.'

Hasn't she heard of computers? I have to admit I was touched by the thought but the mention of her book reminded me of how upset I'd been by all the publicity. It was like ripping the scab off a recent cut.

Ungraciously mumbling a thank you, I called upstairs to the children who were singing into their yellow plastic karaoke microphone. You, of all people, will be pleased to hear that Matilda has now discovered the delights of Abba, so every time we get in the car 'Mamma Mia' echoes through the suburban streets and across the green. Daisy was trying to copy her big sister, but to the tune of 'Money, money, money' she was singing, 'Mummy, Mummy, Mummy in a rich man's world.' Should I be encouraging this? At least we're not onto Britney yet.

To my great surprise they didn't rush downstairs or fling themselves at Sarah. The months apart had emotionally distanced them. Daisy was beginning to forget and Matilda was unforgiving that she had been abandoned. They were polite but not relaxed. Sarah tried all the usual tricks to ingratiate herself and I watched, fascinated to see the change in the girls. They softened a little when she asked them about the summer holidays, and they enthusiastically told her all about the camping trip, competing for attention. Daisy then sat on my knee and started making faces with my mouth while I tried not to laugh.

Sarah only stayed for half an hour. She quickly made her excuses, but as she got to the hallway and picked up her denim jacket from the bottom of the banisters she said to me, 'Listen, Dot, I'm sorry if the book caused you any . . .' she hesitated.

'. . . embarrassment,' I said, finding the word for her.

'I never said it was you. It was a mixture of all my friends' experiences and some personal ones but, I admit, not while I was working for you. I wouldn't have stayed so long if you'd treated me like that. Anyway, it's why I pulled out of the documentary. Nikki told me you were pretty upset, and it hadn't really occurred to me that you would think it was personal. I thought you would understand that it was fiction.'

'The problem wasn't me,' I told her, 'it was everyone else. It's other people's perception. However much you say, "We weren't like that. It wasn't us," they just don't believe you.'

'Well, I'm sorry. Maybe you should write a book about the hell of having nannies.'

'Not a bad idea, but I think I want to move away from domesticity. Thanks for the notebook. God knows when I'll get time to fill it. Maybe in a couple of years when Daisy goes to school full time.'

She went to go and then turned back to say, 'You're doing a great job with the girls. I can't believe how much they've grown up since I last saw them.'

I wanted to hug her, so I did. It was a little awkward but she smiled and gave the girls a kiss each and walked out of our lives, I suspect forever. Is that called closure?

After she'd left I realised what she had said. So Sarah was the one who had pulled out of filming the documentary. Nikki had deliberately misled me into thinking she was the one who had decided not to carry on making the programme. God, she's incorrigible.

To: **Jay@mybestfriendisgay.com**
From: **Dot@noplacelikehome.com**
Subject: **A distinct breeze**

Jay, are you OK? I detect a chilly tone in your e-mail. If something is bothering you, you would tell me, wouldn't you?

To: **Jay@mybestfriendisgay.com**
From: **Dot@noplacelikehome.com**
Subject: **Proverbial spanners**

You can't be serious. Thank goodness you've mentioned it. Yes, I did see Kevin that night at Oscar's and I'm deeply offended at his suggestion that I was all over Luke. More to the point, Kevin and I didn't even speak to each other and I certainly never said that I felt abandoned by you. I know he's never liked me but I think I know why he's trying to drive a wedge between us, which puts you in a difficult position. If he's saying you've got to choose between your friend or your boyfriend then you have to ask yourself why he's doing this, and is that the sort of relationship you need? All I ask is that you don't believe everything he says. Go on seeing him if he's making you happy, but please remember how much I value our friendship and never, ever underestimate how important you are to me.

To: **LukeLloyd@talent.co.uk**
From: **Dot@noplacelikehome.com**
Subject: **Magic moments**

Thank you for the videocassette and note you left in the porch. As I watched it I felt nostalgic, but it seems like years not months have passed since we were all in Cornwall. Luke, please don't complicate things. If it was just about you and me, maybe it would be different but there are too many other people involved. We do have a great time together, you're almost irresistible, but I love Alex and I'm old-fashioned enough to want to try and make my marriage work. Please try to understand.

To: **Bethearthmother@rooted.com**
From: **Dot@noplacelikehome.com**
Subject: **Be prepared**

Have just received a romantic and persuasive note from Luke. He's being very persistent and I'm half-flattered, but also frightened of seeing him, because I can't deny I still have those feelings. As diversionary tactics I'm beginning to plan Christmas. I used to despise those women who finish all their Christmas shopping by the end of October. I prided myself on leaving it all to the last week before Christmas, when the shops are empty and everything is reduced. That was before I had children. I tried it last year and nearly gave myself a nervous breakdown (oops, sorry to mention it) when I couldn't get the purple microscooter Matilda had specifically requested.

Children do complicate things because although we're now in November, they may change their mind about what they want, depending on the last advert they've seen on television. This year I think we're going to be safe with Baby Annabel for both of the girls. She giggles, she cries and – even more delightfully – she burps after drinking her milk. What more could you ask for? I must say that, personally, I draw the line at bodily fluids.

I had an interesting challenge the other day when Molly came to play after school. Kate came to pick her up looking exhausted. I know how she feels – I've been so tired lately, I actually had to have an afternoon nap the other day but she's got the excuse of recovering from a nasty stomach bug. She walked into the kitchen, collapsed onto the sofa and said, 'Thank goodness. I'm feeling rather pleased with myself as I've just bought all the kids' stockings, so it's now just the presents I've got to get.'

Matilda, who was trying to get every last drop of custard,

stopped scraping the bowl and stared at Kate who, immediately realising what she had said, turned beetroot. She looked at me beseechingly as if to say, 'Help. Get me out of this mess.' Molly had already got down from the table to find her shoes, socks and knickers (don't ask, I don't) amidst the pile of dressing-up clothes scattered about Matilda's bedroom.

Matilda demanded, 'What do you mean? What about Father Christmas?'

'I'll explain when they've gone,' I said, beating a hasty retreat and giving myself some valuable time to think as I rushed upstairs to help Molly find her shoes. They left with Kate mouthing at me, 'I'm so sorry,' over their heads.

As soon as the door was closed Matilda, incisive as a prosecuting lawyer, said, 'Molly's mum just said she'd finished buying the kids' stockings, but she doesn't have to do that – it's Father Christmas's job.'

'This year,' I said, desperately thinking on my feet, 'Father Christmas is so busy that he asked Molly's mum to help him out and she agreed. Wasn't that kind of her? Especially when she's not feeling very well.'

'Will Kate be buying my presents?'

'I don't think so.'

'Why not?'

'Because he only needed her to help out a little.'

'Will she have to go and deliver the presents on Christmas Eve or even drive the sleigh?' she continued, warming to her theme.

'No, I think he'll be sorted by then. I think he's planning to recruit some more elves,' I said knowledgeably. Who said I wasn't an inventive mother? But with Matilda you have to follow everything through to a logical conclusion. You can't just palm her off with a lame excuse or half-baked explanations.

'Why don't you offer to help him?' she demanded.

'Well, if he asks, I will,' I replied. She made me sit down immediately and write a letter to him, offering my services, and then sent it up the chimney. As if I don't have enough to do.

Another potential disappointment is the auditions for the Christmas play at school. This year they're doing a play within a play about two children who travel back in time to learn the truth about the Nativity story. Matilda, like all the girls, is desperate to play Mary. In fact she's convinced the part is already hers and is developing her Madonna expression (we're talking Jesus's mother, not the international megastar) and has taken to wearing blue around the house. I've tried to subtly prepare her for a disappointment just in case she isn't cast, pointing out the advantages in being one of the angels (pretty costumes and the possibility of wearing glitter), but my main argument is that they usually go for brunettes to play Mary. This didn't faze her at all, 'I don't mind dyeing my hair. After all, that's what you do, Mama.' You never know, she may get the part.

I've just spent hours pouring over Christmas card catalogues. Do you think I should buy cancer research cards or is that a bit pointed? I don't want people thinking I've become obsessed but having said that, it is a good cause. To be honest I prefer the design on the diabetes charity cards. What a bummer I got the wrong illness. Actually in the spirit of forward planning I've worked out two New Year resolutions already.

The first is to ignore the mountains of catalogues which make you feel that a set of reindeer wall sconces and matching candle holders, festive Father Christmas salt and pepper shakers and packs of shatterproof tree baubles are absolute essentials. I've even been contemplating ordering a Santa Claus draft excluder which looks like Santa's doing the splits, but whose unique selling point is that his cheeks turn red when he sings. I ask you! My second, perhaps more important, resolution is not to talk about cancer unless it's absolutely necessary. I'm going to ban the words, 'When I had cancer . . .' Next year is going to be a cancer-free zone.

Beth, we would love it if you all wanted to come to us for Christmas – the more the merrier – but I need to borrow a copy of Delia's Christmas cookbook.

Chapter Twenty Three

'We have to distrust each other.
It's our only defence against betrayal.'
Tennessee Williams

To: **Delissa@splendidmums.com**
From: **Dot@noplacelikehome.com**
Subject: **Christmas casting**

It's not even Christmas yet and I'm exhausted. Dr Arr has persuaded me to go once a week to get my immune system really strong. I think he's baffled that I haven't been showing a significant improvement. For a while I was feeling fantastic but recently everything has become an effort again.

The really bad news is that Matilda has been cast as an innkeeper in the school play. She's not even *the* innkeeper. She's disappointed and I'm furious, as it's such a waste of her obvious talent. She's so good at remembering lines and singing songs, her timing and sense of rhythm are excellent, but to put her in the back row is criminal. Mr Poppy of course agreed with me, but said it wasn't up to him. I couldn't resist saying something to Mrs Steel, who is in charge of casting. She hardly let me finish my sentence before she manoeuvred me out of the school hall with a brusque, 'We take great care when casting these plays, Mrs Knight, and we thought it was time for someone else to get a share of the limelight. It's not just about acting, you know. It's about building up confidence and fair play. Thank you and good bye.' If ever they need a replacement for Anne Robinson on *The Weakest Link*, Mrs Steel would be perfect.

Kate, Molly's mum, is being wooed by all the children with sweets as Matilda has told them she has a direct line to Father Christmas. I caught Matilda smuggling out a Tridias catalogue with the page corners turned down at the extremely expensive pink-and-purple fairy castle, which she was hoping to show Kate just in case she could put in a good word with Father Christmas. Matilda went to play with Molly last week and Kate rang me afterwards to tell me about a conversation she had with Matilda. She was making up a story about three ducks.

'One of them had cancer and died,' said Matilda with no emotion at all.

Kate was taken aback and didn't say anything but thought she ought to mention it to me. It came as a shock as superficially Matilda seems to have been completely unaffected by my illness. Maybe we need to have a little talk, but I don't want to make things worse or really worry her.

To: **Alex@himindoors.com**
From: **Dot@noplacelikehome.com**
Subject: **Ducks and death**

Have just heard that Matilda has been talking to Molly and her mum, Kate, about ducks, cancer and death. I've never talked to her about the possibility of dying but she's a bright girl and obviously she has picked up on something. Do you think I should talk to her?

To: **Delissa@splendidmums.com**
From: **Dot@noplacelikehome.com**
Subject: **Mission accomplished**

Have just had emotional moment with my eldest daughter. Alex agreed with you and thought that I needed to talk to her, so after their bath and story I sat down on Matilda's bed and said, 'You remember when I was ill. Do you know what was wrong with me?'

'Yes, you had cancer.'

'That's right, and what do you think that means?'

She looked embarrassed and shuffled down under the bedclothes.

'You can say anything you want. I won't be cross and I won't get upset, I promise.'

I wasn't getting anywhere and I thought maybe I shouldn't push it if she didn't want to talk about it. After all, I didn't want to make a big issue of it, I just wanted to reassure her if she was worried. I changed tack.

'Do you know the story about the three ducks?' I asked innocently.

'Oh yes,' she said enthusiastically. 'One of them got cancer and died.' She blanched as soon as she said it and said immediately, 'I'm sorry.'

I tried to reassure her, 'Don't be sorry. Does that worry you? Do you worry that because I had cancer I might die?'

A beat while we looked at each other and then her little face crumpled and the tears started to run down her face, 'I hated it when you were ill. It was horrid. You looked so sad.'

I held her close and said as calmly as I could, 'I know it wasn't much fun, but it's over now and you mustn't worry. There are lots of different sorts of cancer and not everyone who gets cancer dies. Look at me, do I look like someone about to die?'

She looked at me and shook her head. 'But if God loves us, why does he make us ill?'

Good question, I thought to myself. 'Because you can learn from it. You fall over in the playground and you learn not to run in the same place or in the same way.'

'And not to run with 'Enry because he's so rough.'

'That's right. If everything was smooth and easy in life you wouldn't learn anything.'

Somewhere in the back of my mind I remembered a conversation I'd had with Jack when he asked me if I'd learnt anything from being ill. Well, have I?

Matilda seemed content with my explanation. I kissed the top of her head and she smiled as though reassured. Within minutes she'd dropped off to sleep. It was definitely the right thing to do, and the good news is that I can't die now because I've promised Matilda I won't – and I didn't even cross my fingers behind my back.

To: **LukeLloyd@talent.co.uk**
From: **Dot@noplacelikehome.com**
Subject: **Dangerous liaisons**

Luke, you've got to stop calling me. Trust me, distance is what we both need at the moment. Oh, shit . . .

To: **Bethearthmother@rooted.com**
From: **Dot@noplacelikehome.com**
Subject: **Disaster**

I've just been so stupid and spilt my cup of Tension Tamer tea (mix of peppermint, chamomile, cinnamon, ginger and old socks) all over the keys of my laptop. Bubbles appeared on the screen, it was like watching one of those Super 8 black-and-white home movies when the projector snarls up the film and begins to burn the negative. It went all swirly and bubbly, then for a minute it looked like aliens from another planet were trying to establish contact until the screen went blank.

I've tried to mop it up with kitchen towel and, trying not to panic, I rang Alex who, once he realised it was just the laptop and not one of the children I'd chucked scalding tea over, calmly suggested using a hairdryer. I then rang the helpline in some far-flung corner of the world and was talked down by a kindly geek who was very patient with me, not for one second making me feel like the hysterical computer-illiterate idiot I am. I've unscrewed the keyboard and placed it near to the radiator to dry out overnight and they're sending a computer ambulance to collect it in a couple of days. I feel bereft but Alex has kindly let me use his big computer in the study. And that is how the trouble began . . .

I don't know if you feel up to this but I just wanted to get an outside opinion. As I switched on the computer I saw a separate folder entitled 'e-mails to Jessica'. I wouldn't last a second on Temptation Island. Post-production on *Tess* is more or less finished, so why were they still contacting each other? I went downstairs to make myself another cup of tea, this time making sure it didn't go near the computer. I sat staring at the screen. I know Alex's password, just as he knows mine, but I would never expect him to use it. It's like reading someone's diary; you just don't do it unless you expect to read something you'll regret.

Do you remember when we were twelve and I read your diary? I was so upset by the reference to my thunder thighs, and the fact that you thought Susan Simpson was prettier than me. I thought I'd learnt my lesson, but I hadn't. Heart thumping I typed in the password – Matilda. It took seconds to log on and access the list of e-mails, which were endless. I went straight to the last few e-mails on the list, most of which were technical, unemotional and pertinent to the film, but the last one was much more affectionate.

'I've missed you too – why don't we meet up next week after the grade to celebrate? All love, A. X'

OK, it's not exactly a declaration of love, but it suggests a level of intimacy between two work colleagues which is worrying. Do you think I'm overreacting? The problem is, I still don't really know the nature of their relationship. He hasn't been straight with me. He's never taken me in his arms and laughed at me, saying, 'Of course I'm not having an affair with Jessica. How could I look at another woman when I have you?' Oh God, this is eating away at me. I'm going to have to talk to him, but then he'll know that I've read his e-mails. I'm exhausted. I've got to have a lie down.

To: **Bethearthmother@rooted.com**
From: **Dot@noplacelikehome.com**
Subject: **Good advice**

You are absolutely right, I'm just going to stop thinking about Alex and Jessica – I'm being ridiculous.

Good news that Will has been accepted into Mount View, which sounds ideal for him. Don't worry that he hasn't opened up to you yet, as long as he's confiding in Tom and Ella. He's probably worried about upsetting you again after all that's happened. Think what a shock it must have been for him, feeling that he was responsible for making his mother ill. It must have made him even angrier and confirmed his bad opinion of himself. What about writing to him? Both of you might find it easier than talking face to face. I find it helps, if only Matilda and Daisy could read more than words of two syllables.

To: **NikkiSoda@ambitiousproductions.com**
From: **Dot@noplacelikehome.com**
Subject: **When do you have time to work?**

Thank you for e-mail informing me of husband's intimate behaviour with your worst nightmare, aka Jessica Bedmeigh. What would I do without you to mess up my life?

To: **Bethearthmother@rooted.com**
From: **Dot@noplacelikehome.com**
Subject: **Shit and fan**

Now I have no need to tell Alex I read his e-mails because Nikki has just informed me that she saw Alex and Jessica behaving in an intimate manner in a restaurant. What does that mean? Were they snogging or having sex on top of their spotted dick? You can imagine how incensed I was by the time Alex came home.

'I'm going to be calm and fair,' I kept telling myself. Remember, calm and fair, calm and fair.

'Why didn't you tell me you were having lunch with Jessica?' I snarled as he walked through the door.

He looked like a wasp had stung him, 'Oh God, not this again, Dot.'

I was shaking as I said, as proudly as I could, but it came out as a whiny whimper, 'Just be honest with me, Alex, and tell me what's going on. Have you had an affair or are you still having an affair with her? Don't let me carry on like this. It's unfair on both of us.'

He hesitated, watching me as I nervously folded drying-up cloths into a neat pile.

'Come here.' He took me in his arms and looked directly into my eyes, 'Dot, for the last time, I am not having an affair with Jessica.'

I almost believed him. 'Nikki saw you today.'

He turned away, 'That bloody woman. What is it with Nikki? Has it ever occurred to you that she stirs things up because she's a jealous cow?' He took a beer out of the fridge, opened it, took a swig and slumped down onto the sofa. 'OK, you want complete honesty, I'll give it to you. I admit I am attracted to Jessica. I'd have to be made out of stone not to be. But don't tell me you're not attracted to other people? It's natural, just because we're married it doesn't mean that you immediately cut off all feelings.' He paused, checking my face for a response. I was scared of what he was about to say. Whoever said honesty is the best policy had probably never been married.

He continued, 'Yeah, I admit, we do flirt and we have a great working relationship. She thinks I'm good and I'm impressed with her producing skills, and I want to work with her again. It's like a marriage of sorts. You know how rare it is to find that sort of thing at work, and I want to make the most of it. It could be good for all of us, including you. But I have never kissed her or shagged her because I'm married to you, and I love you in spite of your eccentricities.'

I wanted to believe him. He offered me a swig of his beer and then pulled me down onto the sofa beside him.

'Dot, think what we've been through together – the children, your illness, Dad dying – I couldn't have coped without you. We have to trust each other. That's all it's about. Trust.'

He was right. I'd allowed myself to feed on Nikki's poisonous prejudices. It was such a relief for it all to be out in the open. I realise I do trust him, but I have to accept that he is human.

To: **Jay@mybestfriendisgay.com**
From: **Dot@noplacelikehome.com**
Subject: **Impressive displays of self-control**

I know we're having some time out at the moment, but I just wanted to tell you how well I've handled a potentially difficult situation. Since Jack died I've been trying to avoid Luke. We were becoming too intimate and the flirting was becoming uncomfortably serious. I was almost out of control but I can't imagine being unfaithful to Alex, even if Jack's death hadn't brought me to my senses. Up until today I'd been successfully keeping Luke at arm's length, dropping Matilda off early at school, not shopping at the village and taking roundabout detours to make sure I never walked past his house. He e-mails me regularly or drops in cards, tapes – anything to keep up the contact – but today he caught me off guard. Alex decided to take the girls for a jaunt to the Science Museum, and I had a blissful two hours to myself. I had just lain down on the bed, overcome with exhaustion, having written a list of all the things I needed to do when, I heard a knock on the door.

'Bloody Jehovah's Witnesses,' I thought, but they were

persistent so I heaved myself off the bed and opened the door to see Luke.

'Good afternoon, Madam, you're the lucky winner of our pick 'n' mix raffle and your fabulous prize is afternoon tea with local celebrity, Luke Lloyd. Lemon twizzle cake?' He offered me a parcel and smiled slightly nervously. I laughed in spite of my determined efforts not to give him any encouragement. He looked over my shoulder.

'Is everyone out? Can I come in?'

Now what should I have done? I was pleased to see him and it would have been rude to slam the door in his face. Before I knew it he had stepped inside, shut the door, taken my face in his hands and kissed me. There it was again, that rush of warmth – the feeling of being a teenager, plus accompanying alarm bell.

I pulled away. 'No,' I said, as firmly as I could.

He had a look on his face that said, 'Why should I stop?'

'Look, we've got to talk this through.'

'Oh, so now you want to talk,' he replied.

'Shall I put the kettle on?' I said, praying that domestic activity would bring me to my senses.

'I don't think it would suit you,' he joked. 'Sorry, old gag.'

Grimacing, I switched on the kettle and unwrapped the lemon twizzle cake.

'You sit down that side of the table, and I'll sit here.' I indicated a chair, making sure that the table between us would prevent any contact.

He laughed, 'You're making me feel like a dangerous animal. Grrr,' he teased me and then, seeing I didn't smile, he said, ' I promise I won't pounce on you again, without a proper invitation. I've missed you, Dottie.'

With two mugs of steaming tea and the comfort of cake, we talked. I decided to be brutal.

'Luke, what is this all about? Tell me honestly, is this a bit of fun or do you love me madly?' He looked uncomfortable and twisted awkwardly in his chair. 'Do you really want to leave Jules and the boys?'

He stared at me. 'There's something about you, Dot. I've always thought you were special but . . .' he dropped his head '. . . love? I just want . . .' his voice trailed off.

'Yes?' I prompted.

'I don't know what I want.'

'I don't think it's hard to work out. You want what you can't have. But if you could have me you wouldn't want me for long. I think I've always been the one that got away and that's niggled at you all these years. But I'm right, you don't want to leave Jules, do you?'

'No,' he said, deflated. He looked at me like a child looks at their mother when they've ruined their best imaginary game and said, 'Time for bed.' I could see he was angry with me for destroying the illusion. He sighed his resignation. Game over. It was then he began to talk.

'You know, Jules and I met when we were teenagers. She knows me better than anyone. We haven't been together all that time, we've had long breaks when we thought we were in love with other people, but you know something kept pulling us back together. Then she got pregnant with Hamish and it seemed the right thing to do to get married. I know that sounds awful but the baby made us see sense. She's a great mother and good at her job. I can't knock her.'

'She's an architect, right?' I asked, knowing perfectly well as I'd read all those articles in the supermarket magazines, cover to cover.

'Yeah. She's incredibly capable. If anything was to happen to me, I don't think it would change her life that much, or let's just say she'd cope. She's financially independent, she understands the boys, has close friends and family. I sometimes wonder where I fit in?' He was looking extremely sorry for himself.

I sighed. 'I suppose it makes a change from "my wife doesn't understand me". More a case of my wife understands me too well.'

'Yeah. She understands me all right, but she doesn't need me.'

'Are you sure about that?'

We carried on talking and I rather liked this new role as agony aunt, and started thinking I should offer my services to Relate. After an hour he got up to leave. I opened the front door.

'So I suppose a shag is out of the question?' he asked, half-seriously.

'Get out of here,' I replied, grinning as I pushed him out the door onto the path.

'OK, OK, friends it is,' he said as he put his arms up in the air in a gesture of mock surrender. 'Is it OK for friends to kiss goodbye?'

I hesitated, 'Just this once,' and he kissed me on the lips for the last time.

'I'll call you,' he said, and when I looked nervous he added, 'about the programmes.'

'Bye, Luke,' and I shut the door feeling quite pleased with myself.

To: **Jay@mybestfriendisgay.com**
From: **Dot@noplacelikehome.com**
Subject: **The end of the world**

Is Alex with you? Sorry to bother you again but something terrible has just happened. After Luke left it was only a matter of minutes before the door burst open and the girls came rushing in, fighting to be the first to tell me about their afternoon. I took them straight upstairs for a bath and once in their pyjamas they pleaded, 'Can Dadda read to us tonight?' I went downstairs to find Alex crouching in front of the video, and frozen on the screen was a close-up of me laughing into the camera. Alex didn't look up when I entered the room.

'Alex? What are you doing?'

Still without looking at me he said, 'When did you get this?' It was Luke's video of our holiday in Cornwall.

'Oh, it was something Luke dropped off,' I said as innocently as I could.

'Was that before he kissed you?' It wasn't just the image on the screen that was frozen.

'What are you talking about?'

'I saw you. I was driving past, trying to find a parking space, and I saw you. I couldn't believe it but I kept on driving round the block to give me time to think. Thank God the girls were asleep in the back. On your own doorstep, Dot. Christ, you must think me an idiot.' Now he looked at me, and I wished he wouldn't. 'No wonder you can't trust me if you can't trust yourself.'

'Alex, it's not what you think,' I pleaded.

Matilda called down, 'Dadda, will you come and read to us?'

'You go,' he said.

'But it's you they want.'

'Well, you'll have to find some explanation, won't you?' he said, his tone angry and bitter.

Almost in a daze I went upstairs and despite their protests read the girls *Madeline at Christmas*, finding it hard to concentrate on the words. By the time I got downstairs Alex had gone. No note, nothing. Is he with you? Please get him to call so I can explain. I can't believe this is happening.

Chapter Twenty Four

'One fool at least in every married couple.'
Henry Fielding

To: **Alex@himindoors.com**
From: **Dot@noplacelikehome.com**
Subject: **Love means always having to say you're sorry**

I know you're angry with me and I don't deny that I have behaved badly, but not quite as badly as you believe. Alex, I love you with all my heart and I want you to come home. The children are confused but I'm not. Thinking about it, you were right when you said I couldn't trust you because I couldn't trust myself. Maybe I'm naive, but I really did think that when I got married I would stop having feelings for anyone but you. But as you said, human nature isn't like that, and it was such a shock the first time I realised that I was attracted to someone else. I've never been completely unfaithful to you but, yes, I did kiss Luke. I promise you that that was all it ever was and I was never close to sleeping with him. Call it a mid-life crisis, a post-illness madness, or a defence mechanism but I admit I was flattered by the attention, especially when I thought that you were fed up with me and falling for Jessica.

For the past year you and I have been like trains travelling on parallel tracks. We've hardly talked and it's terrifying how quickly our marriage has deteriorated. Perhaps I should have consulted you more when I decided to give up work? Maybe you should have been reassuring when you knew I was jealous of Jessica, and perhaps I'm too demanding, but I need more support and encouragement from you.

God, being ill now feels relatively simple in comparison to all of this emotional upheaval, at least everything was clearly defined. Although it's been a struggle, and I haven't always got it right, it has made me realise what is important. It's you, Alex. You are what matters. Sure, the children mean everything to me but unless you and I are together and happy then everything else feels wrong. I'm so sorry I hurt you, please try to forgive me. Come home and let me show you how much I love you. I want to prove to you that you can trust me. Please, give me a chance.

To: **Jay@mybestfriendisgay.com**
From: **Dot@noplacelikehome.com**
Subject: **Breaking the silence**

Thank you for your e-mail. At least I now know that Alex is staying with you and nobody else, which helps a bit. I'm sorry Kevin is finding it a bit of a strain, but he can't blame me because Alex finished the Shreddies this morning. No doubt he does. I still haven't heard from him, and it's been three agonising days of waiting for the phone to ring, checking messages and e-mails in the hope that he will talk to me. The worst thing is, I found another e-mail from Alex to Jessica, which has made me feel even guiltier, if that's possible. I suppose part of me was hoping to discover some incriminating evidence which could justify what happened between Luke and me, but all I found was this wonderful e-mail to Jessica congratulating her on her engagement.

Why didn't anyone tell me she was getting married? It made me sob when I read what he had written about love and marriage. He described how much he loved me and how our marriage was a partnership based on respect, love and laughter. He ended it hoping that she would be as happy with Ian as he has been with me. I thought I couldn't feel any worse than I did, but I was wrong. A part of me wishes I'd never read it. How could I have been so stupid?

I know you don't want to get involved but, please, could you ask him to call so that I can explain everything? I don't expect him to forgive me, I just want to re-establish contact as much for the children as for myself. They don't really understand why Dadda is not staying at home, and I've told them he's working. What else can I say – 'Your mother has been caught kissing Hamish and Dougal's father, and Dadda wasn't very happy about it'? What an awful mess.

To: **NikkiSoda@ambitiousproductions.com**
From: **Dot@noplacelikehome.com**
Subject: **Work**

Yes, he has left and, no, he's not a bastard. I'm the treacherous one. Can I come and see you this week?

To: **Delissa@splendidmums.com**
From: **Dot@noplacelikehome.com**
Subject: **Mother knows best**

Thank you for your concerned e-mails. Yes, I did go to see Nikki. I had to take the children, much to her disgust, but it was an inset day at Matilda's school and I didn't want to call in any favours, which would mean having to see people. I don't really want to talk to anyone at the moment. Nikki took one look at me and sucked in her breath. I'd forgotten to change out of my Boden pull-ons and hadn't really bothered to look in a mirror. I can't remember the last time I washed my hair, none of it seems very important anymore. The children fell upon the pile of DVDs Nikki has in her office meeting room, and we settled them down in front of Harry Potter while I worried whether they would find it too scary.

Nikki sat me down in her office and sent a runner to get me a hot chocolate made with soya milk from the local Starbucks. I didn't want to waste time, so I came straight to the point, 'Can I come back to work in the New Year?'

She looked radiant, as though all her wishes had come true and that Christmas had come early. For a moment I was flattered that she valued me so highly, but then I began to suspect it was more a question of her being proved right. She never thought I'd make it as a full-time mother.

'Full time?' she asked, rubbing it in.

'I'm not sure, but probably.' I had no idea how things would work out between Alex and me, but this was my first step towards proving to him that I could still be independent, and anyway if, God forbid, we did separate I'd have to start earning my own money.

'Dot, you poor thing. I know how you're feeling. It's awful, isn't it, being abandoned.' I couldn't bear her sycophantic sympathy. After all that's happened, could I really go back to work for her? For a moment I felt like grabbing the children and running out the door, but then commonsense prevailed. At least it's a start, I don't have to stay with her forever, but better the devil you know. Working with Luke is definitely out of the question, especially if

I hope to be reconciled with Alex. I haven't even begun to think about child care.

Nikki leant back in her chair and watched me. 'Do you really want this Dot?'

Oh God, she was going to make me grovel.

'I think you'd find it really hard. Things have moved on since your day, production techniques have changed and the budgets are even tighter. I demand more now from the people who work for me than I did. We've got a new, younger, more dynamic crowd in here. Look at them out there, they even have to fight for their own desks these days.'

'It hasn't even been a year, Nikki, since I left,' I said, astonished by her attitude. But what did I expect? I certainly wasn't going to start begging for a job. So I kept quiet and just stared at her. Was she going to say no?

'I'll think about it and call you,' she said slowly, and I wanted to hit her. How could she be so cruel – talk about kicking a friend when she's down? The decision to go back to work wasn't just a whim. I felt desperate but I wasn't going to show her that. So now I'm waiting for her decision.

Quite simply, you were right. Giving up work was possibly the worst decision I have ever made. If I was working Alex wouldn't be angry with me, I wouldn't have been able to spend so much time with Luke Lloyd, and the children would at least have had a mother and father on speaking terms. Why didn't I listen to you?

To: **Delissa@splendidmums.co**
From: **Dot@noplacelikehome.com**
Subject: **The maternal instinct**

I expected a 'told you so' sort of response, so thanks for being gentle with me. No, you're right, Alex is not entirely blameless but at least he wasn't caught kissing on his own front doorstep.

I suspect you're just being kind when you say you regret not spending enough time with me while I was growing up. It was necessary – you needed to work as Dad's financial contributions were erratic, to say the least. If it makes you feel any better, I don't consider them the lost years but, you're right, it does all pass so quickly. I've taken the opportunity to spend that time with my girls, and on balance I've grown to enjoy it. I'm the first to admit some of it has been like pulling teeth, but most of the time it's been very rewarding. The end result is that I feel more comfortable physically and emotionally with the girls, and as you say, the children seem happy enough.

Maybe my instinct to give up work was right for me just not for Alex. I do feel one of us had to be around, especially considering how hard he has been working over the past year. I can't think straight at the moment but maybe you're right, I should consider part-time work so that the children won't be abandoned by both of us at the same time. Having said that, after the disastrous meeting with Nikki I'm not sure she's going to have me back, and I don't think I really want to work with her again. It makes me feel sick to my stomach. I don't understand how she could be so callous? She's enjoying making me sweat.

I don't know why you're so understanding about her. So what if she's always been jealous of me? It's still no excuse for treating anyone like that, let alone someone you call a friend. I never realised how angry she must have been when I decided to give up work. I expect it made her question the decisions she's made in her life, and judging by the relationship she has with her children I wonder if she thinks she's made a few mistakes. Mind you, I can never imagine Nikki housebound – it would be disastrous. I suppose she's secretly pleased Alex has left. I never thought that she was such an unpleasant, unhappy woman. I just hope she sleeps easily in her bed at night.

And what about my glittering career? It seems even more pointless now than ever. I used to be so proud of my work but when you think about it, what use is it? The sort of programme I used to make was entertaining, sometimes informative, but certainly not life changing. Making television is all-consuming. I remember spending up to a year on one film, and when it was all finished I went out to supper for the first time in ages with Beth and Tom. There was a doctor there with his girlfriend, and he asked me what I'd been working on. It was that film about the children's hospital and I told him that it had been shown the previous night. His eyes glazed over and he said dismissively, 'Oh, I was out, I must have missed it.'

A year of my life gone in fifty minutes. If I am going to go back to work, maybe I should think about doing something more useful but I have no idea what that could be. You're right, for the time being I must concentrate on looking after the girls and myself, and trying to sort out my marriage.

To: **Bethearthmother@rooted.com**
From: **Dot@noplacelikehome.com**
Subject: **Christmas cheer**

Still no news from Alex. The Christmas tree that he ordered arrived yesterday. It's enormous, and we had to persuade the men who delivered it to stay while I rummaged around the cellar trying to find the base. It now has a rather nasty lean, which makes the tower of Pisa look positively straight. It was heartbreaking unwrapping last year's decorations, especially the five boxes of Christmas tree lights that Alex neatly wound together so that the bulbs wouldn't break. A layer of glitter has descended on the house as the girls have been making Christmas cards and it goes everywhere. An X-ray of our lungs at the moment would be luminous.

Mum just wrote me a very emotive e-mail urging me not to go back to work with Nikki, which is ironic when you think about it. It makes my head spin and I feel so tired. She's trying to talk to Alex – she always thinks she can solve everything – but this is something I have to sort out myself. I can't blame her for trying, but I just wish Alex would talk to me. I wish I could just cancel Christmas – I'm certainly going to cancel Nikki's invitation. I doubt if Alex will come on Christmas Day but I know he'll want to see the children. He must be missing them desperately.

It's Matilda's Christmas play tomorrow and many weeks ago, when we were all happy, Jay said he would come with me. I expect he's still cross with me because of conniving Kevin. I can't imagine what it must be like living in that flat at the moment. I expect they spit in disgust whenever my name is mentioned. Or maybe it's worse, and they don't talk about me at all. The only good bit of news over the past few days is that Molly has gone on holiday to Mauritius so Matilda has been given her part and is now no longer a humble innkeeper but the exalted angel Gabriel. She's delighted and didn't have to do any extra work because she knew all the words already. I hope Jay does come tomorrow as I can't bear the thought of facing all those people alone.

To: **Bethearthmother@rooted.com**
From: **Dot@noplacelikehome.com**
Subject: **Can it get any worse?**

It takes a great deal of willpower to get out of bed each morning but today I had the faint hope that I might see Alex, who still hasn't contacted me. There's been no news from Jay either. I got to school early with Daisy, who was determined to wear her red reindeer antlers that come attached to a green plastic hairband. A cassette player in the corner was playing 'O little town of Bethlehem' and I remembered last year when Alex and I had sat close together, relieved that the traumatic year we'd been through was coming to a close. I felt cushioned by love and sympathy but this year everything felt cold. Even the decorations which last year had seemed so charming now looked tacky. The hall began to fill up but no one sat next to us. I tried to cuddle Daisy on my knee but her antlers kept poking into my eye.

Then I heard a familiar voice, 'Is this seat taken?' I looked up and there was Jay. 'Budge over, darling.' It was like a warm wind had blown in. 'Sorry I didn't tell you I was coming but it's all been a bit tricky.' I knew what he meant. 'How are you, lovely?' he asked me.

'Don't be nice to me or I'll cry,' I said, fighting back the tears. I stroked Daisy's head distractedly and then managed to say as calmly as possible, 'I'm fine. How are you doing?'

'Well, you'll be pleased to know that Kevin and I are no longer an item. There must be something in the air, I don't know why they don't just go ahead and call Christmas "break-up time".'

'Oh, I'm so sorry,' I said, not sure whether to be sympathetic. 'Are you all right?'

'Oh God, yes. It had to happen. I couldn't carry on going out with someone you didn't like.' I smiled at him. I know Jay too well.

'So he chucked you.'

Jay did his crestfallen puppy look, and I could see he was really miserable. 'Can you imagine? The man's an idiot. He thought you'd planned it all and deliberately split up with Alex so that he would have to come and live with us and ruin the relationship.'

'How is he?' I asked

'I don't know, it only happened last night, but he hasn't called.'

'No, I mean how is Alex?' It even hurt to say his name. 'He is coming today – isn't he?'

'I don't know, Dot. I didn't see him this morning,' he replied apologetically. Luke Lloyd and his wife walked past holding hands. He smiled at me but I couldn't bring myself to smile back. If only he knew what trouble he'd caused. I watched them take their seats, talking animatedly. His wife was laughing at something he said and pretended to punch his arm in mock rebuke. Jay saw me watching them.

'It's not still going on?' he asked, nodding his head in Luke's direction.

'Don't be silly, but Jay, nothing really happened – you know all there is to know. It was a stupid flirtation. I got carried away with all the attention. Alex is right, I'm impossible. I don't deserve him. I don't want to talk about it, not here anyway.' Jay started looking at the programme. I continued, 'I wrote to him Jay, but he never replied.'

'I thought you didn't want to talk about it?' he said, looking round at the row of seats filling up either side of us.

'Why won't he talk to me?' I asked.

'Wait a minute. How do you mean, you wrote to him? He's never mentioned anything.'

'It was an e-mail, asking him to forgive me and just trying to explain things. Every day I log on, longing to hear the computer tell me in a dead-pan voice, 'You have e-mail.' If the red light flashes my heart pounds against my ribcage, but it's always Delissa or Beth, never Alex. I just want to explain it all to him. I don't mind if he shouts at me and he's angry, I just can't bear the silence.'

Jay looked at me, puzzled, 'Dot, I don't think he's got it. I'm sure he would have mentioned it to me. I've tried not to get involved but obviously we've talked a bit, and I swear he hasn't heard from you since he left. Send it again.' He patted my hand reassuringly but I think he was just being kind. At this point the school band started to play and the children took their positions.

If I'd been in the right mood the play would have been hilarious. Baby Annabel was cast as a frighteningly realistic baby Jesus. To make it authentic they switched her on, to have some natural gurgling baby noises, but it didn't take long before she moved on to the rest of her repertoire, which included glugging and loud belches. Three times Mrs Steel tried to creep onto the stage and switch her off, but Grace (who was playing Mary) kept switching her back on again despite the poisonous looks Mrs Steel sent her way.

Matilda looked splendidly angelic and very beautiful, and had certainly made the most of the glitter opportunity. As Jay whispered to me, Tallulah would have been proud of her – there wasn't a single part of her body that wasn't glistening, from her eyelashes to her toenails. She said her lines clearly, looking very pleased with herself, but as soon as she spotted where we were sitting she started waving frantically, which destroyed the illusion. Beside me a man was mouthing the words to all the songs at his small daughter who was one of Gabriel's cohorts. In between verses he kept pulling a big smile and pointing to his mouth to encourage his daughter to do the same. She was mesmerised by her father, never for a second breaking eye contact. They'd obviously been rehearsing at home for weeks.

I found it hard to concentrate and in between encouraging smiles and waves at Matilda, I kept looking out for Alex but I couldn't see him anywhere. Daisy was getting bored and kept fidgeting. A small group of children were sitting cross-legged in front of the audience. She had spotted them and kept trying to climb down from my lap, eventually I let her go and she went and sat next to a little red-headed girl. As long as I could keep an eye on her I knew she'd be all right.

Once the play was over, the children had been congratulated and bouquets had been exchanged between all those involved in the epic production, we were asked to stay in our seats for a few minutes. Suddenly I saw the back of his leather jacket. It was definitely him. I could tell by his walk and the way that his hair lies on the back of his collar. Alex had obviously watched it all from the back and was walking up to the stage to congratulate Matilda. Daisy had spotted him at the same time and went running into his arms. He scooped her up and gave her a big hug and buried his face in her hair, still making his way towards Matilda. At the side of the stage he put Daisy down, bent down and hugged Matilda while Daisy clung onto his leg. After what seemed like minutes he let them both go. I thought he might be about to bring them over to me but then without so much as a backward glance in my direction he walked out of the school hall.

It felt as though my whole life was disintegrating. Alex couldn't bring himself to look at me or to talk to me. Does he hate me that much? I could feel Jay's awkwardness and I was grateful he didn't say anything. Alex and I are going to have to talk soon, if only to put me out of my misery. How could I have been so stupid?

Jay came home with us, I think he was a bit worried about me. I'm determined the children should not know how terrible I feel but I find it hard keeping up appearances, especially when they ask about Dadda. Matilda seemed oblivious to my despair. She kept singing all the songs that had been in the show and demanding whether I thought she would have been better than Grace at playing Mary. While I was making tea the phone rang. I was sure it would be Alex. Now that he'd seen us he would definitely ring, but it wasn't, it was Professor Harrison. Beth, there is something else I need to tell you, but not yet, until I work out what to do about it.

To: **Jay@mybestfriendisgay.com**
From: **Dot@noplacelikehome.com**
Subject: **Moral support**

Thank you for having a word with Alex. How typical that he didn't get my e-mail, a dot in the wrong place, it's the story of my life. At least it means that he's not totally ignoring my attempts to explain myself. I'll send it again tonight, on second thoughts maybe I'll write him a letter instead and send it by post. It might be more reliable.

To: **NikkiSoda@ambitiousproductions.com**
From: **Dot@noplacelikehome.com**
Subject: **The job**

Thank you for considering me as Series Producer on the second series of *Are You Sitting Comfortably?* but my circumstances have suddenly changed and I don't know whether I can accept. I'll keep you informed and let you know asap.

To: **Bethearthmother@rooted.com**

From: **Dot@noplacelikehome.com**

Subject: **Only connect**

At last I've heard from him, and he wants to take the girls out on Wednesday. His e-mail was short and to the point but it's a start. I hope we get a chance to talk. I never realised how much I loved him until now. I only hope it's not too late.

Chapter Twenty Five

"Tes the hand of Nature, and we women cannot escape it.'
Stella Gibbons, *Cold Comfort Farm*

To: Jay@mybestfriendisgay.com
From: **Dot@noplacelikehome.com**
Subject: **Contact has been established**

Well, he's just been and it was unbelievably painful. He didn't want to talk, he didn't even want to set foot inside the house. The girls were so excited to see him and before I knew it they were gone. All he said was, 'I'll bring them back around five o'clock.' I hate being alone here.

To: Bethearthmother@rooted.com
From: **Dot@noplacelikehome.com**
Subject: **The end**

My life is certainly never dull – exhausting, upsetting but not dull. It was awful seeing Alex so fleetingly. There's so much I need to tell him. It's been so frustrating not knowing what he's thinking or feeling. Beth, I couldn't tell you before but today I was going to have a very important scan. It's been so hard not confiding in anyone, and for the past week I've been feeling frightened and unsure of what to do. I went with the usual mixture of fear of what they might find and a strange curiosity. I sat in the waiting room feeling alone, missing the children and wondering what my future would be. Would I be able to go through it all again, but this time without Alex? It was a terrible thought. How had I got myself into this mess?

There was a long queue of women before it was my turn. Still, this was what I was good at, sitting in waiting rooms, and at least it was peaceful. Some were calmly leafing through the faded copies of *Woman's Realm* circa 1950, others were anxiously scrutinising every single word on the information leaflets, their partners looking awkward. Everything looked tired and tarnished. I started joining the dots on the linoleum floor which was part of a strange design, but when I looked more closely I realised it wasn't a pattern, it was just dirt. The Ladies was out of order and you had to walk down at least two floors to find one that worked. There was no point in waiting for the lift as you could be facing retirement before it arrived.

Eventually they called my name, 'Dorothy Davies.' I had decided to use my maiden name, after all, who knew how things would turn out? Perhaps Alex would want a divorce? How would that work? Would we fight over custody of the children? Would the courts consider me to be an unsuitable mother? Would he start seeing Jessica? Maybe he already has, and I've only myself to blame? With that unbearable thought I pulled open the frayed curtain and went into the cubicle and started unbuttoning my shirt.

The radiographer was a rotund middle-aged woman with extraordinary hair that had been badly dyed and had turned orange in an attempt to hide the grey. She smelt of old ladies' talcum powder and made Nurse Ratchett seem positively sympathetic. Her name badge clipped to her white coat, accompanied by a grim photograph, told me her first name was Joy. The cold gel made me jump and there was no friendly, reassuring banter as the monitor flickered into life registering muscles and arteries. It was as if we had dived under the waves and were scouring the seabed for lost treasure amongst the grey shadows, everything muffled except for the magnified sound of a pulsating heart coming through the loud speaker.

The waiting room was getting noisier and noisier. I could hear shouting outside the cubicle curtain and I thought I could just make out my name, 'Dorothy, she's called Dorothy Knight.'

'There's no one of that name here, Sir, please can you wait outside?'

'I know she's in here somewhere. I have to see her.' It was Alex's voice but how on earth did he know I was here?

'Mama, Mama, are you here?' two little voices I recognised were bellowing excitedly. I looked at the nurse.

'Are they with you?' she asked, as though it confirmed her expectations that I'd be a problem.

'Yes,' I said meekly, worrying how I was going to be able to explain all of this to Alex. I wanted to talk to him but not here, now, like this.

The curtain whipped open. 'In here,' she barked at a startled Alex. 'But you must behave,' she commanded, as much to him as to the children.

They walked round the curtain sheepishly. To say Alex looked anxious would have been an understatement. 'What the . . .' said Alex, but he was silenced by the radiographer.

'There you are, everything looks perfectly normal. Can you see the head? There's the umbilical cord and it looks like baby is sucking his thumb.'

The first sight of my baby will always be with me. It was

extraordinary at only eleven weeks to see it all so clearly. Nobody said anything until Daisy asked, 'What are you all staring at?' To her it was just a jumble of flickering black-and-grey lights, which meant nothing at all. Matilda was trying to work it out, moving her head from side to side.

'Is that a baby?' she asked incredulously.

'Yes,' I replied. 'It's in my tummy. Isn't it incredible?' By now Alex had slumped into the plastic chair designated for partners on these sorts of occasions. Daisy had made her way round the bed and was trying to fiddle with the knobs on the monitor.

Matilda laughed, 'She's trying to change channels. Can we watch the Tweenies?' she asked Mrs Sympathetic, who looked at her as if she was an irritating, dirty little fly that should be swatted immediately.

'Why didn't you tell me?' Alex said quietly.

'How? We haven't exactly been talking.'

'But the letter – you could have said something in the letter.'

'Oh, Alex, how could I? Anyway, I didn't want to tell you like that. I wanted you to come back for me, because you love me, not because I'm having a baby.'

He thought about this but then a shadow of doubt crept across the features I knew so well. He didn't have to say anything. I knew exactly what he was thinking. He was wondering if the baby was his. For a minute I couldn't speak. I was shocked, it was as if I'd been punched in the stomach and left winded by his doubt. The radiographer looked on expressionless. She'd seen it all before and no doubt his accusatory look confirmed her initial impression that I was definitely a slapper. The shock turned into anger.

'For God's sake, how can you think that? I've told you, nothing like that happened with Luke. We just kissed. It's never been more than a kiss. Do you think I'd do that to you? Your opinion of me is worse than I thought. Anyway, you can go now. You've had your gloat. Don't worry about us, we'll be fine. I've always been able to cope before and I'll cope now. Just get out of here.'

The baby's heartbeat continued to pulsate around the cubicle, a reminder that now there was even more at stake. The radiographer clicked to catch the clearest image and started working out the necessary measurements. She wasn't remotely interested in our personal traumas. Alex got up to leave.

'Please don't go, please don't go,' I prayed to myself as I watched him walk towards the curtain. Battling with my hurt pride I called out, 'Alex?'

He stopped just by the curtain. What would he do? I desperately wanted him to stay, to forgive me.

'I'm so sorry. I've been such an idiot,' I said.

He dropped his head but he didn't turn round. What was he thinking? Could he ever forgive me or trust me again? I closed my eyes, willing him to turn round, but I heard footsteps leaving the cubicle and my heart sank. I wanted to howl in despair. I was too frightened to open my eyes, if I kept them closed then maybe, just maybe, I could pretend all this was a bad dream. Silent tears scorched my eyes. Then I felt someone very gently take my hand and kiss it, and when I opened my eyes I saw Alex's face close to mine. It was the radiographer who had left, not Alex.

'I'm sorry,' I whispered.

'Shh,' he said, soothingly, 'I'm sorry too.'

Tears were pouring down my cheeks. 'It must be the hormones,' I said to him through all the tears, and he laughed. It was such a relief to have him with me. 'It's been so awful. I didn't know what to do.'

'I know. I've missed you so much,' he said. As he wiped away my tears with the back of his hand I suddenly realised I had no idea how he had found me.

'But how did you know I was here?'

'We were standing in the queue for the Millennium Wheel when Matilda said, "Mama's got a lump." She'd heard you talking on the phone. I didn't know what to do.'

'You looked so sad,' said Matilda, keen to contribute. 'I heard you say you were going to the hospital.'

'I immediately phoned Jay, but he knew nothing. Then I tried Beth and she said your last e-mail had been a bit strange, but no one knew what was going on. I don't think any of us expected this. We thought it was . . . well, you know.'

Then it dawned on me, 'Oh God, of course, you thought I was coming for a different sort of scan. So what made you come here?'

'I decided to carry on with the girls' day out. Trying to be rational I knew I could always talk to you later when I dropped them off, but as we were waiting in the long queue I couldn't stand it. The thought of you going through that whole experience again on your own was too awful, however badly you might have behaved. So I had to come. We went straight to the Marsden but they had no bookings under your name. And then luckily I saw Professor Harrison, who was in between appointments, and after a bit of persuasion he told me you were here.' He kissed me again and then looked proudly at the monitor.

Matilda, too, was looking at the picture on the screen. 'Is it a boy?' she asked with sudden horror.

'Too early to tell. Why, would you like a little brother?'

'Oh no,' said Matilda, with a look of disgust that suggested she'd rather eat live scorpions than have a boy in the house. Daisy and Matilda clambered onto the bed and Alex and I sat holding hands, all of us watching the screen. It made a wonderful change to stare at a new life made up of healthy cells rather than imminent death in the form of a tumour.

'All right, time's up.' The radiographer brought us back to reality. 'Go on, get up. Get out of here. I haven't got all day to stand around listening to your emotional problems, there's a queue of women waiting to come in.'

As we walked out of the cubicle Alex said, 'A boy would make a change.'

'He'd have to be happy in pink, we can't afford to buy any new clothes.'

'He's not having any of my clothes, especially not my new purple skirt,' said Matilda grumpily.

I bent and kissed her head, 'Don't worry, darling.' I linked my arm in Alex's as we walked out into the tired waiting room, which seemed to have been magically transformed into a room of hope and bright futures. Daisy was standing by the lifts pushing all the buttons. I called to her, 'Daisy, it takes ages. I'm not sure it's even working.' Then, looking at Alex, I said, 'If it is a boy, shall we call him Jack?'

Alex beamed at me and bent forward to kiss me again.

'I prefer Kevin,' said Matilda.

'No,' said Alex and I firmly, together.

There was a ding as, amazingly, the lift doors opened. 'Do you think it's safe?' I asked Alex, looking at it dubiously.

He confidently stepped inside, the girls beside him, and I followed, happy to trust in our future as long as we were all together.

Chapter Twenty Six

'The end is where we start from.'

T.S. Eliot, *Four Quartets*, 'Little Gidding'

To: **Bethearthmother@rooted.com**
From: **Dot@noplacelikehome.com**
Subject: **Seasonal survival**

Well, we made it. This side of Christmas and we're still all together and, would you believe it, I've never felt happier. I had two days of bliss with Alex back in the house, pampering me and helping me prepare for the onslaught on Christmas Day. Wandering dream-like round M&S singing Doris Day's version of 'Walking in a Winter Wonderland', I didn't even get stressed when a pushy woman snatched the last bag of pre-prepared brussel sprouts, right from under my nose. A woman behind me looked on the verge of a nervous breakdown. She kept dropping her pencil as she crossed out yet another item on her extremely long list. When she looked up and saw the precious packet of brussel sprouts, which she'd obviously earmarked for herself, disappearing into the bully's trolley I thought she was going to burst into tears.

Full of seasonal cheer, but mainly sheer happiness that Alex and I are back together again, I went and found a helper who said there were van-loads of pre-packed sprouts waiting to be put out onto the shelves. The highly strung woman laughed with relief and was so grateful she practically flung her arms around me.

Throughout Christmas Eve Alex was tense but I realised it was nothing personal, he was just worried about the transmission of *Tess*, which was scheduled for nine o'clock that evening. I'd offered to invite everyone over to watch it with us but Alex refused, saying rather sweetly, 'I just hope you like it.' As you can imagine, by seven o'clock our house was hardly calm. I was still wrapping presents (must make mental note to start preparations in October next year) and the girls were so excited about the prospect of Father Christmas coming laden with presents, although Daisy started to panic that a strange man would be coming into her bedroom. I reassured her that he would fill the stockings downstairs and would be far too busy to creep upstairs to take a peek at her. We had a protracted argument about whether he'd prefer a glass of wine or milk (we settled on milk as Matilda was worried that the police would arrest Father Christmas for drunken driving).

There was one nasty moment when Alex and I didn't hear Matilda wander into our bedroom and accidently stumble across a bag of presents wrapped in special Father Christmas paper. We both froze when she asked, 'Who are these for?' but thinking quickly, I managed to pretend they were presents for your children. After much deliberation I decided to rewrap the presents just in case she recognised the paper. It was exhausting but necessary. Once they were in bed Alex and I did a lively joint rendition of 'The Night Before Christmas' – I was the narrator and Alex a very convincing Father Christmas. I thought the girls would never go to sleep but soon they stopped calling out and we could get on with our preparations – packing stockings, peeling potatoes and parsnips, laying the table – trying to do everything so that we could have a relaxed Christmas morning.

I suddenly realised that it was five to nine and time for the programme to begin. I felt nervous. What if I hated it? He knows me so well and I'm so bad at lying. We grabbed a bottle of beer each and sat down, dimming the lights, and Alex gave me a nervous kiss as if to put me in a receptive mood for the film. I silently prayed that it would be good but it wasn't good, it was brilliant. I sat amazed. The performances were remarkable and the inventiveness of the shots were dazzling without compromising or interfering with the story. I thought it was a masterpiece, and Alex knew that my praise was genuine, the relief on his face was palpable. The rest of the evening passed in a daze of phonecalls from everyone, ringing to congratulate him, while we tried to get ready for the morning.

As we went to bed at two o'clock he said one more time, 'Did you really like it?'

'Well,' I hesitated, teasing him, 'it was all right, if you like that sort of thing.' He got up and walked out of the bedroom. 'Where are you going,' I laughed.

'I'm going to have words with Father Christmas to cancel your stocking. You don't deserve one.'

Christmas day was full on. How wise you were to go to a country house hotel and let someone else do all the work. It can't be that hard, I thought to myself. After all, it's just a slightly larger roast than usual with some extra trimmings. Christmas morning and the preparations continued right up to the moment the doorbell rang. I think cooking Christmas lunch is a bit like childbirth – no one can tell you how difficult it is. It's one of those female rites of passage surrounded in mystery that even Nigella and Delia can't really prepare you for. I couldn't answer the door as I was wrestling a 14lb turkey back into its tin foil covering while trying not to slip on the pool of grease which had collected beside the oven. Baking trays packed with potatoes and parsnips were trying to escape by sliding out of the oven when I opened the door. I was trapped, delicately balancing the turkey in both hands, my knee jammed against the trays, my tights beginning to singe. An extremely tall silver-haired stranger rescued me.

'Here, let me,' he said in a strong American accent as he deftly picked up two kitchen towels and relieved me of the turkey.

'You must be Carl,' I said disingenuously.

'And you, I presume, are Dorothy? Great to meet you at last.'

My first impression of my mother's boyfriend was good. I liked him. I liked him even more after he took over in the kitchen, saying that cooking the Thanksgiving turkey was his speciality, and he sent me off to the sitting room to have a glass of champagne.

Seconds later the other guests arrived. Alex had driven to collect his mother and she arrived looking elegant in Chanel and carrying an enormous bag stuffed full of presents. This was going to be a hard Christmas for her and for us all without Jack. Alex looked vulnerable as he followed his mother through the door. She was better at playing the game and making an effort. I kissed Alex and held him tightly until someone coughed loudly and said, 'Now that's enough, you two. This is supposed to be a religious celebration.' Jay had arrived, looking festive in revealing red trousers and carrying his own personal bunch of mistletoe and holly which he held up when he saw me and whispered, 'Kiss, or a little prick?' I gave him an exasperated look and he said innocently, 'What?' Was he always like this, or has he been turned by Kevin? It doesn't make me love him less.

Just as the girls were handing out the first presents the doorbell rang. I looked at Alex, puzzled, but went to open the door. It was Nikki. I was dumbfounded. It never crossed my mind that she would still be coming. She was holding an enormous bunch of amaryllis and a bottle of champagne, which she thrust in my direction. She tried to look apologetic, 'You were expecting me, weren't you?'

Delissa came into the hall and put her arms around me and said over my shoulder, 'Nikki, come in. Happy Christmas.' She flashed me a quick reassuring smile as she took Nikki's coat, guiding her quickly past me into the sitting room. I shut the door in shock. I didn't want to celebrate Christmas with that woman. Seething, I went back into the kitchen where Carl was stirring the bread sauce. Within minutes Delissa came in and lightly kissed Carl on the lips. Seeing my furious expression, she said, 'She didn't want to come but I thought it was a good idea. You've known each other too long to start feuding. Listen, you don't want her as an enemy – and look at it from her point of view. She's the one that's really suffering at the moment. She's lost her husband, her children and now a friend. Things can't get much worse.'

'She's only got herself to blame,' I muttered.

'Oh, Dot, can't you be a little bit more generous? She knows she's behaved badly but people do these things when they're miserable. Say what you have to say to her, and then let's all get on and have a good Christmas together.'

Thinking about what Delissa said I went upstairs to put on some lipstick and to get the present you'd bought for Daisy weeks previously and I'd forgotten to put under the tree. As I was coming out of my bedroom Nikki was waiting for me on the landing. 'Sorry' isn't in her vocabulary. I sighed. I'm not great at confrontation but I knew I had to say something.

'Look, I am cross with you. I can't believe you were so horrible, insensitive and cruel when I came to see you. Friends are supposed to help one another.'

Put like that it sounded rather childish, but she looked shamefaced and muttered something under her breath. I thought

I heard a faint hiss as the word I needed to hear bounced off the staircarpet. When she looked up she had tears in her eyes.

'I admit I was a cow. I'm not a nice person. It's not in my nature. I'm not like you, Dot.'

As I watched her disintegrate in front of me I felt my anger dissolve. It was Christmas, after all, Delissa was right again. Also, hadn't I read something recently about the nobility of forgiveness? I gave her a hug and we smiled at each other. As we walked down the stairs I couldn't stop myself from asking, 'What do you mean, you're not like me?' She smiled enigmatically and reached for her champagne.

'Well, for a start, I would never wear those boots with that skirt, but don't worry about it, darling. Happy Christmas.'

She is incorrigible, and maybe I'm stupid but later, as I looked along the table, beautifully decorated with Matilda's alternative place names, with candles in the shape of angels, everyone wearing their ridiculous cracker hats and watching Nikki attempt to act out *Krapp's Last Tape*, I was glad we were all together. The effect was soon ruined when the heads of the angel candles burnt down and they looked like they'd been brutally decapitated, but the children didn't seem to care.

Everyone stayed to help clear up. It took hours to stack the dishwasher, which was bursting with crockery, saucepans and anything we could cram into it. Relieved to have got most of it in, I switched on the machine and there followed an ominous silence. I opened the door, fiddled with the knobs and tried again. Alex took over and changed the fuse and fiddled with more knobs but after half an hour of methodical detective work he declared the machine well and truly dead.

There was a moment as I filled the sink full of water when I thought I might cry with exhaustion. Alex, in a moment of inspiration or possibly because Matilda was nagging him, put on her new S Club 7 CD (a Christmas present from Jay) and the strains of 'Don't Stop Moving' filled the kitchen. We all danced as we washed and dried up countless plates, cutlery and assorted greasy pots and pans. Jay groaned and said, 'I feel like I'm experiencing a Partridge family moment.' It didn't take us long to clear up with the army of helpers. Nikki wafted a tea towel in the general direction of the plates and directed from the sofa. Jay and she left together, and Delissa and Carl were the last the leave. Carl invited us all to go and stay on his ranch in New Mexico – Americans are always so hospitable – but it's a tempting thought. The girls ran down the street shouting their goodbyes, Matilda waving her new Barbie torch, Daisy wearing her purple witch's cloak. Alex and I stood hand-in-hand on the doorstep and although I was tired, I also felt overwhelmingly content.

Six months later . . .

To: **Jay@mybestfriendisgay.com**
From: **Dot@noplacelikehome.com**
Subject: **Postscript**

I know we only spoke on the phone last week but I suddenly felt the urge to write to you. I've hardly touched my computer these past few months and it's strange e-mailing again after all this time. Nowadays there no longer seems the time nor the necessity. Instead I have started writing a diary in the notebook that Nanny Sarah gave to me. I enjoy recording my days, somehow it gives them importance, but also when I become a grandmother I want to look back and remember this time.

I can't believe that the baby is due in only a few weeks. Did I tell you about the bunker Matilda and Daisy have built, complete with provisions (mainly sweets), where they can retreat when it all gets too difficult? Alex has started whistling, which I find intensely irritating, but Beth reassures me it's a sign that he's happy. I love to feel the baby squirming inside but lately, as my time draws nearer, he sometimes lies very still, like he's holding his breath, so I'm quick to give him a prod to check that he's alive. By the time he comes out he'll be black and blue.

No one knows whether this baby could affect my chances of a recurrence – the medical profession remains divided – but I like to feel that he's a positive thing. It's a leap of faith, but so is walking out the front door or getting into a car, and of course there's always that old bus waiting round the corner, ready to run you over. If you stopped to think about all the things that could go wrong, you'd spontaneously combust. This baby, along with Matilda and Daisy, is my insurance for the future. Matilda has just come in, determined that I should be downstairs watching their new show, and has threatened if I don't stop right this minute she really will pull out the . . .

Author's Note

Thank you to the following for their permission to reproduce copyright material:

Dr Spock's Baby and Child Care by Dr Benjamin Spock, excerpt reprinted with the permission of Pocket Books, a division of Simon & Schuster Adult Publishing Group. Copyright © 1945, 1946, 1957, 1968, 1976, 1985, 1992 by Benjamin Spock, MD. Copyright renewed 1973, 1974, 1985, 1996 by Benjamin Spock, MD. Revised and updated material copyright © The Benjamin Spock Trust.

Complete Party Planner by Annabel Karmel, published by Ebury Press. Excerpt reprinted by permission of The Random House Group Limited.

Tunnel of Love by Peter de Vries © 1954 Peter de Vries, excerpt reprinted courtesy of the Estate of Peter de Vries and the Watkins Loomis Agency.

Curriculum Vitae by Muriel Spark, published by Penguin Limited. Excerpt reprinted by permission of David Higham Associates Limited.

The Marx Brothers Scrapbook by Richard Anobile and Groucho Marx, © 1973 by Darien House, Inc. The words of Chico Marx reprinted by permission of HarperCollins Publishers Inc.

Henry Kissinger's words by kind permission of Henry Kissinger.

The Little Prince by Antoine de Saint-Exupéry, © Gallimard 1944. First English edition published by William Heinemann Limited. Excerpt reprinted by permission of Egmont Books Limited, London.

Fear of Flying by Erica Jong, published by Martin Secker & Warburg. Excerpt reprinted by permission of The Random House Group Limited.

Billy Connolly by Duncan Campbell, published by Macmillan 1976, Billy Connolly's words reprinted by kind permission of Billy Connolly.

Thank you to David Higham Associates Limited, Yale University Press and Greenwood Publishing Group for their help in tracing Gertrude Stein's last words.

Camino Real by Tennesse Williams, copyright © 1953 The University of the South. Published by New Directions. Excerpt reprinted by permission of The University of the South, Sewanee, Tennessee.

Cold Comfort Farm by Stella Gibbons, excerpt reproduced with permission of Curtis Brown Group Limited, London, on behalf of the Estate of Stella Gibbons. Copyright © Stella Gibbons 1932.

Four Quartets, copyright © T. S. Eliot, Collected Poems 1909–1962, excerpt reproduced by kind permission of Faber & Faber Limited.

Every reasonable effort has been made to contact all copyright holders, but if there are any errors or omissions, Hodder & Stoughton will be pleased to insert the appropriate acknowledgement in any subsequent printing of this publication.